BY TAFFY BRODESSER-AKNER

Fleishman Is in Trouble

Long Island Compromise

Long Island
Compromise

RANDOM HOUSE

New York

Long Island Compromise

A Novel

TAFFY BRODESSER-AKNER

Published in the United States by Random House, an imprint and division of Penguin Random House LLC, New York.

RANDOM HOUSE and the HOUSE colophon are registered trademarks of Penguin Random House LLC.

The use of lyrics for *The Secret Garden* was granted by Marsha Norman. The Tony Award–winning stage musical adaptation of Frances Hodgson Burnett's book *The Secret Garden* has a book and lyrics by Marsha Norman and music by Lucy Simon. For licensing inquiries and materials, please visit www.concordtheatricals.com.

LIBRARY OF CONGRESS CATALOGING-IN-PUBLICATION DATA

NAMES: Brodesser-Akner, Taffy, author.
TITLE: Long Island compromise / by Taffy Brodesser-Akner.
DESCRIPTION: First edition. | New York: Random House, 2024.
IDENTIFIERS: LCCN 2023059400 (print) | LCCN 2023059401 (ebook) |
ISBN 9780593133491 (hardcover; acid-free paper) |
ISBN 9780593133507 (e-book)
SUBJECTS: LCGFT: Novels.
CLASSIFICATION: LCC PS3602.R63457 L66 2024 (print) |
LCC PS3602.R63457 (ebook) | DDC 813/.6—dc23/eng/20240117
LC record available at https://lccn.loc.gov/2023059400
LC ebook record available at https://lccn.loc.gov/2023059401

Printed in the United States of America on acid-free paper

randomhousebooks.com

1 2 3 4 5 6 7 8 9

FIRST EDITION

Book design by Mary A. Wirth

For my parents

Remember how you made me crazy?

—DON HENLEY, "The Boys of Summer"

Long Island
Compromise

A DYBBUK IN THE WORKS

*D*O YOU WANT to hear a story with a terrible ending?

On Wednesday, March 12, 1980, Carl Fletcher, one of the richest men in the Long Island suburb where we grew up, was kidnapped from his driveway on his way to work.

It had been an unremarkable morning. Carl had awoken and showered and dressed and gone downstairs to kiss his wife, Ruth, goodbye, same as always. Ruth had already presented their two sons, Nathan and Bernard, with their bowls of Product 19 when Carl patted them on the head and left the kitchen and headed out the door into the bright sunlight. The weather was still generally straightforward back then, and spring peeked through the slush of a latest-winter storm that was taking its time to melt. The reflection blinded him a little; his vision was still pocked with dark spots when he inserted the keys into the door of the Cadillac Fleetwood Brougham he'd purchased the previous year.

His brain hadn't yet registered the sound of someone else's footsteps through the slush before a man leapt from behind onto Carl's back and hooded him in one fast, balletic move, turning Carl's world instantly to black. Inside the hood were the amplified sounds of Carl's own suddenly fast breathing and grunting. Someone else—

there were two men—pulled the keys from the lock and settled himself into the driver's seat while the first man struggled with Carl. Now, Carl was a tall man. The two men seemed significantly smaller. It was only the shock of the attack that allowed them to successfully wrest Carl into the footwell of his car.

The Brougham drove away, down and out the C-shaped driveway, away from the giant waterfront Tudor on St. James Drive where the Fletchers lived. It drove through the township of Middle Rock, making a right onto Ocean Vista Road, passing the Fletchers' neighbors' own colossal homes, then over the bridge, then gliding right by, at the 1.8-mile mark, the sixteen-acre estate where Carl had grown up and where his mother was sitting at a Queen Anne desk right at that very moment, writing checks to the electric company and to the synagogue. Then, past the library, past the butcher, past Duplo's Ski and Skate Shop, where Carl's mother had bought him roller skates as a child and where he himself had just recently bought a first tennis racquet for his older son; past the turnoff to the synagogue where Carl had been bar mitzvahed; past the reception hall where he'd gotten married; past the two-block ghetto of auto repair shops, making a right turn onto Shore Turnpike and out of Middle Rock, which, until that moment, was most famous for being the setting of a famous novel from the 1920s (and its author's residence there) and, since, for being the first American suburb to arrive at a Jewish population of fifty percent.

The kidnappers drove for about an hour until they stopped, pulled Carl out of the footwell, and dragged him up a few steps, into somewhere cavernous (the echo of the footsteps told Carl the place was cavernous), then dragged him down two flights of what felt like the same kind of serrated steel-tread stairs they had at the factory that Carl owned, Consolidated Packing Solutions, Ltd. From the steps he was pushed into a small space that he surmised was a closet. The dark became darkest. The Brougham was never found.

Carl was not suspected to be missing until around three o'clock that afternoon. An hour before that, Ruth had looked at the clock and realized that it was time to pick up Nathan from school. She was in the early stages of her third pregnancy and her morning sickness hadn't abated by the afternoon and she was concerned it wasn't actually morning sickness but a virus that had sent her to the couch that morning and kept her there for most of the afternoon, letting Bernard, who was four, watch three reruns of *Gilligan's Island* in a row. She considered calling her friend Linda Messinger and asking her to pick Nathan up, but she'd already asked Linda to take him to school in the morning in the first place with her own six-year-old, Jared. Linda did not yet know that Ruth was pregnant, and so Ruth didn't want to ask her—a two-way favor would have sold Ruth and her condition out, and Ruth didn't want anyone to know this early, not even Linda Messinger, who she wasn't always so sure was rooting for her. She instead called her mother-in-law, Phyllis. Phyllis was a widow with a driver and lived just up the road, a spry fifty-five or fifty (she had destroyed all records of her birth when she turned thirty-six or thirty-one—nobody knew for sure).

While Ruth waited for Nathan, she called the factory to ask Carl if he could pick up eggs and spaghetti on his way home. Carl's secretary, Hannah Zolinski, answered the phone and made noises of delay and then confusion and then finally told Ruth that Carl had never made it into the office that day. Hannah had assumed he was taking a day off. She'd been surprised, she told Ruth, since there was a purchase order that needed fulfilling for the Albertson's account, and Carl had expressed concern the day before that the drafting department was lagging on the order. This would put the factory behind schedule by days or weeks. Hannah hadn't called him at home because, she told Ruth, there was no need to; the drafting department had delivered and everything was running smoothly for Albertson. (Secretly, Hannah was worried that Carl *had* told her he was taking the day off and she hadn't remembered, which would make Carl angry. Hannah had recently become engaged to a man from the factory's engineering department and had already been berated by Carl for her distraction several times in the prior two weeks. Carl, Hannah knew, took pride in a distinct form of management: running "a tight ship," which mostly meant walking around with the baseline assumption that everyone was stealing from him constantly—sometimes in the form of money, but especially in the form of time. This was a lesson passed to him by his own father, who had founded and run the factory all the way up to his death, and this was why Carl rarely took time off, much less spontaneous time, and also why Hannah later told the police that she felt she would have remembered it if Carl had told her he was taking the day.)

Ruth hung up the phone, her finger to her mouth. She stood for a long minute, the phone going dead, then silent, then the dial tone, then the obscene, too-loud clamor of a 1980s kitchen phone off the hook. Her mother-in-law walked in and looked from Ruth to the phone and then back to Ruth.

"What is wrong with you?" Phyllis asked.

Within twenty minutes, the local police arrived. Within an hour, Ruth's mother, Lipshe, entered. Within twenty-four hours, the FBI was setting up camp at Carl and Ruth's home: five full-time agents (two of whom were named John), one of them a woman (Leslie), around the clock, sleeping in the guest rooms and the kids' rooms and the living room. There were three members of the Middle Rock Police Department assigned to the house, but they were mostly useless. Owing to its wealth and relative distance from anything that resembled a working-class neighborhood, Middle Rock was a preternaturally safe place in the 1980s, and the police there had no experience dealing with something as strange and theoretically violent as a suddenly missing person.

Ruth showed the agents recent pictures of Carl from their nephew's bar mitzvah and gave a description: six foot three, meaty but not fat, a prolific head of beautiful brown hair that defied logic—at thirty-three, a mere one on the Hamilton-Norwood baldness scale, same as when she met him—brown eyes that always looked like they were in a squint but were nonetheless kind, and a nose whose apex pointed downward so that he almost always looked like he was slightly repulsed by the thing he was looking at. Ruth's eyes stopped on a picture of the two of them dancing, her looking over her shoulder, perhaps her name being called by someone or just the photographer who took the picture. "This is us dancing," she said. The agents nodded thoughtfully and wrote in their notepads.

And they asked questions: Was anyone *angry* at him? Did anyone have reason to *threaten* him? Did he ever talk about *enemies,* or even something more innocuous, like a random person who hated him? Was there—just hear us out—was there possibly another woman?

"You keep mentioning this Hannah Zolinski," one of the Johns said, checking his notes.

"She's his *secretary*," Ruth said, exasperated. She did not like feeling accused; she did not like that in addition to managing the stress of this absurd situation, she had to also clear her husband's reputation when it seemed very clear to nearly everyone that he was a victim of something. "If you knew how he gets frustrated with her," she tried. Then, quickly, as if this might vindicate him in his absence: "She's engaged! Hannah is recently engaged! To a Socialist!"

It was chaos. Men Ruth had never seen before walking in and around her house. Vans in her driveway. The phone ringing and ringing. Into this walked Phyllis's nephew, Arthur Lindenblatt. He was a wills and trusts lawyer, and, more importantly, the family's wills and trusts lawyer, which made him the family lawyer, since prior to just that moment, the Fletchers had had no need for a lawyer beyond their extensive wills and their massive trusts. Phyllis had called him right after the police had contacted the FBI. He'd been working from home that day at his house in Roslyn because he had a date at the Nassau County courthouse for a will declaration in the late afternoon. He had been headed into his car when his wife, Yvonne, bellowed to him from the doorway and told him that his aunt Phyllis was on the phone and that it was urgent.

Arthur never made it to court that day. He arrived at the Fletchers' house amid one of the first of several tense exchanges between the agents and Phyllis. One of them had just referred to Phyllis as Ruth's mother—"What time did you call your mother again?" asked one of the Johns—and Phyllis was treating them to a long-form lecture on the Fletcher family tree and how it wasn't too complex to keep it all together and how a person should do his job correctly if a person wanted to seem competent to the people relying upon him.

"So you see, this is my daughter-*in-law*," Phyllis was saying when Arthur walked in, wearing his trench coat, his briefcase in hand. "It is *my son* who is missing. This isn't so much to keep straight."

The agents stared between them, more confused than ever. Phyllis and Ruth shared a specific pointiness of the face. They shared chins that curved to a forward point (an aspect that was prettier on Ruth than it was on Phyllis) and noses that had been reshaped by the same plastic surgeon in Manhattan, a doctor known throughout Long Island for being able to coax something parenthesis-shaped—or curly-bracket-shaped even—into not the ski slope that all the Jewish girls thought they wanted but should not have for its dissonance with their other fairly prominent, highly Semitic features, but something more appropriate: the dignified snub nose instead, with its 106-degree nasal tip rotation, narrowed at the end to a slightly wider point that might seem more coherent with the rest of a Jewish face. So many mothers and daughters ordered that same nose from that same doctor that it stands to reason that if Lamarckian evolution theory was real, the daughter's daughter would just be born with that exact new nose, which itself would come to define the American Jewish nose. Phyllis and Ruth were not mother and daughter, obviously, but they both had paid separate visits to this doctor years before they'd ever met. Phyllis and Ruth also shared the same hint-of-mahogany hair and brown eyes, ironed dry at each shampoo (Lamarckian evolution theory would also finally yield straight-haired Jewish girls, though this would stymie the American economy). All to say that Carl had married a version of his mother, and even a gifted federal investigator, if Gentile, might reasonably be mixed up over who was biologically related to whom.

"I can answer any questions," Arthur told the agents, setting down his briefcase and shaking their hands. "Why not let Ruth see to the children?", and Ruth absconded to her bedroom, where her own mother comforted her in Yiddish as Ruth cried into her lap. (Arthur's protectiveness was, at first, interpreted as a need to control informa-

tion and would later be the main reason the agents took a brief interest in him as a possible suspect. But Arthur wasn't controlling; he was
performing from muscle memory. Arthur was a mild, kind man who
was prone to co-dependence and had years of experience by then
defusing his aunt Phyllis's great temper through obeyance and servi-
tude.)

So the agents asked their less gentle questions about the family to
Arthur. These new questions were, of course, about money. For
those agents had perfunctorily sniffed around for women and car ac-
cidents and nervous breakdowns, almost out of politeness, but they
had taken one look at this house—the largest on a block of extremely
robbable homes, the deck that reached over the Long Island Sound
like the Sound was their own personal swimming pool, their own
personal swimming pool, the crescent driveway, the modern appli-
ances, the marble bathrooms, the velvet couches, a Jaguar XJ6
(Ruth's) in the driveway. Then they'd heard from the local police all
about the mother who lived a mile away on a sixteen-acre estate on
the same water and they pretty much knew immediately what was
really going on here, which was that the Fletchers were not just rich
but extraordinarily, absurdly, kidnappably rich.

Meanwhile, Phyllis had set herself up in Carl's study and responded to phone calls from the shul's Sisterhood and from the
women of the Historical Society of Middle Rock (she was the president of both). Phyllis rolled calls to her various connections—the
president of the township, the mayor, their councilman, a state senator who had been helpful on factory matters in the past, one of the
several local representatives that the Fletchers had regularly welcomed to holiday dinners and their children's bar and bat mitzvahs—
all of whom reassured her that there was a multitude of help set on
finding Carl, a task force coming out of every office, that every resource was being deployed, that they knew exactly who she was and
therefore exactly who Carl was. The Johns and Leslie begged Phyllis
to halt her interference and let them run point, but there was no stopping her. Phyllis had a suspicion, a deeply Jewish one borne of events
that had played out in her very lifetime, that actually it was her con-

nections that would help her here instead of the law enforcement that was tasked with it—that the fast and enthusiastic location of her missing son, more and more missing as time went on, would happen not by someone obligated to help her but by someone trying to please her.

By the time the synagogue's Men's Club was forming search parties, the FBI agents were passively condoning them. They saw that they couldn't stop Phyllis's force, so they let it inform their strategy. The agents figured that this might be the kind of thing that showed a potential kidnapper that nobody had a clue where to look, which, in turn, might reassure him and make him lazy. There were all-points bulletins and sketches sent over something called a modem out to various police networks. There were wiretaps and surveillance cameras installed all over the property. There was license plate monitoring on the Long Island Expressway, as though Carl might just be driving back and forth from Middle Rock to Riverhead, Middle Rock to Riverhead.

But nobody could find him. They couldn't even *imagine* where he was. His car was gone; it might as well have been sucked up into the sky. As the first day turned into the second and then the third, the people forming guesses about Carl's whereabouts couldn't even finish their thoughts, the guesses becoming vapor in their mouths before they could even become full sentences. A person couldn't square these scenarios with the gruff, soft, totally bland fixture of Middle Rock who suddenly had a story—who suddenly had a *soul*—the minute he was disappeared from his driveway on a random Wednesday in March.

A KIDNAPPING. IN Middle Rock. A *kidnapping*? In *Middle Rock*? A place that watched the world from a safe distance—a place that got to choose when and how to interact with that world—now inside its grit, inside the dirty, crime-filled movies it had seen at the triplex on Spring Avenue Road, inside of the clandestine cesspool that belonged to tabloid newspapers and the thankfully put-to-bed 1970s and the irredeemable cities they'd long since abandoned. A kidnapping! In Middle Rock!

Both Nathan and Bernard were kept home for the first two days of the family's ordeal. At old Mrs. Annette's playgroup, Bernard Fletcher's cubby sat empty of its usual inordinate amount of Wheat Thins and Fig Newtons. Mrs. Annette thought about Bernard, so curious and fearless. How hard it would be on a boy like that to learn so early why the limits they were constantly struggling to impose on him existed. At Middle Rock Grammar, in classroom 1B, the laminate fiberglass desk of Nathan Fletcher sat empty, too. What a nervous kid Nathan was; surely this would not help. In the faculty lounge a few doors down, Nathan's teacher told the other gals that her sister had dated Carl briefly when the two of them were in high school, and now it seemed like she remembered her sister saying he was prone to depression. Had Carl offed himself? Had Carl run away? Did Carl take all his money and try to go live out his life not under the thumb of his terrifying mother and that oppressive, judgmental wife who always seemed so filled with suspicion at Nathan's parent-teacher conferences? The principal of the elementary school wandered into the lounge to pour himself coffee and mentioned his memories of the Hearst kidnapping, and at this the teachers' eyes became starry: Were there Hearsts in their midst? Were the Fletchers their Hearsts?

Elsewhere: In Walter and Bea Goldberg's new avocado-colored kitchen, Bea closed the clunky door to her humongous new microwave, setting it for three minutes to cook from a recipe book titled *Dinner Like Magic! Five Minutes With Your New Microwave* (published by the company that made the microwave) and dialed her matching avocado-colored long-corded landline phone to ask Marian Greenblatt if she supposed that Carl had run off with that secretary from work that they'd seen at his thirtieth birthday party. Marian, who was standing in her newer, mustard-colored kitchen on her own matching landline phone, staring warily at her own new microwave and wondering how it could possibly *not* give a person cancer, said that her money was on Carl's kook of a sister, Marjorie, being behind all of this. Marian had heard this theory from the caterer's wife, Rona Lipschitz, who reminded Marian that Marjorie had been cut out of her mother's will when she'd been engaged to that con artist years ago, which she knew because Marjorie told anyone who would listen until her mother found out and put an end to it. Then, just a few months before Carl went missing, Marian and her husband, Ned, had run into Marjorie and her *new* boyfriend out to dinner in Manhasset and determined the new boyfriend to be unscrupulous-seeming, though they were careful to say that Marjorie seemed as innocent (clueless) as ever. The Lipschitzes would make no such assumptions about Marjorie. The Lipschitzes had seen too much by then. The Lipschitzes would not even allow a microwave into their home.

Meanwhile, at the Hadassah bowling league that Linda Messinger had coerced Ruth into joining, the women (minus Ruth, of course) sat in their plastic molded seats and breathlessly traded information—not just the kidnapping, but the insanity of the concept of the idea of a kidnapping among them. They were speechless, they kept saying, speechless!

And yet, for all their speechlessness, none of them could stop talking about it. They hadn't even planned on bowling that day; they'd shown up in order to change the setting of their ongoing discussion of these unimaginable events, to share ions of information they'd gathered or inferred or made up, to process what was happening to their friend and to the children—dear Lord, those poor boys—and to their town and therefore to the world. Only Cecilia Mayer was wearing her bowling shoes, though she, too, had arrived with a point of view and began quickly delineating several ways she'd seen on Ruth that all! was! not! well! in her family in the months leading up to this. She had seen Ruth and Carl at Michael Feldman's bar mitzvah and they were not dancing and they did not take advantage of the Viennese dessert table, which, of course, supported the theory that Carl was having an affair and therefore had probably run off with a woman. It was Linda Messinger, loyal to the end, it turned out, who cut Cecilia off and reminded her that not only was there nothing wrong in the Fletcher family, but since when was Cecilia Mayer close enough to the Fletchers to notice anything different about them, exactly? Had she been invited to dinner at their home? Ever? Cecilia began to whine a high-pitched defense of herself, telling Linda to back off and confessing to the group that she, Cecilia, was pregnant, and that Linda shouldn't be criticizing her in her condition! The women shifted their conversation then, gathering around Cecilia to ask the usual questions while Linda Messinger smiled an assassin's grin.

Our grandmothers would often tell us that no matter how much you envy someone, if everyone threw their package of problems into the center of a room and was given a choice of anyone else's, you would, guaranteed, pick up your own. We didn't know if that was always true, especially when it came to the Fletchers, but perhaps now we did. Perhaps now we would truly say that we would pick our own problems over even theirs.

Or would we? It wasn't just the puncture of crime into the community that itself kidnapped the Middle Rock imagination; it was the stench of glamour associated with it. It was the Fletchers' wealth. Their *money*. Middle Rock was the kind of suburb that no longer exists, a community defined by common ethics and values and populated by a variety of middle-to-upper-class people who moved to be among others who shared those same ethics and values. The problem of extremely wealthy people living amid a clamor of plain middle-class people—forcing those middle-class people to contend with not their enormous luck but their remaining dissatisfactions—was a problem solved with the 1990s proliferation of the McMansion. Suddenly the middle class had plenty of space inside their hollow stucco walls to store their delusions. But we're talking about the 1980s here, and Middle Rock still contained its own neighborhood ghettoes—the extremely wealthy on the waterfront and the merely comfortable farther inland. Everyone knew who had a lot of money and who had some; who vacationed where and who had a second home. The Fletchers, in that enormous waterfront house, just down the road from the even more enormous waterfront fenced-off estate where Carl had been raised, well, they were the pinnacle.

But all that money was like the white picket fence around the Fletcher estate: It obscured the view. You couldn't see the Fletchers clearly through the mist of their fortune and whatever it was that you brought to your viewing of it. But now—now, with Carl gone and the streets humming with his disappearance—the people of Middle Rock could finally really see the Fletchers. It was all out in the open now, and the Fletchers' neighbors, under the subterfuge of concern, could finally let their anxieties about their own finances and their own success and their own futures and their own legacies surface right in front of each other, and the ugliest part of themselves found them whispering, late at night, across the pillow to their spouses, not where was Carl Fletcher, or are we in danger, or has the world changed, but: Why not *us*? Why aren't *we* rich enough to be kidnapped?

ON THE FIFTH dawn that Carl was missing, Ruth lay in bed, staring at the walls as the sun came up. The shadows created by the trees outside her second-floor window made a tic-tac-toe board pattern that reminded her of the garden trellis outside the house where Carl grew up. As the room brightened, the shadows were slowly absorbed by the wall they'd been cast against, and she felt like she was losing him all over again. The kids lay next to her: Nathan, who maintained four-limb contact with some part of her; Bernard, who had fallen asleep at the bottom of the bed, sleeping across her feet like a puppy, but not nearly as loyal.

Ruth's thoughts wandered to Brooklyn, where she'd been raised. Each night she lay awake, staring at the ceiling, wondering which of the superstitions that she'd been taught as a girl could have prevented this. She'd stopped summoning those superstitions, those shots in the dark for protection, pretty much completely after she met and married a man whose wealth was its own elaborate system of safeties. She had, as a girl, been taught reams of rituals to forestall injury and demise—to spit three times upon hearing a scary thought; to step into the house with her right foot to avert disaster; to not cut her fingernails and toenails on the same day because that's what's done to you on the day of your burial; to not sit at the corner of a table, lest she not get married for seven years. She'd been taught to whisper "God forbid" over and over, to spit on the ground upon hearing the names of her enemies. But in recent years, since her marriage, she had begun to see all the superstitions that were her heritage as the silly burden of a poor and desperate people who had no control and no explanation of why they were constantly being chased to their death. If all those superstitions were to protect against the dangers that their poverty endowed them with, then money was the solution and it was time for them to finally relax.

But now she saw that the money had tricked her. It had made Ruth, a woman born a mere four years following the liberation of Dachau, believe she was insulated from danger. How could she forget the lessons of her Orthodox girlhood? This was all in God's hands! Look at what happened if you allowed yourself to assume that your good fortune was guaranteed simply because it was vast. Idiot!

The walls were now completely faded of their shadows. It was morning again. Ruth braced herself for another day. She had come to accept that this was not a blip in her life; that whatever this was, however it ended, it would never not have happened. It was time for her to think deeply about it and its inevitable repercussions, to prepare herself: Maybe Carl had fallen in love with another woman, maybe even, yes, Hannah Zolinski, with her small waist and her daffy manner and her dark eyelashes and flushed cheeks. But it could be a million other things, too: Carl kidnapped by Arabs; Carl kidnapped by a psychotic woman who was obsessed with him; maybe Carl and the Cadillac, at the bottom of the Sound; Carl being murdered by his jealous sister, Marjorie, who was supposed to be traveling in Europe with a man everyone suspected to be some kind of grifter; maybe an alien abduction; maybe a fugue state. Maybe he was depressed and drove into the Sound; maybe he was drunk and drove into the Sound;

maybe he was distracted and drove into the Sound. Maybe he was starting a new life somewhere far away, the pressure and predictability of running a family business he never had a choice in, suddenly, yes even at this late date, too miserable for him to endure.

Her thoughts spiraled further. Have you ever lost your child briefly at an amusement park or in a grocery store? Just for a second? It's only right then that you ever truly understand how big and unsearchable the world actually is—how it is far too big to find something in it that is really lost.

Then, at 6:48 A.M., the phone rang.

Ruth's mind went blank and alarmed, but her body knew what to do. She rose from her bed like a doll, in one jointless piece, and found her legs propelling her down the curling staircase into the living room, where Leslie, the female agent, and one of the Johns were wearing large headphones, as calmly as if they'd been sitting there and waiting for hours. John held up a finger of caution and then waved her in slowly.

Ruth sat down and tried to remember what to do: Listen, she was just to listen. Respond normally. Nobody else in the room. Normal normal normal. She picked up.

"Mrs. Fletcher," a man said. He sounded far away and his voice was turned robotic through a filter.

She was quiet for a moment but he seemed to be waiting for her, so when John gave her another small go-ahead nod, she whispered, "Who is this?" Normal normal.

"I am a colonel in the organization known as the Caliphate Freedom Fighters of the Valley of Palestine. We claim responsibility for the bombings in the JCC of Tulsa on February sixth and at the Hamish Middle School in Los Angeles on March first and the execution of Rabbi Shlomo Richtstad of the Congregation Shaare Jacob on January twelfth. We have your Zionist scum husband. He is halfdead by now. I took off all his fingers and his ears but you can have the rest of him back soon if you volunteer to help fund our cause."

"What do you—" Her voice was so high-pitched. She'd never

heard it that way before. She couldn't seem to modulate it. "What do you—"

He cut her off, which was good because she didn't even know what her question was.

"Do not interrupt me," the man said. "Two hundred fifty thousand dollars to the Eastern terminal, luggage carousel six, put it on the belt, at JFK. Noon. If you bring the police, or if you call them, or contact anyone, I'll kill him now."

Ruth gripped the phone with both hands.

"I need to know that he's alive," she said, searching her brain wildly for the way the Johns and Leslie had trained her for this moment, but now she recalled nothing. "I need to speak with him. Let me speak to him!" Leslie nodded. Ruth'd done it right.

"You don't need to know anything, Jew pig. He's barely alive. Another day like this and he'll be done for and it'll be your fault. Do you want that? You have children. You have little Nathan and Bernard." How her blood went cold. "Make this simple. Make it simple!"

The man hung up. The call hadn't lasted long enough for a trace with early 1980s technology. Leslie put her hand on Ruth's shoulder and led her to a dining room chair. Ruth sat down and put her head in her hands. Her husband: his hands, his ears, their luck.

"Why would they think I didn't call the police all these days?" she asked. His hands. His ears. Their luck.

"We just don't know who we're dealing with yet," Leslie said. "If they think you won't call anyone, we have to play it like you haven't called anyone."

The federal agents began a swirl of activity around Ruth as she tried to picture it all. There were several phone calls to some kind of headquarters, after which all the agents stood together in a circle and began to talk quickly and in codes that Ruth didn't understand. She stopped trying when a scream pierced the space, and everyone jumped, the only time Ruth ever saw the agents relent to the tension. The scream was Nathan's. He had awoken to find his mother gone.

At eight A.M., Linda Messinger came to take Nathan to school, same as she had been doing the past two days. Ruth was instructed to bring him out to the car without giving any indication to Linda that "the situation was moving," was how the agents put it. At eight-thirty A.M., one of the Johns went to the Manufacturers Hanover Bank on Spring Avenue Road to tell the bank manager to gather $250,000 in out-of-sequence bills from the vault and to mark them and record their sequencing. At eight-forty-five A.M., Phyllis arrived to help Lipshe take care of Bernard while Ruth made the ransom drop, and Bernard, who understood from the sudden, quick movements in the house that something had changed, saw his mother running toward the car and began one of his epic, seizure-like, trance-like tantrums.

The tantrums had started when Bernard was about eight months old, when he was becoming truly sentient and either failed all lessons of object permanence or rejected the notion that he should ever suffer for a moment without the beloved object that had dared to escape him. For the time up to and including the kidnapping, the object was his mother, and her departure—or her trip to the bathroom, or her falling out of sight for even a second, or even a too-long blink of his eyes—would set him off. The tantrum would start out with the distant rumble of a gathering storm—the inhale—and by the time there was an exhale, Bernard had completed all manner of destruction: ripped clothing, a bloody nose, lungs that were raw and scraped. In the years since he'd learned to talk, the tantrums hadn't abated, though they had become less frequent. The problem was that their severity had become more violent than they'd ever been. The last time he'd had one, which was at someone's pool club on July 4, he had passed out from the wind of his fit, and a lifeguard had had to call in a medic.

Now one was coming, and Ruth and Phyllis made eye contact.

"What should I do?" Ruth asked.

"Don't worry, just go," Lipshe said, in Yiddish.

But Bernard, caught between them and sensing a showdown, unleashed his scream, and, swiftly, the decision was made that he should at least go to the bank with Ruth, because the police would be at the bank, just in case. (Of course, this plan was endorsed by the agents, who were fairly agog at the tantrums they'd witnessed so far that week.) So Ruth put Bernard into the backseat of her Jaguar, and drove to the bank.

She couldn't think. She no longer had instincts. Her world was upside down and she'd outsourced decision-making to anyone who volunteered. Ruth walked into the bank with Bernard's tiny legs wrapped around her waist. She sat in an office while the bank manager brought her tea and tried to make conversation while Bernard hit the desk with a ruler. When the manager asked Bernard to stop, Ruth yelled at them both. She left an interminable thirty minutes later with a large paper bag, like from the grocery store, run-walking to her car, shoving Bernard into the backseat again. From there, she drove to JFK, checking her rearview mirror, holding her head up while she sobbed loudly, barely aware of herself.

Ruth parked and pulled Bernard out of the car, walking so fast to the Eastern terminal with her large paper bag and her son around her waist that she nearly tripped twice. After the second time, she put Bernard down and made him run alongside her. Then, a third time, she dropped the bag, then dove toward it with a combination of a scream and a sob as Bernard watched. For his part, he didn't cry or even react.

Inside, Ruth found the carousel and placed the bag on the belt, though it wasn't moving. She was afraid that she hadn't asked enough questions: Was she just supposed to leave it there? Was she supposed to wait until someone picked it up? What if someone else wondered about a paper grocery bag on the luggage carousel, looked into it and found a small fortune and just took it and the kidnapper never knew she'd dropped it off? She looked around the terminal to try to identify any of the agents she was told would be there, but she couldn't make any of them out. That sleeping custodian? The stewardess on the pay phone? The couple with four teenage children, complaining angrily about lost luggage from a trip in from Rome? Couldn't be. How would an agent have gotten an airport uniform so quickly?

How could they have uniforms? Actual children? No one would use actual children for this. Unless?

She was lost; she was terrified. All she needed was a wink, a nod, an iota of prodding—You're doing it right, Ruth! Keep going, Ruth! But she couldn't continue to look at them because yes, those people could be federal agents or police, but they could also be the kidnappers.

She started to walk away backward, backward, backward until finally, about fifty feet away, she turned around and started walking out of the terminal. Now what, she thought. Now what. NOW WHAT.

Once she was outside, she ran back to her car, and a great panic set in. How could she have agreed to send Nathan to school that day? How could she believe these people who didn't know what they were doing? She looked over her shoulder at her silent, petrified son. How could they have let her bring him along? Because of a *tantrum*? These federal agents were so afraid of a child's tantrum that they sent him along on a *ransom drop*? What kind of people were these? What kind of people were running this operation?

She looked at her watch. Nathan would be home soon, but, in Ruth's state, she felt that would only make him more vulnerable! Even with the agents who stayed in the house, even with Phyllis there! Her children! How could she send Nathan to school? Was she determined to lose everything? She should have walked Carl to the door that day!

She arrived at her car to find a note on the windshield on a scrap of yellow legal pad paper.

TWA TERMINAL 5 LAGWARDIA. BAG CLAIM 9.

She looked around again, frantic. She wanted to scream into the air: Hello! Hello! She was holding Bernard so tightly that he finally began to kick her. She said in a scream that was also a low whisper of vicious hatred, "Don't do that!" Now it was unnerving to her that Bernard didn't cry, that his face didn't change when she did that, and she realized it wasn't that she was just unnerved, it was that she wanted him to cry, to be scared with her. What kind of monster is he, she wondered. Then: What kind of monster am I?

Once again, she threw Bernard into the backseat of the car and drove out of the airport toward LaGuardia, searching her rearview for anyone following her, then realizing that she wouldn't even know if a person following her would be good or bad and so she became scared to look into any of the mirrors and nearly caused an accident on the Grand Central Parkway twice when she tried to change lanes without looking, both times screaming as she swerved, the scream becoming not just the outpouring of the shock of near-collision, but the deep, deranged cry of someone who had held it together for five days and was now fully going insane.

She arrived at LaGuardia and parked, once again running with Bernard through the airport, arriving, and looking around—for what? For her fingerless, earless husband? For his corpse?

Nothing. There was nothing. She went to the baggage claim, only to find there was no baggage claim 9 in TWA's terminal. She began to spin around, left to right, hoping to catch someone—hoping to signal some distress to someone who was watching her. Weren't they supposed to be watching her?

And Bernard was still stone-cold quiet.

She ran back to the parking lot. She realized she didn't know who'd written the note on her windshield—was it the kidnappers, or maybe the FBI? Weren't kidnappers only supposed to communicate in cut-out letters from magazines? Were FBI agents known to be notoriously bad spellers? See? Fully insane!

The only thing left to do was to go home. She placed Bernard in the back of the car, bound again toward Middle Rock, sobbing miserably the whole way, to her home, where Phyllis and Lipshe were waiting for her now, plus twelve more federal agents, plus the local police had returned. They all came out to the car. Ruth got out on wobbly legs, ready to hear the inevitable conclusion of this, which was that her husband was dead.

"What?" Ruth asked. "What? What!" She began to scream what

what what over and over until Leslie found her and pushed down on her shoulders and someone else brought her water. She heard crying. Nathan was there, holding his Bubby Lipshe's hand.

Phyllis took Ruth by the hands.

"We got him," she said, her voice shaking and deep. "We got him!"

What had happened was this: Ten minutes after Ruth had dropped off the money, Carl had been dropped in his dirty clothes, covered in vomit and blood and piss and shit, writhing and convulsing outside the bathroom of the Mobil station that lived in the median of the Northern State Parkway. By then, Carl's blindfold had come loose from the way he'd fallen and he'd been able to wriggle it off for the first time in five days. The sun came at him too fast and hard and he thought he had gone blind. By the time he could see shapes formed through the sunlight, a state trooper who had just been patrolling for speeders was approaching him with his gun drawn. The trooper, seeing that Carl was already bound and handcuffed, holstered his gun and radioed for backup and an ambulance.

Within thirty minutes, Leslie and both Johns were driving Ruth and Phyllis to Long Island Jewish, where Carl was being seen by a team of doctors and trauma nurses and a psychiatrist. Phyllis and Leslie waited in the family lounge with Ruth, who was crying so hard that her diaphragm overtook her and began to predict her sobs for her, drowning out her words. She knew by then that whereas she had long considered that her life was divided between before and after her marriage to Carl—between girlhood and womanhood, between poverty and wealth—now she knew that the divide had only *begun* on their wedding day. The divide was actually this vast thing that included their wedding and their children and ended at this moment, with her in a waiting room and her husband two hallways away from her, her future unknown, and that it started right now, the real division of her life: before the kidnapping and after it.

An hour later, Ruth was brought in to see her husband, lying on the bed, bruised and sedated. She cried and kissed his ears and fingers, which were still very much present and accounted for, though Carl didn't know why she did that. He looked at her hard, searching for something behind her eyes.

"The kids?" he asked in a sob that sounded like a cough. "They didn't tell me. They wouldn't—"

"They're home with my mother," she said.

"They're OK? They're fine? You're fine?"

"We're fine, we're fine. Carl, you were the one who was—" But she didn't finish. It would be a long time until she could say the word to him out loud.

Phyllis was let in second, to her umbrage. She held her son's hand, staring down in what was an exaggeration of labored politeness, until Ruth, who was hovering nearby in shock and bewilderment, realized that Phyllis wanted her to leave the room. Ruth had no fight left in her, so she left, and, as she did, she heard Phyllis lean into Carl, who had begun to cry, and say, "Listen to me, boychick. This happened to your body. This did not happen to you. *Don't let it in.*"

After two days of observation, Carl returned to Middle Rock, but not to the house on St. James Drive. Phyllis moved Carl and Ruth and the kids into one of the sizable caretaker cottages on Phyllis's estate while they waited out Ruth's pregnancy, since they couldn't possibly return to the house, and between Carl's ordeal and its aftermath, they knew that more stress would not be good for Ruth or the baby. Phyllis ordered Arthur to put Carl and Ruth's house up for sale, and Ruth was too tired to object.

Nathan and Bernard settled into a shared bedroom on the second floor of the cottage, and Phyllis and Ruth watched them closely for the next few days. They agreed that the best thing for the kids was to not call attention to anything that had happened, to allow the whole horrible ordeal to fade into history. Ruth continued to send the boys to school and playgroup, and their teachers were instructed to not pay any special attention to the children—to help the Fletchers transmit the message to the two small boys that everything was fine, that nothing had happened, that it had all worked out, just like it always did.

And it seemed to work. Things seemed fine. They seemed better.

Except that Nathan now refused to go outside for recess and a special, dedicated teacher had to stay inside with him in a classroom while he sat beneath the windows so that he couldn't be seen from the outside. And except that Bernard was now wetting the bed. But they were mostly fine.

The Fletchers worked hard to make their world normal again. Phyllis began plans to build a house on the estate where Carl and Ruth and the kids could live permanently. Ruth ultimately agreed, seeing how loath Carl seemed to make big decisions right then and that Phyllis, so confident, knew what was best. Slowly, Ruth resumed taking her fitness walks with Linda Messinger and showing up at the Hadassah bowling league. Phyllis resumed monthly Historical Society meetings. And then, like a triumphant fist to the sky: In October, Ruth gave birth to Jennifer Suzanne Fletcher—Jenny—a daughter.

Meanwhile, the most confounding part: As the FBI began their investigation, they kept arriving at dead ends on the assertions that the kidnapper had made during the ransom call. There was no record of any organization named Caliphate Freedom Fighters of the Valley of Palestine. There were no reported bombings of the JCC of Tulsa in February or ever. There was no such thing as the Hamish Middle School in Los Angeles or anywhere else. And if a rabbi named Shlomo Richtstad had been executed in January, there was no report of it anywhere and no Congregation Shaare Jacob to mourn him.

Then, just three weeks after Carl's return, the FBI was tipped off that the bills, which were marked, had come into play at a Dairy More convenience store in Maryland. Two weeks after that, following a brief sting, Drexel Abraham, a man who had spent the sixteen months prior to the kidnapping driving a truck for Consolidated Packing Solutions, Ltd., was arrested. He had spent ten years prior to that in prison, having received a major sentence for some minor involvement with a Black militia in Oakland in 1967. He had been released from prison only to find that the revolution he'd signed on to fight for had ended before it started, that the exciting movement that had caused his participation in the militia had dissipated, and the hippies had turned into yuppies and the cause was no longer justice but greed and plain old getting by.

Drexel's prison record was enough for the FBI to have taken an early interest in him; it didn't help matters that he'd quit his job at the factory three weeks before the kidnapping and had relocated to Maryland two days after it. When they raided his home, they found $9,479 in the very same marked bills Ruth had run down Spring Avenue Road in a paper grocery bag with. In the spate of confessions that followed, it was revealed that Carl had been kept for the duration of capture in the rarely visited basement of his own factory, in an annexed space where the stockpiles of various epoxies that had been tagged and outlawed were stored.

His own factory.

Nobody could get over that, that he'd been kept exactly under their noses: not the FBI, who hadn't thought to look; not Phyllis, who wondered if she had sentenced Carl to this fate when she'd forced him to continue running the factory after his father died suddenly all those years ago; not Ruth, who could not bear that they'd had the keys to where he'd been, that the world hadn't been so large as they thought; and, according to the shock on his face, certainly not Ike Besser, the factory foreman who had shown up every day to run the factory while his boss had been missing, and who had been the person who hired Drexel Abraham in the first place. Ike had known about Drexel's criminal record but felt that the spirit of the country and the time was the second chance.

"I'll never forgive myself," Ike said to Carl when he visited his boss at home after he was discharged from the hospital. "That you were right down there." He teared up. "Trapped like an animal. Carl, I'll never forgive myself."

"How could you have known?" Carl asked. "I didn't even know. Air I was breathing my whole life, and I didn't even know."

"I'm so sorry," Ike said, now with his face in his hands. "I'm so sorry."

The district attorney told Carl that he wanted to offer Drexel Abraham a reduced sentence in exchange for the other kidnapper, the one they thought might be the mastermind of the affair. It had seemed clear after an interview with Drexel that he was not capable of planning and executing anything like this. But Phyllis said there could be no settlement. Phyllis, who was present every time there was business on the matter of Carl's ordeal, said they could use other means to find out who it was; she would not allow for the idea of Drexel Abraham walking the same streets as her son in any less time than the law owed them.

Then, just a few days later, news came that more of the marked bills had been found when Drexel Abraham's brother, a hospital orderly named Lionel, had used them to purchase a used Datsun in Maryland. The police raided Lionel's home and found $13,587 in an old Royal Dansk cookie tin in Lionel's bedroom. He was arrested immediately, and, over three days of being starved and deprived of sleep in a windowless interrogation room, confessed to planning Carl's kidnapping.

Drexel and Lionel Abraham were each convicted of a class B felony. They received the maximum sentence of twenty-five years, with five additional obstruction-of-justice years for Drexel for not turning in his co-conspirator. The Fletchers went home from the sentencing to celebrate Passover and think about how they were free now, at least for many years.

But they needn't have worried about prison terms. Drexel died three years into his sentence in a prison riot, during which he was crushed by a closing door to his cell. And then, just eighteen months later, his brother Lionel was killed by a swift, undetected bout of pancreatic cancer.

Two years later, the FBI came to visit the house to tell Ruth and Carl that all the trails to the remainder of the money had gone cold. They had no leads, and they were officially closing the case. Carl had hired a private investigator—a former Mossad agent that someone had introduced him to named Gal Plotkin—to try to track that money, and even to monitor large deposits and spends in the region and in Maryland, where Drexel and Lionel had been found. Carl felt like if the money was still out there, he was somehow still in danger.

But he was handling the rest of it all so well. He was working at the factory, the very locus of his imprisonment. He was *functioning*. He was sitting at the dinner table, and maybe sometimes he'd get caught in a middle-distance stare, but he was fine. This had happened to his body, after all, not to him.

One month to the day after he was released from the hospital, Carl returned to work, where no one mentioned that he'd been gone and the only indication that anything had changed was when Hannah Zolinski brought him his coffee and, handing it to him, began to cry so hard she couldn't speak. He stood up and patted her shoulder and said, "Now, now. All of that is over. Now, now. It's done."

THE FLETCHER DISAPPEARANCE, as it became known, was the third-highest domestic ransom ever to date. The second-highest was $650,000 for the kidnapping of the wife of an IBM executive in 1978; the highest was $1 million, for a state senator's nine-year-old daughter in 1974, which had ended in a shoot-out and the kidnapper dead and the girl deaf and mute from the ordeal, now living in a well-appointed institution that looked like a home except for its lack of a family. News of the Fletcher disappearance, in addition to photographs of Carl leaving the hospital, made two national newspapers, four local news programs, and one national prime-time newsmagazine program.

"There's a dybbuk in the works" was an old Fletcher saying about machinery at the factory that had begun to malfunction, one that Carl's father, Zelig, had imported from Poland. The phrase was a cross-contamination of Zelig's factory work and the terrible fables told in the Jewish ghettoes that either warded off or provoked unexplainable happenstance like an infestation of ants in a sugar bowl or Cossacks murdering your siblings in front of you. A dybbuk, as tradition tells us, is a miserable soul that cannot progress to a heavenly rest and instead stays on Earth and takes over someone else's body, displacing the person's soul in order for the miserable soul to do its final bidding. If an aspirator at the factory was malfunctioning, Zelig said there was a dybbuk in the works. If a group of cables all started snapping in short succession, there was a dybbuk in the works.

It was Carl who'd brought this phrase home to his own family, extending it beyond the confines of the factory: When the electricity went out during a storm, there was a dybbuk in the works. When an alarm clock stopped working for no apparent reason. When Nathan couldn't form a sentence for his stammering. When the school called home about Bernard's behavior. When Jenny would refuse to engage in the feminine activities that Ruth thought a daughter should be eager to engage in: shopping, makeup, learning to bake, what Bernard would later refer to as the Great All-Night Nose Job War of 1998. These were a dybbuk in the works, a time when things went more wrong than mere physics and logic could account for.

Eventually, the kidnapping was downgraded to that: A brief period when there was a dybbuk in the works. An inconvenience, a setback, an asterisk to the family legend. A time things went wrong, like when Bernard's appendix burst, or the Holocaust. What were they but a people who could put the past behind them and move on and, most of all, prosper? The ordeal was over. This happened to Carl's body. It didn't happen to him.

This ethos seemed to work. How the Fletchers thrived. The tree they had planted yielded fruit. Nathan was the first Fletcher to graduate from college. He left Middle Rock (reluctantly) for Brandeis, where he met and married a jappy, zaftig girl, then moved back to Middle Rock and settled in as a land use lawyer at his cousin Arthur Lindenblatt's Manhattan law firm.

Beamer, as Bernard roundly came to be known, attended film school at NYU after a storied high school career, where he relieved nearly a full quarter of his class of their virginities. He became a moderately successful screenwriter, most notably of a trilogy of action movies that are, to this day, in constant replay on certain basic cable channels (and sometimes the pay ones, but only the less prestigious ones and only late at night). He finally married when he was thirty-five, a Gentile actress of twenty-six whom he'd met on the set of the second movie in the trilogy, and now had two children.

Jenny, the only Fletcher who had not been born at the time of the kidnapping and had never lived in the St. James Drive house except as an embryo, left Middle Rock the night of her high school graduation. She attended Brown for undergrad, rarely coming home except for the occasional Jewish holiday, or a nephew's bris. She'd shown impressive aptitudes in several areas and was considered gifted before that word meant privileged and merely bright. She was a National Merit Scholar, Phi Beta Kappa, the star of her basketball team (owing to her preternatural Jewish-gigantic height of five foot nine), a two-time Model UN champion, and the recipient of so many science fair gold medals that an engineering think tank tried to recruit her straight out of high school. She helped found the school's robotics team, an extracurricular that was in its infancy in the United States (Middle Rock's team is still a top-placing robotics team in competitions to this day). All that, plus she played the cello, plus she'd so dazzled in her role as Mary in the middle school musical, *The Secret Garden,* that a parent at one performance wondered aloud if the school was now bringing in ringers. Last anyone had heard, she had somehow become a labor organizer in New Haven, where she had attended graduate school, slowly climbing in the ranks until she had some position of authority. If her choice of a career—its Socialistness, but also its smallness—surprised people, her success at it didn't. There was nothing Jenny was ever going to do that she wasn't going to excel at.

And Ruth and Carl remained on that estate with Phyllis, behind that white fence—which was now electrified, of course—the worst part of their lives behind them, never to be visited again.

They were fortunate, the Fletchers. They were lucky. They took every advantage given them and moved endlessly forward toward an enduring future of hope and success, their paths lined with gold, their prior failures and bad luck paved over without consequence. They were the shining realization of the Jewish American dream, people who could load their plates with all that this country had to offer.

Now, obviously, this isn't a terrible ending; this was the best possible ending to a horrific story. But life wasn't over yet, and part of what happened next had to do with the way the Fletchers believed that they had done their time—that actually it was all that they'd been through already that had blessed them to enjoy this eternal sunny day. That the safety and survival they delighted in was *earned* by them, a sort of hazard pay for what they had endured. Carl Fletcher had been kidnapped and not only did this kidnapping not ruin his family; no, the kidnapping became a symbol of the family's fortitude, of their ability to survive in the world. The Fletchers persisted, a beacon of what a person should hope for their family, arm in arm in lockstep down the pathways of happiness and prosperity.

The problem is that they didn't stop to consider what the rest of us knew, which was that they had no right to set the conditions for safety and survival in the first place—that safety and survival might not work that way. They don't care about you. They don't accrue like an Israel bond. The more you bank on them as investments that feed off themselves, the more precarious and insidious their yields.

But what are you going to do? That's how rich people are.

Part 1

FAMILY BUSINESS

YOUR FUTURE NOW

THEN, EARLY IN the morning in late September just a few years ago, Phyllis Fletcher died. It was several days after Yom Kippur, and she lay in her living room, on her marital bed, which had been dragged downstairs by two of the groundskeepers. She was surrounded by her son, Carl; her daughter, Marjorie; her daughter-in-law, Ruth; and a squat, belligerent hospice care worker who hated Phyllis down to both of their spleens. Phyllis's ungrateful grandchildren were nowhere to be found, and though she was delirious owing to her end-of-life medications, she made a note of it. The sun was out and the birds sang like it was any old day, and, as the clock struck ten, Phyllis emitted one last soft, anticlimactic breath that spoke nothing of her legend and succumbed to the autoimmune illness that had come for her in the last year, finally, finally prying her death grip from life. She was either ninety-three or eighty-eight.

Ruth led Carl out of the room, settled him into the kitchen, then made all the necessary phone calls. First to Nathan, then to Jenny, and then, because it was early in California and she didn't want to call Beamer's house and risk getting his wife on the phone, she called the rabbi.

"Baruch dayan ha'emet," the rabbi said. "What a force she was."

"Yes," Ruth said, and they were both silent for a singular moment. That silence contained half a century of mutual, shared dread. Once it was over, they proceeded to make the arrangements.

Eventually, Ruth placed a call to her middle child, but it went to voicemail. She tried again before the hour was up. Then she tried a third time.

Over in Los Angeles, Beamer Fletcher heard the muted vibrational buzz in the distance—his phone, an organ that had been extracted from his grip but somehow continued to endure outside his body—and assumed correctly that it was his mother calling for a third time this morning, a call he would ignore under normal circumstances but especially under this one: naked and hog-tied on the floor of the Radisson Airport Hotel in Los Angeles, getting alternately whipped, taunted, and sodomized and otherwise tortured by the two women he had hired for this task, as he normally was on a Tuesday morning at nine-thirty. As it was, he was having a hard enough time focusing.

The two women had started their work on him just thirty minutes before. They had fed him six pills upon his entrance into the room: four Ambien, one something hexagonal and gray and full of mystery and excitement, one bright orange one, who knows what it did but what a nice pop of color it added! He took them in, straight down the gullet with a vodka assist, and then moved onto his back on the disgusting hotel carpet. The women, whose names were Lady and Beamer couldn't remember, had flipped him over like a pancake and tied him up, flicking him here and there (and there) and pulling his hair. They kissed each other Cinemaxedly while he watched from his bound position and, unable to free himself, began humping the floor in order to achieve his most maximum humiliation, which was all poor Beamer wanted from this experience in the first place. That and a nice, submersive blackout and he would consider the morning a success.

But blackouts don't just come. Like everything else worth achieving in this world, they take hard work and concentration, and today, even this early, Beamer knew he didn't have it in him. He'd felt it when he'd gotten got up that morning; he'd felt it when he sat on the edge of his bed, checking his phone for the message he was waiting for, glancing back worriedly at his still-sleeping wife, turned away from him in a hostile (even unconscious she was hostile!) posture; he'd felt it when he checked his settings to make sure the phone hadn't been in airplane mode and then realized no, really, there were just no notifications. He was bereft and scattered and truly tired in his bones in a way he rarely felt (when he was on all these drugs) and had the inclination to call it and pay the women and go home and go back to bed until his meeting at the studio in the afternoon. He had only kept this appointment here anyway because it's impolite to cancel at the last minute.

More specifically, he had awoken that morning to the brick-stomach realization that in the vacuum of his no-notifications was also the fact that his agent hadn't returned the word he'd left at his office four whole days ago and then again yesterday. Not a disaster, right? Things happen, right? But if your agent is the first early distant warning of where your career should be, five days of a call unreturned is not the sign of your career's health and vigor. It is not the sign of a writer in demand! It is not *not* the sign of a career that's circling the drain. If your agent's belief in his own success is tied directly to the faith he has in you and your talent, then not getting a call back after five days—and also remembering that the last time you got a return call from him, the month before, about the matter of an open writing assignment that you had asked to be put up for, the fact it was not a call actually but a text, and not a real text but a thumbs-up placed upon the text you had sent that hadn't really been asking for approval or disapproval but for a sentence-long answer—yes, it's not great.

None of this was helping, of course, as Beamer tried to ride the wave of what the women had given him down through his debasement and then to his obliteration. He had some experience with circular thinking and rumination, and so he decided to meditate, like his wife, Noelle, had recently suggested he try (Don't think about No-elle right now.). Meditation was about being in the moment, and so Beamer looked up to face his current moment.

"Get up, you piece of shit," his current moment, Lady, was saying.

The hookers Beamer had visited in high school at the strange brothel that existed upstairs from a dental office on Spring Avenue Road were mostly Russian and Polish women, which were fine for right then, but the kind of women Beamer came to enjoy for his depravity were the WASPy ones that looked like the surprised house-wives of the porn he favored—"What are *you* doing here? I'm just trying to make a cake before my kids come home! Hel-*lo!*" But by the time he was twenty-one, then twenty-five, then thirty-five—he was forty-two now—and married to a WASPy girl of his own named Noelle (No, do not think about Noelle right now!), his tastes had morphed toward a new third kind of person. As Noelle came to define his status quo, he now sought the opposite of Noelle: messy where Noelle was neat; dirty where Noelle was groomed; a sphincter that was warm and purple and inviting where Noelle's was pink like a ballerina, hairless, puckered in rebuke, and just about sealed shut. There was no one categorical word for this new kind of person, and especially for Lady and whomsoever she brought to this particular ongoing Tuesday morning appointment; however, if he was forced to describe them, he would say they all lived under the category of *real,* a word the casting directors he knew used to mean "roughed up" or "fat": To cast someone "real" was to cast someone for onetime use.

Not here, though. Beamer and Lady had been a thing for years now, Lady with her straight hair that hung, brown and thick, from a middle part all the way down past her shoulders, at which point the hair turned into a lighter version of brown, then faded into bright blue, then finished at the bottom in hot pink, thoroughly washing its hands of its brunetteness by the time its ends were arrived at; her muted blue eyes that were opaque in a way that is only true for blue eyes when their blueness is the result of a contact lens covering brownness; her wide mouth that had small creases on the sides, like echoes or parentheses; her maple syrup nipples, one pointy like a witch's hat and one flat like a tree stump; her warm body (No! Do not notice her C-section scar!); her permissiveness; her eagerness; that spiked dog's collar she forced him to wear that one time; the way she'd look up at him like whoa, big daddy; her delicious anus. Beyond those particular aspects, he didn't want to think about Lady at all, the way you don't really want to think about where your coffee comes from.

And now the introduction at this old Radisson of this new person named he couldn't remember, Jesus, she was looking like a keeper. This wasn't the first time Lady had brought a friend; sometimes it was a fun surprise, and sometimes it was a disaster, which is its own fun surprise. The new person was wearing a red wig and a blue plastic bra and was missing a tooth, and just the fact of the missing tooth made him almost impossibly hard—like his erection was a comet!— the way she smiled without trying to hide it, the way she poked her tongue through the hole flirtatiously, as though missing a front tooth were universally, undeniably sexy, as opposed to a thing you spend thousands of dollars to fix and hide.

But, yet, my god, now that he looked at it, it sort of was sexy. It *absolutely* was sexy. More people should be missing a front tooth! (Do not picture Noelle with a missing front tooth; do not picture Noelle punching him in the face and his tooth falling out.) He couldn't have imagined the impact of this missing tooth on the whirling hurricane inside his scrotum, how he could feel the semen welling up and cycloning, picking up speed, each little gelatinous paisley lining up eagerly to explode in appreciation of this, a brand-new something for Beamer to remember in a few hours when he had his meeting with the studio, or this evening, as he sat down at his computer, or later tonight at dinner, or when he was heaving away atop his wife romantically and respectfully and totally normally (if she was allowing that on this particular night)—something to reach for when he was next trapped, which was every single minute of his life except for this one.

Lady loosened the scarves that were tied around his wrists and ankles. It was now time to hit the second-act break of this appointment.

"The wall," Lady commanded. He obeyed not because she was forceful but because he knew that was the best she had.

Anyway, Lady. Lady was fun, but even all these years later, it was a struggle to explain to her exactly what the theater of all of this was: If he screamed too loud, if he said stop, it didn't mean she should stop. It meant she should *refuse* to stop. Sometimes she remembered this, but she was not native to a man's degradation and he couldn't figure out a way to tell her how to be except by showing her, one week at a time. And she was either not curious or not capable of understanding exactly what it was that he got out of this, which was that he was not here because he liked being here; he was here because it allowed him to exist as a normal, upright human being out in the world all the other hours of the week. The dominatrix he saw on Thursday nights understood this a little better. But Beamer barely understood it himself, so what could he expect?

And so Beamer crawled over to the wall on that revolting carpet that he knew so well—room 816, his standing room for this weekly event, would look like it was decorated in spin art if you put it under a black light—and faced the wall. Nothing happened for a brutal and wonderful minute and finally, finally there was a gentle, moist pressure being applied to his sphincter.

Now came his reward.

The new person stuck a long, fake fingernail—the acrylic kind that comes in colors and with crystals glued onto them—right up his ass. It had aroused him to look at those terrible nails, but now that one was up his actual rectal cavity, he was wondering exactly how well-glued those crystals were, and also how well-glued that nail was, now that he was really thinking about it, and what exactly is the thing you can explain to an ER doctor or a physician's assistant at an urgent care if you had to get it removed.

See? No focus.

Something was off. Maybe he hadn't timed things right; maybe he had finally built an immunity to all of this. Or maybe he was just too overwhelmed by his troubles to enjoy any of it, though, again, *enjoy-ment* was not the precise word. The blackout phase of the Ambien kept attempting its descent, but he couldn't get it to overtake him the way he needed it to. He tried to breathe. He tried to *feel* this moment. But then he became angry and resentful at having to engage in the kinds of mindfulness techniques that his children brought home from their progressive private school (**Do not think about the chil-dren right now!**). This was what the drugs were for! So that he wouldn't have to practice "techniques"!

Here were the contents of his wandering consciousness: Was this a new bedspread? Was this abstract painting the same in every room of the hotel? How did the artist feel about a great, big deal to mass-produce his ugly painting for the Radisson corporation? Did it make him feel more like an artist or less? If it was in every room here, did it also mean it was in every Radisson? Did they ever clean this room? Had anyone ever died in it? How many other people had fucked amid these pleasant neutrals? How long had he been here already? Was he always here? Did he always exist in this room?

And: Was his career over?

And: Was his wife going to leave him?

And: Why, at forty-two, was he still stuck in this cage of anxieties that he was hoping, by now, would have begun to mellow?

There were too many words forming images in his head. There were too many concerns. My god, how many drugs do you have to take to become the canine part of yourself: wordless, directionless, worry-free—to submit to just feeling, just instinct, just the very mo-ment?

The danger of this kind of mindfulness, of course, is that if you don't like what is happening in your brain in this moment, you revert to either the past or the present.

The past: Beamer had, the night before, arrived home to the in-stinctive sense that something was off. It was just nine-thirty when he walked into the bedroom and found Noelle sleeping, but the air was still filled with an ionic energy that indicated to him that she'd heard him come through the door and had shut off the lights and gone down fast. In the dark, her phone on the night table was still lit from recent use.

"Noelle?" he'd whispered into the room. He'd suddenly been filled with terror, like he was in a horror movie, unsure if it would be reassuring to hear a sound in response. But Noelle's back was to him, and she didn't stir as she might have if she'd really been asleep. In moments like this, the instinct is always to want to be obsequious or overly loving. But just even the inclination to do that is to give yourself away. He knew that. You have to play it cool. Sometimes you have to "allow yourself to sit in the discomfort of the feelings that come without knowing"—this was what was printed on the side of the "mindfulness jar" his son, Wolfie, had brought home from his nursery school. Wolfie could not yet read.

Then, in the morning, he turned to find Noelle still asleep in bed, way past seven-thirty A.M. when the children were supposed to be getting ready for school. He put his hand on her naked arm—she wore gothic, little-girl linen nightgowns that still turned him on for their Puritanism ("What are *you* doing here?")—but she shook him off quickly. No, not asleep. But not willing to admit awakeness, either.

Or, no: on strike. She was on strike.

He'd pulled himself out of bed and gone downstairs to make sure the kids were up and ready. He saw that, minutes before he'd awoken, he had missed a call from his mother, which was just as well. He walked into the kitchen, trying not to let it all get to him. He interacted cheerfully with Ludmilla, the housekeeper, and Paulette, the nanny, both of whom were bustling around, trying to read the tea leaves of their mistress's absence in order to anticipate her mood.

"I just work here," Beamer said with a big, comical shrug, which always made them laugh. He kissed his kids on the forehead and was handed a cup of coffee by Ludmilla. He drank it, fantasizing that she had thrown it in his face and was forcing him to lick it up off the floor.

"I'm a pig!" Wolfie said. He was four and prone to screaming and newly insistent on taking on the identities of animals. Yesterday he'd declared he was a kitten.

"What does a pig do?" Beamer asked.

"Oink, oink."

"You're so silly, Wolfie," his big sister, Liesl, said, loudly and cheerfully. She had, recently, developed the affectation of a game show hostess or a pageant contestant. Beamer worried that she lately only said the kinds of things that you think you're supposed to say. She was seven and wore a large navy bow in the front right side of her long blond hair, hitting at about her ear. Noelle had taken to encouraging Paulette, who was French, to dress the children like tiny Parisian dolls.

While he was in the shower, Noelle had, apparently, gotten out of bed and snuck out of the house. Beamer came downstairs, dressed for his day, and made his voice super-duper casual and said to Ludmilla, "Noelle leave?" and Ludmilla made her face into the Slavic stone she had trained it to be and said, "Yes, Mr. Beamer," and he nodded like that was fine, just fine, and left for the day, too. Honestly, it was a kind of terrorism, this thing Noelle did. Yes, *terrorism* was the word that came to Beamer in that hotel room. Who would be able to focus on ejaculation—who would be able to prance like a centaur toward a blackout—with this kind of terrorism in his midst?

Misery. So, of course, now his mind backed into the only corner it had left: the future. In a few hours, he would finally be receiving notes on a script that had been commissioned and was now in its fourth, and, he hoped, final draft. The script was the really exciting and surprising fourth installment of the action movie that had put Beamer on the map almost twenty years before when he had just finished film school. It was a pretty solid fourth installment of the action movie that had put Beamer on the map almost twenty years before when he had just finished film school. It was an entirely cynical, if properly formatted, fourth installment of the action movie that had put Beamer on the map almost twenty years before when he had just finished film school. For every writer, there is the part of the job that consists of frank surprise that anyone is willing to read your work, much less invest in it. Beamer kept trying to reassure himself that the feelings of dread he had in his loin (where all his feelings lived) were that, and not that other part of being a writer, which is, of course, impending obsolescence.

At the Radisson, he looked up at his own image, there on all fours, in the full-length mirror that covered the door to the bathroom: a dark, ashen head of hair that showed no signs of recession, side-parted in a prep school cut he'd maintained since his bar mitzvah because when it works it works; his mother's former nose that sat just a millimeter too high on his face but, see above; those lips like a satin pillow that someone had laid her head on the middle of, leaving a small dent. His eyes were a surprising sapphire blue, with dark circles beneath them that made him look smoky and sexy and drug-addled. (Though, technically, Beamer's eyes weren't all blue; they contained a streak of brown in the top of the left iris, which he once looked up and learned was called Chimera Syndrome, which, some say, indicated that he'd had a twin in utero and that he'd *eaten* that twin, which tracked enough with his general personality and disproportionate appetites and sense of himself for him to then engage in a rare act of self-preservation and stop reading immediately.)

His appeal—the thing that made him a hometown legend and allowed him into the panties of so many of Middle Rock's daughters—wasn't about his face as much as it was about his entire *being*. Beamer had been born with a thirst for body contact that could not be quelled with body contact; he had been born with blood voluminous enough to throw equal parts of its supply to his penis and to his brain, although perhaps definitely more went to his penis; he had been born with a workman's semen, committed to its indefatigable factory production line, a supply that threatened to become toxic to him were it not relieved like a pressure valve, often and enthusiastically and often and often. The net result was something indescribable, made even more so as he got older and his body took on a side-of-beef *animal* quality—a visible hunger, a bottomless thing that was almost too dirty to describe.

Where was his ejaculation? Where was his blackout? Had he used it all up? A thing about a factory, as he knew well from his upbringing, is that sometimes things go wrong. A dybbuk in the works, his father used to call it. He pictured a little ghoul inside his scrotum and it failed to push him further to the finish line, though it's just that kind of weird shit that normally would. All he knew was that ultimately, a factory triumphs because of supply and demand. He had supply, for sure. He had demand! Here Beamer was, demanding! Here were these two women, demanding! What could be wrong?

No, it was that Noelle was ruining it for him. The thing that happened this morning, he could now see it on a continuum that had been going on for a while now that he had, perhaps falsely, ascribed to her general moodiness. It was bad, this thing; it was not the thing that happened before you, say, renewed your vows or decided to have another baby or generally recommitted to the notion that two people were in it for the duration. No, it was the thing that happened as your marriage came to its sad, slow end.

Noelle was going to leave him. He was sure of it.

They had a couples therapist who had come recommended by Melissa, the wife of his former writing partner, Charlie Messinger. Beamer went, but he wasn't into it. Nobody who has a life built like a fortress can go to therapy, much less couples therapy, much much less with the therapist of the person he had a nonacrimonious but nonetheless sad parting of a partnership with. (In fact, sitting on that couch that he knew Charlie and Melissa had sat on, he often engaged in the mental exercise of replacing Noelle with Charlie and wondering if the mysteries of their own dismantling could be revealed, and therefore resolved as an innocent mistake, a series of misunderstandings, if only they had engaged professional intervention.) Anyway, Beamer was trying. He really was. He was doing the exercises that the therapist kept telling him to do. He was *looking Noelle in the eye* and *repeating back the things she said were her goals.* He was practicing *active listening* and *unconditional positive regard.* He was trying to *remember to tell her* when he was going to be home. He was trying to *reassure* her that those several hours he disappeared for in a day were the result of a kind of tunnel vision he got about work. He was *underpromising and overdelivering.* He was *communicating.* Also: He was *failing at all of this.*

Had he missed an appointment? Had he forgotten a birthday or an anniversary? One of the kids' recitals or sports games? *Did she know?* The question of did she know hovered endlessly around him— whether or not she'd gotten a glimpse into the universe of the subter- fuge that was the life he lived when he wasn't with her and the kids.

The simplest solution would be calling Noelle to ask if everything was OK, if there was any particular new offense that she was upset about. But that would be no help. That was not what they did. Theirs was a marriage, seven years going, in which they moved forward, together, side by side, eyes fixed on the horizon, not ever asking any questions that would rattle the equilibrium (and truly, it was a fragile equilibrium) in which they existed.

And would she even answer a straightforward question? Noelle was a repressed Presbyterian, or just a Presbyterian, and would never share as uncomplicated or direct a thought as "Yes, I'm angry at you, and here is an explanation for why." Her ancestors had left their abil- ity to share their feelings on the *Mayflower* and had never called lost luggage to pick it up.

And all of this was preferable to thinking about his parting with Charlie, if you could believe it.

Focus, Fletcher.

You focus. Because it didn't matter what was being stuck up his ass or jabbed into his perineum on this September Tuesday morning. His problems were unmanageable, and once his mind left that room at the Radisson, once it couldn't be confined to the activities inside it, he would have to contend with his life. Impossible.

And there was that phone again, buzzing. It's amazing how even though all the phones sounded the same, you could pick yours out by the way it felt, the same way they say mothers can pick out their ba- bies' crying in a crowded nursery.

It was his own mother again, he just knew it. But this, too, he tried to push out of his mind. He didn't want the highway of his sexual arousal to cross with the highway of his mother's existence, lest the two highways merge to create a new twelve-lane superhigh-way called Interstate I'm Hot For My Fucking Mother So Please Kill Me Really It Would Be A Favor. (By now Beamer knew there was nothing he couldn't eroticize.)

When would this be over? That hotel room, which was usually for him a heaven, was now a hell. All these drugs and the blackout wouldn't come. Ambien could put you to sleep, for sure. But if you take a bunch of them and push through the twilight blanket that tries to overtake you—its "clinical purpose," which is sleep for the insomniac—on the other side you'll find a wonderland of hours-long hallucination. It was in these hallucinations that his mother's ringing and his wife's glare and Charlie's secession hid like stowaways on the train leaving the station of Beamer's consciousness, running along the side of the last car until finally jumping aboard, sneaking their way into his ride, no matter how fast he was going. This was his least favorite kind of high, the kind where you suddenly understand all the things you didn't realize you already knew, where everything was laid bare and you realized that the state of sobriety was itself a kind of lie we tell ourselves.

"I said now!" Lady said, in her impotent attempt at forcefulness. He hadn't heard her command.

"What?" he asked. "What should I do?"

"I said you have to lick the floor! Pig! Lick the floor!"

Fine, sure, whatever. The hours were running down. He had a busy afternoon scheduled. Maybe he had developed an immunity to the Ambien after all this time. Maybe he needed to clean out and re-turn to it to enjoy it again. He'd done that before. The pain of the secret detox was a pleasure all its own.

He began to lick the carpet, which tasted like chemistry, but he wasn't doing it hard enough or well enough or fast enough, so Lady said, "Harder! Better! Now!"

"Now lick my toes," the red-wigged woman with the missing tooth said. Fine, sure, whatever.

He turned his head to the side to take a breath that was not tainted with hotel carpet, and suddenly, he heard the door open. He turned and saw a man standing in the shadows of the doorframe, but the women weren't turning, and he didn't understand why. He strained to look at the door more closely, but his neck couldn't turn fully and he could only see a little of the person, the man, who was entering.

He heard the footsteps, but the women still didn't seem to notice. They didn't stop their various labors about his body. They must have planned this!

Now the man was standing in front of him. Beamer looked up but all he could see were a pair of running shoes and gray corduroy knees. He strained further and further but couldn't see anything else.

"What the hell—" Beamer screamed.

And then the man crouched down so that he could see Beamer more directly, so that he could say something to him, and finally Beamer caught a glimpse of his face and realized that deep down, he'd known exactly who it was the minute the door opened, perhaps even before that.

"You're coming with me, Bernard," Drexel Abraham said, and from behind his back he pulled out a burlap bag that he began to put over Beamer's head when—

Then, in the grips of whatever opened up inside him in that room and allowed him to reach for what he wanted in the world (Answer: It was probably the drugs that did this), Beamer ejaculated onto the floor and collapsed onto the pool of it. Finally! And finally, finally, the blackout began to descend . . . while . . . he . . .

———

BEAMER WOKE UP on the bed maybe an hour, two hours, three hours later to the girls spooning each other next to him, their vaginal smells strong in the room, and an animal, bodily hatred for himself, a disgusted, cellular self-loathing that was de rigueur for Beamer in these moments. He didn't understand at first why he had awoken except in his dream, Noelle was rushing toward him in her nightgown and she finally opened her mouth almost to eat him or yell at him and instead of talking sounded like a buzz saw.

But it was his actual phone vibrate-ringing again. When he was finally able to discern what was on the screen amid the floaters that bubbled across his eyes, he saw that his mother had called two more times and finally dispatched a written message, a disastrous voice-to-text dictation that she hadn't thought to do a coherence check on before hitting send:

Call Maybach Bean Her

Then—though contained in this *then* was so much more anguish than those four letters could impart—

I don't know water doing that you can't all your other but call Maybach soon period Its detergent

Deep inside his inhale was a shudder. Beamer sneaked out of bed and left cash in both the women's shoes—he liked to think he was a gentleman, but there was no way to ensure that each woman was paid separately and specifically except for the shoe situation—and then extra because he was a fucking monster and knew it.

He checked the time again. Physically, actually, he was feeling pretty good. Ambien was such a good drug. No hangover with Ambien. You are done when you're done, no trace left behind, just a delicious hint of a distant grogginess that felt like rare calm in his body, no smell like when he did speedballs those times, or let's just not even talk about meth, OK, because that would lead to thinking about meth and meth is a thing you can't unthink about once you get started. Wait, did he say that about Ambien already?

He did still smell like those girls, like the biology of copulatory acts, and for that he had to return to the office and shower in his private bathroom. He could shower at the Radisson, of course, but he didn't like risking that it would wake the women up and he'd have to exchange pleasantries and also he knew he would certainly acquire athlete's foot in that horrific bathroom, or maybe a venereal disease from a brushing interaction with the shower curtain. No, he would shower at the office.

He left the hotel and drove in Tesla silence to his office. He had an office in West Hollywood, part of the waning dregs of the writing partnership he and Charlie had had since college. They'd made their money off the three films they'd written that were produced, those movies' residuals, and the handful of specs, open writing assignments, and script punch-ups they'd been hired for, though really Beamer lived off his family money.

The films that had been produced, the ones that Beamer and Charlie were best known for, were a series of action movies called *The Santiago Trilogy.* The first of them, *The Santiago Incident,* was about a rich Mexican kid named Jorge traveling to the Alps one summer who gets kidnapped by a cartel and falls in love with the daughter of the kidnapper. Beamer and Charlie's professors, all of whom agreed that Beamer and Charlie reminded them of younger versions of themselves, had called old friends and set up meetings in Los Angeles before graduation day even came; but it was Carl Fletcher's relationships that had landed them a meeting with an executive named Stan Himmerman, who had grown up with Carl in Middle Rock. If those other guys thought Beamer and Charlie reminded them of themselves, add that Middle Rock dialect and a few references to the beloved Poultry Pantry on Spring Avenue Road—"and they're cash-only to this day!"—and Stan saw them as actual visages of himself from his past. He took them for lunch at the Ivy and left with a handshake sale on their thesis project.

The Santiago Incident was made into a $60 million picture that starred Paul Bixby, a young TV star who had, till then, been a featured neighbor-type in comedies and was making his action debut. The movie, which was called by the *Times* "good, unmemorable fun that occasionally takes itself too seriously (though those moments won't be memorable, either, not to worry)," helped redeem the director Van Vandermeer from the movie jail he was in resulting from a too-expensive failed heist movie that had relegated him to directing soft-core porn for years. But Hollywood is a place for redemption, over and over and over, and Van was welcomed back to the studio with roses thrown at his feet after his old friend Stan slipped him Beamer and Charlie's script and Van saw his future. The movie was number one at the box office for four weeks. Stan Himmerman addressed Beamer and Charlie as "my sons" and told them that he, Stan, was hitching his wagon to Beamer and Charlie's "bright young star" and that they were going to "make history together, my sons, yes we are."

They'd made something, that's for sure. Probably not history. Maybe not even art. Some money, yes. After *The Santiago Incident*'s success, Beamer and Charlie were introduced to an agent named Jeremy Gottlieb, who was also from Long Island (but farther out, Ronkonkoma) and who had just left the desk of the legendary superagent Fran Sacks. Jeremy took all his savings and bought lunch for Beamer and Charlie at the Grill and leaned forward when they spoke and made them his first truly-just-his clients.

Beamer and Charlie were set up at the studio with their deal and told to "think and dream big, my sons" by Stan Himmerman. Beamer and Charlie took this office in West Hollowood and had a shared assistant, a beast of unfettered ambition named Stacy, and it was almost like playing house at a real job, to sit with your desk facing the desk of your lifelong best friend every day and tell fart jokes and talk about ideas and the future and how as soon as they had their next project they could relax and be considered established and then, they said, then they could really start their work.

Or maybe just Charlie said that. Charlie had ideas. He wanted to write anything. He wanted to write action, sure, but also thrillers and dramas and the kind of romantic comedies that were the biggest hits of those days. He had an idea for one about an environmentalist who falls in love with an undercover oil company executive trying to infiltrate their plans for eco-terrorism. He had an idea for a horror movie about a haunted house that looked to whoever was visiting it exactly like the house they grew up in. He had an idea for a mob movie where the son of the main guy falls in love with the son of the rival family's main guy and both families unite in homophobia to destroy their sons' prospects at love. (It was a comedy.)

Stan loved every idea they spoke about. Beamer liked and recognized the ingenuity of Charlie's other ideas, but he couldn't find the energy to pursue them. He was so gratified by *The Santiago Incident*'s success—by its *existence*. He couldn't even name the emotion he felt when he knew that other people were in a room with their hearts beating loudly as Jorge, taken against his will, struggled inside the trunk of a car. But the other stuff, like inspiration or new ideas, simply evaded him.

Technically, the idea for *The Santiago Incident* had been both of theirs, but really Beamer's, a coke-covered idea in the middle of the night in the brownstone the Fletchers owned on 9th Street, which Beamer and Charlie both lived in for college. Here was the idea: "something about a kidnapping." What could Charlie say? It was a good idea. Kidnappings are always fun, right? And Charlie knew about Beamer's father's kidnapping, of course. He and Beamer had been friends since before they could even remember being friends. That was what they said at all those meetings. "We don't even remember becoming best friends." People loved that! Charlie's mother, Linda, had memories of that horrible time. She'd driven their older brothers to school together in the aftermath of Carl's kidnapping and even during it.

But Beamer and Charlie never discussed Beamer's father's kidnapping directly. You don't actually talk about things you know about people; you just live with the knowledge and allow it to ride quietly in the backseat of your relationship. Charlie took Beamer's idea (inkling? notion? half synapse?) and the two of them stayed up for four nights in a row, fueled by the drugs that the one goth guy at the student union had sold them. Did either of them notice that it was Charlie's momentum that got them through the night, through the exciting first act and troublesome second and barely coherent third? Did either of them notice that while Charlie typed, Beamer stood behind him, saying "Yes, right. Exactly!" but did not also contribute any new ideas? Did they notice that he said this "Yes, right. Exactly!" with a kind of instructional authority, like Charlie was receiving what Beamer was communicating through some osmotic process? Did they notice that actually Beamer wasn't communicating at all and that Charlie was the one doing the writing?

Beamer did. The question that lingered for Beamer for years and years was whether or not Charlie did, too.

If Charlie had noticed it, it was an act of lifelong friendship and compassion to assume that this kind of thing might be just the story Beamer would have a hard time with, that a good friend would do the heavy lifting on the script, that the use of the idea was perhaps Beamer's big but only contribution—his initial idea and his lived experience—and that, at the very least, this would be an easy script to get made because it came from some inner truth. (Whether or not *The Santiago Incident* contained any truth, inner or otherwise, is a matter of not much debate.)

And then, four years passed. The haunted house movie was never good enough or high-concept enough or scary enough for Stan. The environmentalist movie was greenlit but never made because of a product placement deal that the studio had with an oil company. The mafia movie was rejected by the studio, which meant that Jeremy could put it out to the market, and then it was sold to an independent producer, made for no money, but never found a distributor.

Stan wanted a sequel to *The Santiago Incident,* and Jeremy Gottlieb agreed it was a good idea to actually do a sure thing. Here was the story of the sequel: In *The Santiago Influence,* Jorge's new girlfriend is kidnapped while they're vacationing in Belgium as revenge for Jorge's triumph during the first movie. It wrote itself, meaning Charlie wrote it again, and it was rushed into production. The *Times* raved that *The Santiago Influence* was "good, derivative fun" and that "the death of art goes down more easily when it's this shiny and action-packed" and "it was strange to see a movie character go from a college kid to an adult without actually maturing when you could have written him any way you wanted to because growth is hard for real people, not movie characters." *The Santiago Influence* was number one at the box office for two weeks during a not particularly competitive, romantic-comedy-heavy summer.

The reviews wore on Charlie, and this annoyed Beamer. They were working screenwriters! They had their second movie in theaters! And another kidnapping movie, to boot! How could that not be enough? But Charlie wanted to write about Middle Rock, about one of the businesses that they'd grown up around—the corrugated cardboard factory family or the people who had put air conditioning into all the Long Island malls, those tiny ideas that led to small businesses that led to big businesses and were the foundation of transport from working class to wealth for their grandparents' generation.

Beamer didn't see it. He didn't understand what was so interesting about that.

"We would do it as a family whose kids all want to take over the factory," Charlie said. "They're each fighting to be the boss."

"Trust me, I am starring in my millionth season of a factory not being interesting," Beamer told him. "It's just a family business. There's no action to it. It can't sustain a story. You are going to have to trust me on this."

And so it went for years. Stops, starts, fights. They couldn't agree on an idea. And in all that time, they didn't finish anything.

Finally, Charlie told Beamer that he needed to do something soon. He'd run out of money. Beamer offered him some of his, but this only wounded Charlie.

"I want to *earn* my money, Beam. I'm a professional at this. I'm a professional man in my thirties."

It was just as well. Beamer himself was living off the proceeds from his family's factory. The factory had been the foundation of the family's wealth, and twenty years before, just as all of manufacturing was leaving for China and Carl was getting ready to phase himself out, it appeared that there would be just enough money left to maintain the estate and perhaps put together a trust for the children. The plan had been to hand the factory over to Ike Besser, the longtime factory foreman, in exchange for proceeds from the remaining business as part of an earn-back plan for Ike to eventually own the factory with his son, Max. Ike was always taken care of by the family with a good salary and participation in the factory's investment matching program, which allowed employees to put money toward both retirement and a stock market fund. And the earn-back plan was a good and generous deal for Ike, put in place years before factories became generally worthless. But then Haulers, a big-box store, inquired about taking over half the factory's operational bandwidth for their emergency, just-in-time manufacturing needs. The Fletchers continued to own and run the factory while on retainer by Haulers. Then, seeing how well-run the factory was, and how much time they saved when not operating in China, Haulers made Consolidated Packing Solutions, Ltd., their exclusive manufacturer of all polystyrene molds for their in-house brands. They gave the Fletchers a $10 million up-front payment and a boatload of stock to cover the concentration risk of having only one client, and the rest of the family was paid in dividends from the factory's excess cash supply. This rejuvenated the factory and stalled Ike's earn-back, though he was reassured it was just a delay, and he was given a $100,000 bonus to compensate him for it and encouraged to invest that money so that when the time came to buy the factory, he could just pay in cash. Ike couldn't say no; who could turn down $100,000? But also, he wasn't being asked. The deal was too much for the Fletchers to pass on. It netted Carl, Ruth, and the kids between $500,000 and $750,000 per quarter apiece, and this was the money that comprised nearly every penny in Beamer's bank account (for the brief moments it remained there after its quarterly drop).

Beamer was grateful for the money. He thought of it as enough to keep him afloat until his career took off on his own terms. But Beamer was also in his thirties, and what Charlie said bothered him. He looked at the hour of his life and saw it was getting late, and thought that it sure would be nice if he was making his way on his own steam by then.

Because by then, he had a house in one of the canyons that was a tax jackpot for Los Angeles County. He had a child by then, and the private school they'd just toured for her cost $52,000 per *year*. He had the nanny, the housekeeper, the weekend nanny, the weekend house-keeper. The house in Carmel. A place in Palm Beach Noelle wanted to buy for her parents. Her fuckup brother's new restaurant that she promised they'd invest in. His and Noelle's cars, then the cars for the nanny and housekeeper. Two trips to Maine per year, first class. One trip to Long Island per year, super-duper first class, as an apology to Noelle and gratitude for her forbearance. One trip to Europe per year, for culture and education for the child who, again, could not yet read, and let's not forget that they wanted to have another child, too. Noelle had her philanthropies, her decorator, her dermatologist, her colonics, her spiritual advisor, her massage therapist, her regular therapist, their couples therapist. He had his entire secret life plus the money it took to cover it up, plus the gifts he bought the family because what kind of person lives like this?

So Charlie and Beamer decided to write another sequel. Within three weeks, *Leaving Santiago* was handed in by its exhausted screen-writers and greenlit immediately. By then, Paul Bixby was forty-six and had been in a car accident and one of his eyeballs was now a pros-thetic made from acrylic, which he sometimes (only sometimes) cov-ered with an eye patch. Charlie and Beamer were going to write toward this, but Van Vandermeer had assured Stan that he could shoot around this, so the movie—in which Jorge's wife (Jorge had a new, younger wife) and adorable toddler daughter are kidnapped—was shot in janky, nonstop format, mostly of Paul's profile, never resting on its aging hero's mutilated face. The *Times* called it "con-fusing" and "a totally nauseating experiment" and "absolutely not worth your time or money, no matter how much expendable of ei-

ther of those resources you have." The movie was number one nowhere except for six hours on the Wednesday in mid-January when
it debuted.

Two more years later, and nothing but ten-page starts, and Jeremy
Gottlieb sat Beamer and Charlie down in his office one afternoon—no
the Grill for them this time—and said that he was concerned about
their output, or, more specifically, their lack thereof. And, then more
awkwardly, that he also had some advice for them.

"Yes?" Charlie asked. "We'll take any advice we could get!"

"This is going to sound like it's out of nowhere," Jeremy began.

"Hit us," Charlie said.

Jeremy took a breath. "I think you should separate as a team," he
said. He looked between the both of them, waiting for it to land. "I
know, this is a surprise. But it's my responsibility to say it. I truly
believe this, in my heart. All partnerships have their season."

Jeremy was now a leading agent at his agency and in line for management of his department. His office had tall windows that overlooked the Hollywood sign when you could see it, and posters of
several of his favorite clients' movies (including *The Santiago Incident*)
and shiny glass surfaces. That day, Beamer and Charlie sat with two
feet of massaged leather couch between them, and Beamer felt his body
seize, though he noticed that he felt no such comparable vibration
through the cushions. But leather isn't a conductor, right? He looked
over at Charlie, who was nodding slowly, appearing to take this in.

"Huh," Charlie said. He did not look at Beamer. "Why do you
think that?"

Beamer opened his mouth and then closed it. Beamer would have
said something stronger; he would have expressed some surprise.
They were almost forty by then. They'd been doing this together
since we can't even remember becoming friends.

"I don't really know what to say," Beamer said.

"I know this feels like it's out of nowhere, but it's not," Jeremy
said. "These partnerships have a season, like I said. They're there to
get each other off the ground. Or to reinvigorate a career that's dried

up. Sometimes a team writes just one script together. Sometimes they're for life. But more often, it's my job to say to you when it's just not working anymore." Beat. "You guys have a trilogy, a legacy, and it's a great tribute to your friendship and the first phase of your life as writers. Right? Am I right?"

Charlie was still nodding slowly. "That's a good point. That makes sense. All this makes sense."

Beamer watched it like he wasn't there. He watched it like a movie.

"I just keep wondering what your careers would look like if you weren't together," Jeremy continued. "It's exciting." Another pause. "A career is an *exciting* thing. It changes. It morphs." This time a really long pause. "You're still both so young. Relatively young. Your best work is ahead of you. Both of you."

"I don't know, Jeremy," Charlie said. "I mean, I trust your advice. Always. You haven't steered us wrong. But—" Charlie turned to Beamer. "What do you think? This is crazy, right? No. This is crazy."

"I don't really know what to think," Beamer said to Jeremy. Then he looked back at Charlie and suddenly saw that he could no longer find the harmony on his face that had been there between them since grade school. Charlie was looking out at Beamer without letting Beamer past his sclera.

Outside the agency, Beamer tried to summon some outrage from Charlie, that their own agent would even bring this suggestion to them. But Charlie was silent, and their walk to their cars from the office—a walk they'd taken a million times before together— suddenly also lacked harmony. By the time the valets had been dispatched, a full six minutes later, Beamer understood that this for sure had been Charlie's idea. Beamer's only remaining act of friendship was to let Charlie go and never mention it again. He couldn't. He was too sad.

After this, Charlie went off to write on his own and immediately became one of Hollywood's most demanded screenwriters. The studio gave him an overall deal, which he'd told Beamer was meager and really just a formality. Stacy, their first assistant, had risen in the power ranks and been hired back by Charlie as his producing partner. Their most recent assistant, Sophie, had stayed on with Beamer.

Charlie and Beamer still called themselves close friends. Their wives were close and the four of them had dinner, oh, once every two months or so. But they now each wrote alone, which is to say that Charlie spent his time writing commissioned, big-budgeted, star-attached scripts and had a two-year wait for his services, and Beamer reenacted his father's kidnapping during scheduled drug-fueled orgies with sex workers.

Then, three years ago, Charlie went into prestige television right at its absolute peak, and was now producing and writing a cable show about a family in Queens whose adult children were engaged in a constant fight for taking over the family factory.

Family Business arrived right on time. It was the first show to synthesize everything that economists (like Charlie's father, an econ professor at Brooklyn College) had been saying for years and show the actual front lines of the disappearance of the middle class. It consumed the culture and the Emmys for its first year on the air; it launched ten thousand think pieces and even was responsible for some renewed labor organizing in the younger generations and at least one piece of legislation regarding inheritance taxes. (The legislation idled in the House but existed nonetheless.) Yes, Charlie had roughly 350 Emmys and Beamer spent his days licking hotel floors and getting anally penetrated by toothless women.

Now Beamer arrived at his office as his phone was ringing once again. He wanted to throw it across the room but instead he just silenced it and put it to his ear so that he could walk past his hostile, judgmental assistant, who sat in an anteroom to his office suite. He wanted to not have to speak to Sophie until he showered, more out of decency than dread, though there certainly was dread. There was always dread.

"No, that's horrible," he said into the phone. Beamer was a person who often took a pretend phone call to deflect interactions, and lately he noticed that the things that came out of his mouth on those phone calls were strange and maybe even tiny cries for help. "I hate that. Stop that."

"Beamer?" Sophie whispered, trying to flag him down. He put a finger up to her, then made that hand into a what-are-you-gonna-do hand, trying to make like he couldn't get out of this call. But Sophie whisper-mouthed anyway: "Your mother!"

"Well, that's just terrible," he said to no one as his pretend phone call took a turn and he began to walk into the office's en-suite bathroom. "Just awful. No, no. I'd never do that."

Sophie's contemptuous eyes were on him as he finished his fake phone call.

As he entered his office, he yelled into the phone, "I can't make these decisions for you!" in case Sophie could still hear. "I fucking hate being asked, honestly. You know that? OK, goodbye. OK, fine, bye."

Beamer made it to the bathroom; he was safe. He took his clothes off and turned on the water. He screamed beyond the bathroom to Sophie that he would be out in a second. He waited for the hot water to beat down on him and make him feel human again, and clean, like he could start his whole life over again, but now he was irritable, having gotten into an argument with no one.

HERE IS THE list of post-*Santiago*, post-Charlie screenplays that Beamer either pitched, outlined, or wrote the first twelve pages of:

1. *Gone by Dinnertime*, a romantic comedy about a man who, years after graduation, kidnaps his high school crush without realizing it.
2. *Monaco*, a *Ronin*-like thriller centered on the car chase of a man trying to race down the man who kidnapped his mother when he was young.
3. *Physical Education*, a fast-moving romp about four teenagers who try to kidnap their math teacher but accidentally end up with their gym teacher.

4. *Stranger Danger,* a G-rated movie about children abducted by space aliens and held in the basement of their UFO for four days.
5. *The Valley,* a movie about the war in Afghanistan in which the 214th Fighting Hawks platoon of the Marines gets ambushed and, yes, kidnapped, and held as prisoners of war.

They all didn't work out for some reason or another. Then, three months ago, Beamer was watching an episode of *Family Business,* trying hard to not see how many of the characters resembled Beamer and his family, and insisting (to himself) that it was some kind of narcissism but was actually pretty hard to ignore: a middle child that had some overlap with Beamer, an uptight older one, an apathetic young one, and the father, slightly spaced out and mostly removed. Some of the genders were changed, and so was the town, but sometimes he'd hear a line of dialogue, or see a familiar genetic habit in one of the actors, and he'd realize he knew beyond reason that Charlie was writing about the Fletchers.

Did it bother him because it was his story, taken without asking? There was a protocol to asking to use someone's biographical information, a gentlemen's agreement, and sometimes Beamer thought he should bring up this terrible breach in gentlemanliness but couldn't find a way. Hell, he hadn't even ever confronted Charlie about using their shared agent to break up! Beamer's own ground was too unsteady, and he couldn't really bring himself to say "The brother who fucks everyone, that has to be based on me, right?"

He was tempted to ask, to take some umbrage, but that wasn't what distracted him when he and Noelle watched it on Sunday nights, which was something Noelle insisted on and he agreed to because it seemed normal (though he would have liked to watch it himself, alone, after the house was dark, on his phone and out of the corner of his eye). No, what really bothered him was that he hadn't recognized his own situation as a perfectly viable story. He hadn't harvested it himself.

He just needed to work. He needed no more time to go by with him, on his own two feet, but with nothing in his hands. Bereft, Beamer approached Jeremy with the idea of a *Santiago* reboot. He knew the IP was a little rusted over, sure, but he also knew that reboots were the lifeblood of modern summer cinema. Jeremy said it wasn't a terrible idea but that Charlie would have to sign off, because the studio was technically allowed to hire just Beamer to write it but, *obviously,* they wouldn't want to upset a writer of Charlie's stature.

Beamer swallowed that *obviously* with some attempt at dignity. Charlie's stature. Beamer said he would be happy to put Charlie's name on it as a producer. Maybe a story-by credit, depending on what the union was allowing or demanding that day. Jeremy said he'd talk to Charlie, and Beamer waited to hear back, trying not to think about the fact that an agent had to ask his lifelong best friend for something on his behalf.

A week later, Jeremy said that Charlie would sign off on another *Santiago.* Even better, Jeremy said, Charlie had said not to worry, that he didn't want his name on it at all, which, well: It wasn't just that Charlie didn't want to be associated with the project with even a tiny story credit, though, yes, what did that mean? It was that maybe some part of Beamer was hoping that Charlie would hear about it and want to come back to him, just this one last time. Maybe a break was all they'd needed.

Beamer got the green light from Stan to write, and he put all this aside and he *wrote.* And the draft? It just poured out of him over the course of two weeks, as though some divine force were reading it to him. Writing had never been this easy or intuitive for him. He thought about that statistic where if you spend ten thousand hours doing something, eventually you'll be an expert at it. Maybe that was what was going on here. He tried to remember to keep this lesson for his children. If you stick to something, even if it's labored, it'll work out eventually, it'll get easier. He thought, for the first time, that maybe there had been some wisdom in his separation from Charlie, that maybe both Jeremy and Charlie could see more clearly that it wasn't just that Beamer had been holding Charlie back; it was that

Charlie had been holding back Beamer, as well. And thus: *Santiago IV: The Valsalva Maneuver* was born.

And now! Four P.M. came and it was time for his meeting. The news he'd been hoping for on his phone was some preview of what Stan thought, an emoji, or a "Wow!" Maybe even something from Jeremy. He was getting ready to leave for Stan's office when Stan, who was now the studio president, changed the location from his office to Beamer's, leaving word that he'd be bringing someone else as well.

Well, this only boded well. Another person at this meeting. Only takes one person to say no. And a studio president? Coming to his office? Beamer was relieved. Beamer had spent the last few hours at his computer, thinking that now he could finally put *Santiago* to rest and go off and do something new, to make his *Family Business,* even though *Family Business* sure seemed like his *Family Business.* He had been watching YouTube videos of magicians and mentalists, in the back of his mind wondering if there would be a viable character there and in the front of his mind knowing that there was something here, something so gratifying in seeing a person make something out of nothing. Maybe he would mention this to Stan. That was when he got an intercom buzz from Sophie.

The office had once belonged to the guy who wrote that movie about the Civil War babies and also collected old-timey memorabilia. He hadn't renovated the office at all and it still had a phone intercom system wired to the front desk that the landlord had offered to remove but that Charlie and Beamer had found charming but that Sophie found unnecessary and degrading to use.

"What is it?" Beamer asked.

"Noelle says you're not picking up your phone? Your mother . . ."

"Oh, I'll call her back."

"Which one? She said not to. She just said to go to Dr. Lorna tonight by yourself. She's stuck in a meeting."

"Noelle wants me to go to Dr. Lorna myself?" Beamer asked.

"Yup."

"What meeting?" Noelle didn't have a job.

He looked at his phone. Another missed call from his mother. He swiped it away and addressed a text to Noelle.

We should just cancel. You don't go to couples therapy alone.

There were three interminable dots and then finally:

We can't cancel this last minute

Then he wrote:

We'll pay. It's fine.

Then she:

Dr. Lorna has a waitlist. Can you just go? Can you just do this thing for me for once?

For once! He nearly dropped the phone. Finally:

I'll be there. Do you even want to tell me why you can't come?

But there was no answer and there was something at the door going on, which meant Stan was there.

"Stan is here," Sophie said into the intercom. "With—you said Anya?—Anya."

"Well, send them in," Beamer said, making his voice folksy and jovial, like he was doing nothing but square dancing and laughing it up in that office, and Sophie opened the door, and led Stan and his guest in. Sophie was holding some kind of wrapped circular thing.

Beamer looked at Stan's guest: a short woman in a large-brimmed safari hat and green cargo shorts, a navy polo shirt, and no makeup.

"Beamer, I want you to meet someone," Stan said. "This is Anya Poroshenko."

"I'm Anya Poroshenko," she said, and shoved her rough hand into his and shook hard. "I'm the new folk!"

Stan and Anya were now settling into the two mostly unused seats across from Beamer's desk. The space used to be occupied by Charlie's desk, and though that was now years ago, there were still cut valleys in the shape of the bottom of Charlie's desk legs in the carpet, just as deep as when they'd hauled that desk out.

"This came for you," Sophie said, placing the wrapped thing on his desk. "Also, your mother keeps calling?"

"Yes, thank you, Sophie," he said. "Remind me later. We should maybe, could you get some water for us, please?"

"None for me," Anya said quickly. "I'm telling you, you could kill whatever planet we're gonna use to replace this planet just based on how much bottled water is given out for every dumb meeting in this town. I wonder if I'll ever get used to it!"

Beamer stared at her.

"It's just so wasteful," she explained.

"Where are you from?" Beamer asked.

"Academia. We use water fountains!"

"I meant where on this planet, on Earth?" Beamer asked.

"Oh, ha, sure, I'm from New Hampshire."

"That's funny, you have a kind of Southern accent? Like, folksy?"

"I don't know what you mean?" Anya said.

"It's just—" Beamer started.

"Where are you from?" Anya asked.

"Oh. Long Island. Middle Rock."

She was expressionless as she said, "I went to college with a lot of people from Middle Rock."

Stan stepped in.

"So, we hired Anya as a consultant to help right our ship a little," Stan said. "She's a big fan and wanted to be here for this meeting." He smiled big, like he did when he was speaking at premieres. Beamer saw that his gums were receding. Stan was so old. Stan was barely holding on to this job. "A big, big fan."

Beamer's phone began to ring—his mother's cell again, he just knew it.

"That's great," Beamer said. "What kind of righting does it need? I'm a writer, maybe I can help." They all laughed.

But Beamer knew what it was, and who she was. There had been a rash of scandals at the studio in the last few years: one racial, several homophobic and transphobic, one about pay and promotions affecting the women and the minuscule number of people of color who worked there, innumerable sexual.

Charlie was the one who had first told Beamer about Anya. He'd been talking about the new process over at the studio the last time they'd had a drink, about a month ago, how now everything was being read as if the writing was to be done in a defensive crouch. He spoke about Anya in particular. She had notes on everything, Charlie said, even though *Family Business* was the studio's biggest unmitigated hit. She was eager to "disrupt" even the most well-planned ongoing storylines and general, viewer-loved plot points with now every social issue she could think of: sexual violence, sexual freedom, sexual terrorism, feminism, racial tension, voting rights, sex positivity, period positivity, pronoun use. Anya had created what she called a "Diversity Worksheet," a veritable bingo board of these issues that each production should aim to include three of in each season: suicide, mental illness, guns, healthcare for all, "grooming," border walls, segregation in schools, redlining, roofies, endometriosis, body positivity, Donald Trump's tax returns, homophobia, Islamophobia, Islamo*philia,* juicing, "the refugee situation," voter suppression, the prevalence of HPV. Plus there were five different kinds of abortion—second-term, back-alley, legal, accidental (!), third-term—that she wanted the shows to address. Anya could not get enough of the various ways there were to abort a pregnancy.

"My show is not supposed to be *pleasant,*" Charlie had said as he waved off the bartender for a second drink. "It's not supposed to be aware of its politics. I'm telling you. They wanted to make the place into *Free to Be . . . You and Me.* I didn't listen to any of the advice. I felt like, I don't know. This is maybe advice for a show that's *not* working? If it's not working, that's when you get all these dumb notes. I ignored her. She went away. Stan's gone so soft. Stan would suck his own dick if he could."

The image of this turned Beamer on in an unseemly way and so he took one more shot, his fifth, and, after he and Charlie parted, jogged around the block twice before he got back into his car.

"Trying to get my hands really into it, dirty as possible," Anya was saying now.

"Sure, sure," Beamer said. Now he smiled at Anya, who slow-blinked an acknowledgment of his smile.

Beamer picked up the wrapped thing that Sophie had given him when she walked Stan and Anya in. He briefly imagined it was a bomb that would explode and he wouldn't have to think about any of this anymore.

"Well, she read your screenplay—she's a huge fan—so maybe now's a good time to jump in," Stan said.

Beamer smiled in a theater of collaboration. "Let's!" he said. "Excited to get this going."

But the thing Sophie had brought in wasn't a bomb. He could see just from its weight and packaging that it was a food item. The label indicated that it had been sent from a fancy bakery in Sherman Oaks. He looked at the packing slip. It was from a producer he'd introduced to Charlie over email, at this producer's beseeching.

"So I'm here to really shake things up," Anya said.

Stan uncrossed his legs and then recrossed them on the other side. In the years since he discovered Beamer, he'd gone bald except for the boomerang of hair that spanned from above one ear around the side to the other. Also in those years, he'd stopped calling Beamer "my son."

"Hey, can we first ask—" Beamer buzzed into his intercom. "Sophie, can we get a cake knife and some plates here?" He untapped the buzzer. "I got this cake and my grandmother always says it's best to have hard conversations over something to eat." Phyllis had never said this. If Bubby Lipshe, his mother's mother, had, he didn't know it; she'd died when he was little and had only spoken Yiddish. But Phyllis Fletcher was not the kind of grandmother who fed you cake.

"Sure thing," Sophie buzzed back.

"I'm not a cop," Anya said. "I'm a resource more than anything. Just trying to get to know people so that we can, you know, 'just do no harm,' if you know what I mean."

"Sure, sure," Beamer said. Then, into the intercom, "That knife?"

"I'm looking, Beamer," Sophie returned.

"I'll be honest with you," Anya said. "I read this new script. I'm not sure this script really works in the current moment."

"Hoo boy," Beamer said, and arranged his face into a wide-open monument to consideration and agreeability. Beamer lifted the ring-shaped pastry Sophie had given him to his nose. It was a baked good, a lethal cocktail of sugar, cinnamon, and warmed, melted fats whose combined scent couldn't be contained by the bakery wrap. For a second, he wondered if he could manage to pull the pastry into his private bathroom and eat it while he sat on the toilet and Stan looked out the window and waited. "I wonder where that knife is."

"We have real issues to address here, Beamer," Stan said. He made a serious face.

Now Beamer was having a sudden, almost violent revulsion response to the shiny spot at the top of Stan's head—how lame the man had become in recent years. How *weak*. How had Beamer not noticed? Stan was scrambling for relevance when every other dinosaur of his race, gender, and class was being made into glue. Stan had hired Anya as a human shield against his irrelevance; the worst part of it was that it was working.

Beamer's eyes went from Anya's to Stan's and back again (though his heart stayed with the wrapped pastry in front of him). What a betrayal. This was the third revision of the script. Beamer had gamely made edits on three versions so far on the understanding that there was an end in sight.

Frankly, he had been expecting to hear he'd done a good job.

"And what are these issues?" Beamer asked. That was when it hit him.

The weight.

The shape.

It was a coffee cake. Oh my god, did Beamer love coffee cake.

"Well," Anya started. "You have a white man playing a Mexican character. He has a French girlfriend who is kidnapped by a Black militia. The action races against time so that the victory is that the girlfriend emerges with her virginity intact. Her virginity is the prize."

Beamer blinked.

"The Black characters aren't even given names."

Blink blink.

"And—I'm sure you know this, but Santiago, actually, is in Chile? Not Mexico? I can't be the first person to bring this up. It would be about a nine-hour flight to get from one to the other."

"I know where Santiago is," Beamer said, more quietly than he'd meant. He did. Technically he did. Right? He'd known that before she'd said it, right? No, of course he did.

"I've had to have a lot of talks about 'representation' since I started," Anya said. "I haven't encountered an actual hate crime yet. Well, not an intentional one, ha ha HA! But this script you wrote, and, well, let's not let the ACLU get its hands on it, ha ha HA HA ha."

"The people have an expectation when they come to a *Santiago* movie," Beamer said, but he heard the weakness in his voice. "This is supposed to be a visit backward, to an old friend, you know? Some comfort food for an aging audience. You know?"

"But that visit doesn't have to be quite so retro, right?" Anya asked. "It could be that the friend has changed over the years, right? He's gotten more progressive. He donates to NPR. He's made some changes in his life. Maybe he canvasses for the sassy new Socialist running as a Democrat? I'm just spitballing here."

"I don't really know how to do that. This is all about character. I can't fundamentally change a character that's existed for three movies. You know? I can't . . . change the name of the movie." He looked to Stan, but Stan was not on his side.

Beamer was unsure what else to say. The only thing he had primacy in was *Santiago,* but now that he was alone on this desert island with nothing but Stan, Anya, and a coffee cake that he couldn't break into, he realized: No, it was Charlie who had primacy in *Santiago*.

"I do have some constructive ideas," Anya said. She pulled out not a cake knife but a small notebook that she kept in one of her shorts' several cargo pockets. She began to flip past a few pages till she got to her list. "What if—you're listening?—what if instead of the plot about Jorge saving his grandchildren, what if it's *not* Jorge at all but a completely new person who is trying to prevent human trafficking, not in Chile or Mexico, because let's be honest, our Latinx friends can speak for themselves, but let's say it's maybe Los Angeles? It's true that there are about fifty million people in the world that are considered enslaved. Do you know that one in five pornographic images on the Internet is of a trafficked minor?"

Now she was going to ruin porn for him!

"What if we ratcheted up the maturity on the *Santiago* movies and made them about something that *matters*?" she continued. "We get people in the door because they think they're seeing some old popcorn fun, and once we have them, we *educate* them."

Triple blink.

"You're not saying anything, Beamer," Anya said. "This is a dialogue, not a lecture!"

"I guess I have to think about it," Beamer said. He was careful to sound like he was truly considering Anya's point of view, a skill he'd bulked up on in couples therapy. "To process it, you know."

"I know the instinct is to get defensive, Beamer," Anya said. "But we have an opportunity to *grow* here."

Beamer was watching Stan carefully. "The more I think about it, the more I think you're right," Beamer said. He searched his mind for a way to cooperate. "I like that trafficking thing."

Anya looked at Stan. "We have our work cut out for us here."

"What do you mean?" Beamer asked. "I like it. I'm saying I like what you're saying!"

"Let's just move on," Anya said. "This must all be a very big shock for you, to have someone asking questions and poking around in your underwear drawer like this."

"No, no. I'm excited about this," Beamer agreed, enthusiastically, though the enthusiasm was for wondering where that fucking knife that Sophie was supposed to bring in was. "I love these ideas. I want this franchise to survive."

"You don't have to love it," said Stan, who was not a coffee cake or a knife for a coffee cake. "You just have to sit with it."

"I *do,* though," he insisted. Then he turned to Anya, who also was not a coffee cake or a knife for a coffee cake. "It's very smart. Times have changed. I get it. I don't want to be a relic. I was trying for this—I wanted to give people continuity. But maybe it needs another hack at it."

Anya put her hands up like don't shoot me. "Your energy is just a little hostile."

"I'm not! My energy isn't hostile. It's excited!" Anya didn't seem to understand that Beamer was willing to consider, like any other writer, that anything he did was a piece of shit, and that he had a threshold of zero for believing that every page should be ripped up or burned. She did not understand that he did not need days or minutes to accept that what he had done was bad and unusable. She did not understand how a person could almost gag on his own shame for something he created when just minutes before he'd thought it was at least salvageable and minutes before that he had thought it was genius of an epic magnitude. Furthermore, was there any way to casually rip open a cake with your hands and not seem like a psycho?

Beamer's phone buzzed again three times in quick succession and he reached over to it in order to shut its sounds off, though he felt in the buzz that it was his mother again. He adjusted his voice before he spoke.

"These are great ideas," he said very slowly, hoping his speed would take care of any kind of perception that he was enraged right then. "I'm going to give it a big think."

He looked at Stan, who nodded vigorously but still wasn't coffee cake. Beamer's phone went off again; he heard the vibration in his spleen this time. All these drugs, but it was the phone that was going to give him the heart attack.

Sophie poked her head in. "Beamer, there's a call for you, I'm sorry—it's urgent?"

Stan stood up. "Seems like you have a fire to put out."

Beamer gave his most castrated, high-pitched goodbye that he hoped didn't seem defensive. When Stan and Anya finally beat it, Beamer let his voice descend to its normal octave. "Where the fuck is that knife?"

"I'm sorry, Beamer. Your mother keeps—"

His cellphone rang. He reached for it and accidentally picked it up.

"Hello?" Beamer heard his mother say.

"Shit," he said.

Beamer waved Sophie away but then made a traffic-cop stop signal for her. He mimed a sawing motion. She nodded: right, right.

"Hi, Mom." Three seconds stretched out like an eternity and Sophie was nowhere so he said fuck it. He wedged a pen into the dermal layer of brown wrapper, taking care not to puncture the plastic wrap he surmised lay beneath.

"It should not be this hard to get in touch with my son!" Ruth said.

What is the feeling that the English language doesn't have a word for, where the expectation of your eyes after so many years of reliable prediction is furnished instead with something different and better?

It wasn't a coffee cake!

It was a cheesecake!

It was a cheesecake with a coffee cake *crust*!

"Beamer, are you there?"

"I'm here, I'm here."

"I have some news to tell you," Ruth said.

The cheesecake had a light layer of raspberry or strawberry across the top, and, on top of that, a swirl of chocolate. How had he not understood that the weight of the thing portended *cheesecake*? Oh my god, it didn't even matter, Beamer loved cheesecake so much—the way the sour of the cheese attacked the sides of the tongue, the way the salt of it assaulted the diameter spread from the sides to the tip so that the sweet could have its way with the entire region. All this at once! Cheesecake!

"Beamer, are you there?"

"Hi, Mom." A card fell from the wrapping and Beamer saw a note from the producer.

"Where have you been? We've been trying to—"

The note read: BEAMER, YOU MAY HAVE CHANGED MY LIFE. THANK YOU FOR THE INTRO TO CHARLIE MESSINGER. YOUR FRIEND FOR LIFE, RONNIE

"Your grandmother dies and I can't even get in touch with you."

"Mom, I live in a different state. I have a job. I was in meetings all morning. I can't be on call every second—"

"Why don't you try again."

"I'm sorry, Mom. I feel awful. Grandma Phyllis. How's Dad?"

"He's not good! He's in shock, I think."

Of course, Phyllis had been in hospice for two months. She'd been dying from a rare disease for nearly a year. *Shock* was a big word for the death of a woman at ninety-three or eighty-eight years old.

"Right. Of course."

Still no Sophie. He looked around for a fork or a spoon. He didn't need a plate. He ripped the plastic off with the starter hole he'd made with the ballpoint pen and then began using his index and middle fingers together to dig in and scoop pieces of the cheesecake into his mouth, one after the other, like he was eating lobster with his hands. There was cheesecake on his face and on his chest by then, but he couldn't stop.

By the time his mother transferred the phone to his father, Beamer had squirreled mounds of cheesecake into his cheeks and so when his father said, "Yes. Bernard, hello," what Carl heard in response was, "Phad. I bupped burd abut Grimma. Um po porry."

A MULHOLLAND BACKFLIP consists of the following: a hit of Ecstasy, followed by a speedball, followed by a handful of Lunesta, followed by a crushed Plexidil—a drug that was only briefly on the market in 2012 and that was designed to treat restless leg syndrome but also accidentally ignited dormant and sometimes nonexistent gambling addictions as a side effect—placed under the tongue. Chase with a Coke Zero. If the Coke Zero is not available, then a Mountain High Super Plus Turbo Charge Blue or a Bombinator Leaded Super Neurofreeze Orange Explosion (only sold in some parts of the Rockies) will work, but not (repeat: not) a Bolt Fahrenheit 1000 Blue-Strawberry Bang Bang Rainbow, which will interact with the Plexidil and perhaps lead to an ischemic event, as is indicated on the long list of contraindications on the Bolt Fahrenheit can.

If the Mulholland Backflip is executed correctly, what it does is light up the pleasure centers of your brain so that you are a veritable slot machine of flashing lightbulbs and energetic noises, which is almost enough to drown out the signs of your burgeoning irrelevance and also the cold war that your wife has been waging upon you for reasons that you cannot determine, since you know that the potential number of reasons for this is so vast that you cannot ask a direct question about it without incriminating yourself.

The thing it also does is make your pupils so large that they don't just overtake your irises; no, they extend far past where you think they should end, particularly in your state. Meaning you're too high to know where your irises should end but you're sure it's not where they are right now.

Beamer was just jetting home five hours later on the fumes of the successful Mulholland Backflip that he'd initiated upon Stan and Anya's departure from his office and that lasted all the way through the couples therapist appointment he had somehow agreed to attend alone. He arrived home to find Noelle in their bedroom, packing, and the children, up beyond their bedtimes, running around the room, rowdy in their travel pajamas.

"It's bad enough that you just disappeared for the entire morning," Noelle was saying. She was closing Wolfie's tiny plaid suitcase. Liesl was jumping on the bed, and her brother was lying on it with his limbs spread out like a starfish so that when Liesl jumped it would propel his body through the air. "I honestly don't understand why we have to leave like thieves in the middle of the night."

"We're not thieves," Beamer said. "It's a red-eye. Normal people take red-eyes. Jews bury their dead immediately. It's how it goes."

"You don't have to lecture me on what Jews do, Beamer. I'm saying if you'd bothered answering the phone all day we could have left hours ago. We could be there now. Instead of disrupting everyone's sleep schedules."

"You made me go to the therapist by myself, Noelle."

"That was two hours ago."

"There was a detour on San Vicente."

"For two hours?" Then, to Liesl, she said, "You should bring your flute. You'll want to practice."

"OK, Mommy!" went Liesl, and ran to get it.

But Noelle looked at Beamer. She was still waiting for an answer.

The truth was that he had had to drive to Encino to leave a note at his dominatrix's house to tell her that he wasn't going to be there on Thursday because the tickets Noelle had had Sophie purchase to get to the funeral had them staying for the shiva, too. He had no way of communicating with the dominatrix, except to leave notes at her door, as he had not yet earned her phone number and she had forbidden him from using the email address he had first used to contact her.

"How about," Beamer said. "Would you like to maybe offer me condolences? Or ask how I'm doing, what with it being my grandmother who just died?"

Liesl came back with her flute case and placed it carefully on the floor and then went to lie on the bed while Wolfie jumped so that now *she'd* fly up with force every time he hit the mattress.

"Kids," Noelle said. "What do we say to Daddy?"

Liesl popped up and made her face into a melodrama of grief. "Oh, Daddy," she said, and jumped over to him on the bed and put her head on his shoulder and her arms around his neck. "Daddy, your grandma is dead. I'm so sorry!"

Wolfie sat up in bed and crawled over to Beamer and put his arms around his waist. "I love you, Daddy."

"We are very sorry," Noelle said.

Beamer hugged his kids back. His grandmother was dead.

Noelle closed Liesl's tiny unicorn suitcase. "That's that," Noelle said. "We're packed. The car comes in forty-five minutes." She sat on the bed and let her jaw jut forward. Noelle insisted they not fight in front of the children, which was fine since they never actually fought at all. You can't fight with someone you don't actually say anything to.

"I had the meeting with Stan," Beamer said. "It was a long, involved meeting."

After a second: "How did it go?"

"Good," Beamer said. "Good. They love it. They have notes, of course. There's this woman now who consults. She wants it to be a little more—aware of the moment, I guess? They loved it, though."

"So they're going to make it?"

"Oh, absolutely. They're definitely going to make it. You know, it's just notes."

Noelle looked around to see if she'd forgotten to put anything in the suitcases but came up with nothing. "What should we do till we leave?" she asked. "We have to keep them up."

The question was for Beamer, but Liesl answered. "Can we read *Are You Sure You've Thought This Through?*"

Beamer, relieved for direction in these dark woods, lay down on the bed and wriggled in between the kids to read them what was currently their favorite book, which had been lying on his bedside table. It was called *Are You Sure You've Thought This Through?* and was about a little boy named Baxter who, on his way to school, encounters danger after danger and makes a bad decision at every turn. A van pulls up alongside Baxter as he's walking to school and tells him that the driver's dog is lost and could he get into the van and help him, since the dog loves kids? Baxter says yes and boards the van, and on the next page it says, *Are You Sure You've Thought This Through?* with no other picture or text, just stark white against dark, a wavy, terrified typeface. Nathan and Alyssa had sent it over as a Chanukah present with a note in Alyssa's swirly handwriting: The boys loved this at Liesl's age!

In the book, a menacing grown-up asks Baxter to keep a secret and come into a closet with him and Baxter does it.

Are You Sure You've Thought This Through?

Baxter steals down to the living room after his parents are asleep and watches four hours of prestige cable, even though he has school the next day.

Are You Sure You've Thought This Through?

Baxter is left to his own devices for breakfast and instead of fixing himself any of the nutritious options available at home, he finds a fast-food drive-thru on his way to school, which he walks through, and orders only bacon with nitrates.

Are You Sure You've Thought This Through?

When the book arrived at the house, Noelle at first thought it was a parody of one of those child safety books and laughed the entire way through; she couldn't fathom that there were people who moved through the world with something like *Are You Sure You've Thought This Through?* as an ethos, or a rallying cry. Beamer had to explain to Noelle that she should know by now that his brother absolutely endorsed this as a way of life, and when she shook her head because yes, OK, but really?, he fell in love with her all over again.

Even at their age, Liesl and Wolfie already knew to laugh along with their parents; they knew that life didn't work like that, that danger wasn't behind every single door but the random twenty-third and fifty-sixth doors—that danger was the rarity and not the condition, which was what made it so scary. They understood, even at their age, that danger was dangerous because it was unpredictable; you couldn't game it like this. Beamer thought of his poor twin nephews being read this same book in the Charles Dickens foreboding of a darkened bedroom, frightened beneath the sheets while his terrified brother reminded them again and again that absolute horrors lay right outside their door. Beamer delighted in his wife's derision of his brother's perpetual state of fear; he bathed luxuriously in her raised eyebrows and wide eyes and air-filled cheeks. He stood with his foot on the neck of his brother's pain. He liked how it made him taller and taller.

As Beamer read to the kids to keep them awake, Noelle sat quietly at the edge of the bed, perhaps so that he could register her displeasure with him. It was even harder for her to convey her emotions than it used to be, owing to how different she'd been looking lately. She had, lately, been fucking with her face, first with some Botox that added pleasantly, he thought, to her Presbyterian remove. But then, more recently, she'd started injecting filler into various regions, puffing out her nasolabial folds, which necessitated then that she inject some into her cheeks so that they'd have dimension. The difference was subtle; she did not yet look like the amphibian version of a fish-woman that so many women in this town looked like by their late forties; she was still just in her early thirties, after all. But he feared she was headed there, since, judging by a cursory glance at the attendees of the school's Curriculum Night, it seemed that this kind of easy treatment caused a dysmorphia, and if a ride down Beverly Drive was any indication, she would soon have lost the plot on what a human face was supposed to look like. Right now her interventions were subtle, but real. Her eyebrows didn't crest in surprise anymore without concerted effort. Her smile no longer extended as widely as it used to. It was disorienting to watch her face and wait for it to react, only to find that it was on a kind of tape delay, and the picture was now fuzzy. For the thousandth time, each time against his will, he thought about a comment his mother made upon her last visit:

"This is all she does?" Ruth had said when Noelle, who had been a charming hostess to his mother, had barely left the room. "That's why her face looks like that. She's bored."

"She's a stay-at-home mother," Beamer said. "So were you."

"I had your father to take care of," she snapped back. "I had plenty to do!"

He didn't say anything, because he didn't want another lecture about how his father's ordeal hijacked her chances at a full life. So instead he said:

"It's not her fault that we have money, Mom."

"There is something so dangerous about having too much money and just enough time," Ruth said, almost to herself.

That was a year ago. Now it was all Beamer could see, yes, that the money had created in Noelle a listlessness; the hours when she wasn't caring for the children or overseeing the household staff were not plentiful enough to engage in a meaningful project. She, like the group of similarly wealthy and listless women she trafficked in at the school, had been experimenting in some kind of self-optimization, where they could transform their faces but also delve, just briefly, into the mysteries of their souls. They started by going to a dermatologist who was also a psychologist, who had a method for prescribing based upon the exact shape a person's face should be—"the face of origin," she called it—but then would also use the concentration of lines these women had to determine what was bothering them so much. It seemed like a revelation to them, but really the revelation was only that someone took the time to sit and listen to them and appear to absorb their human condition instead of ignoring it. The diagnosis would result in a catharsis, and also in some injectable neurotoxins: a fresh start for Noelle, once every three months. She had been so beautiful when they'd first met.

The one good thing to come from the second *Santiago* movie was the young actress who played Jorge's love interest (Jorge aged, but his love interests remained the same age). Noelle was fine-boned and blond. Her beauty was what Beamer could only describe, in the most admiring way, as "nonspecific." Meaning that her face was absolutely pretty, that there could be no argument over it, that it was pure. There were no signs in it of the girls, even the pretty ones, that he'd grown up with—no collapsed nasal columella from a nose job, no eyebrows cut short abruptly of the monobrow they so clearly possessed but for aggressive intervention, no processed, dead-ended hair from overdrying and relaxing treatments. Noelle's teeth were straight and white and broadcasted her good breeding and fine pedigree. Her fingers were long; her feet were perfectly arched; her posture was a marvel.

Noelle Albrecht had been scouted at a mall in Maine when she was a teenager and had become a fixture first in the floral Mennonite wear of the Laura Ashley catalogs, then in the popped collar and chino shorts of the L.L.Bean catalogs. Noelle was an OK model. She was not a great actress. By the time she was cast as Jorge's unrealistically pretty girlfriend in *The Santiago Influence,* she was beginning to make peace with this.

Despite her glorious breeding, she had not come from money. Her father had lost his fortune in an illegal land deal investment. So Noelle, who had a leveraged father and a fuckup brother and an alcoholic mother, was her family's great hope, and when they sent her to Hollywood off her catalog success, they were hoping she would come home with some money. Instead, she got bit roles on teen soaps, which she was aging out of quickly. She was sexually harassed by nearly every producer and director who took a meeting with her, or who passed her in a studio commissary. When she was cast in *The Santiago Influence,* she was surprised and relieved to learn that her sexual harasser would not be the movie's legendarily lecherous director but its handsome co-writer, who gave her the right kind of unsettled feelings and who was, it so happened, extremely wealthy.

Did she marry Beamer for money? How could one possibly know? He knew she was tired of a hustle she wasn't bred for. He knew that she loved how he was bawdy and wild—at least, back then she did. If money was part of the calculation, Beamer didn't mind. He knew he was so flawed and needy, so base and craven, that he felt that the only way he could marry someone like Noelle was if he knew she was getting something tangible in return.

"Did you just say Albrecht?" his mother whispered into the phone when Noelle insisted they call their respective parents from the beach where Beamer proposed to tell them the good news. Noelle's parents had congratulated him heartily and, though he tried, Beamer could not find a convincing way to forestall calling his own home.

"Amazing, right?" Beamer said, his voice full of the invented reflected excitement of his family.

"Is she . . . she's a German?" He could see his mother, standing in the kitchen, her hand on her hip, wearing her old black velvet robe, her lips tight and her nostrils flaring.

"She's from Maine. She reminds me of you! You're going to love her!"

"I lived too long," his mother said.

"We're thinking of doing it at the beach!" Beamer said.

"Noelle Albrecht. *Noelle.* Did we not give you enough? Did we not *love* you enough? Do you need more attention? Is that it?"

"You're just gonna love her, Mom."

"This is the one thing. It's the one thing." Her voice was quiet, like a prayer. She was no longer talking to Beamer. She was now talking to God. "All this freedom, all this opportunity, and all we asked was this one thing."

"Yes, we're just bursting over here as well!" Beamer said. Noelle smiled ridiculously.

"You're going to have to tell your grandmother and your father that, after all your grandfather did to hide away from the Nazis, to sneak out on a boat in the middle of the night, to nearly starve as a stowaway on a boat, that this is what you're doing. I'm going to pretend this conversation never happened."

"I know! She wishes she could meet you already!"

Noelle made a motion that she'd like to speak to his mother the way, just minutes ago, he had spoken to her very cordial and civilized and totally appropriate parents.

"Would you like to speak to her?" he asked boisterously, his throat closing.

"I wish I were dead right now," his mother answered. "Can you imagine that you made your mother wish she was dead?"

"Well, we understand. We'll speak to you tomorrow! Go celebrate!" He hung up. Then, to Noelle, "She could barely keep it together. She had to go run and tell my dad and grandmother."

"That's sweet," Noelle said, because she believed him.

Beamer and Noelle were married five years after they were first engaged in a boisterous, black-tie affair on a ranch in Malibu nine weeks following Noelle's first missed period—their friends, wild with dancing, and their two families, cold and rueful at their separate tables, but for different reasons. Seven months later, their daughter was born.

"Let's name her Liesl, after my grandmother," said his wife, as she cradled the baby in her arms from her bed in the VIP room at Cedars-Sinai. And Beamer inhaled with the despondent anticipation of a man who had just spent the prior half decade trying to educate his family that Albrecht was German the way that Fletcher was German, that Noelle's grandparents had left Germany as soon as they could after World War II, that they were Democrats, that they voted for Al Gore when his vice president was going to be Joseph Lieberman, that they defended the Jews—really that they *loved* the Jews, actually.

"Liesl," Ruth said when Beamer called her from the VIP birthing room.

"A family name!" he said with cheer. "It was Noelle's grandmother!"

"You're trying to kill your grandmother."

"It's actually just a diminutive of Elizabeth. Don't I have an aunt Elizabeth?"

"I don't even know what to say, Bernard. I'm speechless."

"Thank you!" He smiled brightly at Noelle, who was staring at little Liesl, the baby's eyes closed in their newborn exhaustion.

"And the Albrechts just keep forgetting to tell me about all the Jewish families they hid in Germany," his mother said in her fake-curiosity voice. "I keep waiting for those stories. I'm beginning to feel like there are none!"

"You're gonna love her."

"Liesl is the oldest daughter of the Nazi in *The Sound of Music.*"

"OK, I'll let you go spread the news! I texted a picture to your phone!" he said, instead of correcting her and saying that, actually, it was Liesl's boyfriend who was the Nazi.

"I'm going to tell Grandma Phyllis myself. I want to be there in case I need to call for help."

"Well, thank you. Yes, yes, I'll tell her. She'll understand!"

And Beamer hung up and turned to Noelle and said, "She just was beside herself. She couldn't wait to tell all of Middle Rock."

So Liesl it was, and he knew that when he called his mother from the same birthing suite at Cedars three years later, it would have done nothing to prepare her for their chosen son's name, which was Wolfgang, after Noelle's favorite uncle.

"Wolfgang," his mother repeated. "It's like you're playing a joke on me."

"He's as beautiful as his mother and his sister," Beamer said.

"Like, it's a parody of a son marrying a shiksa joke at this point. Liesl and now *Wolfgang*? Is there a camera that's going to jump out! Allen Funt over here! If so, I would like this *Candid Camera* segment to end!"

"You know, I was just saying to Noelle that your father's name was Zev, which means Wolf. Didn't you say that your grandmother called him Volf?"

"Bernard Fletcher, you take my father's name out of your mouth."

"OK, I'll tell her!" And he hung up, turned to Noelle, who was smiling angelically at the baby, and said, "She's so honored."

Now, as Beamer lay awake on the plane to his grandmother's funeral, he looked out from his lay-flat diamond-class bed to his wife's. She was asleep, and when he looked at her without worrying about what she saw in return, he could really see her. The thing she was doing to her face, it broke his heart. It had the countenance of swelling, of puffing out, of crying and distance, and there was a part of him that knew, three Scotches into this flight, that she suffered for being unable to talk about the things that bothered her, a quality he'd been looking for after a lifetime of his mother. Beneath the Scotch cloud, he understood that words were not the only way we communicate. He wanted to reach out and touch her face.

What Ruth didn't understand, what she couldn't realize for as much of a mind-reading witch as she was, was that his marriage and family and even his job represented not just his great success but his lifelong goals: children who did not resemble his own family at any angle, and a wife who served as his very own *Mayflower* to take him to a new world, away from his terrified, haunted family before they drowned him off the shore.

Look what he had. He had a woman who could appropriately discern the threat level, who could mitigate the genetic horror of what he brought into a family. Noelle herself didn't even understand what she was for Beamer. She was a hazmat suit; she was a life raft. She would wash him in newness if only he would let her.

For the millionth time since he married Noelle, but also the millionth time that day, Beamer swore he was not going to fuck this up; he swore he would do better. He wanted to be successful on his own terms. He wanted to be good at his job. He wanted to take care of his body and squeak with pristine health. He wanted to be a father his children would admire. He wanted to deserve his family. He wanted to complete the mission he began all those years ago when he had first carried Noelle over their threshold, which was to successfully transform away from who he was and make himself into someone normal.

His progress had gone slower than he'd hoped, but life wasn't over yet. It was not over yet! Inside him, the booze and the residual drugs that had not yet been flushed by his exhausted liver combined to create in him the hormones of delirious optimism, the feeling of a newborn's potential. He was an excellent husband in the making. He was baptized in the purity of his children. His screenplay, once he made just a few revisions to it, was going to change the world; he was going to prove himself on his own merit. He had merit! He closed his eyes and let the serotonic rush of a wide-open future spread through his lymph, his veins, his muscles, all of his bodily systems, in hopes that they could inoculate him against whatever awaited him upon landing.

Somewhere over one of the states he never learned much about in school, Beamer made devout resolutions to himself as the plane shot through the sky, an unstoppable bullet that was determined for Long Island, no matter how much Scotch he drank.

ALL OF MIDDLE Rock gathered at Temple Beth Israel to pay their second-to-last respects to Phyllis Fletcher.

Inside the sanctuary, Beamer and Noelle took their place in the front pew. Beamer sat with his eyes defocused. There existed for him the real possibility that he would turn into a pillar of salt were he just to turn around and see everyone who had ever known him. He couldn't bear to look to his left and see his big brother, Nathan, crying, and Nathan's wife, Alyssa, comforting him in a way that his own wife would not, were he to have an actual emotion about his grandmother's departure from this Earth. He couldn't bear to look just beyond Nathan and Alyssa to see his sister, Jenny, his one true ally in the family, who had taken on a particular stoniness with him since she had visited him in L.A. almost a year before. He couldn't look to the right because that was where Noelle was sitting, and the dissonance of seeing her unpolluted uprightness against all the messiness of his origins would be too much to bear. He couldn't look at any of them. He could handle a conversation with any of these people; what might be contained in a wordless exchange, however, would absolutely do him in.

Indeed, the one glance he'd taken at his mother had nearly knocked him over. His mother and grandmother, for as long as he remembered, had been a duo of huddled, conniving manipulator worrywarts whose primary job was to manage the ongoing crisis of his catatonic father, and then raise Beamer and his siblings with whatever energy they had left over, which was none. If Ruth had been a loving, caring, expansive woman when she first married and had kids, in the years since Carl's kidnapping, her proximity to her mother-in-law and their shared goal of lying across Carl like he was a grenade had curdled into resemblance. In other words, Beamer's mother had some derision for how controlling his grandmother was; she did not have the self-awareness to understand that she was exactly the same way.

So he looked straight ahead, but with blurry eyes because of course he could not look straight ahead with the full power of his vision, because right in front of him was the cedar box that contained the earthly remains of his grandmother.

Noelle turned and began to ask him something—who someone

was or when they would get started or how long would this whole thing last—but stopped herself.

"Oh, you're crying," she whispered, with such tenderness in her voice. But then, upon closer inspection: "Is that sweat? Beamer, are you *sweating*?"

"It's the humidity. It's the suit."

It was not the humidity; it was not the suit. Beamer and his family had arrived at Newark that morning; after the kidnapping, the Fletchers only ever flew into Newark, despite their extraordinary proximity to both JFK and LaGuardia. Their hired car got them to the estate in Middle Rock an hour later. They drove past the long white gate and turned up the driveway.

The estate that Zelig Fletcher, the polystyrene magnate, had brought Beamer's grandmother to as a young bride nearly seventy-five years before would have been unrecognizable to Zelig now. Somewhere along the way, the lush maze of bushes had become thorny, brittle skeletons full of the foreboding that portends mortality. Phyllis and Zelig's house was the same—painted white brick with stark black shutters—but the roof had shingles that were born in widely different years, patched with care following nor'easter after nor'easter. (Ruth and Carl's house, the one that Beamer was raised in, was the same vintage; built to work with the aesthetic of the other house, but just slightly smaller.)

Elsewhere, it was the reassuring, disgusting feeling of home. The cracked clay of the tennis court. The caretaker cottages were now occupied by the grandchildren of the groundskeepers Zelig and Phyllis had hired decades ago, the grandchildren themselves now taking care of the property. Hidden behind Phyllis's house, the pool house went unused, frozen in the last summer of its active use, circa 2001; the pool, which overlooked the Sound, was fractured and empty. Farther down the driveway, what was once Carl's father's beloved greenhouse was now empty. What was once an impressive collection of ivory-white statues that lined the giant lawn had turned just a slightly more ecru shade of white, and there was a limb missing from one. The white wooden fence that stretched along the road showed signs of decay. The small thicket of strawberry bushes located at the bottom of the estate no longer yielded fruit, and Zelig Fletcher was dead and now so was Phyllis.

Beamer and Noelle alighted from the car and stretched this way and that while Liesl started doing cartwheels on the grass and Wolfgang chased her.

The weather, it was deadly. It was back-to-school, Jewish-holiday crisp, a bright blue sky with fibrous, bright white clouds. It was the weather of optimism and renewal and forgiveness. It was the weather of every fresh start he'd ever had, every lesson he'd ever learned, every first time he'd ever had. It was now also the weather of his grandmother's funeral.

Beamer's parents' house was empty when they arrived. Beamer dropped his and Noelle's bags in his old room and set the kids up in Jenny's old room before he could be told that Jenny was coming in from Connecticut and to please instead could the whole family stay just up the driveway a little farther at Phyllis's house, which was now permanently devoid of Phyllis. No way. No way was Beamer staying in Phyllis's house.

He'd left Noelle to unpack and then wandered into his parents' room, and then into their bathroom, and then into his mother's medicine cabinet, which he groped and clawed around, looking for some new feeling and hoping his parents had some leftover opioids from a root canal or something. All he found was stupid, shitty codeine, which was his least favorite high.

The funeral wasn't until three P.M., so after he and his family took a nap, Beamer volunteered to go get his favorite pizza from Gina's, where he ran into Lisa Beldstein, the butcher's granddaughter, and *is that you* and *I didn't recognize you* and the way she looked at him and what she said: "I thought, no way does any guy in the world carry himself like that except Beamer fuckin' Fletcher, I'd know that guy anywhere." And she'd just gotten a divorce and *could he maybe help her with the soda getting it to the car* because the kids were waiting for pizza and, one thing led to another, and then he was in Lisa Beldstein's garage, fucking her in the backseat of her Lexus with the door open and their legs hanging out and do you see? Do you see why codeine is bad?

He arrived back at the house, and, this time, attacking the guest bathroom on the second floor, he found beneath that bathroom sink, waaaaay in the back, a roll of expired nicotine patches. The sight of them made him want a cigarette, which made him realize that if he smoked, he'd have to quit, which would make these the exact right thing he should put on his body right this minute and maybe, in conjunction with the codeine, it would help get him through the evening and the next day. There had been six expired patches in the box; he put all of them on: one on each biceps, one on each thigh, one on his stomach, and one atop his heart for a soupçon of danger. He heard his parents come in.

"Hi, Mommy," Beamer said. He was happy Noelle was already upstairs; how merciless she was over the fact that the Fletcher kids called their parents Mommy and Daddy.

"Beamer," his mother said. "When did you get here?"

Beamer focused on his mother so he wouldn't have to look at his father.

"Hours ago."

"The kids are upstairs?" Ruth asked.

"They are," he said.

"Hm."

Ruth went to the coffee maker. She had no distaste for her grandchildren; in fact, she loved them, despite their lack of resemblance to her (or perhaps because of it). What she did have was a hierarchical system of caretaking, which meant she was out for Carl first, herself second (to preserve her ability to take care of Carl), then her kids, then her grandkids, then her domestic help, then a stranger in Liberia, then the woman Linda Messinger told her she read about who needed gallbladder surgery in Iowa but was stuck in a snowstorm, then her Jewish daughter-in-law, then her Gentile one.

Now, from a small room off the sanctuary, Carl and Marjorie emerged, led by old Rabbi Weintraub. Carl looked gray in pallor. He had been kept young by his mother's continued endurance; now he was old, and he was crying openly. Beamer had only seen his father cry once before in his life. Of course, their father's crying only made Nathan sob harder, which made the pews shake, which made Jenny look up to the ceiling in annoyance. Beamer finally looked over at Jenny, and the sight of her apathy made him want to hug her and also swallow her so that he could be her or at least contain some aspect of her. But this was a funeral so he turned back to staring down, the only safe place. Carl took a seat next to Ruth, and Marjorie took the seat between him and Alexis, her roommate (went the family euphemism).

"Would there even be a Middle Rock without Phyllis Fletcher?" Rabbi Weintraub said from the bimah. "Indeed, there is probably no one here whose life wasn't affected by her community service: the refurbishment of the religious school. The expansion of the temple's grounds and the playground. Those of us who were here for it will never forget her victory as the town's school board president. Phyllis Fletcher was remarkable. She was a force because she used her understanding of the town's history to inform its future. It's not just people like her, but her in particular, who created such a coherent and *intentional* town, a town that knows its ethic and its values. Truly, I woke up this morning thinking of her tireless work as president of the Historical Society, how she fought the town and the district and then the county for help, with her beloved grandson, Nathan, to restore the lighthouse when the county wanted to replace it with a steel beam. Phyllis knew it was the small reminders of a town's soul that kept that soul intact."

Suddenly, a memory: Beamer finishing up his bar mitzvah lessons—the Fletcher family children received bar mitzvah lessons from the rabbi personally, the only people in Middle Rock who had such an arrangement. Rabbi Weintraub was saying something about the haftorah when he heard a click of footsteps and his face changed from weary wisdom into abject panic.

"Your grandmother is picking you up, Bernard?" he asked. He'd known her footsteps, the ones that arrived on schedule within fifteen minutes following the end of the monthly Sisterhood meetings that took place in the synagogue conference room. She would spend at least an hour soliciting a change she wanted in the synagogue—a new cantor, an evaluation of the acoustics in the sanctuary, a capital campaign to restore the Torah scrolls—coming at him from the Sisterhood and the board that she was the chair of once her presidential term expired. Years later, Rabbi Weintraub would have his daughter program in his cellphone a new ring for Phyllis, so that he could prepare himself emotionally for whatever call he either had to take or return immediately. By the time he stood over her coffin, Rabbi Weintraub had been threatened and intimidated by Phyllis Fletcher more times than any man of holy cloth who eschewed a material life and worked in the service of his community should have to tolerate.

Rabbi Weintraub turned to Nathan. "Nathan, your grandmother confided to me that those months she spent working together with you, watching you use your law degree, were some of her most gratifying. After all your grandfather went through to arrive at this country, after all they did to build a life—that they got to take so much pride in their grandchildren was beyond a reward for her."

Rabbi Weintraub continued: how proud she was of Carl for maintaining the factory in his father's name; what a thrill it was to watch Bernard's movies; how she was so sad that she would never meet Jenny's children, should she ever settle down; that she was so grateful that Ruth took such good care of her Carl; that it was factually correct to say that Marjorie was her daughter.

And, yet, somehow the rabbi seemed to be filled with real emotion when he finished his eulogy. Death floors you every time. He said, "Phyllis was a remarkable woman."

In the front pew, only Carl was convinced.

"I now call up Marjorie, who will speak on behalf of both herself and her brother, Carl," the rabbi said.

Marjorie stood up. Marjorie had the appearance of a frayed wire, a thing in a constant, dangerous state of unravel. She had been born with her father's surprising round blue eyes and her mother's dark hair, but her eyes had gone cloudy and square and scared-looking and the dark of her hair was gone and replaced with a gray crown of overgrown thorns that seemed to swizzle from her head like nerve-thoughts that were twisting away from her brain and then died from the effort.

It is narrowly known that Jews do not dress in traditional American black for funerals, but what Marjorie was wearing was more reminiscent of the costumes she wore when she was briefly in a competitive folk-dancing group while Beamer was in high school. Today, she wore a long necklace with a clear, pear-shaped crystal that hit right at her sternum. Her T-shirt was long-sleeved and white and still a T-shirt. Her floral chiffon skirt contained small bells at the end of the hem and on her feet were sandals, also with bells on them, and that jangled like a sleigh ride up to the bimah. It was her mother's funeral.

She arrived at the shtender and looked out at the crowd for a second, and her eyes momentarily took on a flicker of—was that—triumph.

"My mother," she began. But she stopped. She closed her eyes, then opened them again. Yes, decision. "My mother."

She looked down at Alexis, who gave her a nod of encouragement.

"My mother had a lot of opinions," Marjorie began.

The crowd laughed lightly, and the trickle of laughter first caused Marjorie to startle. It was the startle of a person who had spent her whole life unable to confirm but still absolutely sure that people were making fun of her. The laughter wasn't ridicule, though; Beamer recognized it as the relief of a crowd who now believed they were in for a light and loving remembrance of a woman who had been crazily old for as long as most of them could remember. That's what an old person funeral is like: Someone as old as Phyllis was always going to die, and it was the mourners who dictated the Tragedy of Death vs. Celebration of Life index of the day.

"She said the only proper gift from one Jew to another was an Israel bond. She said you should always buy real estate near an Orthodox shul, since the value will always grow. Also near the water, though that will cost you in insurance." Another light trickling of knowing laughter from the crowd. "She said never to trust the banks, and always keep a little stash of money on the side in case you have to make a run for it. My father taught her that one." More laughter. Who knew Marjorie had this in her? "And also, she had some definitive ideas about how to build a strong girl." She nodded for a second, gathering strength. "But she wasn't always right. She tried, but, ha"—this single-syllable laugh was bitter—"yes, she was, shall we say, a little off on more than one occasion."

Whoops, the crowd had been wrong wrong wrong. In the Tragedy of Death vs. Celebration of Life lottery, the winner was going to be the less frequent but always memorable third option: Character Assassination of the Dead Before She Is Even in the Ground.

"My mother believed that if you constantly denigrated a person and chipped away at her dreams and sense of self, what you would have in the end was someone who could withstand all the abuse that the world had to offer."

And now the room was suddenly silent. Here it was, that exotic creature in the wild, the daughter avenging herself in public over her mother's lifeless, defenseless body.

Marjorie told the story of her first high school dance, how her mother had taken her to New York City to B. Altman to find a new dress, only to leave without buying anything, saying that when nothing was flattering, the key was to look as if you didn't try too hard. She had Marjorie wear her bat mitzvah dress to the dance instead, a silver drop-waist sailor dress. Marjorie was fifteen by then. It was no longer a drop-waist, just an ugly, ill-fitted sailor dress that made her look like a toddler dressed up in Shirley Temple drag.

"I realize now that my mother was trying to show me she loved me then. Some people, they just don't know how to communicate. She saved all her energy for Carl. I used to resent it. I did. I resented it. But then, as you all know, it turned out that it was good they were so close. She didn't have a lot. But what she did have, she gave to him. It turned out he would need it more."

Up on that bimah, Marjorie, who was normally a seismograph for people's regard of her, had quickly become drunk on the wide-scale pronouncement of the category of grievances she frequently referred to (in crowds smaller than this, mostly gathered on folding chairs in a circle) as "her truth." She looked into the audience, expecting understanding, a look that might have been called her signature look, and did not receive it, but she continued anyway. This was her *moment*. She didn't notice what was really in front of her, which was an audience who had recoiled in true horror: Was this what awaited them all from their ungrateful daughters?

The nightmare ended when Marjorie made the mistake of looking at Carl, who was crying with such abandon that she seemed distracted for a minute, and when she returned to the audience, she couldn't quite regain her bearings. She stammered a minute. She tried to refocus. She tried to find her next words but could not and made a noise that sounded like "ack" before the rabbi, sensing a good moment to cut Marjorie off, approached from where he'd been standing stage left, and put his arm around her shoulders and guided her off the stage, though she was still trying to speak into the microphone and was clearly perplexed as to why her grand moment had to end, and why she didn't feel even a little better afterward. She walked past Beamer, past Nathan, whose face was frozen in a near-Munchian scream-panic, past Jenny, whose face was bereft of expression, past Ruth, whose eyes were closed, past Carl, whose head was bowed and whose rended shirt was wet.

"The Fletchers are a great Jewish American family," Rabbi Weintraub was saying now. "They are what our ancestors hoped for us when they abandoned their terrorized homelands and made way for this world. They had to invent who they were, what a Jew could be in America—that's what Phyllis will represent as the years go by, a creative act that allowed us all to live in peace and comfort. But today I am reminded, or maybe I understand for the first time, that she was merely a woman. A beloved mother. A cherished grandmother. An honored aunt. A community builder. A loved one dies, a matriarch, no less, and the world no longer has color for her family. Right now, we, as a community, have to be there for them, the way they have been there for us—the way Phyllis was there for us—all along."

On the way home from the cemetery, Beamer sat in one of two hired limousines, his head against the window. Noelle was checking her face in her compact. Nathan and Alyssa were holding hands solemnly. Jenny sat next to Nathan. Their parents and Marjorie and Alexis and cousin Arthur were in the other car behind them.

"Marjorie really did a number," Beamer said.

He dared to turn to Jenny for affirmation, but she had fallen asleep.

Beamer returned his head to the window and watched as they drove into Middle Rock. If the rabbi was right, and a town had a soul, Middle Rock's had been papered over.

Spring Avenue Road, the main street of his youth, was now in disarray. Half the stores were shut down. Most of the storefronts were a hodgepodge of restaurants. Two of the clothing stores where his mother took him for back-to-school shopping were now chain drugstores. A Starbucks had replaced the ice cream store that Ruth used to bring them to on their way home from camp. The stationery store where Jenny used to buy puffy and scented stickers to trade with her friends had been replaced by one of four shops whose only service was to blow wet, curly hair into dry, straight hair. There were threading salons where the furrier and the bookstore—the bookstore!—had been and a waxing salon where the gadget store had long been standing.

They drove into the residential area. The houses no longer looked the same to him. Whereas he would have categorized them as sort of humble in their opulence before—just big and grand and enough, not unwieldy in their extravagance, now they were a carnival show. The Craftsmans and Colonials and Federalists and Tudors of his youth were still there, but every third one had been razed to make way for something that looked like either a Frankenstein of architectural indecision or an effigy of an important building in another country: a huge expanse of a house that looked like an Italian palazzo or an English castle or the Taj Mahal or a Spanish villa made by someone who had only heard of those things but had never actually seen them. Or a mixed-media half-Tudor half-midcentury-modern disaster complete with a Texan ziggurat and a turret that made no sense.

And the scale! Each lot of land in Middle Rock was inherently gener-ous; the town code stated that houses have to sit on at least half an acre. The lots were still the same size, but now those houses were so large they encroached on the neighboring property lines. And the details were just atrocious: curling wrought-iron gates and shutters that couldn't possibly work and stone-ish siding and my god, the col-umns: Corinthian, Doric, Ionic, tragic.

Now here is a separate paragraph just for the doors. The doors on these homes were huge, at least two whole people high, like they led into a king's chambers or the palace of an ancient ruin. They were elaborately carved and decorated, etched and embellished. Their knockers were comically ornamental: curlicued or in the shape of a cobra that was coiled or like a jaw of teeth. Beamer had only seen doors like this on fantasy television shows that took place in ancient worlds.

As the limo wended farther toward the water, farther toward his parents' house, Beamer thought about his screenplay, or he thought about thinking about his screenplay, and then he thought about fuck-ing Lisa Beldstein. He was trying to distract himself from the image of his father shoveling dirt onto his mother's coffin in a grave next to his father's—a Jewish tradition for the family to throw the initial dirt on the grave—in an area of the cemetery that had plots waiting for him and his siblings and their spouses (but not Noelle). Then he thought about himself in the trunk of the very limo he was sitting in. He pictured himself bound and screaming so that no one could hear, and this kept him in a somewhat tranquil mood as the car passed through the gate and onto the Fletcher estate.

THE LIMO BEAMER was in had the rest of the cars beat by at least several minutes. He left the car and stretched while Noelle hurried inside to check on the children, who were being watched by a neigh-borhood babysitter that his sister-in-law, Alyssa, had arranged for them.

Beamer braced himself and entered. He had just been at Phyllis's house two months ago, when it became clear that she wasn't going to endure much longer. He'd sat next to her as she slept and tried to make himself hold her hand, but he found it was so papery and translucent by then that he couldn't even look at it.

The house was the same study in contrasts as Phyllis herself: equal parts monstrously rich and maniacally frugal. It had an Art Deco cohesiveness to it, but that was because Phyllis and Zelig furnished their home with high-quality sale items on Art Deco's way out. That was Phyllis's gift, to know what might last. There was a certain stiff, faded endurance to the furniture—all in a shade of teal that reverberated between the Vivid Green, Peacock Green, and Beach Glass Pantones, though they were probably the same color at one point and just had different levels of exposure to the sun. Phyllis would never replace the furniture because it had cost them so much in the first place and because she stubbornly took literally the salesman who told her and Zelig, as young newlyweds in hats and gloves in a showroom, that they'd have this stuff "for life." Gold, ringed chandeliers dipping out of a very high ceiling and parquet floors in black and white whose shine hadn't faded, no doubt the result of daily buffing by their household staff of one housekeeper named Marla. This was Phyllis's home as she'd kept it her entire married life.

In the foyer now, he felt a swirl of desperation, just briefly, at his grandmother's absence. It was not that he was so fond of her; it was that this was, perhaps, the first true loss of his life. What does it mean to just disappear? His whole life, he'd been imagining getting taken, but never actually ceasing to be. In his fantasies, the disappeared could always be found. Now, he wanted to run outside, down the giant lawn that they used to call the Impossible Lawn, after a gardener complained about the fact that once he was done mowing it, the other side of it had grown back, it was so large. He wanted to scream. Instead, he rubbed the spot on his heart where the nicotine patch was, in hopes that the friction would activate it further.

The door opened behind Beamer and, slowly, the house filled.

Soon his father was on a low seat in the living room, receiving with sad, tired nods the good wishes and memories of the people he'd known his whole life.

Beamer went upstairs to the bathroom and rifled through Phyllis's medicine cabinet. It was there he found his jackpot: Among the prescription ibuprofen that would be useless to him, he found an amber bottle full of phentermine, which he recognized as diet pills. Speed, good. On the floor, leaning against the toilet, he dry-swallowed two of them. There was a knock at the door.

He stood up and passed through whatever Sisterhood old lady had trudged up to use the bathroom. He absconded to his father's old bedroom, which was embalmed in the Scottish plaids his father had either chosen or not chosen to grow to adulthood amid. He closed the door, away from the smell of smoked fish and coffee and geriatric chemtrails.

He lay on the bed and looked up. The last time he'd slept in this bed was more than thirty years ago, on the terrible day of Nathan's bar mitzvah. Beamer, nine years old, in an itchy suit and strangulating tie, waiting by the window of his parents' house for someone to pull the car around. He had been watching out the window in the living room. The estate had a tent already set up, ready to host the reception that night—the first of the Fletcher grandchildren's bar mitzvahs. It was early morning and there was a mist over the Impossible Lawn. There were trucks up and down the driveway, tables and chairs and lights getting offloaded. Beamer was hypnotized by the action.

Beamer was wearing a yarmulke with Nathan's name woven into the Mets logo. Jenny walked into the living room from outside wearing a royal blue shimmery dress and orange patent leather Mary Janes.

"What?" Beamer asked, because she seemed confused or upset.

"Nothing," Jenny said, and lay down on the floor and fell asleep.

How Beamer loved Jenny—still, even now, even though she was not speaking to him for the first time in their lives. She'd been born into the most confusing moment of his life, a time when they had moved out of their home on St. James Drive abruptly following a brief but violent period of badness where Beamer remembered a scary day that his mother drove him around on highways. That time was only referred to with heated, angry flashes of the eyes and teeth, the imperative to hush and not talk about it. Beamer had felt nothing but impermanence at that time, and his older brother, nervous Nathan, was no help. They two watched the whispering, but no one ever mentioned what had happened again, and they had the instinct not just not to ask, not just to never speak about it even with each other, but to never consciously think about it or remember it or even to assign words to it.

Then, one day, a few months later, his parents disappeared again, and Phyllis came and slept in their bedroom. Beamer didn't know where they were, but knew he shouldn't ask any questions about it, lest the eyes and the teeth flash again. He assumed to himself that now both his parents had been taken, but that for some reason, no one wanted to be honest about it. They returned a day later, though, and now they had a sleeping infant with them.

Beamer took the opportunity, not even five years old, to pronounce Jenny's birth the Fletchers' new start—his new start. As time went on, his father remained remote and cold and his mother still seemed devoted, principally, to her husband and not her children. But Beamer decided that Jenny represented what he could be and not what he was. He would protect her, and, in turn, she would make him new.

Jenny was still sleeping on the floor of the living room on the morning of the bar mitzvah when Nathan, in a suit and yarmulke that matched Beamer's, scurried into the room.

"Aren't we supposed to leave?" Nathan asked. He was more high-pitched than usual. Then, at Jenny: "Why is she sleeping?"

Beamer shrugged.

Grandma Phyllis appeared in the living room. She was wearing her Chanel suit, the only one she owned, and which she would wear to the synagogue portion of all three of her grandchildren's bar mitzvahs.

"Look at how handsome you look," she said to Nathan. Then, to Beamer, "Look at you."

Beamer nudged Jenny awake.

"Everyone into the car," Phyllis said.

Nathan was confused. "We're not going with Mommy and Daddy?"

"They're going to be a little late," she said in her officious way. "Now, into the car."

The children drove with their grandmother over to the temple, where everyone they knew was waiting for them. The boys from Nathan's class all wore the Mets yarmulkes that were provided to them at the door, and the grown-ups who were there smiled extra big at Nathan. As time went on, people took their places and the service began to move, but Carl and Ruth were nowhere to be found.

The service began. No Carl and Ruth. The service continued. No Carl and Ruth. Rabbi Weintraub made a speech about Nathan and his meticulous mind and his ability to do calculations like the best Talmudic scholars—"to worry about things that no one had yet thought to worry about," he said with true affection—and Carl and Ruth were nowhere to be found.

Nathan was called to the Torah (no Carl and Ruth). And the rabbi gave out the aliyot that a person gives to the parents of the child getting bar mitzvahed, but he gave them to Phyllis and to Carl's cousin, Arthur, who took up his duties without a word. Ike Besser, who was the foreman in Carl's factory and who was there with his sloppy, resentful wife, Mindy, and his son, Max, was given an aliyah, too. No Carl and Ruth. Marjorie carried the Torah through the congregation, an honor usually bestowed on the mother. No Carl and Ruth. Nathan's school friends threw candy at him when he was done, and Beamer pelted him with full-body throws that were most vicious—and still no Carl and Ruth.

Nathan gave his speech. There was the kiddush. There was the lunch. There was the return to Phyllis's house, where they all relaxed for two hours with Arthur and Marjorie, talking about how well Nathan had done. Still no Carl and Ruth, and even crazier, still no *mention* of Carl and Ruth. And just like always, Beamer knew somewhere inside him that he shouldn't ask, that if he did, the thing in his family that was already bent beyond its capacity would break.

There was the Mets-themed party, where the DJ was given rush orders to pivot the candle-lighting to now accommodate the Messingers, who stood, absurdly, in place of Nathan's parents. There was limbo, there was Coke and Pepsi, there was a round of musical chairs that was canceled when Nathan's classmates abstained because the game was too babyish, which was just as well, because Nathan's nerves could not accommodate time-pressured activities. The night wound down and everyone danced to "Y.M.C.A." and "We Are Family." Still no Carl and Ruth.

That night, the kids stayed at Phyllis's house. The sleepover had been billed as a special surprise treat, though it was clear that it was a desperate move to keep the kids from their parents. Nathan, Beamer, and Jenny sat in long T-shirts that had belonged to Zelig around the kitchen island, where Phyllis served them hot chocolate.

"Do you know what a dybbuk is?" she asked them. She was leafing through the pile of cards that had been left on the gift table, separating the Israel bonds into a pile while noting their amount on the card written by the family who had given the gift. Phyllis had done at-home events for Israel bonds where she served cocktails and hors d'oeuvres while a representative of the Israeli government made a pitch—the Jewish Tupperware Party of its day—and everyone knew that you only give the Fletchers Israel bonds as gifts.

"Like when Daddy says 'a dybbuk in the works,'" Nathan said, helpfully.

"Yes, exactly," she said. Then, to Beamer and Jenny, "Do you two?"

But Beamer was chugging hot chocolate and Jenny had put her head down on the counter.

"Wake up, Jennifer," Phyllis continued. "Just listen to this. Are you listening? A dybbuk is a spirit that can't rest."

Nathan became very still and whispered, "What does that mean?"

"It's a spirit that wanders and inhabits someone because it hasn't been given the right to ascend to heaven yet."

Beamer was now paying very close attention. He had a thousand questions: Is a dybbuk real? Is it someone you know? Can you prevent it? Is it bad? Is it good?

"I'm using it mostly as a metaphor, Bernard," Phyllis said. He was called Beamer by then, but Phyllis called him Bernard since Bernard was her father's name and that was who he'd been named for. (There was a misunderstanding that Beamer only became Beamer when he began driving in high school and was given a BMW, and then there was a rumor that he was called Beamer because his eyes were hypnotic like high beams. But the actual story was that he was called Beamer from the time he was six, when his little sister tried to say his name and couldn't and said something instead that sounded like Beamer and it took. This baptism by Jenny went well with his overall theory of fresh starts.)

"I'm saying that sometimes something takes him over," Phyllis continued. "A spirit. A demon. He's haunted. Since his ordeal. He does the best he can, but sometimes, a dybbuk takes over. I'm saying you have to get used to the fact that your father has a dybbuk running around inside him. I'm saying he can't always rise to the occasion. You understand me, kids?"

Nobody ever slept at Phyllis's house again.

Now, at the shiva, Beamer's phone made a noise.

Where are you, Noelle texted Beamer. His heart was racing from the phentermine, just like he liked it. He went downstairs. It was seven P.M. now. The room was at capacity with townsfolk who had just finished the shiva minyan and were eating from the pyramid of bagels and heart-shaped whitefish and cream cheese platters that were sent over from the Bagel Man by one of the societies with whom Phyllis had had an affiliation.

In the corner, Jenny was awake and surrounded by her high school friends Erica Mayer and Sarah Messinger-Schlesinger. Erica's mother, Cecilia, who used to wear tight polyester wrap dresses that showcased her nipples nicely, was fussing over Erica's baby. In the foyer,

Ruth and Arthur were discussing something secret, like they always were. Beamer thought about catching Jenny's eye so that they could exchange the usual look about their fantastical longtime theory that their mother and Arthur were in a clandestine romantic relationship, but then thought better of a public testing of Jenny's temperament toward him. On the small chair to his father's left, Marjorie was mopey and Alexis was whispering something comforting to her. Beamer looked for a safe place.

The kitchen seemed like it could work. It had an escape door that emptied out onto the water side of Phyllis's house. Beamer walked in and, nope, wrong choice. Alyssa was telling Noelle about the bar mitzvah she was planning for her twin sons, and how she was debating if she wanted to do a kitchen "reno" before or after the bar mitzvah. "It'll be a mess, but how can I have guests in that kitchen right now? My whole family is coming to stay by me!"

"There you are," Noelle said, when she saw him. She widened her eyes. "Do you think it's time to get the kids to bed? They're exhausted."

"They should be less tired since they're coming from the West Coast, no?" Alyssa asked.

Nearby, Liesl was twirling to make her skirt fly up for the amusement of Nathan's adolescent sons.

"Stop that, Liesl," Noelle hissed. "Stop that!"

"Why don't you get them out of here," Beamer said. "I'll just help clean up."

Noelle was out of there, both kids' hands in hers, before he was done saying that. Alyssa looked bewildered.

Beamer moved back to the living room, just in time to avoid her concerned questions about his well-being and the movie business. But this was a mistake, too, as he landed right in the trap of his father, who was listening to the remaining few of his own father's friends regale Carl with stories of his parents: the story of Beamer's grandfather, the great Zelig, on that boat, coming over to America, and all the people around Carl and Marjorie murmuring what a fighter that Zelig was, and how much of the fighting was about keeping traditions—keeping American Jewry itself alive. And that the Jews like Zelig, well, they broke the mold when they made him, but what does it matter, there were so few of us then and we never replaced ourselves after the Holocaust, except for the ultra-Orthodox Jews. Morrie Beckerman, who was another factory owner (retired) who lived in Middle Rock and was the president of the Factory Owners Association (still) that Carl belonged to, said, "That's not the same as us. As regular Jews. It changes the equation."

Morrie had numbers on his arms. Beamer remembered some holiday meal long ago, looking over and seeing those numbers, the alarm that came over him. He'd known about Morrie's numbers, but for some reason, staring at them as a teenager—he couldn't believe it. He couldn't believe you could number people, but, also, he couldn't believe that Morrie would ever let anyone see them, that he was willing to show how he had been diminished like that. It reminded him of how he'd always known his father's ordeal, but one day he had actually woken up to it as new information, as in: OH MY GOD MY FATHER WAS KIDNAPPED.

"They're Jewish, too, you know," Marjorie said.

"I didn't say they're not," Morrie said. "I said we're going extinct, our kind of Jews. Marrying shiksas and having these half-breed children."

And someone hit Morrie on the knee and jutted a jaw toward Beamer, which caused Beamer to wonder what the hell he was doing in this house when his family was at the other house. He walked determinedly out of the living room, not making eye contact with anyone, nor acknowledging that he saw Charlie's mother, Linda Messinger, who opened her mouth as he passed as if she were about to say hello, but he could not right then deal with questions and comments about Charlie or his perfect wife and thriving career and now a third child, too.

On his way out, he heard one of Phyllis's old friends say to Jenny, "It's true what the rabbi said. She was holding on to see you get married and have children." Jenny was receiving this wordlessly.

Outside, Beamer broke into a jog. He had to get to Noelle, whom he suddenly needed like he now needed nicotine, thanks to those patches. Noelle, who was uncompromised by the ghetto double-breeding that made the Fletchers incurably nearsighted and prone to bronchitis, along with the ridiculous imperative to marry within the same religion, as if doubling down on a million genetic diseases could have possibly been a just God's will. But when he arrived at his parents' house to find them all asleep, he looked at them not through his own eyes but through Morrie Beckerman's. He looked at them from the crack in the door and felt a sudden and deep shame. Look at her. Look at these *children*. Who were they? What did they have to do with Beamer?

("You know what happens when you marry a young shiksa?" Phyllis had asked him, when, in a final plea-threat for him to reconsider, she had appealed not to his conscience but to his vanity. "You end up with an old goya." He still didn't totally understand what that meant, but he thought about it constantly.)

Beamer went to Carl's study, which was not being occupied for the duration of the shiva, and pulled his laptop out of his work bag, and though he had slept as little as anyone else, and perhaps owing to the drug soup that was right now rendering his liver into the consistency of beef jerky, he got to work on his screenplay. He reread the abhorrent, rejected script, hoping he would be able to dismiss Stan and Anya's allegations of cultural insensitivity and overall vapidity.

What he found instead was a sea of shame in which to submerge himself. Suddenly, every line made him cringe. Every instinct that a prior version of himself that existed just a month before had considered righteous and creative was now clearly idiotic and senseless.

Of course Jorge shouldn't be Mexican (but then what?).

Of course the love interest shouldn't be twenty (but then who?).

And what was worse than all that was how bad the writing was. How the sentences were wooden, the premise endemically flawed, the action nonsensical, the characterization nonexistent.

O the self-loathing!

He had to start over. He had to get this right. He had to try, at least. He had to sit and try. His momentum was gone; his chances for a successful future of his own were dwindling. In the darkness of his father's study, where he sat in the glow of his computer like it was a campfire, he had the desperation of a final chance.

He had to get this right.

So he hacked and hacked, for hours, until the revision stars lining the margin of the draft were more prevalent than the blank spaces, and he was perilously close to being in the neighborhood of the zip code of the time zone of being on the verge of a script that would make good use of all he knew about how to write an action movie.

It was four in the morning when Beamer finally looked up from his computer. His parents had come in hours before and gone to bed and so had his sister. He had worked hard, and the diet pills were wearing off and the expired nicotine patches had rendered him completely nauseated and it seemed to him that it was time for his reward. He went downstairs quietly, on tiptoe, in order to privately, secretly eat a bagel, or six bagels, or twelve, whatever would make this all better. In the afternoon, his mother had smelled the whitefish salad and the lox and wondered aloud if it had another day in it and decided to punt the decision to the next day. The prospect of this, of eating fish that might be tainted, held a strange new allure for Beamer, and he wanted to eat all of it and see if he got sick.

A gigantic mirror hung over the entry hall table of the house, so that as you were walking down the stairs from the bedrooms, you could see first your feet, then your legs, then your body, then your face. But a sheet had been draped over the mirror for the duration of the shiva, and every time he descended those stairs while he was home for his grandmother's funeral, Beamer became disturbed and confused when the neural expectation of seeing his body slowly revealed was unmet. And in the brief, disoriented moment before he remembered that this was a shiva house and therefore the mirrors were covered, he immediately believed that of course he had disappeared.

But this time, as he descended the stairs, he stopped and froze because he saw his father at the bottom of them. His father was staring into the covered mirror as if he could see himself. Beamer watched for a minute, undetected, and then turned around and ran up the stairs and turned the hallway's bend, his back up against the wall, panting and hiding from the terror he felt. He listened for thirty-five more minutes before he heard Carl leave his station and go back to bed so that Beamer could finally go downstairs and decimate the kitchen.

THE NEXT NIGHT, after an equally brutal day of socializing with his past and watching his father further dissolve, it was assumed that Beamer and his family were over their jet lag and thus expected to sit for the kosher Chinese dinner that the Sisterhood from the temple had sent over to Phyllis's house. Most of the people had left after the minyan, and between Ruth's and Phyllis's housekeepers—Marla as yet unfired for her forty years of reliable hard work and loyalty—the kitchen was cleaned. The Fletchers, with their children and grandchildren, all sat down, joined by cousin Arthur and by Ike Besser and his wife, Mindy, who wore a fur coat despite the warm weather, and who perhaps had been drinking for the latter half of the afternoon, plus their son, Max, who was Jenny's age.

"Maybe you could travel now that you don't have to take care of Grandma," Jenny said.

"If I could convince him, we'd be in Paris right now!" Ruth said.

The table got quiet for a second, as everyone there tried, unsuccessfully, to picture Carl as a regular person enjoying foreign travel. Ruth passed the sesame chicken to Arthur wordlessly. He received it with his soft smile.

"Is there any more of this?" Mindy asked, draining her glass. "It's divine. What is it, a Boulevardier?"

Jenny and Ruth exchanged a look.

"It's a Manhattan," Ruth said, not looking at Ike.

"Let's drink to Carl not retiring," Mindy said.

"That's enough," Ike said quietly to Mindy.

Ruth stood up and absconded to the kitchen wordlessly with Mindy's glass.

Liesl and Wolfie ran up to Ike. "Can we see your thumb?"

Noelle leapt at them. "Kids! Stop that!" Then, to Ike, "I'm so sorry."

"It's OK," Ike said. He made a dopey face at Liesl and Wolfie and then said in vaudeville exaggeration: "But I only got one!" And he showed them the thumb on his left hand.

"No, the other!" Liesl yelped.

"Liesl!" Noelle was horrified.

"I don't got it!" Ike said, revealing his other hand, which was missing a thumb due to an unfortunate aerator accident that happened at work in the early 1970s.

Liesl and Wolfie screamed and ran away.

"So how's the genius?" Ike asked, turning to Jenny. "How's Connecticut treating you?"

"Going well," Jenny told Ike.

"I always said, 'You can be smart or you can work hard.' It's so rare to have both. This girl? Has both!"

"My dad is jealous of anyone who went to college," Max said.

Ike ruffled Max's hair. "I'm jealous of you!" Ike said to him.

"You must be graduating soon," Jenny said.

"Not soon," Max said. "Three more years."

"Wow, so . . ." Jenny started.

"So it'll be nine years of college, but then I can apply to law school," he said. "Which is fine. It's what it takes."

"That's great, Max," Jenny said. "What kind of law?"

"I was thinking criminal? Litigation? I don't know."

"Leave her be!" Mindy said. She was slurring.

"I asked him!" Jenny said.

"You're out of your league," Mindy said to Max.

The room got quiet again.

Beamer's attention was taken from this roadside tension spectacle by Noelle's hand, placed on his. Once again, he allowed himself to believe that this was some kind of commiseration. It was so good for Noelle to see how fucked up his family was. It was good for her to love him despite it. What if a shiva could bring them close again? Or close for the first time?

But he saw, as soon as he made eye contact with her, that she was not giving support but asking for help. On her side of the table, Alyssa was talking about her twins' bar mitzvah once again.

"Tent, heat, separate catering tent, the whole thing," she was saying. "We are thinking meat lunch, but barbecue for the night? It's a lot of meat! The question is where to put everyone. My family can't travel on *the Sabbath*." The emphasis was for Noelle's benefit. "You know. So they're going to be at our house. Not that our house is ready for prime time!"

Nathan stared straight ahead, miserable.

"Your house is lovely," Noelle said, because she had to.

"Well, it's not exactly what I would call current!"

Ruth returned to the table, setting Mindy's refreshed drink down before her.

"Our house is fine," Nathan said.

"Oh, I know," Alyssa said. "It's just—I never know when the kitchen is going to go. And the plumbing in the guest bathroom . . . The place hasn't been renovated since 1985! And this is our one bar mitzvah . . ."

"It's two!" the older twin, Ari, said. "It's a b'nai mitzvah is what it's called."

"Shut up, stupid," his brother, Josh, answered him. The two were identical, but lately, since puberty, Ari had gotten a little fat while Josh had kept it tight, so it was easier for Beamer to tell them apart.

"I keep trying to tell Nathan that it's actually safer to do the renovation," Alyssa said to Noelle, like Nathan wasn't there. "Like, who knows what condition the electric is in, for example?"

"People did things according to code back then," Nathan said. His voice had taken on the high-pitched panic of a lost argument. "It's *now* that people cut corners. Trust me. I see it at work all the time."

"Liesl," Noelle said. "Do you want to show everyone your symphony?"

Liesl popped up. "Yes, Mommy!" And she ran to the living room.

"Symphony," Alyssa repeated.

"She's practicing for a solo in her school concert," Noelle said.

"A solo," Alyssa repeated again. She looked at her twins. "She's so young to play an instrument."

"It was all her idea," Noelle said. "She's very good at it."

"Are you still fighting the good fight?" Ike asked Jenny.

"I'm trying to, Uncle Ike. I'm trying to. The university doesn't make it easy."

Liesl ran back into the dining room, already uncasing her shiny flute. She looked at her family and saw that she had their attention.

She began to whisper gently into the flute, a delicate, haunting tune that spoke of woods and sprites and fairy tales.

It was mesmerizing. The room was seized by a giant mood shift, a quiet, a surrender. Noelle nodded along with Liesl, and Beamer tried not to look at Liesl too directly, lest he love her too hard. She was so graceful. She bore no trace of him, just her mother: her striking yellow hair, her poise, her exquisite features that you would use to mold a doll.

When the song was over, everyone clapped, and she put her left leg behind her right and curtsied deeply.

"God, why am I crying?" Alyssa asked.

"She's performing for her whole school in the winter concert," Noelle said. "She's very diligent. She practices every day."

"What is that?" Alexis asked.

"It's Mahler," Noelle said. "His fourth."

"Mahler was an antisemite," Ruth said.

"Mahler was not an antisemite," Noelle said, though this was the wrong thing to say.

"He wasn't," Arthur said, before Ruth could react. "He was actually Jewish. He converted to Catholicism because he thought that's what the world would want of him."

"Hm," Ruth said.

"You're thinking of Wagner," Jenny said.

"Leonard Bernstein over here," Ruth answered.

Arthur stood up.

"Where are you going?" Ruth asked, some alarm on her face.

"I have to get home," Arthur said.

"I'll walk you out."

Ruth walked Arthur out. Beamer raised his eyebrows at the floor, wondering if Jenny saw him.

"What if Jenny wants to stay over?" Alyssa said, out of nowhere. "We need that addition. A new kitchen and another bedroom. I don't know why this is such a problem."

"For the bar mitzvah?" Jenny asked. "I'll just stay here."

"You know the dust it kicks up," Nathan said to Alyssa. "Heavy metals. Carcinogens. I'm telling you, I see it every day at work. The lawsuits people file. The kinds of cancer you could get!"

"Of course that shuts down the argument every time!" Alyssa said. "What can I say to that?"

Ruth came in and sat down.

"We're still talking about this?" Ruth asked. "Nathan, renovate. It's OK! My god."

"There's a lot you don't understand, Mommy," Nathan said. "Respectfully."

Noelle's hand gripped tighter on Beamer.

"Can I have a bagel?" Ari asked.

"We had bagels all day, baby," Alyssa said.

"I don't like Chinese food," Ari said. He'd already eaten a pile of lo mein.

"Fine," Alyssa said. She stood up and picked up a bagel from one of the end tables that hadn't yet been cleared by Marla. "Has anyone seen the serrated knife?"

"It's in the kitchen," Ruth said. "Ari, go get it. It's on the counter."

"I'll get it!" Alyssa said.

"Ari can get it," Ruth said, annoyed. "He can handle a knife! He's twelve!" Ruth looked over at Beamer and Noelle for some backup and noticed something on Noelle. "Is that a new necklace?"

Noelle's hand flew to her delicate gold necklace whose tiny charm was the Sanskrit symbol for *om*.

"Oh," Noelle said lightly. "My little cabal gave it to me. That's what Beamer calls my group of friends. My 'cabal.' They gave it to me for my birthday, which was the year anniversary from when we all started visiting this wellness person—well, she's a guru. I can use that word. A legit guru."

"Uh-huh," Ruth said, still looking at the necklace. "I see. Is that Arabic?"

"It's Sanskrit," Beamer said.

"An Arabic language," Ruth said.

"Arabic is actually a Semitic language," Jenny interjected.

"Jennifer," Ruth said.

"No, really," Jenny said. "It's Semitic. Like Hebrew or Aramaic. Sanskrit is Indo-European."

"Don't you start with me," Ruth said.

"See what I'm talking about?" Ike said. "Ha! She knows everything, ladies and germs!"

Ari returned just then, holding the serrated knife by its business end.

"I found it!" Ari said.

Alyssa jumped to her feet. "Ari! No! You're holding it wrong!"

"Yeah, doofus," Josh said.

Nathan jumped up. "Ari! Ari! Listen to me! Put it down! Gently! Careful! Careful!"

He began to approach Ari, who was now frozen still, as if he had just learned he was rigged with a bomb.

"You know better than this," Alyssa said.

(Incidentally, the knife could probably not have caused anyone harm; it could barely cut a bagel.)

Liesl, who had been sitting quietly at her mother's behest, said, "Are you sure you've thought this through?" Then she began to laugh. Noelle stifled her own laugh.

"Exactly," Alyssa said. "Are you sure you thought this through? Your cousins know not to hold a knife like that and they're almost half your age!" Then, in a grave whisper to the table, "Did you know that Baxter was the author's actual son and that he died in a car accident? I just learned that."

Noelle and Beamer shared a look. Finally, a moment of communion. But then, abruptly, Noelle stood up, tripping Beamer's central nervous system wires.

"This is wreaking havoc on the kids' bedtimes," she said. "I'm taking them to the house."

Ruth's face relaxed for a second into weariness.

"Kids?" Noelle said.

Liesl and Wolfgang, who had been eating his third helping of orange chicken, stood up.

"Good night, Grandma! Good night, Grandpa!" Liesl said.

"I'll be right in," Beamer said, because he knew he'd have to address concerns about Noelle's status as a what? Converted Arab? The world's first Presbyterian Arab? He walked them to the door and when he returned:

"In my house," Ruth said in controlled spurts of breath. "She doesn't even have the decency to—it's one thing that she doesn't convert. Everyone converts! You don't even have to mean it! And then she wears *Arab jewelry*? To my mother-in-law's *shiva*. Beamer, your grandfather did not hide in a cabinet for weeks away from the Nazis so that his grandson could bring home a shiksa wife who doesn't even know not to wear Arab jewelry to a shiva."

"She's my wife. She's not an Arab. It's a yoga thing. Everyone in L.A.—you see that symbol everywhere."

"This will not help your cause," Jenny said.

"Of course you see it everywhere," Ruth said. "They're lining up to get us. They're in position."

"First they came for my yoga symbology," Jenny said. "But I was fairly inflexible and so I said nothing."

"Can we not do this in front of the kids?" Nathan asked.

"Can we not do it in front of *me*?" Beamer said. "This is so completely inappropriate."

"I don't like the way Liesl is so eager to please," Ruth said. "She's like one of those pageant kids."

"Mom," Beamer warned.

"That's the kind of girl who ends up in a harem."

"Ruth, please," Alyssa said, jerking her head toward the twins. But it was too late.

"What's a harem?" Josh asked, then pulled out his phone, knowing no one would tell him.

Beamer reached for his phone, which hadn't rung. "Yeah? Hello?" Then, to his family, "Sorry, it's California." Back to the phone: "What bad news. I can't—that is just a nightmare. Horrible. OK, I'll see what I can do." He stood up. "No, I can look right now."

He took his fake phone call outside, closing the door behind him, until it was just him on the quiet estate, standing under the same sky he grew up beneath.

"I'll call you back," he said into the phone, forgetting that no one could hear him.

That night, wired from a renewed supply of now non-expired nicotine patches, Beamer decided to work on his screenplay again. He went outside on his parents' porch with his laptop and sat in the big wicker chair with his feet on the rail. It was Middle Rock's best time, late September, after the holidays. The humidity had dwindled but the heat had remained. It had rained briefly, and his nostrils filled with the petrichor first-day-of-school scent that didn't exist in Los Angeles and that felt like the Earth's own baptism. A sliver of moon hung in the still sky and a breeze came off the water and he felt that he was floating in amniotic fluid, that he somehow had de-individuated from this place the longer he was here, and he didn't know where he ended and his surroundings began. The worst thing was that there, in the middle of the night, he didn't mind it.

He looked at the revisions he'd made the night before. All the changes he'd made were good; they were fine. They undid the damage that Anya had alleged, but once his crimes were gone, what was left was a flat nothing with not one memorable moment or justification for it to exist.

What was there to do? What could he do?

The smell of the petrichor hadn't left his nose. It had settled in and started worming its way up to his brain.

What if—what if—Jorge's next chapter involved him learning that he was Jewish?

Wait, no. That's an abomination. No. What if it was about Jorge having to save his longtime mentor, a Jewish man that we've never met before but would be easy enough to establish, from a kidnapping by a Nazi?

Right.

Yes.

Beamer began to think and walk around the porch. He was picturing Morrie Beckerman's tattoo numbers. He took off his sneakers and socks and scrunched the grass in front of his parents' house with his toes. Just let them criticize him for making his characters Jewish! Just wait till they try to tell him that being Jewish isn't diverse enough! How's the Holocaust for your bingo board, Anya?

What if *Santiago* could be *meaningful,* like Anya had suggested? What if it was about the fight for Jewish longevity, and the dangers that Jews are always in? The character from Jorge's past would be older than Jorge, a wise mentor and friend. This man—we'll call him, I don't know, ~~Morris~~, no Mort, yes, Mort!—he gets kidnapped himself and that's when he has to call his old friend Jorge. The student becomes the master!

He returned to the porch and opened his laptop again. He discarded his revised screenplay, just deleted it right there. No revisions. He pulled up a blank document instead.

Ready.

Over five fevered hours, he banged out the first twelve pages of his new screenplay, which, in a moment of phentermine-fueled inspiration, he knew should be called . . . are you ready? . . . *The Santiago Mitzvah.* Mort Silverman is taken in the night on his way home from teaching a class at ~~Harvard~~, no ~~Princeton~~, no Yale. Jorge is alerted to it, only to find that Mort's been hunted by Nazis for years, that Mort Silverman isn't really his name. In fact, Mort is actually named Ruben Steinberg and ~~he has been wanted for the murder of a Nazi when~~ ~~he was a child in a concentration camp~~ no when he grew to learn that his father had been killed by a Nazi in a concentration camp, no he wants to stop running from the Nazis who have been chasing him in revenge for liberating Bergen-Belsen, no Auschwitz, no Dachau. He's been in hiding, but he's tired of hiding, and now that he's made, all bets are off. Jorge is looking for him, but the main clues lie with Mort's daughter, Sarah, Rachel, Rebecca, Leah, who had had no idea that her father was living under an assumed identity, no who pretends she had no idea that her father was living under an assumed identity. She's young and beautiful (but doesn't know it) and brainy and will absolutely have sex with Jorge (in his eye patch) in a moment of anguish, when her need for comfort overcomes her common sense. But she'll do it on her terms!

They say it's the darkest before the dawn, but it's not actually true. Right before dawn, there's a sense of loss and betrayal, that just when you had made peace with the one thing now it was going to change. The sun was coming up over Middle Rock, but Beamer was so amped he could not imagine going to bed.

He stood up and stretched. He shook out his legs. He walked around the porch, then wandered into the house, where he saw his father's car keys on the hook. He took them off and headed to the garage and took his father's car into town.

The stores on Spring Avenue Road had mostly turned over, but in the haze of the near-morning, he saw the town he grew up in, and then he saw himself on every corner, at every age.

He saw his young self and Charlie, thirteen years old, walking past the pediatric dentist's office with painted clowns in the window, joking in bursting whisper about the brothel that Ethan Lipschitz told them lived above it. They walked, eating their slices from Gina's, which, at thirteen, was an act of brazen disregard for Beamer's mother, who said the consumption of pizza while walking was "too Brooklyn" for her to abide.

"He said Joy and Dawn's father went in there," Charlie told him as they stopped and looked up at the window above the painted-balloon-filled one of the pediatric dentist. "That guy. It seems right!"

"That's so funny," Beamer said. "Because I heard your mom works there."

"She does. She was telling me that your dad is her best customer."

Beamer and Charlie stared up and a curtain moved in the window. A woman in her forties with bleached hair and black eyebrows looked down at them and winked. Charlie broke into a run, but Beamer stayed for a second, his eyes locked with the woman's.

It was four insomnolent nights spent thinking of the contrast between the woman's hair and eyebrows later when he told his mother he had to be at Charlie's house to play Atari. Beamer rode his bike to town, leaned it up against the dentist's now-closed-for-the-night door, and entered the vestibule to its side. He climbed the steps up and up until he arrived at what looked like another office with a waiting room and a desk. A young woman, much younger than the woman in the window, sat at a desk that had no paper or pens on it.

"How old are you?" she asked. She had a Russian accent.

He was thirteen, but had never felt more ten years old in his life.

"Eighteen," he said.

"You couldn't be more than sixteen," she said with a quiet laugh. "Come with me. I'm sixteen, too."

She led him toward the back, where the design of the place mimicked the design of the dentist's office below—incidentally, the dentist that Beamer went to himself. He was taken into a room where a much older woman with red hair (but black eyebrows!) was wearing a filmy black negligee and was propped on her elbow on a daybed, reading a *People* magazine with Demi Moore on the cover. The room was the same shape as one of the examining rooms below him, and you could see where a dentist's chair had been ripped from the floor. The woman sighed and sat up and looked Beamer over.

Now Beamer drove by the high school. It was six A.M. by then and the marching band was practicing on the field, the way they did during football season, because it was the only time they had without actual athletes running around. He got out of his car and sat on the hood, listening to them play "Baba O'Riley."

"Teenage wasteland," he whispered along with them. "It's only teenage wasteland."

Again, he saw himself as a young person. It was Beamer's junior year of high school, and the Fletchers, including Phyllis, were filing into the middle school auditorium with a hundred other families, to see the school's production of *The Secret Garden*. It was a rare outing for all of them. Ruth and Phyllis sat on each side of Carl, while Beamer looked around for girls he'd want to have sex with in a couple of years. Nathan, home from college, sat next to him.

"It's starting," Ruth said.

Erica Mayer came out, dressed absurdly like a gothic ghost in a white gown.

"Clusters of crocus, purple and gold," she sang.

Then Jenny appeared, standing under a spotlight in an embroidered dress and a bow in her hair.

"My name is Mary Lennox," Jenny said. "Where has everyone gone? Where's my Ayah?"

In the audience, her family was riveted. So was everyone else. Jenny's command of the stage, her talent, her presence—everything that made Jenny a generally spectacular person—all there on one contained platform.

Beamer, so proud, looked over to his parents and what he saw that was most staggering was his generally stoic, distracted father, now with his mouth open, his face totally absorbed in the action. Beamer shuddered and looked away.

On stage, a kid playing the hunchback Archibald came into his son's room while he was sleeping to read to him.

"When we left off last night," Archibald read, "the hideous dragon had carried the maid to his cave in the moonlight. He gnashed his teeth, breathed his fire. The heath quaked and we trembled in fear." Then he began to sing: *"Someone must save this sweet raven-haired maiden, though surely the cost will be steep."*

Beamer dared to peer over at Carl again. He had never seen his father this animated: laughing, crying, moved. He watched as Phyllis and Ruth shared a look. Phyllis's was disapproval, but Ruth, who was still young and still had some optimism to her, was more neutral.

Now Carl was crying.

Crying.

And then he was on his feet, calling out, "Bravo!" when the line of pre-teens took their awkward bow.

Bravo.

Afterward, they stood on the front steps of the school while people passed and called out how terrific Jenny was. She stood, holding three bouquets of roses, handling the praise like a pro.

"That was just so amazing," Carl was saying. "Jenny, you were— that play. That play was just beautiful. I've never seen anything like it."

Jenny and Beamer shared a look over how weird their father was being.

"You know, it's on Broadway now, Dad," Jenny said. "You should see it if you loved it so much."

"It is? Just incredible. Gosh, I loved it. I can't believe I'm still—" He wiped away moisture that had accumulated on his face.

The next day, Beamer accompanied his father to the record store on Spring Avenue Road.

"I'm looking for the soundtrack to *The Secret Garden*," Carl told the teenager behind the counter. "It's a musical."

Beamer looked over at the rock section and saw the blond-haired, black-browed prostitute from the brothel. She smiled at him. He turned away in a panic.

"Record or tape?" the teenager asked.

"Cassette," Carl said.

For the next few weeks, Carl listened to his new tape all day. He borrowed Beamer's cassette player. He sang—*he sang*—loudly as he got to know the lyrics, a booming boffo bass that filled the house and his car and even his small office that was situated up above the action of the factory so that he could watch his employees through large glass windows, and so that his employees could look up at him in bewilderment.

"Get back to work," Ike said to them, and stood there to make sure his command was obeyed.

At home, the sound of music and the family's patriarch reverberated off its walls, but it didn't warm the place; no, it chilled it. The other occupants of the house moved around as though a hitman had a gun trained on them.

"When is this going to stop?" Jenny finally whispered at the kitchen table one morning as Carl bellowed a song about planting in the spring.

"I don't know!" Ruth hissed.

And then, out of what seemed like nowhere, Ruth threw the plate that she'd been washing down into the sink, splintering it. Ruth, whose economy of motion and essential practicality would never allow for a dramatic gesture if it resulted in cleanup, much less the impossible cleanup of glass.

As they tiptoed around the cheerful-seeming, normal-seeming man that you could not have convinced a regular observer was having some kind of slow and extended nervous breakdown, the man himself doubled down. He asked, for his birthday that year, that they all go to see *The Secret Garden* on Broadway.

"This is a mistake," Phyllis said to Ruth, now at the kitchen table, while Beamer drank Coke and Jenny did homework with her head on the table. Ruth was cooking dinner. "He is becoming emotional. You know what the doctor said."

"It was more than ten years ago," Ruth said. "Maybe this is the next step of his healing. Maybe he's going to heal."

"He's doing fine," Phyllis insisted. "He's functioning. But if you open this up—he's running around, singing, for god's sake."

"What do you want me to do? You want me to say no?" Ruth's back was to the room as she sliced a carrot. "Saying no is crazier than saying yes."

"We have to keep him calm," Phyllis said. "It's Pandora's box. That's what the doctor said."

Ruth turned around. "What if he's OK? What if this is just normal and good? What if this is him moving on?"

Phyllis tightened her lips.

"People heal, Phyllis," Ruth said.

From his study, Carl sang, *"She has her eyes! She has my Lily's hazel eyes!"*

"Does that sound healed to you?" Phyllis asked. "Does that sound *right*?" She looked over at Jenny, whose eyes had closed. "She's asleep again. You should talk to a doctor about it."

"What do you tell him? A man is singing along to a soundtrack?"

"No, I mean about Jenny and the sleeping."

"There's nothing to do," Ruth said, and went back to cooking.

A month later, they all went to Broadway. They arrived early and took their seats and the curtain rose. To say that Carl was enthralled is merely because there are limits to what words can do. Beamer watched as his father took on the held-breath, slack-jawed countenance of someone approaching the Temple Mount for ritual sacrifice.

"Someone must save this sweet raven-haired maiden." It was Mandy Patinkin who played Archibald on Broadway. Carl could now mouth the words along with him, not wildly, no longer crooning, but the crazed whispering of silent prayer. Mandy Patinkin approached the footlights. It was like they were singing to each other.

Beamer didn't remember much after that, except that he was awoken late that night by a scream. He walked out of his room to see his grandmother trudging up the steps while his mother waited in the doorway of her and Carl's bedroom.

"I told you!" Phyllis said. "I told you!"

Beamer heard the scream again. It wasn't really a scream, actually, but a howl. He looked past his mother into her bedroom to find Carl, facedown on the bed, wailing into a pillow.

"Go to bed, Beamer," Ruth said, as Phyllis plowed by her.

Once Phyllis was in, Ruth closed the door, leaving Beamer alone in the hallway. He wasn't sure what he'd just seen, but he knew it was bad. He walked over and into Jenny's room, which was even closer to his parents' bedroom than his was. She was asleep. He sat at the far foot of her bed, on the corner.

"Jenny," he whisper-shouted. "Jenny!"

She didn't open her eyes. "What is it?"

"You didn't hear that? You didn't hear Daddy yelling?"

"I didn't."

"It was loud. It was—" But Jenny was asleep again.

"I cannot wait to leave this place," Beamer said. But no one was listening.

Now Beamer returned to the estate. It was still early enough that there was a haze settled over the Impossible Lawn. He remembered the rager he'd thrown during his senior year of high school, when his parents were at Brandeis for homecoming weekend with Nathan and he'd been left in charge of Jenny. He remembered Sarah Messinger and Erica Mayer and Jenny loitering in the kitchen like they were big while Melissa Simpkin, who was not yet Charlie's wife, threw up in the bushes outside. He remembered Joy and Dawn, whom they called the Palmolive twins, singing along to the CD that was blaring from the living room, which was playing "Boys of Summer" by Don Henley. It went, *"But I can see you, your brown skin shining in the sun."*

Erica Mayer was scavenging for a drink.

"I am so thirsty," she said. "It's so hot."

"The air-conditioning is broken," Beamer said.

He remembered Ethan Lipschitz and Boris Goldman, drinking beer and telling the room about their travails the night before, when they got two Catholic school girls that they'd met at the movie theater in Douglaston to come to Boris's car and let them feel them up.

"And then the one who was with me—" Boris began.

"The chubby one," Ethan said.

"She just wasn't skinny. She was fine. She said, 'We can't do anything else because we're *Catholic.*'"

"It's so hot," Erica said again.

"It's October," Ethan said.

"I didn't make it this hot, Ethan."

"Drink this," Jenny said, handing over a bottle of Moscato. "It's like 7UP."

Erica poured the wine into a red Solo cup, gulped it down, and then poured another cup, saying, "Oh my god, this is so good."

"They were virgins?" Beamer asked. He sat down on the kitchen counter while people came in and out looking for beer.

"Well, see, listen," Ethan said. "They were like, 'We can't go all the way, but we could do it up the butt.'"

"That's disgusting," Jenny said.

"So what happened?" Beamer asked.

"So I said, 'You mean you won't do it regular but you'll do it up the butt because you think you're going to get to heaven and God is going to say, 'Wow! You showed me!'"

"Yeah," Boris said. "I was like, 'You're going to get there and God is going to say, 'What do you think I am, a fucking idiot?'"

They all laughed. Erica was still drinking Moscato and Sarah and Jenny were laughing.

"Heeeeeeeeeey!" Charlie screamed from the other room, but nobody knew why.

"And they say, 'It's the butt, or nothing,'" Boris said. "And we look at each other and that's that."

"You did it in one car?" Beamer said.

"Would you have said no?" Ethan asked.

"God, this is so good," Erica said. "We should drink this all the time!"

"I'm driving by your house, though I know you're not home!" Joy and Dawn sang from the living room.

"I'm going to find Charlie," Sarah said, and made for the living room.

"I said, 'We'll call it the Queens Compromise,' since we were in Douglaston. Right on the border."

"The tall one, which was mine, said, 'We'll call it the Long Island Compromise, because you're Jewish,'" Ethan said.

They all laughed.

"First they came for my butthole, but I was a virgin, so I said nothing," Beamer said.

Erica sat down on the counter and put her head on Beamer's shoulder.

"You OK, champ?" he asked her.

"I can see you, your brown skin shining in the sun," Erica answered.

"You're weird," Beamer said.

"You're weird," she said back.

He didn't look to see if Jenny was watching this interaction. Then Erica turned to him.

"I think someone's in the bathroom. Can I go upstairs?"

He knew that look.

"Yeah, I'll show you," he said, as if she didn't know.

He stood up and then Erica stood up and they started up the stairs together.

Now Beamer parked the car and headed to the house. He was exhausted. The memories, the violent way they wouldn't stop. How could you start on your fresh start when you were standing in the graveyard of your past? As he walked up to the house, Noelle came out to greet him, dressed already.

"Your mother just asked me if I'd converted to Muslim, Beamer," she said. "I can't be here anymore. I'm sorry. I just can't."

"Yes," he said, bounding up the porch. "Let's get out of here. Right away!"

A few hours later, Sophie had booked them four tickets back to Los Angeles and a car was driving them off the estate to Newark. Beamer, who was tired from being up all night, closed his eyes and thought of fresh starts.

"Those days are gone forever" went the song that played over and over in his head until he touched down in Los Angeles. *"I should just let them go."*

NOW PICTURE THIS: In a montage, under a flowery kind of music that has both some gravitas but also layered, plucky notes of optimism, Beamer returned home to Los Angeles and began to pursue his fresh start.

He ripped all the patches from his body, even the one he only found three days later in the shower. He flushed some pills down the toilet. (Remember, the pain of the secret detox held a pleasure of its own.)

He woke up early and sat with Liesl in the living room, his hands folded, leaning forward, watching her face, her form, her execution as she performed Mahler's Fourth Symphony over and over in anticipation of her solo.

Noelle moved in and out of the room, making corrections to Liesl's posture, getting Wolfie out of bed.

"Just amazing," Beamer said to Liesl.

Liesl's perfect face smiled, a pure reaction to a pure impulse.

"Am I good enough, Daddy?" she asked.

"You're good enough for anything," he said. "Do you understand that you are beyond my dreams for what a person should be?"

She came over and sat on his lap and put her arms around his neck. She laughed the way she'd seen her mother laugh, with her head pulled back, aiming at the sky.

"I don't know if I'm good enough yet," she said. "I don't know what will happen in front of all those people." She stood up. "I'm going to do it again."

But he stopped her. "You know, there's a point where you're done practicing. You know that?"

"That's not what Mommy says."

"Well, of course your mother is always right, but it seems to me you are handing in a flawless performance. Actually, you know what is also true?"

"What, Daddy?"

"That if you work hard on something—I know this for sure— that if you work hard, and you truly put all your best energy into doing something as well as you possibly could, and you don't make excuses, and you just really show up, the road will rise up to meet you."

"What does that mean?"

"It means that some force in the universe will help you complete it, because you've already put so much good, hard work into it. And the universe loves good, completed work, so it will help you finish right."

"But am I good?"

"My girl, you are so good. You are perfect to me. I feel so bad for all the other parents who will have to see their children not be as good as you. I feel bad for all the other parents who think they love their daughters as much as I love you."

Noelle was calling Liesl from the kitchen now.

"I'm coming, Mommy!"

She laid her flute inside its velvet coffin and kissed her father on his cheek and ran.

His phone rang. It was Nathan. He looked at his watch.

"Nathan, what is it?"

"Oh, hi. Hey, Beamer. I'm sorry to bother you." Nathan spoke quietly, which only annoyed Beamer more.

"What is it? Is everything OK?"

"Beam, do you remember that time Grandma told us about the dybbuk?" Now Nathan was actually whispering.

"What? What do you mean?"

"No, I mean when we were kids. After my bar mitzvah?"

"Nathan, it's early here. I—"

"We went to sleep over at her house after my bar mitzvah and she told us about the dybbuk?"

"I have no idea what you're talking about."

"You don't?"

"I'm pretty sure that never happened."

"Grandma told us about it."

"I don't know what you're talking about. I have to go."

In the silence of the cavernous living room, he needed to restore the feelings that he'd had before Nathan called and stole them and so he took out his phone and poked around until he figured out how to make Mahler's Fourth into his ringtone. He could still feel his daughter's kiss burning through his cheek for the next few minutes and tried not to think about how he was raised to think that it was hard to love your children, that it took enormous effort to focus on them and show them they were special—that even if you could pull that off, what a burden it was to you, the parent. Actually, he thought for the millionth time, it was quite easy.

The next day, he was still thinking about how if you work hard at something, it will summon benevolent forces while he continued his own good work. He returned to the Radisson one last time, asking ahead that Lady show up just by herself. He sat on the bed and told her he was grateful for all the time they'd spent together, but that he was now ending their weekly visits. He told her that she had been an instrumental part of his mental health these last years, and she smiled sadly and nodded and confirmed that he was paying for this session. He paid her for the next twenty-five sessions, in fact, because Beamer was a good employer and believed in a decent severance.

At a stoplight on his way home, Beamer deleted the contact information for his college student drug dealer, his Ukrainian drug dealer, his pharmacology student drug dealer.

He almost didn't show up to his Thursday night appointment, knowing that the only way to fully break with his dominatrix was to never see her again; this, too, caused him an exquisite kind of agony. He was wistful remembering the first time he drove up to her house, which was a small, Spanish-tile bungalow that looked like all the other Spanish-tile bungalows on the wide, greenery-starved Valley street under the foreboding Valley night. He had found this woman soon after he'd arrived in Los Angeles, all those many years ago, from an ad she'd placed on a blog with a white sans serif typeface against a black background. It said:

I'LL TIE YOU UP, SCUMBAG

So he'd gotten in touch immediately. She emailed him back, telling him to knock at her door every Thursday at seven P.M. and she'd see if she was interested in opening it.

He'd spent every Thursday for three weeks knocking at her door. She never opened it, but on the fourth Thursday, she left a note. It said:

BRING ME GIFTS

So then he knocked at her door and left her a gift at the same time—every Thursday at seven P.M. One day it was flowers. Then it was jewelry. Then, one day, just as he was about to give up, the woman left a note at the door during the time that Beamer was due. It said:

NEXT TIME WEAR NOTHING

And if Beamer could be given a time machine and told he could go to literally any point in time—that includes when Baby Hitler was born and also the moment his father left for the office that day in 1980—Beamer would have just fast-forwarded to the six days, twenty-three hours, and fifty-nine minutes later when his life could finally begin. How he could not wait to be standing outside her door, naked on the sidewalk!

She was not what he had been taught to expect from all the literature (blog posts) he'd read about BDSM and about domination and submission in general. He knew from the time he'd been to that brothel, and the Russian women there who had wrestled him and choked him, that he liked a certain amount of pain, but when he read experiences from other people, he could not locate himself in their desires.

Now, that could be because so much of BDSM blogging exists to justify the need for no justification in a fetish or a kink; it exists not purely to explain, but to explain that the explanation would only set the dominators and submissives of the world back (and only the submissives would enjoy that).

So there was the problem: He wanted the pain but he did not want the subculture. He did not care if a person wore vinyl or a mask.

He was sort of into the fact that he didn't know her name, but that was probably more so that he could not fully flesh out her existence or allow himself to wonder in full why she was doing this, since the answer in these trades was always depressing. (Truly, he once saw a green tricycle on her lawn, and it took him months of drug use to destroy that particular synapse.)

No, he just wanted the pain.

And he didn't want to have to work for it. He could easily have joined one of at least twenty fight clubs he knew of in the area, all of which were populated purely by Hollywood executives and which took place in CrossFit gyms after midnight. But he didn't want to defend himself. He didn't want to win. He certainly didn't want to bruise.

So he took this next best thing, the thing society does have in place, which was this dominatrix. And sometimes she whipped him and sometimes she sodomized him with foreign objects and it was all fine. All he had to do was pretend he was into the control, dom-sub part of it. Pretend you're into that, that you need the authority, and you can get bound up anytime you want—trapped, subdued. There's no other real service system for getting tied up at will.

But then they went into a new unit of interaction, when perhaps she sensed he was getting bored. Sure, the gig was that she had to appear that she could take it or leave it, but, capitalism being what it is, she adjusted her routine. She began to play-act different roles every week, a rotating career fair that bewildered and amused him—and that he consented to, so long as there was enough brutal force.

She was a farmer and he had to be milked before her daddy woke up and found him engorged.

She was a shoe designer testing high heels to make sure they didn't break off when inserted into the rectum.

She was a snake who bit him.

She was an acupuncturist who poked him with needles.

She was a blind candle maker who was clumsy with hot wax.

She was a cardiologist who experimented with stopping and starting the heart by suffocating her patients by sitting on their faces.

She was a nurse who had to give him rectal exams without lube.

She was a massage therapist in school to learn a brutal new mode of therapy called Sustained Energetic Fascia something. It required him lying down on something like a massage table—usually it was a metal bed frame with a dirty mattress in the middle of the room, something real rusty and filled with tetanus. He lay down, face first, and she subjected him to a pain he had never felt before. She began at the bottom of his left leg, attaching her thumbs to some kind of ligament or band that was sensitive to just the touch. She pushed down hard and up, she twisted and turned his very fascia, until he was howling in a high-pitched pain, begging, screaming, "YOU MOTHERFUCKER," but she didn't relent. Instead, she did it again and again, and then started on his other leg. She did all four limbs. She did his back. She flipped him over and did all four limbs again.

In her slow hand, the pain was excruciating. It was unfathomable. It was what he'd been looking for this entire time.

She did this for several weeks in a row. He didn't know if she repeated this routine because he seemed so gratified by it, and some version of the customer is always right, or if maybe she really was in massage therapy school, trying to find something legit to grow into as whoever the owner of that green tricycle was came further online.

Either way, he didn't ask. It wasn't important. There are only two reasons to want that kind of pain: because you feel you deserve it, or because of the life-affirming quality of its disappearance. That second one is probably the most optimistic-seeming thing you could say about this predilection of Beamer's.

That final night, she pulled out an actual massage table. Maybe something inside her knew that this was their last go. He hadn't told her that he planned to do it yet—he was waiting for the end to do that—but she had some experience with goodbyes and knew one was coming.

There, on the massage table, each terrible immersion into pain lasted so long, each little bout of it, that he got to know the pain. He saw how observation changed it; how just acknowledging it changed it. He felt the pain and then it would disappear. It was so interesting!

He could finally really be *inside* the pain, not just catching accidental whiffs of it. He had time to hold the pain in his hands, to move it around, to examine it and pet it and snuggle it up to himself and get to know it.

It was important to understand what he was saying goodbye to.

Now that music, the montage music, swells: He wakes at five A.M. the next day and drives to his office in the deep violet glow of dawn, thinking this, now *this* is the magic hour. He sits at his computer and begins to type and when he finally looks up he finds that the sun has gone up and then down. He breathes in the righteous vitamin air of a hard-won day of work. He remembers that, actually, spending a day just writing will pass the time without need of vice—that he gets actual bodily pleasure from it. He drives home, sitting in the canyon traffic with all the other commuters, his vision a straight line, never wandering and never diverting from the path home. He feels a thrum of emptiness somewhere in his limbic system, and that's the withdrawal. Luckily, his addictions are such a highly diversified portfolio that the withdrawal doesn't know where to point and instead is just a dull echo of a memory. He pulls up to the house. He enters the home and performs all husbandry and fatherdry. He kisses his wife and eats dinner at the table and reads to his children. He wakes up the next morning and he does this exact same thing all over again, and he thinks that maybe if he does this one or two or three dozen more times, it will start to feel normal to him.

Then the music fades and it is two months later and he types FADE OUT onto page 118 of *The Santiago Mitzvah*. He rereads it through blurred eyes, every move of it reassuring to him, though of course he scrolls faster and faster as he goes through, as any meticulousness he ever possessed is on life support. He runs a spell-check. He sends it to Jeremy Gottlieb and then thinks that there could be no harm in sending it over to Charlie, just as a first read. Who better? Who knows both the intricacies and truth of the *Santiago* story so well? Who knows better Beamer's own weaknesses, and who better to steer him toward the kinds of victories that *Santiago* represents, at least to him?

Hey can I send you over the new stgo to read?

There are three dots, then an answer:

Can't wait

It's all so simple, Beamer realizes. What has he been afraid of?
Two days later, he checks in with Charlie.

You have a chance to read yet, bro?

There are three dots, but then nothing.
He could sit tight. It's fine. It's good to let things settle a little.
Two mornings later, though, he wakes, feeling indignant:

I have to hand this thing in

The three dots, and then, after a good, tortured minute, finally, an
answer:

I read! Let's talk! Tomorrow morning?

THAT NIGHT, BEAMER drove around until it was time to go home to
pick Noelle up for their couples therapy. But when he got there, it
was to Noelle sitting at the table, alone in a quiet house.
    "Where is everyone?" Beamer asked.
    "Paulette took them to the park and then to Josie's for dinner,"
Noelle said. She wouldn't look at him.
    "What's going on? Is everything—did something happen?"
    "Dr. Lorna canceled. She said she can't see us anymore."
    "What?"
    "She wouldn't say why."
    Beamer was still standing in the doorway of the kitchen.
    "I guess this happens, right? They get busy or—"

She was quiet.

"Or maybe it's because we canceled for the last few times? Or—if she just let you know today, maybe she's sick. Or quitting. Maybe she's tired of this kind of work. Frankly, it seems exhausting."

"What do you think that means about us, Beamer?" Noelle sounded like a teacher running out of patience.

"That maybe she thought we didn't need her so much?" He thought maybe she'd laugh at this. She didn't. "I don't know, Noelle. I have no idea what happened."

But Beamer did know what happened.

That time, right when his grandmother died, when Noelle sent him to couples therapy on his own. Dr. Lorna, whose office was done up in soothing pastel tones, sat with her hands cradling each other, one above the other, waiting for him to speak. He hated this. He thought a *hello* and *how are you* were a nice way to start a session, but no.

"Noelle couldn't be here. She's stuck across town."

Dr. Lorna nodded but didn't politely ask for details. Therapists were so smug.

"She wanted to be here, though. She just sent me. If that's even OK to do? I mean, it feels like cheating." He laughed too loudly at this.

Dr. Lorna nodded. So smug.

How can he explain what went on from there? It all happened so fast. He began talking about their "communication style." Noelle didn't speak to him for two days at a time and he couldn't even figure out why—that was their communication style. He talked about his "love language" (the funding of her hobbies, which now included that pumping poison into her face until its distortions made her feel better). He talked about these things but there were still so many minutes to go. He boldly turned to the clock that was next to him, the one that was unspoken of and just for the therapist to sneak looks at—the worst part of therapy, the way they do their surreptitious glance—and, realizing there were still thirty full minutes left, said, "I don't really have that much else. I'm not sure why she's so unhappy."

Dr. Lorna finally spoke. "Are you happy?"

Beamer didn't like that question. He didn't think happiness was a goal. It was like all the emotions—fleeting—and chasing it seemed to be a fool's errand nonpareil.

"I'm busy. Busy is good. I don't think about happiness a lot."

"Why not?"

He thought for a minute and then spread out his hands. He was outside this moment right then and not in it. "Happiness just . . . It's fine. It means that I'm never unhappy, because I don't live in a paradigm in which happiness is at one end of a spectrum. If it doesn't exist, it can't be on the agenda."

"There's no agenda, Beamer," she said. "There's no paradigm. There's just life, right? And trying to get through it."

"Noelle says that, too," he said. Maybe they should have a male counselor. Maybe this was just a man-woman thing and a man could understand and possibly even explain to Noelle that it's fine for a man to take a call or miss a dinner. There's a lot to do! "It's just a saying, you know?"

"Do you ever think about counting your blessings?" Dr. Lorna asked. "Do you ever think about looking around and making an actual list of ways that your life is good?"

Beamer laughed, one brutal syllable. "Jews don't do that."

"Do you speak with your own therapist about that?" she asked.

Beamer could feel his "therapist's" French tickler on his balls when she asked that.

"We talk about everything," he said. Then, "I'm just under a lot of stress." He looked at the clock again, which he was pretty sure had ticked backward.

"You keep looking at the clock."

"Yeah," he said. "I don't know why therapists don't want you to know what time it is. Why that's information you just get for yourself and I'm locked in a bubble."

"You feel locked in right now?"

He didn't answer.

"You could leave anytime, you know," she said.

"Right. So you could then tell Noelle in our next session that that's what I did."

Dr. Lorna had nothing to say to that. For a moment, he wondered what it would be like to just sit there and not say a word. To take a nap, maybe. To use this time to actually rest on her couch.

But then he wondered if he could just say something that was true, something that was in his mouth already. Here, let's go; let's try it.

"I am so scared of Noelle sometimes," he said. "No, all the time. I'm always scared of her. She holds the key. She holds all these cards. And she could just pull them away at any point. I always know that."

"That seems stressful," Dr. Lorna said.

"Yes, it's stressful. It's really stressful."

And then, once he started talking about it, he couldn't stop. Noelle was too angry at him lately to express any genuine interest beyond the facts; along with her animosity for Beamer came her total freeze-out of his family—a family she'd been kind to despite their early treatment of her, and who she felt no longer deserved favors.

"You're not going to repeat the things I say here, right?" he asked Dr. Lorna. Because now he was revved up and there was nowhere to sink his penis and no one to hit him and barely a trace of the afternoon's Mulholland Backflip. He was a caged animal and he was no longer operating rationally.

"I . . . won't," she said.

And so he told her everything. He told her about his drug use, including the ones he was on at that very minute. He told her about his anger and sadness about Charlie, how it opened the door to his own insecurities about his talent and abilities. He told her about how hard he tried to keep it together. He told her everything.

"You really *really* can't say anything, right?"

"I cannot. I will not."

"Are you sure?" He was suddenly overcome with remorse.

"I can't," Dr. Lorna said. "But you should—you should think about the implications of the secrets you're keeping. It's not a marriage." And again, "Do you talk to your own therapist about this?"

But now that it was all out, he honestly couldn't stop. He explained that his therapist was not a therapist but a dominatrix in Encino whom he saw every week, lest the world begin to take on the photonegative realm it did when he wasn't seeing to his debasement. See? Everything.

Then he said one more time, "Are you sure you won't tell her?"

By then, Dr. Lorna was speechless. She did not look at the clock when she said, "Our time is up." But she didn't say it in the fake-sad-face way she usually did. Her face conveyed pure shock.

And so no, he was not surprised to hear that Dr. Lorna was not seeing them, but he was not on this particular night going to be the person who told Noelle why.

"You know what?" he asked. "I didn't like her anyway. She was very judgmental."

"Well, she didn't like us, either, apparently," Noelle said. "I think it's like surgeons and their statistics. She dropped us because she doesn't have any hope in us."

And maybe that was true. But here's a counterpoint: At the bottom of your lies, when you cannot swim down farther because there is no farther to swim down, the brain finds optimism.

What if he could be saved? What if, having unburdened himself to Dr. Lorna, the cancer was now hers and not his? What if he was freed, having given it away? Noelle didn't even understand that he was in the middle of his fresh start.

There was something about the two of them in this kitchen, just the two of them. He thought back to the beach where he'd proposed. He could see her face there clearly. He could see now the horrible things she'd done to her face since then, but he could also reconcile the two faces as belonging to the same person. It broke his heart all over again.

"Well, I for one am glad that we have a night off," Beamer said. "What if we just went to dinner or a movie and maybe you could remember that you once liked me?" He tried to make this light but he couldn't.

Noelle just sat there.

"C'mon," he said. "We can go to that place in Brentwood, with the caviar hot dogs."

"We'll never get a reservation."

"We'll get a reservation."

"Maybe we should just stay home," she said. "Liesl's recital is to-morrow."

"Date night. Isn't that what Dr. Lorna was always saying? Or is the idea that we use our date night to have a therapist say we need a date night? Seems like a racket to me. Come. Stand up. Let's go."

Finally, she acquiesced. But when they arrived at the place in Brentwood, there was a two-hour wait, reduced to ninety minutes when Beamer gave the maître d' a fifty-dollar bill. Beamer and No-elle stood outside and the silence became perilous until Noelle spoke suddenly.

"You know, the person I see is near here."

"Which person?" Beamer asked.

"The reader. The tarot cards. While we wait, maybe we could—"

"You go to a tarot reader now?"

"It's fun. It's interesting. We all go. Just, please? She's probably not even there."

They walked to a mini-mall three blocks away, where a storefront on the second floor that read YOUR FUTURE NOW flashed pink neon.

"This is where you go?" Beamer asked.

"It's like Thai restaurants. The best ones are in mini-malls. I don't know why."

"I thought you go to that dermatologist."

"I do. But then the cabal and I started doing this, too. It's—you'll see."

Beamer began to feel his exhaustion as they walked up the stairs.

The woman who answered the door and greeted his wife with a warmth and intimacy that startled him seemed to be formed of six different ethnicities. She was wearing pink sweatpants that said JUICY across the rear and a fake football jersey that said PINK where it normally had a player's name. She was either thirty or sixty, with dark eyebrows and brittle bleached hair like the Middle Rock prostitutes; she had fake eyelashes that made her eyes look like they were being eaten by tarantulas.

She embraced Noelle with a hug that included points of contact at the cheek, breast, pelvis, and knees. Beamer could smell the kind of rank cigarette smoke coming off her that wouldn't go away with a mere shower.

"You brought him!" the woman said when they finally stopped hugging. She had a voice that was so croaky it was like it had already been replaced by its inevitable voice prosthesis.

"I brought him," Noelle confirmed. "Here he is."

The psychic, who did not even introduce herself to Beamer, said, "I've been telling her to bring you for months! I said I can't look into his soul unless his soul is here! I tell her it doesn't work like that, like in the movies! A sweatshirt doesn't work. A hair clipping doesn't work. Only in the movies, I told her! I'm a medium. I'm not God!" She crossed herself when she said that, looking up to where she supposed God was.

Beamer had no idea that Noelle had brought his sweatshirt or hair clippings to this woman.

"Let me take a look at him," the psychic said.

When had she cut his hair?

"He's all yours," Noelle answered.

Beamer sat down in a room that reminded him of an Indian restaurant he and Charlie used to go to in Manhattan when he was in college. It was dark, with Christmas lights strung in four different directions. There was a giant, imposing television, a daybed that sat too close to the screen, and a pack of More Lights on the table. He stared at the cigarettes.

The woman looked him over, head to toe, seriously. Her eyes were cloudy with something like the beginning of glaucoma.

"Mmmmmm," she said.

"What is it?" Noelle asked.

She stopped and looked Beamer in the eyes in a sustained and deep way that he could barely fathom. He froze, just froze. He became so afraid suddenly, as if the woman could actually know something about him, that he wanted to turn and run.

"Your third eye," she said. "It's not clear."

"I don't know what that means," Beamer said.

"It's your creativity. It's stopping you from doing what you have to do. You're paralyzed. You can't think."

"I just finished a screenplay and I'm tired," he said. "That's probably it."

But she ignored him, looking instead at his forehead like it had a stain on it. "It's got a lot of muck on it, your third eye. You haven't seen clearly in many years. You let other people see for you."

"I don't know—I don't know what that means."

"I can't tell if you're a good person," she said.

"What kind of thing is that to say?" Beamer asked.

"It's not clear. There are so many layers on top of you that I can't see you. So many clouds around you. I've never seen anything like it." She began to pick imagined clouds out from around him, pulling them like pieces of cotton and discarding them. "Every time I get one, another grows back!"

She gave up. She sat down and took out a gigantic deck of thick tarot cards. Without taking her eyes off him, she began to draw cards. She laid each one down in front of him.

"This is the Empress. This is the Emperor. This is the Ten of Cups. This is the Ten of Pentacles. Hm. Oh. OK. Oh. Hm."

"What do they mean?" Noelle asked. Right then Beamer hated Noelle for a brief but violent flash. He hated her stupidity for believing in any of this shit; he hated her sedition, that she would even ask.

The woman laid one last card out.

"This is the Devil." She looked up at Noelle. "Noelle, this is not good."

Beamer stood up.

"We have our name on a list. This was fun, but we have dinner. Noelle, come on, we have dinner. What do I owe you?"

He didn't wait for an answer. He just rushed outside. He had been having such a good day. He had been filled with hope. He walked downstairs and waited on the blacktop, in a spot in the parking lot marked RESERVED FOR OWNER. He wished the owner would drive in now and run him over.

Five minutes later, Noelle came downstairs. She was crying.

"Noelle, that woman is a huckster and a charlatan. She's a predator!"

Noelle shook her head, unable to speak.

"What? She wants to scare you into coming back. She's a thief, Noelle. She's not your family." He put his hands out like search me. "Look at me. I have no clouds around me! She knows you have money and she's taking advantage of you! How do you not see this?"

Finally, Noelle spoke. "You take advantage of me. You take advantage of the fact that I don't ask."

He opened his mouth to object, but he didn't say anything. Instead, he looked at her in that parking lot and saw her face, how she'd changed. A heavenly light shone through her, a light that his mother had guaranteed him could never exist in her. Screw his mother. "I know you think I don't ask because I can't. It's not that." Tears began to make their way from her eyes down her cheeks. "It's because it's beneath me to ask, Beamer. The minute I have to ask . . ." She didn't finish.

He put a hand up to touch her swollen, hard cheek. Looking at his wife, he did the brave thing and had mercy on her and granted her that she wasn't making all of this up.

"I don't know if you would love me if you knew me," he said. He could not remember ever being this tired.

"Those cards, Beamer. They mean divorce. They mean separation. They mean *termination*. There was no hope in those cards." Now she was crying harder, and Beamer felt so desperate he wanted to suffocate her to make her suffering stop.

He put his hands on her shoulders. He felt her soft blond hair in his hands. He was overcome with a sense of unity about the two of them—of certainty. She was his chronic condition, but he was hers.

"We are not those divorce cards, Noelle," Beamer said. "Those cards aren't even divorce cards. The deck is every possibility. That's us, Noelle. Noelle, we are *all* the cards. Don't you see that? Me and you. We're the entire deck."

He hugged her to him. She was a rag doll. He held on to her, hugging her, and infusing her with every modicum of hope he had. It wasn't a lot, but she could have all of it.

It was an endless moment while he prayed for her to listen, to soften, to forgive, to decide, but it didn't come for so long and he thought it was over. But then her eyes met his . . .

"Do you think the table's ready?" she asked.

. . . and knew he had one last chance.

———

THE NEXT DAY was the day of Liesl's recital.

"I'm going to meet Charlie," Beamer told Noelle in the morning. "I'll drop the kids on the way. I'll see you tonight at the school?"

"They only allow one car because it's a schoolwide thing," Noelle said. "So do you want me to pick you up at the office?"

"I'll pick you up," he said. "Five. So we have time, in case there's traffic."

Noelle looked tired but not angry. He'd take it.

Beamer played the Mahler in the car. In the backseat, Wolfie played with his little backpack and Liesl smoothed out the shimmering light blue dress that she was wearing for that evening while she chattered. "The other kids, the other musicians, have to wear dark blue and white, but me and the boy with the piano solo get to wear light blue. To stand out."

"I've never seen you nervous before," he said.

"I've never felt like this before!" she said.

"I'm nervous, too!" Wolfie said, and Beamer and Liesl laughed.

"I cannot wait to see you tonight," he said as they exited to the school. "You are going to be terrific."

Charlie was already at the corner booth, sending messages on his phone, when Beamer walked into the diner, on his own phone, speaking to no one.

"A total disaster," Beamer was saying to the nobody he was talking to.

With a nod to Charlie, he sat down.

"Do what you have to do," Beamer said into the phone. "OK, great. Bye."

He hung up on nothing.

"Everything OK?" Charlie asked. He looked so healthy, in jeans and a white button-down shirt, and—what was the word?—grown up.

"Everything's fine, you know, just the usual," Beamer said. "How are you?"

"Melissa's due any day. I'm shooting the fifth episode. Don't think I'm going to make it to the end of the episode by the time this baby comes, though!"

"That's exciting," Beamer said. "It's exciting. A third. Just like in your house."

"And yours! Melissa convinced me. I was fine with two, but, you know. By now I have faith that the third will be the same kind of exponential thing in a good way."

Beamer was filled with a brief but electric longing to be Charlie's third child.

"So!" Charlie said. "*Santiago!*"

Beamer took a deep and dramatic breath. "*Santiago,*" he answered.

"It's so crazy to think that we've been thinking about this guy for how many years? Twenty, right? More? Like, we change but he stays the same."

". . . Right." Beamer didn't know or like where this was going.

"I guess . . ." Charlie began. "I guess my question when I was reading it was, like—listen, you have to forgive me."

"Speak your mind," Beamer either said or tried to say.

"I guess, what are you doing here?"

"What do you mean?"

"I mean, why are you writing this?"

"That's your feedback? Wow!"

"Don't be defensive."

"What kind of question is that? Why *wouldn't* I be defensive?"

"I'm not saying anything bad. It's a passable script. I mean, it's good. It's just—I spoke to Jeremy about it."

"I don't know if he's read it."

"He read it. We talked about it."

There is a gulf between your agent not getting back to you and your agent talking about your work behind your back with your former writing partner without even acknowledging receipt of the thing in the first place. Beamer realized he'd just now drowned in this gulf.

"What did you say?" Beamer asked. "What did he say? Maybe someone could tell me!"

"It's fine. You know? It's like not really of the time, but there's always someone who will see something like this if people will make it, or it'll go straight to VOD or streaming or whatever, but—I guess you have to take my question at its face value. Why are you doing this?"

"Because it's our story?"

"Don't get angry."

"What do you want me to be, Charlie? I asked you to read this. I thought we might have a nice conversation, maybe walk down memory lane a little, maybe, I don't know, you could reassure me that you were not the thing that . . . But now you can't even find something to say about this that's even *polite*? Not even a compliment sandwich? It's *adequate*?"

"I said passable."

"Oh, much better!"

"Will you let me finish?" Charlie said. "God, you make it so hard to actually have a conversation. I'm, like, sweating."

"Is this a conversation?"

"Yes, I ask a question. You answer it. Why do you want to make this movie? Why do you want to write it?" Then, with open hands and a kinder expression, he said, "I'm not saying this to be cruel. It's a totally fine screenplay, like I said. It has some strange anachronisms. But I was reading it, and I could kind of see Mort as your dad? I know this is like a fault line, so I won't say the thing we never talk about even as we talk about it but I guess my question is—wait, let me back up. I wrote those movies with you because we were young and getting our feet wet, right?"

"Right."

"So now, we kind of know what we're doing and I guess I went back to the idea of: Why did I want to be a writer in the first place? Right? Like, is the end game that we just do the same thing over and over? Is the end game us just trying to figure out what a studio wants and then mold ourselves to fit? I don't think so. I think we used to think that, but I think we don't need to anymore."

"Right, uh-huh. Listen, if you hated it—"

"It's not that I hated it, Beam." Charlie wore tortoiseshell glasses, and now he took them off and put them on the table while he rubbed the bridge of his nose. "It's that you're not supposed to do your first project forever. You didn't become a writer to keep writing the same shit all the time. This is fine, I swear. It's a little weird when the girlfriend gets kidnapped while Jorge's also looking for Mort? Like, two kidnappings at the same time? But that's not what I'm talking about. I'm saying—" He closed his eyes and then opened them and took a deep breath. "Beamer, you don't need to do this."

Beamer didn't move.

"You're so rich, dude. You have money that just comes to you from being born. You can write whatever you want. Me? I was doing all that *Santiago* stuff—"

"For money?"

"No, not—well, yes. I needed money. But I was also figuring out how to do this. I wanted to do it well. And that's what people wanted in the nineties, those kinds of scripts. I don't think anyone expects you to land on your magnum opus or whatever with the first thing you've done, particularly not if it's a shallow little action movie with two-dimensional characters."

The betrayal that coursed through Beamer just then.

"Santiago is not in Mexico, you know," Charlie said. "How did we get away with any of this? We're lucky people will still take meetings with us."

Beamer took this in. Charlie was watching him to see how this was landing, and Beamer said, "I think, Charlie, that you've become a snob. We loved this stuff. We watched it all the time. We—"

"Right. When we were young. And we made this franchise for people like us. And this is what there was. But, I guess, who did we *become*? Now that I have some money. Now that I have some skills. What is the thing I want to say to the world? What would I make for the people so that they might understand me? Understand who I am? Catharsis, drama, something new, something that advances on the form."

"And that's *Family Business.*"

"Right," Charlie said. "That's *Family Business.*"

"Which is the story you had burning in you."

"Right." But now Charlie didn't like where this was going.

"Even though it's about my family?"

"I'm sorry, what?"

"Well, obviously. *Family Business.* It's about my family. You took my family's story. The factory. My grandparents. My brother and sister."

"Not really!"

"Not really? Are you kidding me? Charlie."

"It's just—it's just a family, you know? A rich family. It's not you guys."

"It's not you guys, either."

"No, it's not," Charlie said. He put his glasses back on. "My father is an economics professor who retired five years ago. He paints. My mother never worked. They live in the same tiny shithole that I grew up in, far from the shore, surrounded by rich people, while he's alone with his intellect and can't take his wife or kids on a vacation. *Family Business* is his gripe. It's what I grew up listening to."

"It's his gripe with my family?" Beamer asked.

"No, no. *No.* Just—it's his gripe with all the families. It's the thing that fueled him, everyone having so much more money than he did. I guess I never forgot that. But it's not you. It's not you guys. Not literally." Charlie looked down at his hands. "Or maybe, I don't know. Somewhere deep down you symbolize to me all the other people who had so much when I was growing up. Maybe it became my gripe, too. Maybe this whole show is a composite of the people I knew, but maybe you are the closest one of them to me, and so you can see yourself a little more sharply. I don't know. I just know that if I had what you had, I would not be rewriting *Santiago.* That's what I'm trying to say here. You should think and look inside and ask yourself: Do I want to contribute another *Santiago* movie, or do I have something to say to the world? I . . . I have to think you have something you've been trying to say to the world. Beam, I know you do."

"I just wanted to know if it was good, Charlie."

"It doesn't matter if it's good. It's not the thing you should be writing. Beamer, do you hear me? Don't do this. Write your own thing. The thing you *obviously* have always needed to write."

When the conversation was finally over, and Charlie had to go back to set, Beamer stayed at the table for one hour, then another, then another. He was trying to remember what he was thinking all those years ago when he and Charlie filled out their NYU applications. The two of them, sitting at the Messingers' kitchen table, taking turns at a typewriter to answer NYU's paragraphs about what they wanted to do in the world. How could Beamer not remember what he said then? Was he cribbing from Charlie as far back as that?

In the diner, he didn't do anything except stare straight ahead until the waitress told him that they needed the table for the lunch rush. He paid the bill and walked out.

Frankly, he had been expecting to hear he'd done a good job.

BEAMER STAGGERED OVER to his office, unsure what to do next. He couldn't sit still. He couldn't bear to look at his computer. But mostly he couldn't get what Charlie had said out of his head. He "obviously" had something to say. Obviously? *Obviously?* He couldn't begin to imagine what Charlie might have been talking about. He wished he'd asked. How lame is that, that he wished he'd asked?

He walked around the room. He looked at his shelves, at the books he hadn't read. He knelt on the floor and rifled through his desk drawer, the one that was on the bottom and could hold files if it weren't busy holding his junk. He moved around old contracts and magazines until he found an old amber bottle of Modafinil, which he'd stolen from Noelle when she was going through a bout of depression (but told the doctor that she was simply sleepy). These, which were uppers, were so long expired that he took three, so that he could feel their effects sooner and in a more pronounced way, since sometimes the efficacy of a drug was diminished over time which is why it was important to

NOPE! NOT WITH THESE! THESE WORKED!

Exciting. Exhilarating. Perfect. OK! He dug around the desk for some more.

His phone went off just then. It was a text from Jenny.

Have you gotten your distribution?

He pressed the button that darkened the phone's screen. He was on the precipice of something, maybe. Or a doorstep to a precipice of something. He should write about this thing. Or, should he write about what happened to his father? Was his father's k-i-d-n-a-p-p-i-n-g the thing that Charlie thought he obviously had to write about? What had he been writing about all this time but kidnappings?

He tried to imagine what else it was he could write, but nothing came to him except for the night before. Right before the psychic had told Noelle that Beamer was bad, she'd said something about his third eye. Yes, his third eye. That was the problem. There were answers in front of him, obvious things he couldn't see. His third eye was blocked. Of course! What else made sense? It made sense. He was not a person who would normally believe in a mini-mall psychic's wisdom, but right then he was someone who would believe in anything.

CUT TO: Within a few minutes, he was back in his car, in the parking lot, staring up at the YOUR FUTURE NOW neon sign, debating what to do. On the one hand, he wisely did not want to encounter a woman who clearly had his number. But on the other hand, she had his number and maybe also the solution.

He looked at his phone and he saw a text from Noelle:

Still on time? I want to stop and get her flowers for after.

He added a thumbs-up to her text and then put the phone aside because the psychic woman came outside in her terrible outfit from the night before. She stood on the second-floor balcony, lit a cigarette, and looked out grievously onto the horizon.

Slowly, like he was trying not to scare a bug before he killed it, he got out of his car. The minute the door closed:

"Hi there," he called up to her.

She squinted down at him. "Who's that?"

"It's Beamer Fletcher," he called up. He put up don't-shoot-me hands.

"You're Noelle's husband," she said. She sprung into a karate posture of defense; it was not the first time an angry husband showed up. He noticed that in her nonsmoking hand she was holding an asthma inhaler.

"I'm not here—I'm not here because of the divorce thing. Or you calling me . . . what you said about me—I have another question."

She relaxed a little. "What do you want? Does Noelle know you're here?"

"No, no. I mean, she doesn't not know. She's home. I was just driving by and I just—I wanted to follow up on something?"

He started stepping forward, but she became alarmed.

"Why don't you stay down there for a minute?" she said.

"I'm not going to hurt you. I'm going to ask you—that thing you said about my third eye. What was it? What does that mean?"

"Oh," she said. She relaxed again. "Come up here. You can come up. You have cash?"

"I can get some."

Inside her small room, the gigantic TV was on a reality show about people who work on a boat having sex with each other.

"Sit down," said the woman.

"What's your name?"

"Phyllis," she said.

He nearly choked.

"Phyllis. OK, Phyllis. Phyllis, I need help figuring this out. Because it's true. I have a third eye problem. Like you said. It's clouded. I can't see anything anymore. Everything is right beyond it, like I can see it but I can't make it out? It's true. Everything you said was true."

"Phyllis is always right, baby." She reached for his hand but he pulled it back.

"I need to see it," she said. "I need to look."

Slowly, he put his hand in front of her and watched her face. He imagined the palm of his hand was a map of his indiscretions.

She nodded.

"What is it?" he asked.

"What I'm seeing is that you don't have to be this way. I'm seeing that the thing that makes you a bad husband to that poor girl is also what is blocking your third eye."

"What is the thing? What are you supposed to do about it? How do you fix it?"

Phyllis continued to stare down. "Did you take something this morning?"

"What do you mean?"

"Are you on a medication?"

"No, nothing like that."

"I want to see the veins on your arm. They tell a story sometimes." She rolled up his sleeve. "What's this?"

"It's just a nicotine patch," he said.

"You're quitting smoking?"

"Yes."

She looked dubious. Then she said, "You know, I already see you. I see what your problems are. I see what you do to that poor girl—"

He tried to object but realized he didn't actually know what she knew, nor what her proof for what she knew was. Then, "Listen, I just had a question. If you can't answer it—"

"Give me ten thousand dollars."

"I'm sorry, what?"

"Give me ten thousand dollars. I see you can't do anything until you clear out that third eye. I can do it for you."

"For ten thousand dollars."

"Yes, that's the price. You said you have cash."

He should have parked a block away; he shouldn't have let her see his car.

"I don't have that right now," he said. "Nobody has that. Nobody carries ten thousand dollars on them."

"You have it. You're gonna try to tell me you don't have it?"

Again, he was confused as to what she knew from Noelle, what she knew from being a psychic (yes, he could hear himself), and what was just her charlatan grifter bullying.

"You want to shop around for this?" she asked. "Clearing a third eye, it's not easy. There are layers. There are clouds. There are forces you have to go to war with. A lot of people can't even diagnose it!"

"How—how do you do it?" Beamer asked.

"I do it! I just do it! Don't ask me my secrets!"

Here is what this woman had going for her: Her name was somehow Phyllis. She had not so far been incorrect about anything. If she was saying that his third eye, the wellspring of his talent, was cloudy or whatever, what proof did he have that she was wrong? What do they say about atheists in foxholes? What they say about atheists in foxholes is that they will give you ten thousand dollars to clear their third eye on the off chance that a problem can be solved with witchery.

He sent her the money right there, from his bank's quick-pay app on his phone, bypassing all its warnings about fraud and coercion and trickery and all the people in the world who would like to take advantage of you. As he sent it and waited for the beep on her phone to confirm she'd received the money, he saw out of his periphery that his balance was unusually low. Something about that made his heart grip. It was either a sign he shouldn't have done that, or a sign that he was right to. He tried to remember what day it was, how long it would be till his quarterly factory payout dropped, but he realized he couldn't even conjure what month it was.

"How long will this take?" Beamer asked.

"It's a process. An art, not a science. I have to try a few things." She looked around her room, then caught focus on a small table near the door. She stood up and walked across the room and picked up a small piece of twine, something left over from some packing.

"Take this," she said. She handed it to him.

"What is it?"

"It's our rope. It's our connection. I have a matching one. I'm going to do some work with it."

"Is that all? That's it?"

"It's more than that. It's holy, this rope. Of course it's more than that. Look at it at three o'clock today. You make sure at that time that you are open and available and willing."

"For what?"

"Just make sure. Be open. Be available. Be *willing*."

Why is it that only the implausible ever felt true to him?

CUT TO: Beamer sitting in his car and looking at his phone. Jenny had sent another message.

I haven't gotten it yet.

His vision narrowed and he drove back to the office. He wanted to be at his desk when three P.M. came and his third eye was cleared.

CUT TO: Beamer at his desk. He realized he hadn't eaten yet that day, but he'd been through enough Yom Kippurs to know that revelation was alleged to happen upon an empty vessel.

The hour was approaching. It was two-thirty.

He tried to feel what was in the air for him. He closed his eyes.

Something about the moment—the gloam of his conversation with
Charlie, the suffocating constriction of his blood vessels—laid bare
for him that the problem had been the willy-nilly insertion of the
kidnapping as a plot point in any other story. The violence of a disappearance. But what was the real story?

Are you there? (Jenny again.)

Then it was three P.M., and was it a coincidence that it was right
then that he realized it? It couldn't be. He should write a kidnapping,
yes, but different from the *Santiago* movies.

It shouldn't be wild and commercial. It should be the exact opposite:

*It should be a small story about a young boy who is waiting in the car
for his mother to run an errand in the bank when suddenly the car is stolen
by a thief who doesn't realize that the boy is in the back.*

He sat down at his computer. Ready. Go. Wait, did he say that
already?

He realized that the Modafinil, which quelled his appetite, might
be making him woozy. It was important to eat no matter what.

CUT TO: He stood in line at Chipotle, where Noelle would
never agree to order from, visit, or even pass on the street, as the
story continued to come.

*The mother left the boy in the car to run an errand, to go to the Wald-
baum's or something, even though she could have easily brought him in
shopping with her, but the mother hates how slow the boy can be and how
he always wants to fill the cart with foods that aren't chicken and rice. The
boy sits and waits but when the driver's-side door opens, the person who
gets in isn't his mother but a scary man.*

This hasn't ever happened I don't think. Hello? (ibid.)

*The boy is scared and so he hides in the footwell and only when the
thief arrives at the factory does he discover that he has a stowaway. The
thief takes him into the factory and chains him to the radiator and the boy*

remembers nothing after that except that it happened—that it was a fact that it happened. Then, one day, there are some glowing beams and these cops show up and he's saved. But they never find the kidnapper.

CUT TO: Beamer back at his computer, but just as he was about to start typing, he saw a nicotine patch on the floor, then another. A small trail of curdled patches that must have fallen off. He had to go to a drugstore to get more. He was now as addicted to nicotine as someone who'd been smoking four packs of Camels for twenty years. As he took out his phone to pay, he saw:

Call me back when you can. I think something weird is going on. (And again.)

He couldn't call Jenny back, though. He was finally in touch with the magic. The magic and absolutely not the buffet of drugs he'd taken. No, he could feel it. He was available and open and stuff. He could feel *Santiago* leaving him. He felt *Santiago* drifting away. He didn't need *Santiago* anymore. He had his own thing he was *obviously* trying to say. He could make success off his own wind. He didn't need to stand on Charlie's shoulders. He had his own shoulders. He *was* the shoulders. He was all shoulders now.

So: The kid grows up to be so incredibly fucked up—all he wants to do is eat the world and hope that in the eating of it he becomes less malnourished, that somehow in all of the eating he will find the vitamin his body so needs. But no matter what, he finds that he's unable to get enough because there isn't *enough, not in the whole world.*

Food. Was it possible he should eat again? He'd only had a burrito the size of a toddler and some (all) of the chips they give you, plus he got extra chips with the guacamole he ordered. He couldn't leave his desk again, though. He had to write. But he also had to keep his energy up. He pulled up his phone to text Sophie, but he saw another text from Jenny.

Ok I just spoke to Nathan. We have to call him. Something is up.

Then, immediately after that, another text, from Noelle:

Are you running late?

The kid who is now a man meets a woman, a sexy lawyer (she doesn't know that she's sexy, but she does know that she's a lawyer), who finds him irresistibly charming and attractive and falls in love with him. She sees how haunted he is by what happened to him so she looks into his case and finds some clues now that DNA evidence is available and easy to read. Then, one day, she comes to him, and kneels at his feet. He is now a famous basketball player, but he is still broken inside. She tells him what she's learned, which is that the kidnapper was someone he'd always known. It was his father. The person who took him in the car, the person who chained him up. His own father.

Now the phone rang. Jenny. He let it go to voicemail.

Yes, his father! His father is the kidnapper! It all makes sense! The boy now goes to confront his father. His father cries immediately. He's spent all these years waiting for his boy to learn the truth about what happened and now he knows. The boy can't handle any more of this, so he goes to the mother and takes her by the shoulders. He screams at her, "Why did you put me in the backseat in the first place? Why couldn't you care about my safety?"

Now the phone rang again. It was Noelle.

She cries and cries and begs for his forgiveness. She puts a knife to her chest. The boy struggles with her, grabs it away from her. The mother is left at his feet, begging for forgiveness.

Beamer. Call me. It's serious.

But just as he was about to write the first word, he realized he shouldn't be writing this on a computer. No, this project deserves longhand, with a special, fetishized kind of pen.

CUT TO: A specialty stationery store, which was just a mile away.

CUT TO: Back at his desk, ready to write. His nervous system activated his forearms, which ignited his wrists, which sent currents to his fingers, but just as the words were about to start from them, he jumped out of his seat. Nope! Not yet! Not quite yet!

He knew this story. He knew its value. He had something of value and it had come from his own mind. The magic was still in him, or it was in him for the first time. He knew, just knew, that he could set this thing up anywhere and anyone who even got to hear the pitch would feel lucky. They'd talk for decades about how they were in the room when Beamer Fletcher pitched—no, dictated the terms of!—his masterpiece.

He also knew something else for the first time: It was not that he was clumsily throwing kidnappings into innocuous screenplays because he was lazy or afraid of the real story. No, it was that he wanted to show what a kidnapping actually is, which is something that walks into your life—whichever life—and steals it.

He was still sweating from this revelation—fraudulent charlatan, pump the brakes, please!—when the next truth hit him so hard that he did sit down because his legs had nearly given out.

What if.

It came to him like a punch in the stomach.

Mandy Patinkin.

We are going to be late. (From Noelle.)

Mandy Patinkin should play his father.

She is going to look out into that audience and not see her parents. Not me or you.

This was the role Mandy Patinkin was born to play! He could picture his father, his father who looked a little, no a lot, like Mandy, finally understanding that all of Beamer's work was a love letter to Carl, that he had a son who loved and understood him. A son who had been scared in that backseat of his mother's car, right along with Carl himself, neither of them sure of where they were or why any of this was happening to them.

Beamer you should call me. It appears we are totally fucked. (From Jenny.)

What is wrong with you? Call me back. (Also from Jenny.)

Hi-ho! Can we get on the phone? (Nathan.)

The school just called. She is freaking out. I'm in an Uber. Are you at least meeting me there? (Noelle.)

He stared at his legal pad for forty-seven minutes without blinking once! His hand ached already just from holding the pen. How long since he'd written longhand? There were so many strong beginnings, so many ways to start. Every time he almost wrote out one of them, he backed off. It was terrible the way one decision narrows the rest; it was terrible the way the words looked different on the page than they had looked in your head.

The phone rang three times, him sending it to voicemail at the first sound. He was under a magic spell, a newly cleaned third eye. He could not be disturbed. The thing that came out of him, he knew, was going to be gold, no platinum, no diamond!

. . .

. . .

. . .

Beamer what the fuck is wrong with you call me back (Jenny.)

. . .

. . .

This is totally unforgivable. I will never forgive you for this. I will not make your excuses to her. (Noelle.)

Perhaps this was a multiprong fix, this new third eye. Perhaps the first thing you feel is the old spunk back in your gut. Maybe the next

step was being able to put at least maybe literally one literal word
onto an actual page? Made sense!

But there had to be something he could do in the meantime.
Think, Fletcher.

Frankly this is part of the reason I cannot take you anymore
(Jenny again.)

The phone rang again, and again he pushed it to voicemail.

What if he was doing this backward? What if the key was to first
attach Mandy to the project, get it greenlit, and then Beamer could
write it at his leisure? Happens all the time. An actor blesses the project, says he wants in, and the script comes as a by-product of this
partnership. Yes. Beamer stood up. He had to tell someone. He
looked at his phone. It wasn't enough.

Pick up the fucking phone (Noelle.)

His agency was a good mile away from Beamer's office, the agency
that housed Jeremy Gottlieb, and also the agent who represented
Mandy Patinkin. Mandy was represented by a partner agent named
Fran Sacks, the same one whose desk Jeremy had been leaving when
he met Beamer and Charlie.

He texted Jeremy:

I'm coming over

Beamer left the office and headed toward his car, but then, remembering how a person has to keep up his body, he broke into a
jog. It's just a mile! Jogging is good!

It was the latest part of the afternoon, and the sun was beating
down the way it always did in L.A.—a relentless taskmaster right up
until the minute it disappeared at night. But Beamer wanted it. He
wanted to feel the sun on his head, the heat in his body, the smog in
his lungs. Look at him! Jogging!

He arrived at the agency, where the receptionist told him to wait in the lobby. As luck would have it, Beamer saw Fran Sacks heading down the hall.

"Fran!" Beamer jumped up to intercept him at the elevator.

Fran, who was seventy-two years old, looked up from his phone and squinted hard at this person flagging him down, a preemptive greeting on his face, trying to place Beamer.

"Beamer Fletcher," Beamer said, extending his hand. Fran took it.

"Right, hello, Beamer. Charlie Messinger's friend."

"Well. Yes. I'm also a client. We were partners, actually, Charlie and me. We're taking some time off."

"Right, right. How are you? I'm so sorry, I'm on my way to a dinner—oh, your phone is going off."

"That's an early dinner! Ha!" Then, realizing Fran was still looking at Beamer's phone: "Oh, it's nothing. I'm not here to—I'm having a meeting myself with Jeremy Gottlieb. *My* agent." Sounds right.

Fran looked at his watch.

"Just, it's so funny I'm running into you," Beamer continued quickly. "I was wondering. I have this great project for Mandy Patinkin. A kidnapping, but with heart. A family drama. An epic. Something I could really tell from my soul, you know?"

Fran was still smiling, but his eyes took on caution.

"I'm sorry, I don't—should we talk later? I can have my office set up . . . ?"

"It's Mandy Patinkin," Beamer said. "It's for the starring role. Number one on the call sheet. It's perfect for him. It's a great, great role."

"You know, we're looking for something for Jeff Goldblum."

"Oh, Jeff is great. He's great. I'm sorry, but I really just see Mandy for this."

"Oh, Mandy is finishing up nearly a decade on a spy thriller. I think he wants to take some time off. Spend it with his family. But if the project is right, well . . . I'll talk to Jeremy as soon as I . . ."

"Great, great, good to get this packaged up right, am I right?" Beamer laughed too loud and they said their goodbyes. "Synergy.

Packaging. A dirty word! But we're not babes in the woods, are we, Fran?" But Fran was taillights by then.

Beamer sat on the couch for another twenty (twelve) minutes when the receptionist said, "I don't know where he is. I'm sorry, Beamer."

"We were having coffee! A drink. Dinner," Beamer said, until he remembered that that wasn't true. "I'll wait here." But then, after ten (forty) more minutes, he stood up. "I guess we got our signals crossed," he said, and walked out.

On his way out, Beamer bumped into Seth Horowitz, a producer on a constellation of teen shows, who was now producing a sci-fi movie about discovering life on Jupiter.

"Don't ask Mandy Patinkin," Beamer said. "He's not taking offers."

Seth laughed. "Right. I just heard about it from Charlie. That Patinkin is doing a thing for *Family Business*? Oh and hey: You're writing a new *Santiago*?"

Spoke to Mommy. She says she can't get in touch with Arthur.
He went on some trip. She doesn't know what to do.

"I wrote a new *Santiago*. But no, I'm writing something new now. Original. No IP. Oh-riginal."

"Right, right. Yeah, Charlie's pretty excited about Patinkin. Who doesn't love Patinkin? 'My name is Inigo Montoya!'" He looked at the phone in Beamer's hand. "Hey, do you want to get that?" Which is how Beamer realized Noelle was calling him again.

On his jog back to his office, he was stopped at the corner of Santa Monica and Martel by a West Hollywood police officer directing traffic. He jogged in place and heard his phone ring. He almost fumbled it taking it out of his pocket, what with his overall nervousness (plus the jogging and the drugs).

It was Jenny. He ignored it.

But with his phone out, he decided to make a call himself.

"Fran Sacks's office," said the assistant.

"Beamer Fletcher here."

"I don't understand. Hello? Say that again?"

"I'm fine. Running. Just tell him it's Beamer Fletcher and I heard that Mandy is actually taking offers? On *Family Business*? So maybe there's a mix-up here, and I'd love to just clear it up. I feel like it's his obligation to convey this offer to Mandy. You know? Legally? Yes. Thank you. Yes. This is a special role. A career-maker, if you will. OK, sure, bye. Yes, bye!" He jogged farther in the direction of his office, feeling pretty good about all this.

Now CUT TO: Thirty minutes later, Beamer back at his own desk and calling Fran Sacks's office again, this time saying he was Charlie Messinger. Fran got on the phone immediately.

"It's a really juicy role," Beamer said.

"Charlie?"

"Beamer Fletcher." In his boyhood, his enthusiasm and charm went a long way toward erasing the ways he was too much. "You know what I was thinking? I was thinking about the diversity initiatives everywhere now. How come Jews are never part of that? I grew up, my father has a factory—swastikas."

"A factory that made swastikas?" Fran asked.

"No, no," Beamer laughed. "They make polystyrene. Like styrofoam molds for shipping? Insulation. The place would get vandalized, though. That's what I'm saying. It's going to be such a juicy part—he's going to come in and educate everyone on the fact that Jews aren't just these rich assholes, you know?" He let that sink in. "I'm writing it *for him*. I'm writing it *myself*. For *him*."

After a long pause, Fran spoke. "You doing OK, Beamer?"

"I'm just really into this, you know? I feel a big wind coming and I want to be part of it. Inspiration. I want to *be* the wind, you know?"

It sometimes takes people a beat to realize what you're offering them.

CUT TO: Beamer was staring at his cellphone and thumbing away Noelle's inquiries when it rang. It was Charlie.

"Are you calling the agency and pretending to be me?" Charlie asked.

"What?"

"I know, it's crazy. Jeremy just said it. Is it true?"

"You spoke to Jeremy?"

"Just, is something going on, Beamer?"

"Are you casting Mandy Patinkin in *Family Business*?"

"What?"

His phone was going off like a pinball machine. He switched it to silent.

"I'm doing it, Charlie. I'm writing something about my childhood. I'm calling it *The Backseat*. Action, but emotional, you know? An indie feel."

"I don't know if Mandy Patinkin is action material."

"What are you talking about?" Beamer was flabbergasted. "He's a great actor. A once-in-a-lifetime— Do you know I saw him in *The Secret Garden* on Broadway in high school? He was great. He is one of the greats." Then, "You know, Charlie, people love those movies. They love the *Santiago*s, too. You shouldn't really tarnish our legacy."

"Of course they do. Of course. It's just, it's unexpected. Mandy for this."

"Bruce Willis was basically a goofball dramedy guy when they cast him in *Die Hard*. Forget that. Paul was a sitcom star when he got Jorge. That role made his career."

"It's really none of my business. Just, if you're calling and saying you're me?"

"Charlie. It's offensive. Don't say it again."

Silence.

"I'm sorry, Beamer. I'm sorry. I guess—I don't know, maybe I misunderstood. Hey, are you OK? You sound . . . intense?"

"Please don't judge me on how I sound when my lifelong best friend accuses me of stealing his identity!" Charlie was quiet. "Seriously, Charlie. Your ego has grown with your paychecks. You would like my new script."

"I'm sure! Send it over when it's done!"

"You will like it. It's serious and good and it advances the conversation and it even meets diversity checklists! If you add Jews to them! But seriously, bro, you really inspired me with your talk."

"I . . . it's Melissa calling on the other line. I have to go. Let's catch up soon. I'd love to read it. Bye. OK. Bye."

He realized that he had to leave for Liesl's recital, so he took two more Modafinil and affixed three more nicotine patches to his stomach and one to his forehead, just to see, and got in the car. He remembered that Jeremy's home was on the way to the school, and he looked at the time and thought maybe he had a minute to just stop there and clear the air and also ask him why he wasn't calling him back. He stopped at a donut shop, one of the cheap mini-mall ones, because you can't show up empty-handed. He still felt not even a spark of appetite—boy, did these things work!—though he had the compulsion to dance the woman behind the counter around the room and then dry-hump her just seven or eight times.

CUT TO: Beamer in his car, realizing that two dozen donuts for a man with one husband and no kids was overkill and that he should eat one or two of them so that it doesn't look weird. He sat in a spot in the parking lot reserved for employees only, tonguing colored sprinkles off pink icing.

He started to wonder if—if—what *if* Modafinil is like the Ambien, where if you do the thing they're there to undo you get to a higher rung of satisfaction. What if your appetite is killed by an upper but then you go to an In-N-Out Burger drive-thru anyway?

He had to know. And luckily, he knew exactly where there was an In-N-Out Burger so that he could see.

CUT TO: The In-N-Out drive-thru on Sunset, where he waited in line in his car, feeling pretty good about the spirit of experimentation he was embarking upon. He ordered a Double-Double, fries, and a shake, just to make sure he had the American standard experience. He pulled over in the parking lot in the parking spot of desperation that the place kept for if you couldn't even wait till you got home and he went to work on his meal.

Now his phone rang. He couldn't see the number because his eyes had become too blurry and he was driving. He picked it up anyway.

"Yo," he said.

"Beamer, it's Jeremy. Listen, we have to talk. You need to stay away from Fran. And from Mandy Patinkin. I don't need to tell you this, right?"

"Is that the strategy? Stay away? Create some heat and hope he comes to us?"

"No, Beam. There's no strategy. Fran's asking you to, uh, he's asking you to stop. To cease and desist."

"That's bullshit. I ran into him and then I called him."

"Pretending you were Charlie."

"His assistant misunderstood. Honestly. Is that how he reacts to getting a once-in-a-lifetime opportunity for his client? To play a role that will honor his heritage? Wow."

"Beamer, you have to—"

"I gotta go."

"No, you listen to me. I'm not your agent anymore. Fran is making me fire you. The agency is firing you. Do you understand that? Do you understand? I'm sorry I couldn't get you a sixteen-million-dollar deal. I'm sorry that things fell apart. But you have to pull it together, man. You just do."

For a long second, Beamer was quiet. Then:

"Charlie has a sixteen-million-dollar deal?"

"Beamer . . ."

"I gotta go."

Beamer hung up and turned on La Brea and turned in to the McDonald's. His sphincter was pulsating pleasurably, signs of a storm brewing. He knew what was coming. Soon there would be burning jets of diarrhea, but Not! Just! Yet!

"Welcome shfaleraejropaeijsd help you?"

Finally!

"I'll have a Quarter Pounder with Cheese, a Filet-O-Fish, and two Big Macs, a Diet Coke, two large fries, and a Sunkist"—for that fine, fine finish—"and let's say six McNuggets. No, thirty."

"They come twenty."

"Make it forty!"

CUT TO: Seven minutes later, still in the parking lot, his hazards on. He licked a finger and started on his way home, but realized he forgot to order his absolute favorite—*Are You Sure You've Thought This Through?*, he thought with a chuckle—and so ran on through one more time for a McChicken and one of those tiny boxed apple pies that he used to enjoy in concert with one another. (He also ordered a Happy Meal, pretending he'd forgotten to pick it up for a phantom child in the backseat the round before ["I won't forget this time, kiddo!" he yelled to nobody], but his energy was wasted because the woman didn't appear to remember him or care.) He ate the McChicken and thought yes, it really does feel like coming home somehow.

He arrived in Malibu but wasn't sure how. No problem. He wanted to watch the sunset, though it was dark already and he wasn't sure how he'd miscalculated it. He remembered something. He pulled over and called Sophie.

"Beamer?"

"Yeah, hi, how are you?" He was so gassy from all that he had eaten that there was a drumline of flatulence shooting from his throbbing rectum.

"I'm—are you OK? Your voice sounds weird."

"Oh, no. Sure. Will you please do me a favor and track down Mandy Patinkin's address?"

"In upstate New York, I think, right?"

"He has a place here. I want to send him something and his agent is on vacation. For the movie. Fran Sacks said he'd get it for me—don't call his office, they're in the middle of a merger, you didn't hear it from me, but, let's just not bother them. Just get it for me?"

"It's just, maybe we should wait till morning . . ."

"Just get it, will you?"

Fifteen minutes later, she texted him an address in the Palisades.

He drove around the twisting streets. He nearly ran over Diane Keaton, who was out for a brisk walk. He passed Ben Affleck's house twice, though he could have sworn he was driving in a straight line. Maybe he'd been around the world? Maybe he'd traversed the world?

How had it gotten so dark so fast? He stopped at an intersection, and in the quiet came a thought:

It was how they don't tell you how long the tail is on self-destruction—how you could self-destruct over and over and for so, so long without even coming close to the end, which, of course, is destruction itself. He marveled at this, how many chances there were to turn back when you saw the signs, which was exactly how many times you chose not to.

In the seat next to him, his phone went off again, again from Jenny:

> There's no money anymore. I didn't want to tell you like this, but you won't answer the phone.

"Someone must save this sweet raven-haired maiden," he sang, opera-style, as he pulled up into the driveway of a Spanish-style home. He put the car in park and then put the car in park and then put the car in park. He got out of the car and looked out. It was a house on the water, raised up high on a hill, so that the tide could never get them. This is where Mandy Patinkin should live, he thought. This was a safe place for him.

The door opened. It was Mandy Patinkin himself, about to take his dog for a walk.

"Who are you?" Mandy asked. Then he looked over Beamer's shoulder. "What the hell are you—"

Beamer turned around and saw his car, driving itself backward, down the driveway. He watched speechless, with his mouth open. He turned back to Mandy, who also turned to him again and repeated himself.

"What the hell is going on? Who are you? What is on your forehead?"

In response, Beamer raised his hand like an opera singer serenading his audience, but when he opened his mouth, he spoke like a lawyer.

"Someone must save this sweet raven-haired maiden," he said.

His phone rang just then, to the tune of Mahler's Fourth Symphony, and for a second, he was relieved to realize he'd made Liesl's concert in time, and he looked around to find Noelle so that he could parade his reassurance against her doubts about him, but the only person he could find was Mandy Patinkin, who had somehow shown up, too—though maybe not so surprised, since he sure seemed like a nice guy.

That's when Beamer collapsed.

THE HARD LIFE
BUFFET

W HAT HAD HAPPENED to the Fletchers' money was this: A
private equity firm had purchased fifty-one percent of Haulers, the
big-box store that held Consolidated Packing Solutions, Ltd., in an
exclusive contract, and had taken it private either overnight or when
the Fletchers weren't looking. The private equity firm's stated goal
was to optimize Haulers's operational spending; their mostly unstated
goal was to then sell it again once it started turning a bigger profit.

The first thing their efficiency consultants did was ask why Haulers's in-house appliance brand was operating a factory domestically at
a cost of six times what it would cost to simply buy the product over-
seas and have it imported. That led to the efficiency consultants' conclusion, which was that the assets of the business, appraised at 2.3
times the purchase price of the entire company, were worth far more
sold off in an auction than as a component of an actual running business with an anemic profit margin of six percent.

The Consolidated Packing Solutions, Ltd., contract was one of
those assets.

And so it was resolved: Haulers would become a logistics company going forward, ceasing production of their own line of appli-
ances for the first time since they were founded in 1921. Their shelves

would now be lined with products made in China, the Philippines, Thailand, Vietnam, Myanmar, and Cambodia. Most importantly, the items would be shipped on cargo boats packed in whatever combination of styrofoam mold or packing peanuts already existed.

The problem wasn't just that Consolidated Packing Solutions, Ltd., was one of the last remaining polystyrene (or otherwise) factories in the United States. It was that Haulers still retained that exclusive contract on the place, which they now hoped to sell at auction to any other big-box store, though the very thing that had made Haulers vulnerable to private equity in the first place was that no other company was dumb enough to manufacture domestically anymore.

So it was settled. Consolidated Packing Solutions, Ltd., would complete the three dozen or so orders it had outstanding and then it would stand fallow, pending a sale of the contract.

Now, the Fletchers were not preternaturally rich. They were just regular rich, or the richest people we knew. Had they invested better, perhaps the private equity drama would not have even touched them; perhaps they would have even divested from the factory long ago, allowing Ike his earn-back of the factory, and moving on. It had not been a secret that the dominance of the domestic factory would one day come to an end, and Phyllis, who had overseen the management of the family money, had made some minor investments, but she had not been immune to the paranoia that her husband, Zelig, had implanted in her—that institutions were corrupt, that governments turn, that children will fuck up anything you give them, et cetera. Her own father had lost all his savings in the crash of '29.

In other words, the Fletchers' money wasn't terribly diversified. The cash payout from the initial Haulers purchase had been used mostly to acquire homes in the forms of irrevocable trusts, so that they technically belonged to the children but were controlled by Arthur. There were a few thousand dollars in savings bonds lying around from weddings and bar mitzvahs that seemed more trouble to cash in than not. And the cash that the factory spat out quarterly went to the maintenance of the family and the estate.

And the Fletcher children had not been immune to the inertia of all rich kids, which was to lack the imagination that the money could ever possibly stop coming in. They spent their money like third-generation American children do: quickly, and without thinking too hard about it. Beamer was leveraged because of his lifestyle; Nathan had the closest thing in the family to an investment portfolio but also a predilection for buying massive amounts of insurance. And Jenny, who had always been the most disdainful of the money, had given most of hers away.

Besides, they thought, the Haulers stock was like a secret savings plan. Until it went bankrupt it was like a secret savings plan!

And yet it was Jenny who noticed that the money was gone first. For a variety of reasons—but presumably because she was the most organized of her siblings—she noticed almost immediately that no cash drop had been made into her account on the fifteenth of the month. After trying to get in touch with Beamer, and choosing not to talk to Nathan for how nuts he was liable to go, she finally called her mother to say that her quarterly payout had not appeared in her bank account, a deposit that was more reliable than most of the things she'd come to expect in this world. Her mother checked the calendar to see if there was a bank holiday that would have delayed the payment. She called the family accountant, but he said there was no delay. The money simply hadn't come in that month.

Ruth didn't know what to do. Normally, she would call Arthur, but Arthur was god knows where. Arthur, a founding name partner in his law firm and the executor of the trust that held the factory and the mastermind of the family fortune—"He knows where the bodies are buried," Phyllis used to say. "I know where *everything* is buried," he would answer, and Phyllis would laugh. He had taken a sudden sabbatical, and a strange one: To the shock of everyone who knew him, he'd left town following Phyllis's funeral with no forwarding address and just a simple note left on Ruth's desk saying that he was going away, that he didn't know when he'd return, that she should not hope to be in touch with him during this time, that she should call the law firm if she had any issues with any legal needs.

"*Legal* needs?" she said to the air when she finished the letter.

The following week, Nathan, who worked at the very same firm—no accident there—told Ruth that the partners had arrived at work the next day to find Arthur's cellphone on his desk. When Ruth heard that, she put her head in her hands and cried. This made Nathan sufficiently uncomfortable to abscond to the bathroom for the next forty-five minutes.

"And then what happened?" Jenny asked now. Now Ruth was in her kitchen with Nathan, whom she'd called over urgently, and was on speakerphone with Jenny.

"They won't tell me where Arthur is," Ruth said from the kitchen in Middle Rock. "They say they don't know. He's the only one who understands all of this. I spoke to Arnie. He's the partner doing Arthur's work. He just kept saying there's nothing to do. There's no money coming. It's done."

"What's going to happen to the factory?" Jenny asked.

"The factory? What's going to happen to *your family*, Jennifer."

"What about the workers?" Jenny asked.

"Norma Rae over here."

"These people worked for us for decades, and what are we doing for them?"

"We're laying them off, Jennifer," Ruth said. "In three months. When the last of the jobs is finished. That's what Ike thinks it will take. We're giving them a month of severance and thanking them for their hard work."

"This is bullshit," Jenny said. "They deserve better."

"When the implications of all of this hit you, Jennifer, and you can think of what this will be like for your family, and not just for the men you've only said passing hellos to your whole life but who are somehow more important to you than your own flesh and blood, you call me. I'll be homeless, so call the cell."

"We have plenty of money, Mom."

"You do. Nathan does. You were smart. You saved it. But Beamer? I don't know. And us! We don't get those payments. We only got the money up front. And then we gave it all away to you kids."

"To them, not me," Jenny said.

"Don't start. You don't need a house until you have a family. You're going to raise a family in New Haven? In a slum?"

"What about Ike?" Jenny asked.

"He understands that things didn't go according to plan."

"But he was supposed to take over! You promised him!"

"Jennifer. I cannot have this fight with you. We took very good care of him. Do you know how much it costs to mow the lawn here?"

"Then move! People who have financial precarity don't live on huge properties."

"Your father is in a fragile state right now since your grandmother died. I don't think a move would be good."

"I'm sorry, but when is he not in a fragile state!"

"Jennifer Suzanne Fletcher."

Nathan remained silent, now with his eyes squeezed shut.

"There is nothing to do," Ruth repeated to Nathan there in her kitchen, with Jenny listening in. "And when you speak to your brother, if he bothers returning your calls, you tell him also there's nothing to do." The slow rumble in her voice began, a weather vane pointing directly to that coming shriek. "You kids, I don't know what you're going to do. I hope you held on to some money. I don't know how to help you. You're grown-ups. You have to figure this out." And now, here we go, the shrieking aria: "I grew up poor. Do you know what that's like?"

Jenny grumbled something about having to go to a meeting and hung up. Ruth stared at the phone for a second, biting her lip, and Nathan stood up.

"I have to get home," he said. "Alyssa's waiting for dinner for me."

"Hm," Ruth replied.

But at home, Nathan stayed parked in the driveway and called his childhood friend Mickey Mayer, who also still lived in Middle Rock.

"Yo," Mickey said.

"Hi-ho, Mickey-moto," Nathan said, with labored cheer.

Either the dinnertime phone call or the terror in Nathan's voice or both found Mickey in a very bad mood.

"What is it?" Mickey was breathless and it occurred to Nathan that he had called and interrupted either exercise or s-e-x, Nathan couldn't tell. "Unh. Unh. Unh."

Nathan closed his eyes and inhaled through his nose for two counts and out for four, like the meditation app on his phone that he tried to remember to use told him to. You wouldn't make those noises into a phone if you were having sex, right? You wouldn't pick up the phone if you were having sex, right?

"Are you there? Unh."

"I'm here," Nathan said. "I have to talk to you about that, uh—a, uh, a distribution. A disbursement. Of my money."

"Unh, huck, unh." Mickey had never been nice to Nathan. Mickey had been Nathan's most ardent and zealous bully since they were first thrust together as children. It was the kind of cruelty that forged in them a lifelong friendship, with Nathan on the hamster wheel of trying to secure approbation and approval without ever really asking himself why. Such is the complicated stew of childhood friendships.

But recently Mickey had become even more aggressive. He was training for some kind of -athon and had been working out for several hours a day, all of which led to a new, more advanced kind of belligerence. (Also, he was taking some questionable supplements and perhaps experimenting with a growth hormone harvested from the pituitary glands of rabid raccoons.)

"Can I just tell you what I need?" Nathan asked. "Or, uh, or do I have to fill out, like, a form?"

"Fuck." Nathan heard a loud clang. Dumbbells hitting the floor. Thank god. He'd been exercising. Thank god thank god thank god. He didn't want to think of sweet Penny Mayer lying there . . . forget it! Don't think about that!

"Nathan," Mickey was saying. "We are getting the full ten percent growth this year. Full ten percent. You want a disbursement *now*?"

"Not all of it, of course. Just I was thinking that—"

Mickey slowed down and made his voice light and casual. "Are you investing somewhere else?" But Mickey wasn't asking; he was accusing. "It's OK if you are, but I'd like to know. I think after all this time I deserve to know."

"Right-o. No, of course not. Of course I'd tell you. No, it's that—" Nathan stopped. What was he to say? "I'm thinking of doing a little bit of a reh-no-vation on the ole HQ. Kids' bar mitzvah coming down the pike, and I thought maybe I should be a teaspoon more liquid. You know? A tablespoon more liquid."

"Listen," Mickey said. "We're hitting peak growth. Conservative, like you like. I don't get it. You have plenty of cash. Lord knows you have plenty of cash! And don't forget your income. You have an income! You're a lawyer, for Christ's sake! Seriously, my advice is to hold."

"I'm very happy with the growth! I'm not leaving you! This isn't about that. I'm just, it's just a small payout for right now—"

"Listen," Mickey said again. "Can I call you in a minute. Penny needs me for some shit with the kids."

"Sure, I—when should we—"

"I'll call you when I'm done."

"Great, so that should be, what, twenty minutes or so? I'm about to sit down for—"

And the phone took on the muted silence of nothing in the background and Nathan tried hard not to think about being the kind of person you could just hang up on into his late forties.

"Are you hungry?" Alyssa asked when Nathan finally walked into the house. Ari was at the kitchen table and his twin brother, Josh, was at the dining room table, both of them practicing different sections of the haftorah they'd divided for their bar mitzvah. "We ate but there's some left."

"I ate," Nathan said, though of course he hadn't. But he wasn't hungry and could feel the mounting offensive of his activated bowel. His IBS could not withstand such sneak attacks as were being visited upon it tonight.

"Your mother cooked for you?" Alyssa was dubious. Then she asked, "Were you at the CVS? Tell me the truth."

Nathan had received an elevated blood pressure reading two years before at his biannual physical—just one, once. He'd left in a panic and bought several at-home blood pressure reading kits, which had *not* been the advice of the doctor, who knew him well enough to say, "Nathan, it's just one reading. It doesn't mean anything. We'll monitor it. It's fine," and had given him a prescription for beta-blockers just in case. Nathan was terrified of the pills—just the existence of the pills and his belief that they would hurt him before they could help him—and instead started assiduously monitoring his blood pressure once an hour on each blood pressure machine, calculating the means and freaking out over the minute disparities in the numbers. Alyssa got wind of this and confiscated all four devices that she found; he had an emergency one he kept in his study. Then she found that one, and he was contrite when he was caught, maybe too contrite for Alyssa's taste—he'd apologized as though he'd been found with his penis inside the housekeeper's mouth—and now she regularly accused him of going to the local pharmacy, which had a pay blood pressure monitor. She was correct about sixty-five percent of the time she accused him. But not today!

"I didn't! I wasn't!"

"We don't lie to each other, right?" she said.

"I have some casework I have to finish before the paralegals go home," he said, and kissed her at the corkscrew crown of her hair and absconded into his home office, where he closed the door, listened for a second to make sure he was alone, and sat in the dark and imagined his doom.

Nathan tried Mickey again at eight-thirty P.M., this time via text message.

Hi-ho! I need to talk to you! Time-sensitive!

The three terrifying dots appeared for longer than Nathan could bear. Mickey's ultimate answer:

Bro. Dinner. Call u later.

Later, Ari and Josh were on their separate, parallel iPads in the den and Alyssa was buzzing through the house, as she did at the ten o'clock hour, flexing her astonishing economy of motion as she picked up, arranged, stabilized, prepared the house for another day.

"Are you winding down?" Alyssa asked him. "You really shouldn't be looking at your phone. You know how you get those weird dreams if you—"

"I just have a call to make," he answered. "I'll find a place."

But despite the ginormosity of the house, Nathan couldn't find a corner alone. There was no room Alyssa wasn't going to pop up in for just a brief moment as she restored towels to their hooks, shoes to their closets, dishes to their rightful sink, papers to desks, laundry to its correct drawers. Nowhere was safe from her be-legginged mien.

Finally, he found a plausible hiding place, the corner of the upstairs guest bathroom, where he texted Mickey again. Forty minutes later there was still no response, so Nathan went to bed.

But did Nathan sleep? He did not. He lay awake, his eyes never closing, watching a rainstorm's midnight ambush, the shadows of the trees on his bedroom wall jousting chaotically, then the sound of the rain slowing in predawn to a light patter. He was still up when the light changed in his room as finally the morning came and he could be awake with the world, which made him feel a little more normal.

He arose to no text messages or missed calls from Mickey (but it was still early!) and showered and dressed and boarded the passenger seat of his family's Acura 2017 MDX, which was the Insurance Institute for Highway Safety's Top Safety Pick+ that year, and, that year, received a Five Star Overall Rating from the National Highway Traffic and Safety Administration.

"Come on, come on," he urged his family. His sons were dragging toward the car and Alyssa was taking her time locking the door.

"We're not running late!" Alyssa said, though she broke into a jog. The tyranny of Nathan's anxiety was often easier for her to acquiesce to.

Nathan inserted the male component of the seatbelt into its attendant female component, and sat and listened for the three clicks of the remaining seatbelts that needed fastening throughout the car. In the stillness of the listening, however, he realized he was stepping on something that elicited a crinkling quality in the passenger footwell.

"Oh no, I think I stepped on some—"

He reached down to see what it was and saw that it was a glossy page full of swatches of variations on the color beige: Sand, Dust, Lint, Hazy, Wood, Résumé Paper, Oatmeal, Wheat Germ—

The page was snatched from Nathan's hand and frisbeed to the backseat in a singular discus throw by Alyssa before Nathan could react.

"What was that?" Nathan asked.

She pulled onto the road, which was still wet from the midnight thunderstorm. "Did you hear the rain last night, kids?" Then, to Nathan, "When do you think we'll get some snow?"

"I hope there were no downed branches," he answered. "Scratch that. I hope there are no trees that are going to fall."

"Nathan," Alyssa said, with a head jerk to the back.

But it was too late. The frequency of Nathan's alarm had found and syncopated with his son's.

"Can that happen?" Ari asked. "Can a tree just fall like that?"

Alyssa answered fast. "It doesn't. Is that something you worry about? There's no reason for you to worry about that."

But Ari knew where to get the terrible truth. "Dad?" he asked.

Nathan knew the correct answer but he also knew the right answer. The correct answer was that of course a tree can fall. Of course a random confluence of events could result in grave injury or immediate (or excruciatingly slow) death. Of course our demise is imminent, and the only constant is that we never know exactly how imminent. Just ask someone who died a minute ago! It's a miracle that we woke up this morning! That's the correct answer. The right answer, on the other hand, was to say: Not to worry, son. It's all fine.

Things like that don't happen. We will all live forever in peace and health and prosperity.

Guess which answer Nathan gave?

Nathan Fletcher had grown from that little boy making twenty-four-hour four-point contact with his mother during his father's kidnapping into not so much a whole man but a collection of tics: a composite panic attack whose brain lived in both the unspeakable past and the terrifying future and rarely in a particular current moment unless that moment contained more fear than the past and future put together and therefore deserved his complete attention. It was the fear that always felt like the truth to him.

"You never know what kind of damage a storm can do to the integrity of a tree," Nathan said. "Mostly because you have no way of knowing what the tree's been through already, see? Some of these trees are three hundred years old!"

"Which doesn't mean that a tree is going to fall into our house . . ." Alyssa said, equal parts warning and wear.

"Right-o," Nathan said. He sat for a still moment, trying his hardest to yield to the plea in her voice. He loved his wife. In calmer moments, before he was triggered with these kinds of questions, he was convinced she was right that a child shouldn't concern himself with what he can't help. But there was a dark, boiling chasm between what he knew and what he knew for sure. So:

"These trees have been growing for hundreds of years," Nathan said. "We don't know how much they've rotted inside. Again, it's about integrity. The integrity of the tree."

Alyssa made a noise, and Nathan felt like OK, OK, but: Isn't this what parenting is? Making sure your children knew about all the dangers of the world?

In the pause where Ari took in the implications of this, Alyssa puffed up her cheeks.

"So a tree can just tip?" he asked. "What if I'm standing under it? What if it falls on our house when we're sleeping?" Alyssa began to release the air from her cheeks slowly, like a balloon deflating endlessly. "What if you're sleeping?"

Then Nathan was filled with the sadness that often visited him as a parent, the sadness that came when he had made sure his children were finally alert and listening and as scared as he knew they should be. Now they had the information he felt they needed and he wished desperately that he could have kept it from them.

"I think the big oak in the backyard is directly across from your room," Josh said to Ari.

"Joshua!" Alyssa said.

"It's an old oak," Josh said. "Who knows what it's been through?"

"Josh," Nathan said, with warning in his voice. But he could not disagree.

"Do you remember when we tried to make a tree house on it? But Dad said it wasn't stable enough?"

"That was just a theory Dad had!" Alyssa said, her eyes jumping to the rearview. "We didn't know that for sure! Ari, we don't know for sure! Do you hear me?"

"Alyssa!" Nathan grabbed the wheel. "The road!"

(There was no one else on the road. You should see how wide those streets are.)

Alyssa wrenched back the wheel and stopped at the street's stop sign. They both sat, breathing at the windshield for a minute. Finally, Nathan turned around and looked at Ari:

"I'm not saying it'll smash into your room in the middle of the night."

Alyssa appeared to relax.

"I'm saying we just don't know."

"OK!" Alyssa fairly shouted. They had pulled up to the train station. "Here we are!"

Nathan preferred the 7:59 for what he believed were obvious reasons: It was the only one of the two morning rush-hour trains that originated from Middle Rock Station and therefore started out empty and therefore Nathan could sit in the seat closest to the doors, but facing away from them, behind the divider. He had long since ascertained that this was the safest seat on the train. It was close to two evacuation areas, plus, in the case of derailment, the divider would be solid enough for him to use as a shield against projectiles before he ran for the exit.

Nathan was a familiar sight on the train, clutching his briefcase to his chest, openly fretting. Physically, he resembled Beamer enough for their differences to be comical. He had the same blue eyes as his brother, but whereas Beamer's were sultry with their dark circles beneath them, Nathan's dark circles called to mind a terrified comic book raccoon. Nathan was taller than his brother, but skinnier, owing to his sensitive stomach. And whereas Beamer's hair showed no signs of deterioration, Nathan was already knee-deep in the kind of male-pattern hair loss that threatened an eventuality in which Nathan would have to make some real decisions about arrangement regarding the little hair he would soon have left.

On the train, Nathan looked at his phone. Nothing. He texted Mickey again:

Hi-ho! Must have missed you last night. Talk now?

He stared at the text for a second before he hit send. When he finally did it, his stomach lurched as though he were in free fall.

Here was the truth: Unbeknownst to Alyssa, Nathan's money was no longer at the J.P. Morgan fund that he'd been squirreling it away in for the last fifteen years. He'd withdrawn it when his childhood best friend (though "best" and "friend" are doing hard work there) started his own fund after leaving a large brokerage house. It was not easy to convince Nathan to do this, of course. Mickey Mayer leveraged his years of friendship with Nathan (tense), the long relationship between their sisters (tenuous), and their parents' mutual regard (dubious) to woo Nathan away from J.P. Morgan. But it was not with any of this that Mickey was able to convince Nathan to give him his money to invest. It was not with promises of large returns. It was not even with the bull's-eye siren song of investment conservatism that he serenaded Nathan with while other investor types sang of cascading returns. No, it was with his usual bullying.

"You know my children, Nathan," Mickey had said. "You know

me my whole life. Our sisters are friends. Our mothers are best friends." Actually Jenny was barely in touch with Erica Mayer and actually Ruth hated Cecilia Mayer. "I know you. I know everything wrong with you, and everything that stops you from making good decisions. And it's a lot, if I may say so. A lot." Then, "What the fuck is wrong with you? What's wrong with you that you don't want a ten percent yield? You *want* withdrawal fees?" Then, "Are you—is something wrong with you? That guy takes advantage of you. If I'd known you liked being taken advantage of . . . If I'd known you were a little bitch who likes when people take advantage of you . . ."

"I don't know, Mickey," Nathan had said then. "I have a good relationship with the guy at J.P."

But Mickey ignored him. "And the best thing about it is that it's just me," he continued. "And you know where I live. You know where that other guy lives? Do you know his name?"

"Barry Silverman."

"Barry Silverman. Ha! Listen, those guys only care about money. I care about your future. If you don't do this, you're a bigger fucking idiot than I thought."

It was true that Nathan had known Mickey for his whole life. And yes, he knew where Mickey lived. And Mickey's plan, as shown on a special iPad Mickey brought over to the house when Alyssa was out with the kids, was of a mild incline, not the spiky EKG of a graph that the J.P. Morgan portal showed when Nathan's stomach was base enough to check.

But that's making this sound like the decision was logical and inevitable. It was not. For as long as he could remember, Nathan's habit was to black out a little when Mickey berated him, his body playing possum to endure the strike. Nathan often emerged from this blackout to find that he'd agreed to whatever Mickey wanted just to make it stop. And thus, Nathan became Mickey's first customer.

The train went in and out of robust cellular signal. Nathan watched his phone like a stock ticker. He sat back and tried to do his breathing. Then he tried to do his counting. Then he tried to do his sub-aural humming. Then he tried to do his body scan. Then he tried to do a guided meditation from memory because you would have to be pretty stupid to put earphones in and close your eyes on a train with strangers who could plan your mugging or death right there in front of your face while you were distracted.

When Nathan's train finally deposited him into Penn Station, he took the escalator up to the main level. He looked at his phone as he surfaced.

We need to talk, Alyssa texted. Ari is freaking out about a tree falling into his room.

Nathan's office, where he worked as a land use attorney, sat just a few blocks north of the Eighth Avenue exit. To get there, he would have to take an additional escalator up to the street. But he didn't get on that escalator. Instead, he walked toward the subway and went through the turnstile and got on the microbe spore biodome coaster that was the 1 train and headed downtown to Houston Street. There, he alighted, trudging up the stairs.

Can this wait? he typed back to Alyssa when he finally surfaced to find that her text message was still the most recent. I have an important meeting and i'm just walking into the office.

He put his phone into his pocket and walked toward Film Forum, where he checked the day's listings and bought a single ticket to the first show, which would begin at noon.

NATHAN HAD SPENT every day of the prior two weeks in a movie theater, mostly in the Village, far out of range of any possible accidental meeting with any possible acquaintances. He sat in his favorite seat, the most north-northeast one to the screen, which measured 9144 mm to the closest exit sign, in accordance with New York City building code. It was from there you could leave most easily in case of a fire, and, should the call you were waiting on finally come in, it was from there you could most swiftly jump up and leave without disturbing your fellow moviegoers, though he was generally the only person in the theater at a matinee on a weekday in the early winter.

Today, however, there was one other man about his age, and two older women, watching *How to Succeed in Business Without Really Trying* in the theater with him. It was Nathan's third viewing of the movie that week. Film Forum only showed three or four movies at a time, and he'd been doing the rotation, but he found that *How to Succeed in Business* worked best for flooding his prefrontal cortex in the front of his brain with data and stimulation, which helped, in turn, to stimulate the amygdala in the back of his brain, which was trying to process exactly how he became someone who pretended he was going to work every day and instead headed to a dark movie theater.

He would not have called his journey there a straight line, but consider for yourself:

Just six months before this, Nathan had been walking past the main conference room on the obscene forty-sixth floor of the building where his law firm was located. He liked to avoid looking directly into that conference room owing to its equally obscene floor-to-ceiling windows, but as he passed, he saw inside that a dozen or so people were gathered, all partners it seemed, holding champagne flutes aloft. At the center of it was Dominic Romano.

Nathan had been en route to his office, and he passed his assistant, Nancy, whom he shared with four associates, and asked what was going on.

"Dominic Romano made partner," Nancy said.

"Dominic Romano did?" Nathan stared into the conference room. His father's cousin, Arthur, was standing, looking out the window, his hands in his pockets, slightly outside the celebration. Arthur turned slightly and looked over his shoulder, perhaps feeling Nathan's eyes on him. He gave Nathan a tiny shrug and turned back to the window. Dominic Romano had been two years behind Nathan in law school.

Not just that, but Dominic had started at the firm six years after Nathan. And then, before Nathan knew it, Dominic Romano was on the partner track while Nathan was still just an associate. Then, *four* years later, Dominic got his father-in-law to bring his chain of venture capital–backed hardware stores to the firm and now, suddenly, Dominic was a partner!

Nathan had gone home and told Alyssa about it, and she looked at him hard, nodding, her eyebrows forming an empathetic steeple.

"You're on partner track, too, though, right?" she asked. The question destabilized him.

"Oh sure," he'd said. "Well, I'm not on partner track per se. More like the track to partner track."

"Uh-huh," she said with just her mouth.

"It's totally normal."

All Nathan had ever wanted was stability. And law school, though, yes, competitive, fit his needs and his temperament. It was the promise of a secure future. It was books and papers and tests. It was deadlines and listening. It was finding the tiny hole inside the larger hole that you could only see if you could be very still and look very carefully from every which way—a gift he absolutely had from all the years of worry. And it was a business that would give him a decent income, so that he could forget about the money that came to him every quarter and keep that for what he called a rainy day out loud but thought of as his very own doomsday bunker.

Then the second year of law school came and it was time for him to figure out an internship and then a job, which meant he needed to pick a concentration.

He couldn't do bankruptcy law because he couldn't be around the anxiety of people enduring bankruptcy. He couldn't do criminal law because no thanks he did not want to be around criminals. There was family law but he didn't want to be around fighting. There was wills and trusts, like his cousin Arthur, but wills were about dying, and he could not spend his day talking about dying when he already spent the day thinking about it.

"Well, what kind of thing do you like to do all day?" Arthur asked when Nathan came to him for advice. "Do you see yourself as a good negotiator?"

A shiver ran through young Nathan.

"Do you see yourself going to court?"

Whatever happened to Nathan's face just then was an indicator that no, Nathan would not like to go to court.

Arthur told him about contract law (but there's still client inter-face), immigration law (what?), labor law (but there's still negotia-tion), don't even say itigation-lay.

Then Arthur told him about land use. The statutes and regula-tions and ordinances. The amendments to the statutes and regula-tions and ordinances. The case law. The amendments to the case law. Precedent. Newer precedent. The treatises. The applications. The pre-applications to fill out before you can submit the applications. The permits. The permits to fill out the permits. The piles of paper. Land use had so much delicious paper that you could bury yourself in it, and once you lay beneath the laws and regulations and ordinances and statutes and loopholes, if things went wrong, no one could find you beneath all that paper!

Sure, there were hearings to go to. And most land use lawyers had to go to court and negotiate with project opponents and neighboring property owners. But there was an entire category of land use lawyer who just sat under the piles of paper, doing research and filling out forms and finding workarounds and marking up documents. That was Nathan.

Listening to Arthur talk about land use, Nathan's face became the googly-eyed face of a man in love, drunk on the promise of a life of low-risk, nonconfrontational tedium.

So Arthur hired Nathan out of law school, of course he had. Ar-thur served Ruth above all, so he cleared the way to give his second cousin a running start.

Nathan excelled! He did OK. He held on to his job. He had a cer-tain gift for research, and the patience that comes with knowing that the more work you do outside a courtroom, the likelier you are to never have to enter one. As such, he was instrumental in many of the firm's many successes, such as:

- The local university that was buying tax-built homeless shelters to convert into dorms
- The Mouse n' More Play-All-Day Arcade in downtown Brooklyn that now has a liquor license and a CBD vending machine
- The Valu-Mart on 34th Street (a client) that can sell cannabis while its competitor, the Shop-Now just nine storefronts down (not a client), is somehow subject to blue laws and has to be closed on Sundays
- Five housing projects' worth of low-income housing in the easternmost impoverished section of Brooklyn that were eliminated and replaced with Burger Kings

Et cetera, et cetera, ad infinitum.

For all of those projects, Nathan did the paperwork. He did the research, the filling out of forms, the drafting of necessary findings, the filing in triplicate. He wrote up approvals for use by the engineering departments, the municipal zoning committees, the city councils. He walked down the halls of the firm without looking up from the fourteenth volume of a book of arcane case law that hadn't been opened in a dozen years. He did the kind of meticulous scavenging for detail that nobody else was willing to do but that is needed in the kind of subversions of good-faith, ethical laws that land use lawyers constantly have to obliterate for their clients' gain. He was so busy his brain didn't make any room for the moral bankruptcy of his job. Remember, he helped convert homeless shelters into dorms.

But that's also all he did. He was never part of the creation of plans, the honing of business, the production and expansion of *work*. He couldn't fathom meeting with a client. He couldn't abide the idea of going to court. He didn't advance, and he never thought about it, because honestly? He never looked up. He never counted the days or the years. He considered himself lucky that he liked how he spent his time. His grandfather had done hard labor in a factory in order to create his own factory; his father had toiled in management at that factory, so that he could furnish his own children with the dream of enjoying how you spent your day. America!

And that may have been a huge relief from Nathan's point of view, but from management's, it made him slightly forgettable to everyone he worked with. People think that getting fired is the opposite of promotion, but it's actually this—stasis—that's promotion's opposite.

But he'd chosen that. He'd de facto chosen that. Dominic Romano's ascent shouldn't have bothered Nathan so much, but it coincided with two momentous factors in Nathan's life. One was that his grandmother was sick, and when he went to visit her each week in her living room he would learn that the sentimentality and softening he'd heard affected the aged and dying was continuing to evade her.

"You're my oldest grandson," she'd say. "You're the leader of this family once your parents are gone." She could no longer lift her head. The home healthcare worker sat in the corner of the room, nodding off. "I can't believe I won't live to see you make something of yourself."

"She must be delirious," he'd say to the aide.

"Sounds fine to me," the woman would reply.

Nathan would try to soothe his grandmother and tell her that his parents were still young and healthy, that he was a lawyer at his firm—at Arthur's firm! At Arthur's reputable firm!—and that he was actually doing quite well.

"I'm telling you, the time will go faster than you think," his grandmother said. Her veins told all kinds of ugly secrets about what awaits us. "You didn't know your grandfather. What he did for you. What he did so you would have these choices. You have to *make* these choices, Nathan. You have to make them."

"I'm plugging away every day. It's a competitive field, for sure. I'm—"

"You are not listening to me, Nathan. You think I don't know but I know. Listen to me!"

Despite what her home healthcare worker said, he allowed himself to think that she was lost and confused, that her aggression was the result of her hospice medications (though weren't those supposed to make you tranquil?). But when he arrived at his own home after those visits and sat next to his children on the couch and watched them play their videogames, he began to reconsider. Ari was into fantasy role-playing games where various kinds of creatures, including humans, murdered each other in archaic ways, with arrows and poisons and hexes. Josh liked a sports game or a first-person shooter, or, preferably, to combine those things so that a soccer player was opening fire with a submachine gun amid a match. His sons were quite different from each other.

But they were also different from him. Ari was temperamentally like Nathan, meaning he was a nervous wreck, too, but Nathan would never have played videogames growing up. His anxiety had translated into hiding in corners with books, arming himself with information—not this . . . inertia. Not a childhood waiting out childhood, passing the time with no thoughts or ambitions. Neither of his children was interested in anything other than videogames. They didn't read. They weren't curious about the world. When they were done shooting up soccer arenas or igniting armies of trolls against regiments of elves—and they were only ever done because their mother had limits on their game console's use—they took out their phones and submitted passively to a stream of a hodgepodge of random entertainment created by other people.

"By this age, I'd read all the Lord of the Rings and all the Narnias," Nathan lamented to Alyssa at night when they'd finally wrestled iPhones and iPads from the kids' hands and sent them to bed. "I even tried building my own computer when I was, like, ten."

"I was raised differently," she'd say. They were in bed, too, by now, lying prone on their stomachs and facing each other across from their pillows, whispering. "I think it's all the money. You know? Like, what's going to light a fire under them? The thing that lit a fire under me was that I wanted a life different from my parents."

"I didn't!" Nathan said.

"You know what they say," Alyssa said. "First generation builds the house, second generation lives in it, third generation burns it down."

"Which generation are the kids?" Nathan whispered.

"Well, it's funny. On my side they're the second, since I didn't have any money. But on your side they're the third. Or are they fourth? And it seems like your side might be winning."

"You'd rather they were raised like you were?"

"I didn't say that. You're the one complaining. The thing you're talking about seems like a reasonable sacrifice for not being afraid all the time. There are worse things than being spoiled and lazy."

"Like what?"

"Like being poor," she said.

Nathan would then turn off his lamp because he knew the next thing she would talk about was the one thing she believed could mitigate their children from becoming full-on monsters, which was a more assiduous approach to religion.

"I have an early morning," he'd say, and turn his face away from her. The things that weren't worth talking about.

But in the dark, he'd rail against the idea that it had to be this way. When he was young, there was an imperative to read, to learn, to engage, to *pursue*. His grandparents' friends were entrepreneurs or philosophy professors or lawyers who argued in front of the Supreme Court. They were authors and playwrights and people who took advantage of all that their own parents' wartime suffering and survival allowed them to have. Then, his parents' generation, it was dermatologists and contract lawyers, all the way down, but still: Their common impetuses were hard work and forward momentum, digging out of the deficit that the war and immigration generations had landed them in. Nathan had to spend two summers at his family's factory, learning a trade—"learning what hard work is," said his parents. He was sent to programming classes, back at the dawn of personal computing, to learn fungible computer languages like C++ and Pascal. He was forced to take piano lessons, a value that seemed invented, as no one in his family was particularly musical or music-loving. He was taken to after-school French classes (French!), after-school chess lessons, after-school karate (don't ask). He was encouraged to dream about his future, to pursue big things for himself. He was trusted to want to be a whole person.

In his own way, he succeeded at that. But now, as he watched his children resentfully drop their controllers to pick up their phones or homework or drag their feet to their bar mitzvah lessons, he realized that his grandmother was right. He was older than he thought he was, which meant his kids were, too. There they were, right in front of him, the recipients of even more incredible opportunity than he had been given, but they either didn't know it or they didn't care—or more likely, they didn't think in that language. Nathan hadn't even made them go to work with him for the summers, the way his father had. He now briefly wondered if he should insist they go to work in the factory, just to get their hands dirty. But it was a nonstarter. Alyssa had insisted they go to Jewish sleepaway camp if they were going to attend the local public school. He didn't object. He was going to let them pursue what they wanted to! Isn't that the Jewish American dream? But now he saw that that was only a good idea if they were like him. Now he understood, maybe too late, what had happened. His wife insulated his children from *criticism* and *hurt feelings,* she protected their *emotional health,* she pursued a *growth mindset.* His grandmother was right. His children were useless. (Though, of course, technically his grandmother had called *him* useless, not his children.)

It was the next day, as his grandmother continued to waste away in the center of her living room, and his children sat in their classrooms drooling onto their phones as they awaited the morning bell, that Nathan arrived at work even earlier than usual, and walked into Arthur's anteroom. Arthur was already there, having had a partner breakfast and an early meeting with a trustee.

"Hi-ho," Nathan said, his head ducking into Arthur's office's airspace.

"Nathan," Arthur greeted him, some concern on his face. "Is everything OK with your mother?"

"Of course, of course," Nathan said, allowing his body to follow his head and sitting down across from Arthur at his desk. "It's just, I wanted to pick your brain. I've been thinking. I was thinking about Dominic Romano, about him making partner . . ."

"Ah, right, yes," Arthur said. He took off his glasses and smiled gently. "Listen. Everyone is different. Dom Romano is a shark. Not everyone can be like that, Nathan. It doesn't mean you're not valuable. You are a valuable cog in the department."

"Well, yes, sure, right. It's just—I don't know how you measure value. I think if I do what I do and people find it valuable, perhaps, I don't know, there are ways of making that known, you know?" Nathan looked to the side of Arthur's shoulder as he spoke, unable to meet his eyes.

"Yes," Arthur said, his voice soft. "But sometimes the way you show someone that they're valuable is by making sure that someone can work within the parameters of what they're able to do. You make them comfortable in their limitations. Allow them to do what they're capable of. Do you understand me?"

After a second, Nathan said, "Right-o," but it was barely a whisper. Then he thought of Dominic Romano's smug face and brought himself to look squarely at Arthur. "But now the guy who was years behind me in law school and hasn't even been working here for as long as I have is my superior. What if I became someone who met with clients? Like someone who went to court. What if I *tried* it?"

Arthur took a breath and gathered himself before he spoke.

"Here's the thing, Nathan," he said. "Land use is a political category of law. You're not just lawyers, according to the State of New York. You're *lobbyists*. And lobbying just might not be your thing. The kind of aggressive ambition that Dom has, that's not you." Then, off Nathan's frown, "Which is not bad! Nathan, a firm needs a guy like you. A guy who wants to be away from the action. Stay buried in the books. Find the loopholes. You're invaluable for that."

"OK, well, there we are again talking about value. If I'm so valuable, if there's truly a need for what I do, then maybe I don't have to be so aggressive in order to get a promotion? I've just . . . I've been an associate for a long time." Then, before Arthur could say it, "It's not about money. You know it's not about money. It's that money is the thing that society uses to show how we value a person, and the last time I got a raise . . ."

"You get a raise every year."

"I get an inflation raise. That's not the same thing. And I'm still just an associate. No one else my age is an associate."

Arthur had nothing left to say, and Nathan had said what he wanted to, so he stood up and walked away, exhausted from this, the most heated confrontation he'd ever had with anyone in his whole life.

But then, a week later, Nathan was sorting through the final submittal package for NYU's proposal to acquire a church to turn it into a dorm/frozen yogurt shop for students. It's nearly impossible to turn a church with an active congregation into a dorm and frozen yogurt dispensary in New York City because of the city's wariness about eliminating houses of faith, which generally can't afford to stay amid the chain pharmacies that have become the lifeblood of the place. But Nathan had figured out that if you pay off the congregation and find them a new house of worship (in this case, a dilapidated and condemned building in East New York that was a Workmen's Circle/Arbeter Ring in the 1950s before it was a rape-crisis-center-cum-failed-co-working-space) and then replace them with the congregation of a different religion (allowable via *Yeti v. Smith,* 1982), and then the new religion (ibid.), which you made up in the first place (allowable via *Koresh vs. Brotherhood of St. Matthew's,* 1992), which is then allowed to convert out of the religion, then wait ninety days' worth of empty Saturdays and Sundays (and Wednesday afternoons, which was the made-up Sabbath of the made-up religion that the firm had inserted into the space, in this particular case)—then and only then could any commercial entity purchase the building for residential, educational, or restaurateurial use. Did the city clerk who stamped the final Certificate of Occupancy for the place seem thrilled by these technically allowable leaps of logic? No. Did he say to the paralegal who picked up the certificate that he should be ashamed to work for "those pirate fiends who are ruining this city"? Sure. But this wasn't kindergarten; no, this was land use.

He had just sent the final NYU paperwork off for notarizing when Dominic Romano's new, just-for-him assistant told Nathan that Mr. Romano would like to see him in his office.

Nathan felt his gastric contents rise out of his esophageal sphincter and splash upward to his pharynx and up and up as he headed down the long hall. There was no reason for Dominic to want to see him.

"Hi-ho," Nathan said, poking his head inside the door.

Dominic didn't look away from his computer as he waved Nathan in.

"Have a seat, Nathan," Dominic said. "Thanks for rushing on over."

"I was just—is there something you needed?" Nathan asked. "I was finishing the final NYU packet for submission."

"Great, great, no. I just wanted to—I was going to meet with everyone, now that I'm here somehow." Dominic finally looked away from his computer and rolled his eyes around the office to indicate where he somehow was. "I want to get to know my team. Of course, we know each other. Years now."

"Years now."

"And I know you got along with Sim."

"Right-o."

"He's worked hard. I'm glad he's getting a break."

"He's worked hard," Nathan agreed.

"Tough thing about his divorce. Good to take some time off." Then, "Also, your uncle Arthur was talking to me—"

"He's my father's cousin. He's not my uncle. My first cousin once removed. We're more peers like that. Just, technically."

"Right, sure." Dominic wore shirts that were blue but had a white collar. His blazer was off right now, and his cuffs, which were also white, were rolled up to reveal his hairy, masculine arms and his gold watch. "We were talking about what great work you do on the non-client-facing side of things. You were always a bookworm, even in school."

"Well, it was law school. Lot of books to read."

"Right, sure. But what I'm saying is that Arthur and I agreed that that kind of work, it doesn't come with much glory, but maybe it should come with reward. Maybe you should be rewarded."

Nathan's throat dried up.

"Now, your uncle thinks I should just promote you, but where's the sense in that, am I right? I told him you don't want all that nepotism. You want to make it on your own."

". . . Right. Right-o."

"I remember in school. You had that apartment. A brownstone in the Village, if I recall? I lived at home, on Staten Island, at my parents' house, straight to the end. I *worked*. You know? I worked, first in the cafeteria. I worked in the gym, cleaning up after people, like the towels and stuff. Once, these two guys were having sex in the shower. I was there when they were caught by the gym manager. The guy made me clean up the mess."

"Oh wow. That's, that sounds . . . wow."

"I didn't come from money. I took a ferry every day. Twice. I was the first person in my family to go to college."

"That's interesting, Dominic, because, you know, so was I. I didn't realize we had that in common. My father didn't go to college. Or, rather, he was in his junior year of college when his mother called him to say that his father had dropped dead of a heart attack—he wasn't even fifty years old, my grandfather! Right there in the factory he owned. So my father came home, and he ran the factory. Didn't graduate. And I was the first person to graduate college in the end."

"Jewish people, it's a little different."

"No, what? I'm not—I wasn't talking about . . . what do you mean?"

"You know what someone once told me?"

Nathan could feel his ascending colon tying itself into a slipknot with his transverse colon and descending colon.

"What's that, Dominic?"

"That an Italian's a dumb Jew. Isn't that funny?"

Nathan couldn't move.

"Which is funny to think because here I am, being asked to help you along. Then again, it was a Jew who told me that."

"I don't know if I'd agree with that assessment. About Italian Americans. You know. Jews and Italian Americans have so much in common. Well, not everything—"

"You're going to bring up the Holocaust. How innovative."

"Oh. No. Not at all. What I was just thinking was about immigrant experiences. You know, my family, my grandfather came over here with no money. He had just this idea for polystyrene molds. How to make them. And then he just worked hard."

Dominic waited politely for Nathan to finish. After the dumbschmuck moment of silence that followed, he said, "I'm going to give you an opportunity here. I know you don't ever want to be the guy dining clients. As if you could. But there's more you can do. I'm giving you an opportunity."

"That's so nice. Really. Thank you."

"I'm putting you on Giant's."

"You're—"

"Giant's. Yes."

But Nathan couldn't believe it. Dominic was putting Nathan on the Giant's case? Giant's? Giant's!

Giant's was the iconic home supply/clothing/presswood coffee table/stationery/shoe/lawn mower/toilet bowl cleaner/medication/ sanitary product/auto repair/cosmetics/food/belt/nursing bra/*Call of Duty: Modern Warfare*/clothing hook in the shape of a pig snout/ diaper/2000 Flushes/wine cooler store that had overtaken the Eastern Seaboard in the prior decade. It was also the land use department's most important name-brand client, the one responsible for the lights staying on on the forty-sixth floor and for the low-rate mortgages on partners' third and fourth homes, their second Porsches and private school tuitions, their secret Canadian families.

Nathan didn't know what to do with himself.

"Wow, Dominic. Thank you," he said. "Just wow." Then, "What will I be doing?"

Dominic continued. "The Yellowton Giant's needs a C of O."

"Huh," Nathan said, nodding vigorously. "Sure. There are problems? I hadn't heard of any problems on the C of O."

"No, no," Dominic said. "It's just that we need someone to oversee it. Make sure it all goes OK. We're almost there!"

"Ah. I understand. Hm. Well, see . . . we're not usually involved in that?"

"Sometimes we are. We've needed to sometimes. Discretionary approval and all that."

"OK, but then it's like, first-years. Or paralegals."

Dominic allowed a brief flash of exhaustion to pass his face in a way that reminded Nathan of how his mother sometimes looked at him.

"Nathan, a name partner asked me to give his nephew some more work to do to justify a promotion. Help me out here. Is there something else you feel you can offer our business with the Yellowton Giant's?"

Nathan sat, continuing his vociferous nodding, but in the direction of his own feet, trying to compute.

"A promotion?" he asked.

Dominic briefly closed his eyes and shook his head.

"Yes," Dominic said. "I'm going to give you a promotion. When you're done with this task. Senior associate. Congratulations, Nathan."

Dominic stood up and Nathan was powerless not to stand, too. Dominic reached his hand out for shaking and then sat down and turned back to his computer. The meeting was over.

On the train home that night, Nathan held two things equally. One was that he'd never been so insulted in all his life, and the second was that he was getting a promotion!

He told Alyssa the news.

"Senior associate!" she said. "That's something! That's cause to celebrate!" She called to the kids that they were going out to dinner.

"Well, it's not final yet. You know? It's not final. I'm being put on the Giant's case. Which is its own promotion! It's the firm's biggest client, right? But they need me to do some stuff, and then, well, it's just a formality."

"Let's celebrate anyway."

They went to the kosher Chinese, since Alyssa liked to both support kosher businesses and discourage the eating of high treif, and Chinese food was a land mine of high treif.

Once they were seated and had ordered, Alyssa said, "So. Now we're talking. Is this like a partner thing? Or is it a partner-track thing? Or?"

Nathan looked from her face to off beyond her shoulder and realized he didn't know.

"It's a promotion. I guess all promotions are a partner-track thing?"

But the next day, he went to see Dominic again, poking his head into his door.

"Hi-ho, boss!" Nathan said.

Dominic looked up. "Did we have a meeting?"

"Oh, I just have a question or two about the uh, the ole promotion you mentioned yesterday."

Dominic hesitated for a second, then waved Nathan in from the doorway.

"Just, my wife asked a question last night I realized I didn't know the answer to."

"Sure, sure," Dominic said. "I have about two minutes, though . . ."

"Is senior associate a partner-track position?" Nathan's voice had squeaked higher than it had when he had practiced.

Dominic leaned back in his chair. "Well, all positions are partner track at a law firm, right? Technically, right? If you're a lawyer. Which you are."

"I'm saying specifically senior associate."

"Well, I'll be honest with you, Nathan. I don't know. It's not a title anyone else has."

"It's not a—"

"Right. You're our first senior associate."

"But, materially, does that mean—"

"Hey, can we talk about this later? I know you have some big things this week. Let's talk when the C of O is complete. Sound good?"

But it wasn't a question.

ONE MONDAY MORNING, just over three months to the day after his meeting with Dominic, Nathan told Alyssa he didn't need a ride to the train and instead took his own Acura 2017 MDX onto the Long Island Distressway and headed east instead of west.

It was time to complete his crucible.

That the Yellowton Giant's even existed was something of a coup. The superstore giant Giant's had been trying to get a toehold in the Hamptons-adjacent parts of Eastern Long Island for years. The people of the region, both wealthy and working-class, needed a place to buy their packs of underwear and batteries and medications and snowblowers alongside their giant cartons of Frosted Flakes and their reading glasses. In that sense, that region of Long Island was a bull's-eye for the company. It was where their constituency needed to shop, and where the wealthy liked to shop—but the latter only under the cover of distance. The wealthy didn't like to be reminded of the kind of neighbors they kept, the kind that also purchased their produce and their formalwear there.

For nobody was immune to the magic of a Giant's. Once you entered one of the humongous, kelly green stores and were greeted by their iconic lizard mascot, a mass of possibilities opened up—about your life, about your soul, about all the stuff that could finally make you feel something in the neighborhood akin to happiness. Nobody understood why or how this kind of maximalist consumerism activated their dopamine systems like it did. The thing about dopamine, though, is that once it's activated, you don't really care how it got that way. That's how dopamine works.

The store's corporate management did understand it, though. And it vexed them so to think of how much money they were missing out on each day that Eastern Long Island's potential profits were being spent at the combination of the area's Costcos and Sam's Clubs and Walmarts and Targets. Because there was no way the more upscale sections of Long Island were going to allow the store (and the shopping population it was a beacon to) directly onto their turf, and for a variety of reasons that had mostly to do with zoning laws, it was also impossible to find land that could accommodate the store in the more working-class areas.

So Giant's hired Plotz Lindenblatt. Sim Lustig, the managing partner in charge of the land use department, asked his most promising associate, Dominic Romano, to help the firm locate a township that might be hospitable to a Giant's. Almost immediately, Dom found the tiny, misshapen hamlet called Yellowton.

Yellowton occupied a mere 7.43-mile radius from its center. But it was an important 7.43 miles to the people who lived there, and they protected those miles with a uniquely Long Island savagery.

The residential area of the town was filled with small, mostly dilapidated saltbox homes that had historically housed sailors and fishermen and dockworkers and anyone else associated with the horrible sea—the sea that was so sought after by the city folk for its views, but that was, for others, a cruel and uncaring workplace with no HR department to which a person could report malfeasance and abuse. Sea people no longer made up a majority of the population in Yellowton now that fishing was corporatized and outsourced, though; now the service industry jobs outnumbered the water jobs, and unemployment outnumbered all of it.

The town was run by a council of elders, installed generations ago to uphold a set of immutable bylaws that had been written to ensure that every generation, in their youthful ignorance and abject greed, could never make a deal that would alter the town's mostly Irish, English, and German population.

The laws did this in a variety of ways. The condominium that the builder from Manhattan wanted to put up would raise rents all

around and put homeowners in danger of local inflation, so no outside builders, not on your life, said the bylaws. The twenty-four-
room beachfront inn that the craft hotelier wanted to start
construction on? It would cut off access to at least two docks and
cause the Meet Shack (sic, if formerly unintended) to have to upgrade
to all-FDA-approved, non–Grade C, nonexpired ingredients just to
compete with whatever restaurant they installed in the hotel, so you
can build near the docks when hell freezes over, said the bylaws. The
seafood-forward offshoot of the fancy Manhattan steakhouse, which
would bring people to the rest of the stores on Main Street and give
the town actual tourism money? There's plenty of seafood in these
parts already, so no redundant restaurants in the town limits, and
while you're at it, go fuck yourself, you Manhattan fucks, said the
bylaws.

But the land use lawyer's creed is that all ancient, well-thought-
out, devoutly upheld bylaws are merely an opening bid. So Dominic
Romano, the plucky associate put in charge of town relations, got to
work. He mounted an offensive of bribery, manipulation, and charm
that was so intense that the people of Yellowton couldn't even remember when the lawyer from the city who was trying to corrode
their town values started showing up—no, somehow, over the course
of time, he had become a trusted advisor to them, and a friend. By
the time they clocked Dominic as a mainstay there, they had come to
agree that Giant's was a benevolent, neighbor-minded corporation
and that they were a worthy community for its benevolences. In fact,
they couldn't remember why they'd held out for so long! What could
anyone possibly have against purveyors of low prices and temporary,
China-made goods? What could anyone have against true American
convenience? Not to mention the jobs jobs jobs! How could they
complain? They could not complain. Not when they had a new
Giant's-branded football field at the high school; not when they had
a new "Giant's Presents . . . The Yellowton Al Fresco Dining Patio
Experience"—essentially an outdoor food court—in front of the
town center's newly refurbished Giant's fountain. Not when Giant's
held a 5K run/walk that paid people a hundred dollars just for show-

ing up. You didn't even need to run or walk it! You could just be in the cheering section, or walking by the cheering section, or accidentally using a crosswalk nearby, and the hundred dollars was yours!

But while the Yellowton townsfolk came around to a hard yes on a local Giant's, the Yellowton town council would not. The Yellowton charter stated that there could be only one (1) consumer establishment within its 7.43-mile radius per shopping category—say, one gas station or one grocery store, or, as above, one lobsteria—but not more than that. So if there wasn't a store that sold the kinds of tires that Giant's sold, but Giant's also sold baby carrots and there was already another store that sold baby carrots, it didn't matter that there was still room for competition for tires; no, they'd edged themselves out of contention with the baby carrots. Denied. As a result, there was no new construction in Yellowton. There was no developing in Yellowton. There was barely even passing through Yellowton if you weren't from there.

Then, a miracle! In an act of precision timing, Gremin Walt, one of the elders of the town and the head of the town council, died in a suicide pact with a fellow councilman and former commercial fishing boat steward named Billy Moore. Gremin and Billy had, apparently, been engaged in a years-long sexual relationship (despite their presumably monogamous heterosexual marriages) and were being extorted by Tenley Squib, a third member of the council, who had found out about the affair when, one night, he returned to the town meeting hall to retrieve his forgotten pack of Pall Malls and saw Gremin giving Billy a handy in the community room. Within a month, Gremin and Billy were dead.

Dominic, who had attended the memorial services because by then he was a Yellowton fixture himself, had overheard one of Tenley's three daughters bragging to someone about how her father just bought a new boat and so Dominic had a paralegal call in an anonymous tip to the local police. The call he made said that Tenley should be looked at as a suspicious player in the extortion and deaths of Gremin and Billy. The police interview and subsequent trip-up and confession of Tenley Squib lasted fewer than seven minutes. He was indicted for extortion. (That's how good Dominic was at this job. It had been a hunch.)

"Those cocksuckers were affrontin' to God," Tenley said solemnly to the judge, who, despite this airtight argument, convicted him and sentenced him to five years in prison.

Yellowton was teetering at the edge of anarchy. The town council had been whittled down to just the three children of Billy, Gremin, and Tenley—not surprisingly, the succession rules required blood-lines all the way down—all of whom were bored with this dumb fucking town and, most important, they were totally broke. They fought, they canceled meetings haphazardly, they threw flaming bags of dogshit (one hopes it was dogshit) into each other's windows, they showed up at hearings drunk, and all of this made for a vulner-able breeding ground for Dominic Romano. Dominic recognized that all this chaos had left the town exhausted, and he came to the next council meeting with an offer to fund "local programs" to "re-juvenate the community."

"What kind of local programs?" asked Lewis Squib, the son of Tenley. He was an island on the council; the bylaws did not have an asterisk for the son of the council member who had extorted and therefore instigated the suicide pact of two other members. Billy's and Gremin's sons, consumed not just with their hatred for Lewis but with the awkward nature of their own new relationship as sons of lovers, brooded in the corner.

Dominic straightened up. "Well, really, thing is, we don't pretend to understand what will rejuvenate a certain community. We partner *with* you instead. We let *you* decide. We hand over the cash and *let you decide.* Partnership."

Lewis Squib, who had thirty-seven thousand dollars in credit card debt and two child support liens on a salary he only intermittently earned, looked down the lunch table at the rest of the council, none of whom would return his gaze, in the very community room of Yellowton's town hall where the meetings were held and where Billy and Gremin were discovered expressing their love. They sat beneath a banner that stated that all lives mattered, an American flag, a thin blue line flag, and a state-mandated poster of Martin Luther King, Jr.

"Partnership," Lewis repeated.

"Yes, partnership," Dominic reassured him.

The deal was locked. Giant's would be allowed on the very borders of Yellowton, so that the store's parking lot, which accounted for the majority square footage of the property, was the only part of the store inside Yellowton; the actual goods were technically being sold in the adjacent town, owing to the fact that the adjacent town's land use drama was that they had room for a store like Giant's but had already used up the maximum allotment for land that was allowed to go to parking spaces. That's land use law at its finest!

Plans for construction were immediately under way, and at Plotz Lindenblatt, cases of champagne arrived from Giant's corporate for seven days in a row—one day for every year they'd been trying to get a toehold there. The company sent everyone in the entire firm gray T-shirts that included the now-amended list of Giant's that existed in Suffolk and Nassau Counties: PATCHOGUE & HUNTINGTON & OYSTER BAY & YELLOWTON. The writing was all in white except for where it said YELLOWTON, which was, of course, yellow.

Then it was a year later, and the Yellowton Giant's was nearing its realization as an actual, open-for-business store. There was no more construction to be done. The store was filled with shelves; the shelves were filled with products; the staff was hired from in and around Yellowton; the wheel stops were installed in the parking lots; signs that said COMPACT ONLY were painted on those spots, though of course, no one meant it. And Nathan Fletcher, who had been introduced to the project just three months earlier, had worked on his one small part with a vigor that allowed him to drown out the information that he knew for positive sure, which was that babysitting a Certificate of Occupancy was not an important task.

Never mind! Never mind, he told himself the whole way through. He would *make* it important work. And the work itself—it was not all bad. Nothing alleviated the sadness and misgiving like the paperwork did. Nothing made you believe you were moving forward when you absolutely were not like paperwork. Nathan's love for paperwork, his understanding of its rigors and demands, its emotional neutrality, its lines and boxes—it was a storybook love, a Vows section love, a movie love, a love for all time.

And then, the C of O became a machine that went of itself. Suddenly, all forms finally filled out, he spent the next months scrupulously performing the tasks that were required to obtain this, the final hammer blow in the Yellowton Giant's. He went to all of the inspection meetings, though, again, a paralegal could have accompanied the contractors and electrical engineers and plumbers that were needed for those approvals. He vetted each of the private local companies that Giant's hired to help lend to their "local jobs initiative" that they'd guaranteed upon their handshake deals with the town, from Bart's Plumbing to the unfortunately named Flawless Floors. (Paula, who owned Flawless Floors, didn't like Nathan after speaking to him for a full minute in the rigors of her Long Island accent, trying to enunciate over the diphthong *au* that sounded more *awwww* and, combined with the dropped *r* that's native to all classes in the region, resulted in Nathan having to untangle his way through this introduction: "I'm Pawla from Flawless Flaws." And Nathan, who heard it before he saw it, at first said, "It's so interesting. How can a flaw be flawless?" like it was an existential conundrum and Paula kept saying, "No. Flaw? Flaw. Like you wawk on." Nathan was used to a dropped *r* and a problematic cawffee diphthong—it was deployed by everyone he knew, from his parents to his English teachers, his whole life—but this, this was something.)

A wave of approvals, a tsunami of double-checking, an eddy of stamps. And then it was done. The meetings were done. The paperwork was done. A task completed, start to finish. Mission accomplished, as one of his favorite presidents—or at least the one he empathized with most—once said.

Finally came the day where he was to visit the town hall for the last time and pick up that pesky certificate. Senior associate, ahora!

He found the clerk in the tiny Department of Buildings annex at the town hall, chewing gum and staring into space. She looked at him blankly when he walked in.

"Hi there, here to pick up the C of O," he said.

She tilted her head from one side to the other, like a windshield wiper. "For . . . who?"

Nathan had been to this office at least six times in the last three months, and had made different requests of this specific woman each time. Plus, the Giant's was the only permit that had made it to the processing point in four years, meaning that Nathan was the only person to have walked into this office in all that time and still she had no idea who he was.

"Nathan Fletcher? Here to pick up the C of O for Giant's?"

The woman pushed a few pieces of paper on her otherwise completely bare desk and said, "I have nothing here."

Again, there was not one other commercial C of O file on her desk. For years.

"My office got a call that it was ready. It's for Giant's. The Certificate of Occupancy?"

"I heard you."

"Right-o." Nathan waited another few seconds, but nothing. "Well, where is it, do you think?"

"It's not here." Then she saw a Post-it on the corner of her desk, and she turned to a second table where there was a single manila envelope beneath an index card that read REJECTED. She pulled the folder, but she had obscenely long, fake fingernails that were decorated with four-leaf clovers and, were those?, yes, tiny pineapples, and she fumbled for a second.

"Here it is," she finally said. She leafed through pages, angling her wrists to use as fingers so that her hands could be functional despite those fingernails.

"Thank you," Nathan said politely after a full ten seconds went by.

She looked up. "Oh, I don't have anything for you. It was rejected."

"What? How could it be rejected?"

"I just do the paperwork. It says at the bottom here COUNCIL WITHDREW PERMIT."

"What? This is crazy. On what grounds?"

She blinked at him and ran a tongue over her teeth.

"Then why did you call my office to say it was done?"

She began to suck at something in her teeth. "Because it is. It's done."

Nathan's collar was wet by the time he got outside the town hall, where he stood, not really sure how to proceed. He should call Dominic, he knew. But he wanted to first anticipate what Dominic would tell him to do and therefore already be on his way to doing it. He looked up and down the street. It was quiet. What would Dominic do here? Decision-making was such anathema to Nathan that he drew a blank.

Nope. He was not calling Dominic. He was not going to fail at a job you couldn't fail at. He was tasked with picking up the Certificate of Occupancy, and he was going to have answers. Once a C of O is rejected, it takes months before a new one will be considered. He could not be associated with this level of disaster.

Today was supposed to have been a triumphant day. Today he was supposed to stand atop of all that paperwork with his fist pumped toward the sky!

Muscle memory allowed Nathan to get into his car. His breathing was shallow and his hands were shaking but he was somehow able to get onto the expressway and drive along, talking aloud to himself about how these things were out of his control, and he had to handle conflict, and it was all going to be fine. He realized he was going a cool 25 in the right lane so he sped up to a brazen 38 and looked into the rearview mirror in order to change to the middle lane, and that's when he saw it.

A shadow moved at the lower right edge of the mirror, jumping out of view so that Nathan couldn't see it.

He swerved! He twisted quickly to see who or what it was that was hiding, but by the time he looked back over his right shoulder, it had moved to the left.

He saw a sign that said Exit 50 and pulled over. He parked on the first road off the highway, in front of a columned McMansion. He jumped out of the car and forced himself to look into the backseat, but it was empty.

He looked up and down the road. Nothing.

Had he been seeing things?

He got back into the car and locked the door. He took out his phone, swiping across the field of icons to find the full page and a half dedicated to meditation apps. He located his new favorite, Hale, and opened it up. All it was was an animated flower that blossomed and receded, blossomed and receded while he exhaled, inhaled and exhaled, inhaled.

This was making it worse. He went over to the tab that said GUIDED MEDITATION and pulled up an Australian man's voice, telling him to proceed through a body scan, going over his body from top to bottom to "feel the locus of the tensions, and dissolve it."

Which, sure.

Nathan closed his eyes in his car and tried to participate in the exercise. But at the top of his head, he felt a throbbing that he imagined might be blood trying to get past a blockage, probably a blood clot in his brain. He moved on to his jaw, which clicked when he moved it, and it reminded him of a pervasive fear he had that his teeth were going to fall out. He reached his neck, where he felt a thumping so hard and had so much difficulty in swallowing that he knew—*he knew*—that there was a budding tumor inside his throat and that it was only a matter of time before—

THIS WASN'T WORKING! He didn't know who this worked for, but it wasn't him. And as he opened his eyes, he saw something in the corner of his rearview mirror move again. This time it was outside the rear windshield.

He stopped and froze. He moved his eyes to look at the mirror directly, but it was gone. He turned his head to the right, but then was sure the thing he'd seen was on his left. He turned fast again. Now it passed the rearview mirror, he was sure, and the only recourse was to take his still-running car and jam it the hell out of there. The cortisol in him made a tunnel for his vision and he drove 65 through a school zone trying to get at whatever it was that had been there, menacing him.

He arrived at a stoplight. He twisted this way and that, looking for whoever was there to get him—to hood him and take him away. But there was nothing. His heart still raced in the unique powerlessness of a person who has spent most of his life well aware that someone could just come and pluck you out of your life and hold you captive for as long as they wanted. He pulled over again when he realized he was sobbing.

A smell overtook the car. It was Chanel N°5 and the No Frills brand deodorant that combined to create the scent that preceded his grandmother into any room. It was so powerful and overwhelming just then—so truly real—that it occurred to him that his grandmother was what was in the rearview mirror. His grandmother was trying to get him a message. Was he crazy? He was as crazy as the scent in the car, which was unmistakable. It was a dybbuk!

He found his phone and called his brother, but Beamer didn't seem to remember their grandmother telling them about the dybbuk. He thought about calling Jenny, but he couldn't take any more rejection, particularly from his younger siblings, who were supposed to look up to him. Theoretically, they were supposed to look up to him!

In the silence of the car, he knew what he had to do. He couldn't bring this C of O problem back to Dominic. He had to fix it himself. He had to get answers.

He had to find Lewis Squib.

So Nathan turned around and took the terrifying route back east to Yellowton. Then he was driving down Yellowton's Main Street, trying to remember where the turnoff was so that he could find Lewis Squib's boat slip.

A few wrong turns and he remembered. Lewis Squib's boat slip was right behind the bait shop Lewis owned and which he'd inherited when his father was incarcerated.

Nathan leaned over the boat. He wasn't sure exactly how you

were supposed to knock on someone's boat. Do you board yourself onto the boat and knock at the cabin door? Nathan stood and stood and finally, a man his age carrying a rope walked by and said, "Squib's at his shop. Just saw him." Nathan thanked the man and, with some relief, walked down the dock, away from the water, and into Squib's Squpplies, where he was immediately overwhelmed with the smell of old, rotted fish guts and the sight of Lewis Squib.

Lewis was the fuckup youngest child and only son of Tenley Squib. Tenley himself had been a fourth-generation Yellowton fisherman who, by the time of his death, owned and ran six fishing boats that kept the family comfortable, despite his family's best efforts. Besides that, Lewis had to his name about four hundred total strands of greasy hair, plus a dandruffy goatee that was beginning to show gray.

Lewis narrowed his eyes at Nathan when the door jangled. He was alone in the shop, behind the counter, leafing through a copy of a magazine that was just called *Trout.*

"You a cop?" he asked.

"Mr. Squib," he said. "It's me. It's Nathan Fletcher. You and I have met? Several times? I'm with Plotz Lindenblatt? The law firm that represents Giant's?"

Lewis narrowed his eyes further.

"Mr. Squib," Nathan started. "*Lewis.* We've met before. Several times. I work for Giant's? I work with Mr. Romano? At Plotz Lindenblatt . . ." His confidence, tenuous as it was, was fading.

Lewis tilted his head back and to the right and now stared those narrowed eyes down Nathan's face. "I never met you."

Nathan tried again. "I'm here because your name was on the Certificate of Occupancy denial I just found at the Department of Buildings in Yellowton."

"Sure. OK. Right. You're the lawyer."

"Yes, right. I'm saying that we were waiting for one last permit to be approved before we open our Giant's in a few weeks. Remember? And I'm here because we were supposed to close that case up today. We were supposed to get that permit. It's called a Certificate of Occupancy and it's the final permit we need to open the store."

Lewis reached behind the counter for something and Nathan wheezed in a gulp of air. This was it. He knew it. Lewis was going to kill him. Ruth flashed before his eyes before he realized how weird that was and replaced the image of her with one of Alyssa and the twins in penance. But it was just a Mountain Dew that Lewis pulled from beneath the counter.

"So, that permit?" Nathan asked. "If you still haven't signed it, or if you checked off the wrong marker on it, it's easy to fix that. I can even help you. If you have some time now—"

"Oh yeah. I have some time." Lewis smiled. Then he started laughing.

"I really just think there's been a mix-up on the forms," Nathan said.

"There was no mix-up. Me and the council, we changed our minds."

"You . . . changed your minds?"

"Yeppers. We can do that, right?"

"Well, technically, but you already didn't. You already approved this project. I know that Giant's—I know they've donated vigorously to your causes in town."

"Yeah, well, I did some measuring last week. Turns out, your Giant's is in violation of the bylaws."

"Which bylaw? I'm well acquainted with the bylaws." Nathan knew they'd subverted a bunch of them and just wanted to know which one this imbecile had somehow caught.

"Where you can't build two liquor stores in town limits."

"But it's already there. It's built. It passed its inspections. It's ready."

"You know we can't change the bylaws! It would not be right. It would not be the right thing to do in my father's honor. My father would be very angry to learn that the Giant's was in the same town lines as the liquor."

"But we are borrowing land from the next town."

"But there's overlap."

"It's .347 of a yard. We know this."

"That's not the same as zero!" Lewis was getting angry. "You think because I didn't go to law school or come from Manhattan that I can't do anything? Can you fish? Can you run a small business like this?"

"I'm actually also from Long Island."

"Where?"

"Farther west. Middle Rock."

"Fanc-ee! Didn't realize we had a true crown prince in here! Thank you so much for gracing us!" He made a dumb curtsy.

"Mr. Squib, I'm going to lose my job for this. For not coming back to work with the Certificate of Occupancy that I was sent for, that I was told was ready. That you OKed! A million times!"

"You don't have to yell," Lewis said. "We can be civilized."

"So?" Nathan asked. "That's it? Can I at least get a meeting with the council?"

Lewis laughed. "You can try, but the next meeting is scheduled for March. Petey Walt is on a salmon boat in Alaska."

"We're supposed to open in less than three weeks. People have been hired. Food has been ordered. Is there any way we could talk—"

Lewis laughed again. "I'm done talking with you big dummies. That Giant's was meant to destroy my town, and me and the rest of the council, we're not having it. Now if you don't have to buy any bait, I think I'm gonna close. It's almost quitting time anyway."

The sign on the store said that Squib's Squpplies was open till four. It was only noon.

Nathan froze in panic. This could not be how it ended for the C of O. This could not be how it ended for the Giant's. This could not be how it ended for him. He had to make a decision. He had to *act*.

"Let me take you to lunch," Nathan said, though he said it with his bowel already aflame.

"This is on you?"

"I'm paying. I'm just—I'm sure we can work something out."

"Follow me."

Nathan drove behind Lewis through town, then back toward the water, finally stopping at a rock-'n'-roll-themed restaurant. It so happened that Nathan knew enough about this place, since it was the copyright and intellectual property departments of Plotz Lindenblatt that the Hard Rock Cafe had hired when faced with a Suffolk County–based rip-off of its famed restaurant concept. It was quite a story. The restaurant received a judge's order to stop its opening but proceeded anyway, hastily changing its name to the Hard Life Buffet.

Nathan parked his car but didn't leave it yet. Something was happening to him. He became short of breath—and noticed a sharp pain in his chest at the bottom of the breath he was now gulping for.

This wasn't a new sensation for him. He'd been taken to emergency rooms with heart attacks so far three times in his relatively short life, all of which turned out to be mere (mere!) panic attacks. At night, he lay awake, trying to make Alyssa understand that because of this history, he was destined to die of an actual heart attack that everyone mistook for a panic attack. He sat in his car and scanned his body, trying to do a cool assessment of his symptoms. Nothing in his feet. Nothing in his ankles. Nothing in his legs (that was a big one), knees, thighs, buttocks. But when he got to his hips, he felt his wallet against his thigh and recalled that he had one of the beta-blockers the doctor had prescribed in his wallet—that carrying it was the solution that Alyssa had devised.

"It'll be reassuring to know you have it," she'd said, as she folded it into a tiny square of paper, the way criminals transport diamonds in movies. "An insurance policy. You love insurance."

Now he took the pill from his wallet. He knew that when he was in a state, as he was now, pills that could help him actually seemed like they were going to kill him. But life is a series of mitigating risks, of choices, of priorities, a flow chart of lessening threats. He could not sit down with this man just as he was. So he hit override and shoved the pill into his mouth and quickly dry-swallowed the pill and left the car. Movement would help. If you could make your body move faster than your heart, you'll never notice that you're FREAKING OUT.

Lewis was already inside when Nathan entered. The restaurant was pandemonium; it was mayhem; it was not even one P.M. The room was dark and themed like a night where you're lost and drunk without cab fare, with relics of musicians on the wall, the irrelevance of those musicians somehow mitigated just by the fact that something they once touched was now suspended in a frame with an engraved plate beneath it. The music was loud and clubby so that the host had to scream to seat you, adding to the sensory assault. They should have had occupational therapists standing at the door to help people integrate in and out of that restaurant.

They were seated in a booth. A tired-looking waitress came over and Lewis shouted something at her, but Nathan couldn't hear what. He could still hear his heart beating in his ears loudest, but now he was sure the beat was erratic. Not a good sign.

Lewis explained his position from beneath an In Memoriam poster of the dead member of Mötley Crüe. Nathan leaned forward, trying to read his lips and discern the sound of his voice through the thumping of the music.

"What?" Nathan shouted. "What?" He was worried his own shrieking might push his heart over the edge.

An order of Whiskey Bacon Double Mayo Slam Jams was brought to the table by a waiter who was their second waiter either because there had been a shift change or because Lewis had ordered this appetizer by telling the first waiter not to be a cheap ass-muncher.

"Yo," Lewis said to the waiter, who had almost cleared the area safely.

"Yes, sir," the waiter said, his upper lip twitching.

"I need some hot sauce and some mayonnaise." The waiter blinked briefly and scrammed. Nathan could feel animal fat congealing in his own veins, and he was nowhere near touching one of the Slam Jams.

"I'm just saying I know the law," Lewis said. "The law is that you can't have two liquor stores in the town. Now you do. And Split Connor's store is still up and running. And that seems like a real shame in light of the fact that you already built your big store."

"So what do you, uh, think?" Nathan asked. "What are you, uh, saying?" Asking questions felt safe. The way Lewis looked at him over that red nose, his tongue slightly visible from between his lips, which stayed half an inch open as default.

"I'm saying that you can't pick up a store big as yours and move it by any kind of distance to make it legal," Lewis said. "And you can't even pick up a store small as Split's. That's physics."

The waiter returned with a bottle of hot sauce and a coleslaw cup of mayonnaise, which had been poured from a squirt vat so that it had a kind of custard whip and peak to it.

"Well, it doesn't sound like so much, that little distance," Nathan said. "It sounds more like if we remeasured we might find it was borderline. And there's, uh, there's room in the law for borderline." Though there was not. "In case you didn't know that."

Lewis laughed. "I think if I were to let Split know about this, he could make sure that store of yours never got open. Because I've known Split a long time. And you know what he hates?"

"What does Split hate?"

"He hates Giant's. He hates new things. He hates when someone comes in and steals from him."

Lewis picked up one of his disgusting appetizers and plunged it into the mayonnaise cup, getting some on three of his fingers. Nathan heaved. Lewis took a bite and Nathan could hear a squirting sound above all this noise and heaved again.

Lewis spoke with his third and an as-yet-unswallowed second bite of Slam Jam in his mouth. "You want one of these? They're good."

"No, thank you."

"I think I'm gonna get some loaded skins, too."

Before Nathan could understand he meant potato skins, he pictured bodies emptied of their bones and organs and other systems and just filled with mayonnaise.

"So what are you suggesting here?" Nathan asked. A Queen song that he hated came on.

"I've known Split my whole life," Lewis said. "He and my father were fishing buddies, and they bowled together. I dated one of his daughters."

"OK."

"I'm suggesting that Split Connor doesn't know any of this yet, and that Split Connor may hate Giant's. But you know what I hate?"

Nathan blinked.

"Split Connor." Lewis stopped the waiter again and ordered not just the skins but now a Razm'taz Cheeseboyger for his entrée. "So you see what I'm saying?"

"Right-o," Nathan said to Lewis over the Queen song. "I understand your position. I do. But it's illegal for me to pay you for looking the other way. I'm sure you—you must know that."

"And I'm sure you know that not abiding by a town's laws once you know you're in violation of them also has a name, right?"

Nathan was quiet. The potato skins arrived. Nathan had been waiting out the last of the Slam Jam order to speak again, so that when Lewis spoke back, it would be with an empty mouth. No such luck. Lewis took a bite of the skins and shifted the food to the left side of his mouth so he could speak.

"Are you gonna not say anything?" Lewis's oration launched the Bac-Os that decorated the potato skins out of his mouth and into the air and onto Nathan's plate, which contained a chicken breast and steamed vegetables, which Nathan had ordered out of desperation and not noticed had arrived and now would never ever no fucking way even look at, much less touch. He actually probably wouldn't be eating again ever in his life, now that he thought about it. He was starting to feel dizzy. He couldn't breathe at all now.

But Lewis wasn't having it. "I thought you were the guy." He looked Nathan up and down. "Are you the guy? Are you really the guy?"

"Well, obviously I have to go back to the office and talk to my—" Nathan began.

"Are you OK?" Lewis asked.

"Know where the gentlemen's room is?"

Lewis pointed with his chin but didn't stop chewing. As Nathan stood up and walked away, he heard Lewis ask the waiter for two orders of Russian Wings Roulette and three orders of Southwest Artichoke Guac 'n' Dip, all to go, but on the same bill.

Nathan pretended not to hear. He entered the bathroom, then the first stall—he'd read in one of the kids' Fun Facts compendia years before that the first stall was actually the least used because people assumed it was the most used, and he never forgot it—and put the lid down and just sat.

For the millionth time in his life, and also that day, he considered that life was just completely untenable.

The fact was that the moment had arrived. Something was being asked of him. He was being given not just a test but an opportunity.

If his circumstances and the temperament that kept him in them was a constant, so was his lack of opportunity to transcend them, sitting in an office all day, reading arcane volumes of land use law. His colleagues were constantly out there, making deals, doing the dance along legal and ethical lines that anyone who wants to succeed in this business—Oh, Arthur, how could you not tell him that this was what it would take to succeed here?—either knew how to do or was willing to learn.

This was his moment to do. This was his moment to learn.

All he had to do was say yes and he could ascend and join his colleagues in their mansions in the sky.

He went back over the years: elementary school, junior high school, high school, college, law school, adulthood. He went back to a school dance when Miriam Sterngelb sat across from him, clearly giving him the come-hither, but he couldn't bear the fear of rejection. The fact that he hadn't even really applied to Columbia for law school—he'd just had Arthur call the dean. That he never tried out for a school athletic team except for volleyball, which had an automatic acceptance policy because of low male enrollment. The fact that Alyssa had to propose to *him*. Nathan was so consumed his whole life with keeping everything calm and safe that, as a result, he'd never taken any risk, never done anything whose outcome was unknown, and sitting there on a lidded toilet in that disgusting bathroom while someone in the next stall paid a steep price for a Bangin' Onion, he knew that this was his chance. Maybe even his last chance.

Was this what his grandmother had been trying to tell him on her deathbed?

He took a deep breath and expected the panic to enter, but no. It was . . . calm. Calm overtook him. Calm like a battle cry. Calm like a clarion call. Was it God? Was it fate?

No. It was the beta-blocker. The beta-blocker was kicking in.

Now the flatulence in the next stall wasn't horrific to him; now it was a trumpet sounding reveille. It was a call to arms. He stood up and his heart rate stayed slow and steady.

Yes, he thought. I am the guy. I'm the guy!

Nathan left the stall and washed his hands for forty-five seconds, looking himself in the eye in the mirror, not recognizing the m-a-n staring back at him.

He walked back to the booth like he was in a Western. He felt like a spy, an assassin, a civil servant who didn't give a shit. He was sweatless, dry as a desert, his breathing steady. God, it was like he had taken over somebody's body. Beamer's—no, not Beamer's. Beamer had hunger. It was like he was *Jenny*. No affect. No anxiety. No attachment. No problem.

He sat down. Lewis had ordered a gigantic red soda.

"I'm the guy," he said.

"Good," Lewis said.

An obscene hair metal song was playing, and Nathan beat his fingers along with it on the table, the coolest motherfucker you ever saw.

"Lewis," Nathan said. "Do you have a charity that you like? Because I can make a donation to that charity. Or I can help you figure out what kind of charity you'd like the best."

"Charity begins in the home, Nathan-boy," Lewis said, and there was a pause as he sounded a long, luxurious fart that never seemed to end. Lewis stared at him, almost daring him to either acknowledge or complain about the fart, but Nathan was stone-cold still. "Charity. Begins. In. The. Home."

"Right-o," Nathan said. "Sure thing. That's exactly what I'm saying. What if we set up a charity in your home, say a charity for homes, like for homeless people, and I'd give you a lot of money to put into it right now. And you could use it for homeless people however you decide is exactly the right way to spend it on them. Let me put it this way: Whatever you want, you can have. Just tell me how much and where to put it."

His heart rate never went above sixty-six beats per minute.

That was how easy it was. This was how the world worked, now he understood. Nathan was finally seeing the other side. That if you could be momentarily unsafe in your head, there was even more safety guaranteed to you for miles. He would go home and fuck his wife like a king. If she was in the mood to do that!

That afternoon, Nathan left the Hard Life Buffet, his lymph flooded with the unfamiliar hormones of bravery and the alien synapses of success. He walked out thinking that it hadn't been so bad as he thought it would be. He hadn't realized that if you could just leap over the not even very high bar of risk and chance that, on the other side, the re-wards would dissolve the fear. How had nobody ever told him that?

It had started raining while he was inside. He put the folder with the rejected Certificate of Occupancy inside his jacket and his hand on his head like a visor and looked up. If there had been storm clouds coming, he hadn't noticed.

Within a day, he would be called into the same conference room where Dominic Romano had celebrated making partner and played a tape recording of himself attempting to bribe and extort Lewis Squib, that obscene song playing in the foreground.

But that day, after he left the Hard Life Buffet, he just looked around at the boats in the water, the empty bottles of beer on the beach, and the drunk teenager in a bra top hanging off the shoulder of a much older man as they stumbled down the slip, trying to out-run the rain, and he thought about how easy it always was to forget that this was Long Island, too.

———

NATHAN HADN'T BEEN fired—not exactly, anyway. Or at least not formally; at least not yet. He was on what was technically called "un-paid administrative leave" while he waited for a panel of his superiors to convene to determine the level of discipline he'd earned when he'd totally accidentally and yet somehow intentionally bribed a government official. He waited to hear if he'd be fired. He waited to hear if they were going to recommend disbarment. The beta-blocker had long since worn off.

It wasn't that he wasn't telling Alyssa. He just needed to shore things up a little before he sprang it all on her. Alyssa had grown up poor in New Jersey with an Orthodox father whose equal parts faith in God and his own talent as a clarinetist had proven disastrous to his family. Hershey Semansky would get piecemeal orchestral jobs at weddings and galas but never be able to work at, say, Lincoln Center or the Met or even off-Broadway, because religious law wouldn't permit him to work on a Friday night, a Saturday, or any of the holidays, wherever the Jewish calendar randomly and chaotically placed them. He therefore was never able to accrue enough hours to join the union, and the wallpaper in Alyssa's childhood home seemed to be made up of strained conversations and gritted-teeth fights about money, though Alyssa herself characterized them as a happy family. Alyssa's mother, Elaine, a speech therapist by trade, worked needlepointing tallis bags for bar mitzvahs in between helping kids iron out their stammers and lisps in order to make ends meet, all while raising her five children. Her father worked miserably doing substitute music teaching at local schools, waiting for a big break that he could not accept even if it ever did come.

Alyssa had revealed these circumstances to Nathan one night, on their way back from her first-ever visit to Middle Rock, back when they were freshmen at Brandeis. They'd met during orientation, that first week. Nathan had been flailing for two whole days in a new environment and with a problematically unhygienic roommate when he attended a Shabbat dinner at the Hillel House, where he met one Alyssa Semansky.

Alyssa had cheeks ruddy with cheer, a confident, big-boned presence, and the booming energetic warmth of a camp counselor. By Yom Kippur, which Nathan did not return to Middle Rock for, they were inseparable. The custodial handoff between Ruth and Alyssa had gone seamlessly, particularly since Ruth had been so relieved to have discharged her oldest and neediest child into the wilderness and Alyssa had been so eager to find someone who wanted and needed her attention and her *leadership.*

But Ruth had known something was up since Nathan came home for Rosh Hashanah. The day after the holiday was a Sunday, and she was cooking bacon and eggs for the family. She noticed that Nathan wasn't eating it.

"Are you not hungry?" she asked Nathan.

"I'm eating eggs," he said. He wasn't looking at her. "It's fine."

"What's wrong with the bacon?"

"Nothing," he said, miserably. "I'm just not."

"You love bacon," Ruth said.

Jenny and Beamer exchanged a look across the table. Their mother was sometimes a witch.

"I just don't want bacon!" Nathan said.

It took forty-five seconds before the truth was laid out right there next to the swine. He'd been going to the Hillel, fine he'd been going to the Hillel with a girl, fine he'd started calling this girl his girlfriend and she was from a religious house and wanted to be with him and for them to live the same way she grew up.

"We shouldn't eat bacon anyway," Nathan said. "We're Jews."

"We're Jews who eat bacon," Ruth said. "That's who we are." But here was her psychopath voice, at the beginning of its roil. "I was raised in an Orthodox home. It was miserable. You want that kind of misery?" Now here came the yelling. "You want to bring Tupperware to my house with food you can eat? You want to watch your brother and sister and their children eat bagels and lox at my house while your children are left out and always know they're not like us?"

Ruth demanded to meet this Alyssa, so Nathan brought her home for Thanksgiving. On the train ride back to school, Nathan braced himself for a conversation about his family's relative lack of accommodations for her observance, particularly on Saturday, when she said she wanted to go to synagogue and Phyllis had said, "It's Thanksgiving weekend, dear." Alyssa was quiet, staring out the window of the train. Finally, when the train passed into New England, Nathan told her he was sorry, that *he* was going to be respectful of her observance, that he hadn't known that his family would react to her that way since they were so into being Jewish, et cetera, but she turned to him and explained the life of precariousness she'd experienced, how she was pulled out of class all the time because her parents sent her to private Jewish day school but didn't pay tuition on time, how she couldn't go to camp because her parents couldn't afford it, how she'd had to move all around Livingston, one rental to the next, her whole life. Seeing where the Fletchers lived, seeing how they lived—she was stunned. She said to Nathan that she had plenty of conviction, and she was hoping this didn't sound shallow and terrible, but that she'd trade the faith she was raised with for the security he was raised with in a second.

Nathan, who was so relieved that he wouldn't have to defy his mother, told her then for the first time that he loved her. He told her he would take care of her. He watched as she believed him. Why shouldn't she? He kept his word, and mostly she kept hers. She'd moved to Middle Rock, two hours from her parents if there was no traffic. She'd abandoned most of her ritual, even if, around the bar mitzvah, she had started audibly questioning that decision.

But what he got from her in return! He had a person of his very own, to take care of him and love him the most. He'd grown up invisible to his father, bewildered by the exasperation he seemed to cause in his mother. Forget Beamer and Jenny—they were their own faction, always whispering together in a huddle, them against the world. Alyssa was his, and in return, he would be hers, honestly and faithfully.

Which is to say that she had kept her end of the bargain, her vows, her marital agreement. How could he possibly now not tell her that he'd lost his job? How could he tell her that the rest of the family might be broke? It was too cruel.

The answer was that he could not put her through any of this unnecessarily. He had to know for sure what their true, independent financial situation was. Imagine growing up like that.

In the movie theater, Nathan's phone vibrated and he emitted a small yelp.

The other man in the theater looked over his shoulder. On the screen, Robert Morse sang, "Mediocrity is not a mortal sin!" He looked down and saw a text from Mickey:

Yo. Sorry about that. Crazy night. Working from home today. Meet me late lunch at 2 tomorrow? Place in my building?

Nathan added a thumbs-up to the text, and then, in case that wasn't clear, responded:

I'll be there!

On the train home that afternoon, Nathan looked forlornly out the window as he passed all the pastoral suburbs: Bayside, Douglaston, Little Neck. Everyone inside the train had no problems. Everyone on every platform he passed was living a blessed life and had nothing on their minds. It had been more than two months since he'd been put on ice at the firm. He had turned over his files and was waiting. He kept looking for news about the Yellowton Giant's—he had hope that if the store could still be opened, all would be forgotten—but the day came and went when it was supposed to have its opening, and there was not a word, not even in the local papers.

At least he still had his money.

He wondered if his family would need him now. He wondered if he would have to chip in to support them. He entered into a brief fantasy in which he sat in his mother's kitchen and slid a check across the table to her and she looked at it and then at him and then she cried and told him that she always knew that maybe Beamer was handsome and charming and talented, and maybe Jenny was just the right amount of smart and aloof to make people crazy about her, but Nathan—it was Nathan who was the one.

But just as soon, he wondered how he'd reconcile his lack of income with giving all his money away to his family. How would he live? How would he pay for his sons' bar mitzvah? How would he pay the property taxes on that house?

He was home too early. He stood on the sidewalk and took a deep breath of icy air before he got in a taxi and directed it home.

He would tell Alyssa that he'd had a light day, that the work stuff he was worrying about wasn't so bad after all. He paid the driver and tried to relax his forehead as he entered his home through the back entrance. And this is what he walked into:

A collage of images that came like photos falling on the ground.

It was Alyssa.

In the kitchen.

Was that a man's voice? She was with a man.

With a man.

"Nathan!" she cried.

Textiles.

A pack of Kent cigarettes.

Nathan's eyes tried to take in the scene. There was his wife, sitting at the kitchen table, tiles in front of her, with a man.

"Mee zeh?" the man asked. He was shaved bald, maybe fifty, wearing jeans. Of course he was Israeli.

"Nathan, I was just getting an estimate—"

"So this is what you were doing all day?" he asked. "I'm working all day and the very thing we agreed on, the very thing we talked about just this morning—"

She closed her eyes and sighed miserably. "Oh, Nathan."

Nathan took it all in: the tiles, the swatches, the Israeli contractor, the renovation that they had absolutely agreed to not pursue. When he spoke, this is what he said:

"I thought we didn't lie to each other."

———

THE NEXT DAY, when Nathan went to meet Mickey, he was exhausted and defeated. Of course he hadn't slept. Of course he'd been made to feel angry at Alyssa's infidelity ("Well, what else should I call it?"), and then of course he'd been made to feel sad and ashamed that he had been depriving her of something she so wanted.

He'd spent the evening at first ranting, but then apologizing, then quietly contrite, trying to be helpful as he goaded the twins to do their various bar mitzvah lessons and then watched over their shoulders as they played their various role-playing games, his stomach liquid and trembling. He thought of the beta-blockers in his medicine cabinet but would not consider them. He was still living with the consequences of his prior sojourn into drug experimentation.

So he was bleary and not quite sharp, but he was not dragging his feet as a waiter dressed in a tuxedo showed Nathan to Mickey's daily table.

Owing to his own natural chemistry, Nathan's suit was rumpled and sweaty. He arrived at the table to find that Mickey was *not* rumpled and sweaty. Mickey was in a clean navy suit that fell exactly where it was supposed to, according to the men's magazines that Nathan used to read in the waiting room of his regular visits to his doctors—too short on the legs, hitting at just the ankle, you'd think, but then look at him: He looked perfect. He looked like a spy! And was it too tight around the middle? It was not! Did it bunch when he sat? It did not! Mickey had a visual coherence. Sleek suit, power-shaved skull, icy blue eyes, a smile you had to earn.

"My man," Mickey said, standing up. He took Nathan's right hand with his own right hand, like he was preparing to arm-wrestle him, and instead pulled him in hard and close to his chest so that Nathan almost impaled himself on one of the fancy chairs at the table. It was smooth, swift gestures like that that always underlined to Nathan how much a part of the world Mickey was, and how Nathan felt that he was always just catching up.

"Now," Mickey said, as Nathan sat down. "What the fuck can I do for you, my friend?"

Nathan opened his mouth to speak but Mickey cut him off.

"I'm glad you wanted to have lunch," Mickey said. "I have been meaning to take you out and celebrate with you for a while now."

"Celebrate, right-o. Of course. Well, I'm not so much here to celebrate as—"

"You probably think I'm talking investment. No. I grew up

watching you and your family, and my parents, they were living so close to the edge all the time. It was so stressful. Do you remember my mother had that clothing store? It was always something, trying to get rich. But I'd come to your house. That place, the way everyone was calm. Your tennis lessons. You'd think I'd be bitter. No. I was *grateful* for it. It gave me something to aspire to."

A busboy came over with a glass of ice for Mickey and an empty glass for Nathan. Mickey was on some kind of diet in which he didn't eat till one P.M., and then, when he did, it was only modules of what his nutritionist called elder-meat (bison, among other hard-to-find proteins) and one root vegetable. He could eat young coconut and drink olive oil for the rest of the day but nothing else; he could only consume water in the form of ice, something Nathan didn't quite understand but Mickey explained that it had to do with a cutting-edge theory regarding metabolism and heat inside the body. All of this amounted to Mickey being generally malnourished and close to what Nathan had to imagine was overall nonspecific organ failure, which Nathan was sure accounted for at least half of how unpredictable and moody he was.

The busboy hesitated before pouring Nathan's water, but Nathan gave him a nod of reassurance that he, like most people, still wanted water.

"We are here because, well, what can I say?" Mickey began, his hands spread wide and his lips mushed together. "I have to thank you, Nathan."

"Well," Nathan said, hoping Mickey would expound.

"Yes, I want to thank you. I just celebrated my hundred-millionth dollar invested. You were the first. You took a chance on me. After I left the bank, I was really lost. And you, my old friend, you had faith."

"Of course, of course. It's good to see you settled. I just—I need a disbursement."

Nathan's salmon and Mickey's food arrived.

Nathan squinted at Mickey's plate. "What did you order?" he asked.

"Kangaroo," Mickey said. "The filet. They only have the filet here. They special-order it for me because I come here every day." He began to dig in.

"Did you say kangaroo?" Nathan's general gastroenterology had been too much through the wringer lately. "Did you say you were eating the filet of a kangaroo?"

"Mmm," Mickey said. "Most people, they hear kangaroo and they say, 'Awww, how could you eat those adorable little guys?' You know, in Australia, they're rodents."

"So there's this thing—"

"Isn't that nuts? Kangaroos are the rodents of Australia! Like, there's a population problem. But we think they're these adorable, fun, like boxing things? That's good PR! Heh. But they have this terrific enzyme in them called I don't remember but it turns muscle into fat."

"Wait, why would you want your muscle to turn into fat?"

"You're not up on the science, Nathan," Mickey said. "The science says that we should be building as much fat as possible so that our metabolism can always be in a struggle, a fight for its life. It's not intuitive. The science of optimization is not intuitive. People don't want you to know this. Like, have you ever almost drowned?"

"I think so." Nathan could not remember a time he'd almost drowned and yet felt sure that at some point he had.

"Do you ever feel more alive than when you're fighting for your life? You know? That's your metabolism. It wants to survive drowning in fat."

The busboy refilled Nathan's glass from a pitcher of water. Mickey watched Nathan watch the busboy, and then turned to Nathan's glass with longing.

"Man, I'd love some actual water," Mickey said. "Some Aych. Too. Oh."

"Ice is just water, right?" Nathan asked. "Technically speaking?"

"My trainer says hydration is a myth. Oversold to the American public. Ice cools the body and gets metabolized optimally. Like in the ice age. Everyone was healthy back then. You don't need all this water. Bottled water company propaganda. Evian, Poland Spring, Aquafina, et cetera. Sucker's bet." He sat back and considered his own argument, as if he was having a conversation with himself. "Of course, water is a generally good element to consume, but he said that since I'm training for my triathlon plus, it'll only slow me down. If you just have ice, it kind of eats itself as it evaporates in your body."

"You're doing a triathlon?"

"Plus. Oh, it's the regular three sports, but then a combat sport, then an additional brain challenge." He counted them out. "Biking, running, swimming, like a triathlon, but then a quick jousting match, then a chess match. Body and mind."

"Right-o," Nathan said. "Amazing."

Mickey made prayer hands.

"Anyway," Nathan said. "I was asking about the money?"

"Right. Yes, you had so much faith to invest with me."

"Ain't that the truth." Nathan made a laughing sound, though his face wouldn't acquiesce to laughter. "Listen. I need that disbursement. Nothing crazy. But I've had a thing come up. It's . . . it's urgent."

"Oh no." Mickey made his face a teddy bear of concern. "Is everything OK? Alyssa? The boys?"

"Everything's fine," Nathan said. "Just that Alyssa wants to do a kitchen renovation. You know how it is."

"Is that it? What do you need? Ten thou? Less?"

"Sure, yeah. Well, perhaps more. Maybe more."

"Penny redid the kitchen. It was about 35K. Maybe a little more. Your house is bigger." He laughed big. "But not for long! Nothing like all those construction people in it to make you feel like you live in a Lower East Side tenement, let me tell you! You sure you want to do this?"

"So you can just get me the money? That's really all I—"

"Oh sure, sure. I think, if I'm right, this is your first disbursement? It's hard to keep it straight. Which client wants how much. Don't ask me who. I can't tell you!"

"It's my first, yes. I was hoping I wouldn't take any out till retirement, just live on the ole salary, but happy wife, happy life, right!"

"And I guess your parents aren't helping you on this?"

"Well, why would they?"

"Right, right. OK, so if it's your first disbursement, we'll need to set up a transfer. You know how that is. The paranoia of the banks. So over the course of the next week, we'll take a small deposit out of your bank. This is called *verification*. So if you see some strange withdrawals, ten or four cents here or there, that just means it's working. If you don't see them, it means your bank is giving us a hard time." Then, "Hey, Natie, do you think your parents are happy with their money guy? Maybe they'd want to move their money closer to home."

Nathan shuddered. He opened his mouth, unsure of what he was about to say when, mercifully, Mickey's phone rang.

"I'm sorry, I have to take this. I'll have my assistant send the paperwork. No big deal. Just gimme a sec here."

Mickey walked away from the table, leaving Nathan with his salmon, which he could not bear to look at. Eventually, enough time went by that the check came, so Nathan paid it.

THEN HE WAITED. He watched his bank account, waiting for any signs of verification, but a week went by, then another, and nothing happened. First, there was a problem because Mickey's assistant was out on vacation, then Mickey was at a training sesh for his triathlon plus. For the next two weeks, Nathan waited and followed up with Mickey, and Mickey claimed that it was just a bad time because of the race.

The renovation was now fully under way; now he didn't even want to be at home, listening to the kids fight about preparing for their bar mitzvah. Now their home was a mess. There was dirt everywhere, dust in the air, visible in thick, opaque beams when it was hit by sunlight coming through the plastic-wrapped windows in the mornings. The drywall was down. The pipes were exposed. There were sinkholes in the kitchen tile floor with a dozen-foot drop into the foundation so that when you looked into it, you felt like you were falling into a dark abyss. Every day, Yoav, the contractor, and a varying band of misfit Israelis showed up whatever time they wanted to and told them that the job would be done in two weeks, in six weeks, in twelve weeks—then back to eight weeks. Yoav shushed Alyssa and told her to relax, and Nathan wanted to know how she, the president of the Jewish Feminists for Zionism club at Brandeis, tolerated this, but her only answer was a gigantic, shrugging "They're Israeli."

It was a lot to take. The week before, he'd come home to a flood in the kitchen that was encroaching on the living room. He'd had the plumber come at great expense to drain the house, but Yoav did not arrive till ten A.M. the next morning, when Nathan was livid.

"I don't know what happened!" Yoav said. "Pipes is old!"

"Well, I'm burning mad," Nathan said, though the truth was that he was actually burning scared. He had the feeling he was at the beginning of a dismal, terrible thing. He was right.

A few days later, Nathan took the boys to school, determined to come home and amass all his nerve and tell Alyssa, in a quiet moment, all that had been going on. It had been going on too long, and his lie was now too great, no matter his good intentions. Poor Alyssa, who had thought she'd finally found safety in Nathan.

But there she was, in the driveway, waiting to tell him something.

"I need you to stay calm," she said.

"What is it?" he asked.

"Can you be calm?"

"Of course I can be calm."

"No, really."

"Alyssa. What is it?"

"I have to tell you something," she said, and his body seized. "There is a crack in the foundation. They found it digging through the floor."

Nathan began to breathe quickly and, in response, Alyssa began to talk faster.

"The house would have *collapsed* in a few years," she said. Then, seeing that this had the opposite effect of what she was hoping, she tried to make him see. "No, it's good news. It's good news! *We found it and we can fix it and what a relief and a good thing we did this renovation.*"

HE WAS PRESCRIBED BETA-BLOCKERS FOR HIS BLOOD PRESSURE! DID ANYONE REALIZE THAT????

And then, like a gift from God, distraction.

One night, he was called to his mother's house to join her on her fitness walk around the estate.

He'd arrived at the ostensible post-work, post-commute hour of six-thirty P.M., having just come from seeing *Dog Day Afternoon* for a second day in a row, still wearing his suit. He walked into his parents' house. His mother called that she'd be downstairs in a minute, so he sat next to his father, who was in the living room watching a documentary about a Jewish musician who survived the Holocaust by pretending he was a painter and painting portraits of Hitler's cabinet.

"How was your day, Dad?" Nathan asked.

"Did you know about this guy?" Carl asked.

"I didn't. No."

"So interesting."

His father, who was too delicate to ask him about his own day, but who could absorb an untold amount of Holocaust stories, which is as close to describing the modern Jewish condition as you can get.

"Siskel and Ebert over here," Ruth said as she entered the room. Then, to Nathan, "Are you coming?"

Outside, they began their walk.

"You wanted to ask me something?" Nathan reminded her, his eyes darting everywhere. The clocks hadn't yet changed and it was still getting dark in the late afternoon, and he felt that they were too exposed to lurking, unseeable dangers as they huffed around the ring that inner-circled the estate.

"Meanwhile," his mother said. "*Meanwhile,* I'm frantic about how we're going to at least make sure we can survive. Us! Just the two of us! Forget you kids. Forget Marjorie." Then, "We're going to sell the brownstone."

"The brownstone, right."

"I thought—I was so stupid—I thought maybe one day when your grandmother died we'd go and live there. I always wanted to. We could go to the theater and museums and live right there in the Village." She emitted a bitter laugh. "So stupid." Then, before he could react, "You haven't heard anything from Arthur?"

"No, nothing. Nothing at the office. He's just on . . . a sabbatical."

"Still, a sabbatical, usually they check in."

"That's—I don't know if that's true. I don't know the rules of a sabbatical."

Ruth stopped right there and put her hands on her hips. They were now at the farthest point they could be from her house. If someone jumped out from behind the greenhouse, no one would hear them scream. Ruth looked at it across the lawn and shook her head.

"I want to know if we can sell the factory," she finally said.

She began walking again. A faraway synapse signaled to Nathan that he should follow, so he broke into a jog.

"What about Ike?" he asked.

"He can't sell it. He's a factory foreman, not a real estate lawyer."

"No, I mean, is he angry? He had an agreement with Dad."

"Whoever buys it would be smart to keep Ike on."

"But Ike was going to buy it from Dad. From us."

"Then Ike can buy it. Go ahead. Offer it to him first if you want to humiliate him. Nathan! He doesn't have the kind of money we're going to need."

"I know, but—"

"Things change." Uh-oh, psychopath voice. "Things change all the time. We didn't create this situation!"

"Don't get upset. It'll be OK." He put his hand on her shoulder, but she jerked it away.

"Dr. Joyce Brothers over here. I just need you to handle it, Nathan. Arthur isn't here. I have nobody. We won't get a good price on that brownstone. We never updated it; it's a terrible market. I have no idea what we can get for the factory. I don't even know who to call."

"Nobody will want the factory," Nathan said. "It's a polystyrene factory. I'm not even sure you could get any of the laws Dad's grand-father grandfathered in on passed on to someone else. They have environmental laws now. A change of ownership—but it's not just even that. It's that you can't use it because we're under an exclusivity contract with these people. They're not even people anymore. They're a corpora-tion. No, they're private equity now. You can't even face your ac-cuser over there. They're just sharks who will do what's best for their bottom line."

"But what if we sold it? Then it would be someone else's prob-lem."

"Who exactly is going to buy a factory that no one can use any-more?" Then he said, "I don't know, Mom. I have all this work. And the bar mitzvah is coming up. And this renovation, it's such a head-ache, and I promised I'd get all the permits expedited. Alyssa's wor-ried it won't be done by the bar mitzvah. Her family is coming. You know."

"You didn't need a renovation," his mother said. "You need to save your money right now." She breathed out hard and looked at the sky. "We don't have a choice, Nathan. We just don't have a choice anymore."

"I just—"

She stopped again. When she turned to him now, she did so se-ductively. "Do you remember the lighthouse? How you helped your grandmother with the lighthouse? She was so proud of you. We all were. You were the hero of that story. Do you remember that?"

He remembered. It had been a terrible time in Nathan's life, when Alyssa was undergoing terrifying, life-threatening hormone injec-tions and IVF treatments, crying each night and praying to God to give her a baby. And Nathan—all he could do while he was up all night was worry about the risk to Alyssa's health with all the crap they were pumping into her, and these procedures that always carried with them the risk of a coma, or death, or a coma that ended in death.

So Nathan had gone to work. He came home and comforted his wife, desperate to help her but not able to. And in the corner of his home office, after she went to sleep, he found some success restoring his hometown's dignity and helping his grandmother complete her final life's work. Yes, he thought wistfully, he was the hero of that story.

"You can't landmark a factory, Mom."

"Why not? It's an American institution. There aren't any left."

"Because even if that mattered, you'll make it impossible to sell in the future. Even if you could landmark it. Which you couldn't."

But soon they parted. He had nothing else to say to his mother now, and there were not so many times he could have been called the hero of a story that he didn't not want to drive home in the afterglow of it. God, how he loved the seductive version of his mother.

So Nathan got to work. He no longer went to the movies during the day, waiting out the firm's ethics review to conclude. Now he sought refuge at a quiet Hungarian coffee shop in the Village, where he researched the laws for selling old factories.

He spoke to his many contacts in commercial real estate on zoning and landmarking issues. He met with the least unscrupulous of them, a man named Benny Marina, in Benny's office in Sheepshead Bay. Benny was a commercial real estate agent who had overseen the sale and transition of at least two factories that Nathan knew about.

"It's rubber?" Benny asked.

"Polystyrene."

"Styrofoam?"

"We say polystyrene."

"Why?" Benny asked.

"It's political to say styrofoam. Bad reputation."

"Aha."

"We do molds, mostly," Nathan said. "Insulation molds for shipping. It has a good staff. Loyal employees. A really knowledgeable foreman and his son, they run it. They do a good job. This contract will be sold to someone and the factory will work again. Isn't there anyone who can see the reward here?"

Benny thought for a second. "I know a guy. Nessman. He special-izes in this."

"In what?"

"Problematic sales. Not necessarily property, but businesses."

"Problematic," Nathan repeated. He took down this Nessman's number.

Three days later, Nathan, Benny, Ike, and Ike's son, Max, waited in front of the factory as the man he assumed was Nessman limped up the steps to the factory door. He wore a billowing suit and metal-framed, dirty-lensed bifocals that were shaped like opposing paral-lelograms.

Ike and Nathan introduced themselves.

"And this is my son, Max," Ike said. He clapped his hands to-gether. "Shall I show you around?"

Consolidated Packing Solutions, Ltd., was housed in a large, rect-angular building—one story high with a seventy-five-foot ceiling and a singular, glass-enclosed office space at the top. The floor was divided into two sections, one side for the manufacturing, filled with giant drums of polystyrene pellets that got poured into humongous steel machines, which injected air into the pellets once they were heated so that they could puff up to be specifically shaped foam molds, designed to insulate delicate items in shipping. The other side was for the more patrician tasks of drafting, engineering, and accounts payable.

It was a shock for Nathan to see the inside; he hadn't been inside in quite a few years. It wasn't that it looked that different. It was that Nathan hadn't been in such a blue-collar space in so long that he'd forgotten that it was just this blue-collar space that gave him his white-collar life.

Ike led them through the engineering department, the drafting department, accounting. He led them through the floor that held the giant aerators and compression machines and the hundred-gallon drums of polystyrene pellets. During his forced apprenticeship, Na-than had been scared of all the activity and sounds and alarm bells that went off during a day of working there. Now, with his entire career on the line, he wondered if he could have managed to have seen the value in such simple, straightforward work.

As they walked through the steampunk machinery of it all, Nessman shook his head despondently at every turn: An inaccessible bathroom ("But if you're handicapped, you can't work here in the first place!" Nathan said. "It's a factory!"). An inefficient drainage system for the melted offshoot that was not in compliance with a 2008 law ("Well, now, it's in total compliance with the 1976 law, when it was renovated, and the code isn't exactly clear about . . ." Nathan said, though Nessman gave him an over-the-glasses look that stopped him midsentence).

"You're still allowed to use a high-steam fuel injector here?" Nessman asked as they passed the big brass cylinder.

"We were grandfathered in," Nathan said.

Nathan pretended he had to take a call when it was time to tour the basement.

They continued upstairs, into Carl's old office, which was glass on all sides so that Carl, and his father before him, could more easily see any of the workers slacking off. It was now occupied by Ike, though he always sat where old Hannah Zolinski, the secretary, used to sit, as if Carl might return to work any day.

Nessman leaned down and picked up a stray packing peanut. He pinched it between his hands. It was shiny and squeaked against itself. He held the specimen up to eye level for Benny and Nathan, as if they had never seen a packing peanut.

"You make styrofoam," he said. Then, almost to himself, he said, "It's shocking to me that you're still allowed to make styrofoam." Then he added, "It would be one thing if you wanted to just sell the building. That I could probably help you with. But I have to say, I specialize in selling a business you could squeeze just a little bit more out of. I don't see how I could sell this." Nessman looked at Ike over his dirty glasses, then at Nathan. "Your foreman is missing a finger."

"He's been compensated," Nathan said. "He's been well taken care of. This is a family business for him, too. His father was the prior foreman of the factory."

The tour finally ended outside where the ground was depressed—the Rainbow River, they used to call it. When Nathan was doing his forced apprenticeship in high school, his father had brought him out here for lunch each day and told him the story about how his own father had brought him out here for lunch as well. Back then, Nathan remembered, the multicolored swirl of chemical runoff was mesmerizing, a thing of beauty that he didn't yet know to fear.

The area became a park bench and a fountain built over what was unfixable grassland after a random inspection in 2002 resulted in a summons and a fine. Nessman looked at it and said, "Well, this is nice." But Nessman's face quickly changed. He looked down, realizing his feet were partially submerged in a muck. His tan shoes were covered in blue-green whorls of color. He bent down and touched the ground. When he stood up, his fingers were purple.

"I'm not sure what to tell you," Nessman said. "Do the people in this area know what you've done to their groundwater?"

"The factory was grandfathered in under a variety of manufacturing laws," Nathan said again. "We employ more than eighty-five workers."

"You keep saying you were grandfathered in," Nessman said. "Those were bribes, right? They were probably the only reason this factory was attractive to Haulers. But the grandfathered laws won't transfer with a sale. The environmental laws now—who is going to want to take on a styrofoam factory that needs this much remediation? You can't sell this without being beholden to one point three million in compliance fixes minimum. Your best bet is to cut your losses and just get out."

Polystyrene, Nathan said in his head. He sat down on the bench. He was suddenly very tired.

"This place isn't just worthless," Nessman said. "It's a liability."

WHEN NATHAN BECAME nervous or triggered or went into what psychoneuroendocrinologists call hypervigilance, the most anxious part of his brain (there was steep competition for this) imagined different kinds of horrific, humiliating behaviors he could enact right then that would make each circumstance markedly worse. During his own bar mitzvah, his state was so heightened that he wondered what it might be like to run up behind Rabbi Weintraub and lift him up and scream, "Come here, you big, adorable lug!" on his way back to the bimah from opening the ark. When he got married, right at that moment, he imagined pulling his zipper down and waving his penis about, screaming, "Par-tay! Par-tay!" When Nessman was talking to him about the fate of his family's factory, he had the overwhelming urge to tap him on the nose and say, one word per tap, "That. Is. Adorable."

He needed to be alone after that meeting, but there was nowhere to go. He began the drive home, but when he arrived in Middle Rock, he remembered that his home was no longer a sanctuary. His home was now a nightmare. There was drilling all the time, and dust everywhere—heavy metals and sundry carcinogens having a party in the air. Just the noise. Just the arrogant, mocking tone of voice of Yoav, the contractor, whom Nathan hated down to his liver.

And Alyssa? She was gone to him, too. Each night she ordered takeout, then fell into bed exhausted, then pulled herself up to sitting and went through iPad displays of the different ways a person can have a kitchen. A universe of backsplashes. A geological survey of marble. The lighting fixtures you can hang over a kitchen island— they could be old-timey and filamenty; they could be Deco or modern. The kitchen could be made into something that might appear to be in a farmhouse, with a giant sink and wooden cabinets, or it could be something that looked like it belonged on a spaceship. In order to pick what your style was you had to have a more definitive sense of yourself and your tastes, to not feel like such an impostor, and here is where Alyssa failed.

But forget matters of taste! There were a million other choices to make. There had been innovations in dishwashers that made it so that for a mere six thousand dollars, you would not be able to detect that the dishwasher was working unless you had eyes on it and could follow the displays of lights. There had been innovations in cabinets in which you could slam one of them and it wouldn't make a noise (this one Nathan loved). There was a way to have a faucet that lay beneath the surface of the kitchen island and only surfaced like a rose growing in fast-motion when summoned.

At night, Nathan fantasized about a reality in which he could apply for a permit to zone their house for some specific use that would force the renovation to stop and have the kitchen restored to before the name Yoav ever entered their home, when all was fine and his grandmother hadn't died and Nathan had his job and his paperwork and everyone was happy or at least oblivious.

He was too miserable. He needed a way out of this misery. Twice a day he thought: Maybe it was time to come clean. Not because it was the right thing to do but because it would alleviate his misery. Nobody could comfort him like Alyssa. Nobody was rooting for him like Alyssa. His mother had always made him feel ashamed of his love for her, but Alyssa's metrics were simple: Good is good, bad is bad, love is good, Nathan is good and wanted.

Maybe it was only having a truly honest conversation with Alyssa that would help. Maybe there would be something redemptive in how she still loved him, how she'd ultimately understand why he lied. He had been planning to tell her everything after he got his money from Mickey, but Mickey had ever more excuses, and he never prioritized Nathan because Mickey was being Mickey, taking Nathan for granted and elevating his other clients ahead of his most loyal, most imprisoned friend. Meanwhile, Nathan was desperate for his wife, for her loving and understanding. He couldn't bear the weight of all this anxiety if it came with all these lies. Yes, he thought now, maybe it was time to tell Alyssa what was going on, both in his job and in the family finances.

He'd actually tried the week before, but he'd walked in on her having a conversation with Lily Schlesinger, who was telling her that if she didn't like the renovation, she could undo certain parts, that just knowing that would rid her of her decision paralysis. But Alyssa, who had never truly gotten comfortable in a life with money, stared at her like she was an alien and shook her head. She was always trying to figure out a way to understand the wealth, to have its comforts be manifest to her. He saw on her face that she didn't know if what Lily was suggesting was correct or as ridiculous as it sounded. This broke his heart.

He left his car and slammed the door. He took out his keys and opened the door to his house.

Yes, it was time to tell her everything. It was time to tell Alyssa what he knew. He would tell her about the family money. He would tell her about his job. But he arrived at the cordoned-off kitchen to find her inside with Yoav. She was making a noise, like a moaning. The kids were in school by now. He only now remembered that Yoav's truck was in the driveway, but no other cars were there.

Nathan ripped open the plastic to see inside the kitchen.

Alyssa began to cry: tired tears of exhaustion and fear.

"What is it?" Nathan asked. His heart was nearly stopped.

"Nathan," she said, turning and running and putting her arms around him.

"What? What is it? Is it my mother?" He immediately wished he'd asked if it was the kids.

When she spoke, he could hardly hear her through her sobs.

"Nathan. They found asbestos. This whole time, the kids—asbestos."

He stood in the ruins of his home, his wife collapsed in sobs at his chest, and for a moment, he was the tallest person in the room—the only one who had seen all of this coming.

Is now where you start? Do you tell her now?

Like hell you do.

"Pack everything up," Nathan said. "We're getting out of here. We're going to my mom."

——

PHYLLIS'S HOUSE STOOD empty and foreboding at the top of the estate, just waiting to receive the occupants of both Acura 2017 MDXes that ambled their way up the driveway, filled with the earthly possessions of Nathan Fletcher's family.

Nathan gave himself the gift of telling Alyssa that he was taking three weeks off of work in light of this and in light of the kids' impending bar mitzvah. She was so distracted with the planning, not to mention their home disaster and sudden move, that she didn't ask questions.

Each night, Nathan and Alyssa would bring the kids over to his parents' house for dinner, and Nathan would try to goose conversation with his father. His father seemed so old lately, and what was Nathan expecting? That he had suddenly become someone who talked about his life? Or at all?

"You know, when Grandpa was a kid, the gas station was a playground," Nathan would say. And his father would nod, looking far away, and Ruth would sigh and stand up and clear the table.

At night, back at his grandmother's house, Alyssa would stay up in the living room on her laptop, using software to plan seating, checking with the party planner to make sure that yarmulkes were ordered, that flowers were ordered, that benchers were ordered, that honors were distributed, that the egg salad at the shul would have dill but no scallions.

And Nathan found himself believing he really was on a vacation, convinced equally by the upending of his home, the change of scenery, and the way the brain morphs under stress.

"Is this house safe, Dad?" Ari asked one night, as Nathan tucked him into Marjorie's old bed.

"It's the safest," Nathan said. "Nothing could happen here. The fence is electrified. The gate is locked."

"But the problem wasn't from people coming," Ari said. "It was from inside the house."

"There are plenty of alarms. Nobody will bother us here."

"But what about poisons?"

"What do you mean, poisons?"

"Like in our house, all the poisons?"

Nathan looked at the boy. His sons looked so much alike in the face, but Ari's eyes were wide where Josh's were beady.

"We were very lucky. We found them. Sometimes, you find something and it's good because it's just a canary in the coal mine of what these old houses could contain."

"What does that mean? A canary . . . ?"

"A canary in the coal mine."

"*What does that mean?*" Ari whispered.

"It's just a saying. It used to be that they made sure it was safe for miners to go down into the mines for coal by sending a canary in. If the canary died, you knew it wasn't safe. There wasn't enough oxygen."

Ari's eyes were so big it felt like they could never close. "They killed the canaries?"

"Yes, to make sure it would be safe for the miners."

"That's not a good reason."

Nathan shook his head. "You are right. It's terrible. I never thought about it that way." He blew air out of his mouth. "It's terrible what people think of."

Nathan lay down next to Ari. There are few things more validating than to see someone who is like you and love them instead of hate them. That was a surprising thing about fatherhood that Nathan had not anticipated.

"Will you sleep with me, Dad?"

"Sure, I'll stay with you for a while. Sure thing."

But once Ari was asleep, Nathan could not stop his legs from wandering over to his mother's house to hear more drama: how Beamer would never return her calls (typical); how Jenny was being her petulant self (annoying). How warm was the bond between his mother and him when she was ranting about others (pathetic?).

Nathan listened, and once she had exhausted herself, he walked back up the hill to his grandmother's house alone, where he had somehow ended up living for the time being, locking its perimeter and then looking out over the Sound.

And in the late night, when he went to bed, he dreamed of his grandmother—almost every single night that they stayed there. In one dream, he was floating in the pool, back when it had water in it, and then suddenly he started sinking and sinking, and at the bottom of the pool, where he found himself, he realized that he had landed on his grandmother's dead body. He would try to rush back up to the surface, but he couldn't. The water was too heavy.

In another dream, he was sitting shiva in her living room, but it was unclear for whom and he was panicked that his parents had died, but also realized it could be so much worse. It was in this dream that Phyllis came to pay her respects.

"I'm so sorry for your loss."

"But who?" Nathan said. She was huge compared to him because he was sitting in one of shiva's tiny, low seats. "Who died?"

"I didn't know you had it in you, boychick," Phyllis said, and he realized that that was exactly what she said at the reception that the Historical Society threw after the Cobbleway Park Lighthouse restoration was completed. "You reminded me of your grandfather for a minute. They used to force him to study Talmud in school. The Nazis were shooting everyone, and your grandfather, Zelig, was forced to hide in a basement and study Talmud. But you know what?" She put her finger to her temple and tapped. "It made him smart. He hated it but he also knew that it was what helped him escape. Learning the loopholes. Seeing the themes. You see?"

Nathan didn't, but he didn't care; it was so nice to be bathed in approbation. He stopped caring who died and asked her to say it again and again.

"I didn't know you had that in you, boychick," she said.

"I didn't know you had that in you, boychick," she said again.

In the dream, he leaned over her and snuggled up to her, inhaling deeply so he could smell the Chanel N°5 and No Frills brew again.

"It's just like the lighthouse, boychick," she said. "You have to see it's just like the lighthouse."

He woke up in the middle of the night during these dreams. Alyssa turned over, disturbed but still asleep. Nathan stood up and wandered the house again, afraid of every corner but unsure who he could ask for protection.

That was when he remembered the dybbuk again. What if these weren't dreams? What if his grandmother was a dybbuk, coming to haunt him? To punish him for not being better—for not listening to her?

"I tried," he said to the air, but his own voice falling on nothing scared him further.

He went back to bed and this time he slept till the afternoon. When he came downstairs, Alyssa asked him if he was feeling OK.

"I'm fine. I think it's just all getting to me."

"Hm. OK! Do you think you could pick the kids up at shul? They're at their lesson."

"Sure, sure. I'll just shower."

Nathan parked at the synagogue and went to the rabbi's chambers, where he could hear his sons practicing inside. He was fifteen minutes early.

The place had not changed since he was a bar mitzvah student. He'd taken lessons in that very office. He'd done eight years of Hebrew School prior to that. As he sat waiting for his sons to finish, he remembered his favorite teacher, a nice morah named Laura, who taught them when Nathan was in fifth grade. They were doing a unit on the Shema, the nighttime prayer to keep the person going to sleep safe through the night.

Morah Laura stood luminous in her calf-length skirt in the middle of the room, where she spoke with joy and eye contact about the prayer: "It will protect you. You say it when you're scared, and it protects you!"

Nathan, at eleven, was the only boy in class paying attention. The others were writing notes to girls or playing hangman with each other. One in the corner made armpit farts when Morah Laura turned her back. But Morah Laura was too dreamy to care. Her recent engagement to a rabbinical student from Teaneck had filled her with a zeal for Judaics that is normally conspicuously absent in a Hebrew School teacher.

He looked down at his prayer book, which had the words in a seraphic Hebrew, an italic transliteration, and then, finally, a small English translation: "Hear O Israel! The Lord is God! The Lord is One!" He raised his hand.

"Yes, Nathan." Morah Laura had a round, full face and a dimple in her chin.

"What does it protect you from?"

Morah Laura came alive. "Oh, everything," she said. "It protects you from *everything*." She told a story about a man who was falling out of a skyscraper window and said the Shema, only to find a wind that overtook him and escorted him gently to Earth, standing upright.

"And he was fine?" Nathan whispered. He didn't raise his hand; he might as well have been alone with her. "He lived?"

"He lived and became a great rabbi. He's very famous." She looked out at the greater class. The boy next to Nathan was wiping boogers on his desk but Nathan didn't care. "Here, everyone. Take your right hand and put it over your eyes."

She put her hand over her eyes. So did Nathan, though being blindfolded was one of his fears. No one else in the room did it. Instead, they took Morah Laura's brief blindness to make blow job gestures at her and give her the finger.

"Shema Yisrael Adonai Elohaynu Adonai Echad!" she intoned. She took her hand off her eyes in time for all the thrusting eleven-year-old boys to sit down. "Now you do it." She put her hand over her eyes again and recited the prayer again, this time accompanied by the girls and by Nathan.

Nathan walked home that afternoon with Bernard, who had been ejected from class early on in the day for drawing naughty pictures. It was one of those late-winter days that wasn't just warm but smelled like spring, and Nathan was trying to stay inside the special golden moment of Morah Laura, but Bernard had dropped his Trapper Keeper on the ground and was kicking it down Cutland Road.

"What are you *doing*?" Nathan asked. He was going to get in trouble for this, he just knew it.

Bernard didn't answer him. Instead, he took one more big kick and one of the unconfiscated pictures of his Hebrew teacher, Morah Rochelle, came flying out and feather-landed in front of them. Morah Rochelle was in her seventies, and Bernard had drawn her—

quite competently, actually—wearing a dress that she was lifting in the picture and that depicted her as having a penis. Nathan bent down to pick it up.

"You can't do this," Nathan said. "You'll get in trouble."

"Fuck off," Bernard said. He was seven.

They walked and walked and walked. It was their mother's attempt at them becoming independent. Ruth, who, by age seven, was crossing Coney Island Avenue in Brooklyn, also worried that she was raising children who didn't know how to cross a street or find their way home. When Bernard started Hebrew School that year, Ruth insisted that the two now begin to walk the mile home. Naturally, Nathan objected to this with every tattered nerve he had, but Ruth insisted, and Carl, well, Carl couldn't summon the energy to disagree with Ruth on anything.

They arrived at Ocean Vista Road, the big street to cross to get to their house. Bernard kicked his notebook one last time into the intersection and began to pursue it when a landscaping truck drove through the crosswalk and ran over the notebook. Bernard was just a yard away.

Over on the sidewalk, Nathan watched this, paralyzed. He hadn't been able to move when he clearly saw his brother walking into traffic and the landscaping truck not slowing down. He even saw himself not moving, but no amount of rebuke could make his body jump into action. So he put his hands over his eyes and said, "Shema Yisrael Adonai Elohaynu Adonai Echad!" And when he removed his hand, he saw his brother, Bernard, unharmed.

That night, Nathan lay in bed, shuddering over and over in memory of having saved his brother. Morah Laura had been right. This stuff was powerful. But now he was burdened by its power. If you knew that you had the power to keep your family safe, what was your obligation?

So that night, he put his hand over his eyes and said Shema for his own safety. Then he turned his hand so that the palm side faced outward and he said Shema for each of the members of his family. First it was his immediate family. He said it once for Ruth and then for

Carl, and then for Bernard and then for Jenny. But then he realized that if his grandmother died right then, it would be because he didn't say it. So he said it for Grandma Phyllis. And also for Bubby Lipshe, since it wouldn't be fair if she died and Grandma Phyllis got to live. Then he'd say it for Ruth's four brothers and sisters, then their children, his cousins, who numbered twelve. Then he'd say it for Cousin Arthur. Then he'd say it for Arthur's wife, Cousin Yvonne. Then he'd say it for Grandma Phyllis's two brothers, Phil and Milton. Both Phil and Milton were married, so he'd say it for their wives. Then he'd say it for his aunt Marjorie. He even said it for Ike Besser and his wife, Mindy, and their son, Max, though they were *like* family, and not *technically* family. And then once he said it for them once, he realized he was stuck saying it for all of them forever.

So he did. He did this every night for years. And by the time he was done, he'd have taken a full seventy-five minutes each night to say Shema for each family member he had, not so much because it mattered to him that they live, but because he now knew he was in charge of it. It was the only time in his childhood that Nathan ever felt that he had any power.

Now, as Nathan waited in the anteroom to the rabbi's chamber for his children to come out of their lesson, the rabbi's office burst open and his sons grunted by him. Rabbi Weintraub followed them out and Nathan stood up.

"Nathan, what a pleasure," the rabbi said.

"How are they doing?"

"You know, distracted, nervous. You remember. You have a big month. The bar mitzvah. Your grandmother's unveiling. It was so considerate of Alyssa to plan those together, so that your whole family could be here. She's very special. I'm sure you know."

"She's very thoughtful. I was worried that we should wait the whole year. Like, maybe it's bad luck to do an unveiling before the year is up."

"I don't think it really matters. In fact, the chassidim think you should put a headstone up immediately, that a soul can't rest until it is judged, and it's not judged till a stone is up."

Nathan swallowed.

"Are you doing OK?" Rabbi Weintraub asked. "You look a little anemic."

"Can I ask you something, Rabbi?"

"Anything."

"This is going to sound strange. Do you—do we—believe in dybbuks?"

The rabbi sat down on the bench that Nathan had been sitting on, and Nathan sat back down himself.

"What a question," Rabbi Weintraub said. "Do we believe in an unrested spirit that possesses and animates a body? I guess some of the mystics would say yes. The more practical people would say no. It's a big question. Belief. Who knows? You have some rabbis who don't think you need to believe in God anymore. But—where is this coming from?"

"I just was remembering a thing my grandmother told me when I was young, after my bar mitzvah, actually. I keep dreaming about her. I keep wondering if—I have these dreams about her."

"I think a dybbuk has to possess an actual body. I think other than that, it's your brain doing some mourning. It's you missing her."

Nathan closed his eyes and shook his head. "There's just so much changing, Rabbi. The kids are getting older. And my family—my house is in shambles. I just really don't know what's going to happen."

The rabbi nodded. "Do you know who Gershom Scholem was? He was a Jewish philosopher. He wrote about Kabbalah and Shabbtai Zvi and antinomianism. He spoke once about something called a plastic hour, that there are these times in our lives when everything is soft and malleable. We tend to suffer during these times, but his point was that actually, these plastic hours are times when you can make actual change."

"What change?"

"Whatever change is necessary. For the better. This is a time when you can become better. I know you went through a lot with your family. More than anyone should. You know what I think when I look at you? When I look at any of the families in my congregation?"

Nathan waited.

"I think that every family is its own Bible story. Every family is its own mythology. The people that were written about in the Torah—that's just a document from a period of time. If the Torah had gone on, perhaps we'd all be included in it. Perhaps there would be a Book of the Fletchers."

Nathan's phone rang.

"Excuse me." He pulled his phone out of his pocket and saw that it was Mickey calling. Thank god. One problem solved. To the rabbi, he said, "I'm so sorry. This is important."

The rabbi waved him off, and Nathan stood in the entry hall of the synagogue. "Hello? Mickey? Hello?"

He couldn't hear anything but something muffled.

"Yes! Yes, Mickey, hello!" he said.

He heard a faraway voice.

"Mickey," Nathan said. "I can't hear you. Everything A-OK?"

But the voice on the other end wasn't Mickey's. It was a woman, and he could barely make out the words she was saying.

"Oh, Nathan," he finally understood.

"Penny. Penny! Are you OK?"

"Oh, Nathan," she said again. "I saw you were trying to call. I don't know what to do, I don't know if I should be calling back. I don't know what to do!"

"Penny. What is it?"

Penny's voice broke and he heard now that she was crying.

"It's Mickey," she said. "Nathan, he's in the hospital."

NATHAN ARRIVED AT Long Island Jewish to find his lifelong friend, Mickey, in a private hospital bed with his eyes taped closed with some kind of opaque Scotch tape, and five different machines monitoring his vital signs. Penny was holding Mickey's hand, looking gravely at him.

Nathan stood in the doorway.

"Penny," he said. But Penny didn't seem to hear him, so devoted in her vigil was she.

"Penny," he said again.

She looked up.

"Nathan." She wiped her eyes with her free hand. "Oh, Nathan."

Now she stood up and held her arms out. She was short, with straight hair that clung flat and close to her face and bangs that covered half of it, as if her face didn't want to cause too much trouble.

"They don't know when he's going to wake up, Nathan."

"What happened?" Nathan looked at Mickey's inanimate face again and shuddered.

"He overtrained. He didn't even make it to the race. He was dressed and then he was standing there and then he collapsed."

Nathan stared at his big, bad friend, now just lying terrifyingly inert.

"I kept telling him, it's not normal to not drink water. It's not normal to just eat kangaroo! He kept saying they have some enzyme!" She sat down again, staring at him. "He kept saying not to worry, shh shh don't worry, Penny. And now look."

"Why—why are his eyes taped shut?"

She took a heavy breath and looked up at Nathan. "He had taken so many performance drugs that his eyes were stuck open. They say they'll close on their own when that stuff is out of his system."

According to the doctor, beneath the visage of health and manhood that Nathan had seen at lunch, Mickey's body had been eating away at itself under his draconian regimen. His adrenal glands altered, affecting his heart rate. His liver began secreting a hormone that was starting to make his body hair fall out. His liver had grown cysts that were so bloated with serous fluid that they had obliterated the architecture of his liver. His cerebrospinal fluid was twice as viscous as it should have been and now was the consistency of strawberry preserves.

"I'm sure he'll be fine," Nathan said, more to make her stop describing his insides.

Penny looked at Mickey again.

"Do you think so?"

"Oh, for sure." Nathan was sweating. "It's Mickey."

"He's been under so much pressure lately," she said.

Penny sat down and took Mickey's hand again.

"He was so grateful to you, Nathan," Penny said, looking at her husband. "Is. He is so grateful to you."

"We've been friends a long time."

"Well, a lot of people say they're friends but not a lot of people invest in someone who just had his broker's license revoked."

"Right-o," Nathan said. Then: "What's that now?"

"I know he has his issues. I know he has sharp elbows and whatever else they said about him." She stared at him wistfully. "But you're going to tell me that at all of Goldman, he's the worst one? The most dishonest one? I mean, do you read the news?"

"Honesty? They said he was dishonest?"

"A lot of people left him for dead. You know? Only a true friend like you would stand by him like this when everyone left him for dead."

Nathan couldn't speak.

"It wasn't enough to fire him," Penny said. "They had to also sic the government on him!"

"The what's that? Did you say the *government*? Like the SEC?"

"No, something about the SEC being too overloaded, so they outsourced it to . . ." Penny was trying to remember.

Nathan could barely get the words out. "The Department of Justice?"

"Right, yes." She sniffed. "They fired him! It's enough! Am I right?" She shook her head. "Do you know why they fired him?"

Nathan was just about to scream.

"They fired him," she said, "because he didn't take enough vacation. Can you believe that?"

"It doesn't really sound right, actually."

"I guess in America now, if you don't take vacation, if you don't slack off, if you try your hardest for your clients, well, that's just not good enough! Forget innovation! It's burnout! Everyone's so burned out that they have to mandate vacation now! And if you refuse to go on a vacation, you're fired because everyone else feels threatened by your hard work." Her eyes began to well as she stared harder into her husband's vegetablarian face. "Nathan, he just wanted to do his best for his clients."

It was so hot in that room just then that Nathan wanted to jump out the window. Had it been this hot the minute before? Was there some kind of terrorist attack on the hospital? Smoke coming through the vents? But then, he realized that the heat was coming from inside him, an internal furnace turned up to 150. The terrorists were him; they were inside him. They'd been inside him the whole time.

"Your investment brought him back," Penny was saying. "He was so depressed all the time after it happened. But he felt like with you—with your trust in him, he could really build back a life. Which is a miracle. But I keep telling him, 'You're talented. People will see that. Just one client at a time.'"

"So, well, that's—am I just the one client, then?"

Penny laughed a little through her tears.

"Oh, Nathan. You're so funny."

"Hey, uh—do you think I can speak to like his secretary or something? I've been waiting on a disbursement and of course I don't want to—"

"He doesn't have a secretary yet. Grass roots, he calls it. He wanted everything to be grass roots."

A doctor came in flanked by interns.

"Hello there, how is our patient?" asked the doctor, but it seemed like a dumb question.

Penny stood up and started talking to the doctor, and Nathan made some noises about wanting to give them their privacy.

Outside the door of Mickey's room, Nathan was wild-eyed and foamy.

"Sir, are you OK?" a passing nurse asked him. "Should you be in your room?"

"I was, uh, I was visiting a friend." He looked down at himself. "I'm wearing street clothes."

The nurse made crazy-weirdo eyes and continued walking.

Nathan stood still, unable to move, until he remembered the spores of illness that hung in the air at a hospital. Next to him was a hand sanitizer dispenser, but a thing people don't think about is how dirty the actual dispensers can be if they're touched mostly by people who are seeking out hand sanitizer. He ran to the elevator.

He emerged into the parking lot. An ambulance brushed by him (with fifteen feet of clearance), nearly killing him (not nearly killing him). He had no idea what to do next.

He took his phone out and called his mother.

"What is it, Nathan?"

"Do you remember the guy from the—the guy who helped look for the money after Dad?"

"The Israeli? The Mossad guy? Uh, yes, right. It's—right, I'll look it up."

"Can I have his number?"

"What do you need his number for?"

"Oh, it's a work thing. It's, you know, the big guns."

"Julius Rosenberg over here."

By the time his mother sent him over the contact information for a Gal Plotkin, he was in his car. Nathan texted him:

Hi-ho. Nathan Fletcher here. You know my parents? From middle rock? A long time ago. Need help urgently. On a personal issue.

Within a few hours, Nathan was giving Plotkin details, and Plotkin was asking him to give him a day.

Nathan waited. Yes, he knew: He should have had enough money just from many years of his extremely decent salary at the firm, it's true. But first you have to take into account that the cost of living in Middle Rock was just untenable. Then you have to take into account the cars. Add to that Alyssa's group tennis lessons. Add to that Alyssa's *private* tennis lessons that allowed her to stay in that same group as Lily Schlesinger, who was the symbol of the person Alyssa felt she should be, and had been herself playing tennis since she was six. The renovation. The tutors. The after-school sports. The after-school private tuba lessons. The replacement tuba for the (somehow?) lost tuba. The summer camps. The summer trips. The bar mitzvah—the catering, the clothing, the lessons, the hype men, the DJs (plural!), the way they were flying Alyssa's grandparents in from Israel *first class* for the event. The money they sent Alyssa's family on occasion. The pool club. The beach club. The orthodontia. That Alyssa had started going gray at thirty-two and now had to get her roots done every three weeks and a draconian relaxing treatment that made her hair very curly instead of too curly, done every three months or so.

You have to take into account that he hadn't drawn that extremely decent salary in now months.

And then there was Nathan's secret little hobby: the insurances. A thing that Alyssa did not necessarily know was that her husband's commitment to buying insurance technically met the criteria for addiction. Nathan Fletcher owned—though you own it only in your head—home insurance, life insurance, flood insurance, car insurance, just like anyone else. But he also had supplemental health insurance. He had bedbug insurance, lawn insurance, earthquake insurance. He had liability insurance, an umbrella policy, critical illness insurance, comprehensive insurance, maritime insurance (the kids took sailing lessons at Cobbleway Park), personal malpractice insurance. It goes without saying that he had kidnapping insurance. He had a special insurance to cover the insurances he already had, should one of those insurance companies go belly up.

What was there to do? The person he would call in this circumstance was Arthur, but Arthur was nowhere to be found. He was gone. Nathan didn't have a father who could help, just the surrogate one—a substitute at times, maybe. Nathan had for so long looked the other way on the borderline inappropriate, yes maybe actually highly inappropriate relationship that his mother had with Arthur, and in exchange, Arthur *helped* him. Arthur *calmed* him. Arthur answered his questions. Arthur wasn't just supposed to leave in the middle of the night like a thief, especially when he was the only one who could possibly help Nathan figure out how to handle this, yes, he'll say it, no, this time he means it: CATASTROPHE.

One sleepless, foodless day spent mostly inside the bathroom later, he was standing with a former (probably a former) Israeli spy in a Korean grocery in an aisle that appeared to sell only variations on peeled chestnuts. Gal Plotkin was a short, compact, muscular man, with gray curly hair, and creases around his mouth and eyes, and an old vertical scar on his left cheek. He explained to Nathan that his friend—his "friend"—Mickey had been fired from Goldman.

"I figured," Nathan said. "But why? She said it was because he never took vacation! Who ever heard of that?"

"No," said Gal. "It's true. It was for vacation refusal."

"Vacation refusal is real?"

"Well," Plotkin said. And he explained:

Finance companies mandate several consecutive-day weeks of vacation per year, and yes, Mickey had refused, but not for the Conservative bootstraps reasons that Penny had suggested. It turned out that Mickey, who had been a star trader on the derivatives desk, had been fired ostensibly for the minor offense of refusing to take the FINRA-mandated "at least 10 consecutive vacation days away from the office per annum," engineered to uncover complex illicit trading schemes that would unravel without ten days of active management.

Well, it worked. Mickey's license was revoked because he was, in fact, running a complex illicit trading scheme. He had been hedging his one-way bets by entering imaginary and not-fully-offsetting opposite-way bets into the bank's oversight computer system so it appeared his total capital at risk was minimal, when, in fact, it was extremely not minimal—it was maximal, actually—resulting in his positions being liquidated, catastrophic investor losses, the aforementioned termination, and now an ongoing Department of Justice investigation.

Mickey might have intended to set up a fund with Nathan as an investor, but that didn't happen. Instead, he merely took the several millions of dollars that Nathan had given him and lived off it, renting an office in Manhattan, upgrading his wardrobe, having high-end marsupial lunches. It appeared that he had hopes of using Nathan's cash to convey a more monied appearance so that he could attract more clients—at a rented house in Sag Harbor, at a vacation in Monaco, during a full month at a resort in West Palm Beach. He had used Nathan's money for all of it.

"I can't believe you figured this out so quickly" was all Nathan could say.

"It wasn't a very complex scheme, as these things go," Plotkin said. "I am imagining that he thought that he would earn back the money with other investors. We see it a lot. He just didn't do that. I don't know why. Can you ask him?"

"He's . . . in a coma," Nathan said, only barely believing it himself. "So what do I do? How do I get my money back?"

Plotkin blew air out of his nose in a tight, one-beat facsimile of a laugh.

"You either go to the authorities, or you ask for it back." For the first time there was sympathy on his face. "But neither will result in you seeing your money again."

"Neither will . . . " Nathan's instinct was to repeat the words since they didn't make sense to him.

"Mr. Fletcher," said Plotkin. "Your money is gone."

SEMANTIC
EVACUATION

ACCORDING TO THE hometown report that every Middle Rock student has to write in fourth grade, the township of what is now called Middle Rock was founded in 1694, but it wasn't until 1702 that Duty Williamson arrived on its shores.

Duty was the eleventh daughter of a Devonshire preacher who had named all his daughters after Christian virtues. At fourteen, when finally her family was able to marry her off, Duty headed to the New World with her husband, an anemic apprentice in her father's parish actually named Peter P. Parish. It was Duty who suggested they land on the peninsula of Long Island that she spotted from the sea and named instantly, before even docking, as "a lush and floraly spread whose sumptuous beauty belies its deep serpentine sin." It was Duty who gave the call for their several servants and many slaves to shoot indiscriminately at the Matinecock Indians, so that they could safely settle and begin to help spread the good news of Christian brotherly love. And it was Duty who demanded a plot of land overlooking the Long Island Sound, and who was chased off the first acre in which she tried to plant her flag, and then the next one, and then the next one after that. One by one, she went to the giant estates that lined the coast of the peninsula, and one by one she was told that there was plenty of land to be had in the interior and to please find her way off the premises before the owner called upon his own slaves to chase her off themselves.

So Duty and Peter were sent inland, basically to about where Spring Avenue Road is right now. They set up a church on the same spot which is now occupied by Middle Rock's third CVS, and the only one that's open twenty-four hours. The Parishes had sixteen children of their own, and it is said that with each child, Duty grew more and more insane. She had never recovered from the "frank lack of Christian characteristick" that her landsmen displayed, and now, into her late twenties, it was all she talked about. Each Sunday, while her husband preached, Duty would shout from the pews, "A most unwelcoming flock!" over and over while Peter closed his eyes and tried to picture St. Paul.

During the week, Duty rode through town on her horse, sitting in the cradle of her enviable calfskin saddle, which her husband had procured to placate her. But she was not to be placated! No, instead she rode past all the estates that overlooked the Sound, screaming about Christ's rights to land and Christ's right to evict in the name of his servants, and how she and Peter had been sent in Christ's name to occupy the land. She stopped intermittently at people's front doors, her six youngest children trailing behind her, screaming about hellfire.

Finally, John Constable, who had a plum piece of land that looked straight into Connecticut, and who therefore was the recipient of more than several of Duty's visits, had had enough. His own wife reported that she could hear Goodwife Parish screaming even long after her rounds had adjourned for the day. So John went to Reverend Parish's church one day and demanded he order his wife to cease her ranting and try to restore some peace.

"Uh, I've tried that," Reverend Parish said.

"We are prepared to offer her that in the stead of land, we will call the entire peninsula after her good name," John said. "We will call it Duty's Spit," *spit* being another name for *peninsula*.

"Really, she just wants the land," the Reverend Parish pleaded.

He was born weak of will, and Duty had ironed out any small bits of stamina that he'd had. By the time he was thirty, he looked like he was seventy. "Can you please just give her the land instead?"

"No."

"What if I excommunicate you?"

"I will have my slaves murder you and your family. I will have them choke you with apples and put you onto a spit"—here *spit* means the stick you poke through an animal before you cook it— "and eat you for a fortnight feast!"

Reverend Parish pursed his lips and squinted his eyes, and nodded in consideration. "Naming should be good. Let's try it."

And so the area was named Duty's Spit, but as time went by, it was recommended that *spit* be removed from the name of the region, because of spit's alternative meaning as saliva, and a hundred years after the death of Duty Parish, who did indeed, as anyone could have predicted, die in a Colonial version of a shootout with the police, *Spit* was replaced with *Head,* which is also a name for a peninsula.

Over the years, Duty's Head became populated by wealthy people from New York City who, like Columbus, erroneously believed they'd discovered the Hamptons. Long Island itself eventually became highly populated, mostly by more white people. The natives were either killed or driven to Connecticut, where they found refuge on or around dedicated reservations, only to be remembered in the naming of an errant public park or a middle school.

And each part of Long Island came to represent something different. The south shore grew into a highly populated, working-class community of mostly Irish immigrants. The north shore was more spacious, for the wealthier German and Italian immigrants. Duty's Head became Duty Head when the train system that would not accommodate an apostrophe on its signage was erected, then became Middle Rock immediately when the mayor went to cut the ribbon on that new train station and heard someone say the name Duty Head aloud.

Middle Rock was the northest, the most spacious, the wealthiest. Even as time went on, those large estates that Duty coveted were not diced into smaller plots, and even the interior plots of land remained large: A polo field where the high school now is. A golf course where the row of synagogues now sits. A high-end pedestrian shopping mall was built just outside the city limits.

In other words, Middle Rock was always about money.

The John Constable estate passed through his relatives' hands over the generations, until, in 1945, his great-great-great-great-great-grandson, who had gotten himself into more than $1 million of casino gambling debt, sold it to a newly flush immigrant named Zelig Fletcher.

Zelig Fletcher had come over to America from Poland as a stowaway in the bowels of an ocean liner in 1942. Two of his brothers had already perished in concentration camps by 1941, and two other brothers had been sent to a work camp in Siberia, though, as the months went on and he didn't hear from them, he imagined that that was no longer true. He imagined that they were gone, the way everyone was gone. He had seen his own father shot in the street for sneezing while a Nazi was talking to him, and that was not even the worst thing that had happened to him by the time he was twenty-one.

Zelig had been hiding for weeks in the basement lab of the abandoned university's science building when a young man wearing a tattered yarmulke sought the same shelter. There the young man, whose name was Chaim, found Zelig, starved and malnourished, hallucinating that bright beams of light were coming to take him away—beams he imagined were the souls of his dead parents and brothers, eager to take him to a layer of atmosphere that hovered above the Earth, where they would feed him and hide him. Yes, by then he could not imagine freedom, just a safer hiding spot.

Chaim had spent his first two hours in the lab sitting inside a cabinet, waiting out whoever he worried was following him. Afterward, he heard a gasping—a death rattle, it seemed—from beneath a desk and crawled with terrified trepidation to investigate it. What Chaim found was Zelig, tall but diminished, unable to hold up his head, and yammering nonsense in Yiddish. Chaim took the last of his own water and applied it to Zelig's mouth. Chaim shared with him half of a potato and then gave him a boiled egg, which he'd purchased on the black market two days before.

They stayed in the lab for two days, saving their strength by not moving or talking very much. Chaim, who was a chemist, was able to rig the lab sink so that it produced something that looked like water, and then he'd boil it in a beaker.

The next day, Chaim began to vomit uncontrollably. It was unclear why, whether it was something from the water or because he had some kind of illness he'd brought in from the streets. Zelig asked what he should do—if there was something he could do to help, or failing help, if there was someone he should get word to.

But Chaim had the black eyes of the doomed. He knew he'd been on borrowed time for the last few years; all of them had been. He told Zelig about a ship that was leaving for the United States in a few days. He told Zelig his plan to go to America and create an insulation material out of a special polymer formula he had. The insulation could be used for warmth or for shock absorption, since it was porous and light but also sturdy. Chaim was going to go to the United States to meet his wife, who had made it out the year before, pregnant with their first child.

But Chaim grew even sicker overnight with whatever it was he had: typhus, dysentery, malnutrition, exposure. By morning, he couldn't even stand up. By the next morning, he would no longer take water.

By then, he hadn't spoken in a day. His last words were "Do, nemen dem"—"Here, take this." It was in the dark of night and Zelig couldn't see what was being put into his hand but when he woke after a terrified sleep, he found it was still there and that Chaim was dead.

Zelig looked down at the gift that had been the young man's last act: a handwritten note with the time and date of the ocean liner's departure, a code word in order to secure passage on it—*freyheyt* was the word—and also the formula for the polymer that he'd told Zelig about. Zelig took the yarmulke from Chaim's head and wrapped the dead boy in one of the sheets that had been draped over the lab equipment before the place had been abandoned. He said kaddish for Chaim, because he knew Chaim would want that, and waited for sundown so that he could head to the port.

That night, Zelig met the boat at the port in Gdańsk wearing the young man's yarmulke. At the dock, he walked over to a dozen Jewish men in long black coats and long beards and black hats who were standing together and said the code word and was welcomed to their group. They spoke to Zelig in Yiddish and encouraged him to join them. Zelig introduced himself as Chaim, a chemistry student from the university. One of them gave him a coat, since the weather was snowy and Zelig had been inside since the autumn. Another gave him the hat he'd been carrying—a fur shtreimel that had belonged to his father. And then they also gave him a prayer book. The men didn't ask what had happened to him; in those days, you didn't ask those things of a man who looked like that because what did it matter? The details might have been different but the story was always the same.

The men assembled to pray, and Zelig began to pray with them, just to fit in and not set off any suspicions. He prayed and he prayed the whole time he was with them, three times a day like he had been taught in school. And then, for all practical purposes, he wasn't an impostor anymore.

The passage took forty-seven days, and when the ship's passengers disembarked, they were too starved and exhausted to be as terrified or grateful as they should have been. On that last morning, in front of the Statue of Liberty, Zelig prayed with the minyan one last time, and he paused in his prayers to consider God. God had tortured him, and then God had saved him. God had cursed him, but then He had blessed him. They were even, Zelig decided. But it was best they never spoke again. Before he even cleared immigration, he had thrown the prayer book away. (Years later, when Zelig's widow, Phyllis, searched her brain for what exactly God was punishing her for when her only son was abducted, she landed on this story—the heretical throwing away of holy printed matter, the renouncing of God. A man educated to know God's power, and he curses Him! If only Zelig had lived to see the consequences of his actions!)

Once Zelig cleared customs, he followed a few of his fellow passengers to the Lower East Side, where he was given government bread and tipped off about several factories that hired men who stood out front each morning. He didn't pursue any of those jobs. Instead, he found a rubber factory on Essex Street and approached, hoping for work. He was one of throngs of Jewish and Italian men lining up for a job there, and on the third day, when the crowd thinned because of a tip that there was work in a corset factory, Zelig was plucked from the group and set on an assembly line making domed cups for toilet plungers.

There were no safety regulations at the factory, and so each day, as twenty-six men beside him poured depolymerized rubber into cup-shaped molds, they waited to see who would get hurt, and how badly. Several times each week, Zelig would hear a scream and look up to see one of his fellow line workers, his hands coated in the rubber, fingernails melted. On Zelig's first day, a man named Ivan had hot rubber spill all over his hand, up his arm, to the elbow. Two months later, the man who stood on the line next to Zelig, Lazer Besser, told him that he'd seen Ivan's wife in the street the other day. She worked now doing laundry, because Ivan stayed at home screaming for God to take him every day, every night holding a blade to his wrists, every morning cursing himself for his cowardice.

At the factory, every day a person was taken out by the foreman, never to be seen again. And every day, Zelig, who had always been good with numbers, saw that soon it would be his turn. He had to get out.

The factory owner, a fat Jew who could sweat in any kind of weather, left daily for lunch at home at noon. Zelig's lunch break was 12:37 to 12:49 P.M. Zelig would wait outside the factory, eating his cabbage sandwich, hoping that one day the factory owner would return from his lunch in time for Zelig to catch him.

Seven months later, it finally happened.

The factory owner was returning to the factory, and Zelig, who made four dollars a day doing work that was statistically guaranteed to disable him, blocked him from entrance.

"What is this?" asked the owner, some panic in his eyes.

"Formula for polymer," Zelig sputtered. "To make efficient the ship."

"What?" the owner said, relaxing a little. As factory owners went, he was a nice man.

Zelig opened his mouth but nothing came out. It had all been so clear in his head. He had practiced this sentence for months. But now he froze. After all that, he froze.

"Vus?" the owner said. Yiddish. OK.

The truth was that Zelig's English was good by then. He'd been spending nights teaching himself chemical engineering via used textbooks he'd purchased at a secondhand store near City College. Other people in the factory went out at night to find booze or a girl to marry, but Zelig sat alone on his stoop in the light of a sodium lantern, an English dictionary on one thigh and a textbook on the other.

Zelig told him his idea, which was to create polystyrene molds in order to guarantee safe postal transit for delicate objects. He showed him the formula that Chaim had given him, and explained how adding a hydrofluorocarbon during polymerization would allow a new shipping product with not many competitors on the market. It was not the same business as rubber, no, but it was the same business as molds, and it required much of the same equipment.

The factory owner was interested and asked to see how it would be done. Zelig showed how you could use the same machines to create a weightless, fluffy glove for an object that would hold that object in place with just the slightest amount of shock-absorbing give, without ever letting anything actually hurt the object.

Even better: Polystyrene molds were not just less expensive and less dangerous to manufacture; they also created a product that was light as air, and therefore less expensive to ship. Zelig explained how this could expand his business: They could move away from producing a product that many needed into a product that *everyone* needed in order to ship the products that only the many needed.

The factory owner wasn't just nice; he was also smart. He knew to not be threatened by ideas and talent but to commandeer them and the people who showed up with them. More, you reward them, lest you risk creating your own vengeful competition. Together, he and Zelig reserved a corner of the factory to start their new experiment. Then, slowly, over the next few years, rubber molds were eclipsed by the factory's new business, which was creating foam molds to fit fragile objects which, hitherto, had broken during the shipping process.

Zelig was soon appointed factory foreman. He worked hard and lived lean; he made himself essential to the entire operation. Within a few years, he'd saved up his money and told his boss that he wanted to buy the factory from him. The owner only had daughters, and they and their husbands had moved to cities outside New York, plus his wife had asthma and wanted to follow their oldest daughter to suburban New Jersey. He took what money Zelig had, with an agreement to share profits for the next ten years as an earn-back of where he was short. They shook hands, and Consolidated Packing Solutions, Ltd., now belonged to Zelig Fletcher.

Soon Zelig had real money, and he went home to his one-room apartment in Brooklyn and stared at all of it because he would never trust banks after what happened to him in Poland. FDIC insurance sounded like exactly the kind of trick a government uses to confiscate your wealth.

He promoted his old pal, Lazer, who was still on the assembly line, and who had just gotten married, to be his own foreman. He paid him a good salary and took him into his confidence, the way the factory owner had done with Zelig. Then, some of the zoning laws in Manhattan changed and Zelig found an empty space in Elmhurst, Queens—a former textiles factory—and he moved the operation there. But there were no good subways to Queens from Brooklyn, where Lazer lived, too, and Lazer's wife, Manya, didn't like Brooklyn anyway, so they moved to one of the nicer parts of Queens, a small garden apartment in Little Neck, just on the border of Long Island. There was green space in the communal backyard, which was all they wanted for when they had children. Two years later, they finally would: a son named Isaac, whom they called Ike.

That first year they lived in Queens, Lazer and Manya invited

Zelig for an American Thanksgiving. Zelig got lost on his way there, and ended up diverted on Shore Turnpike, the road that leads to Middle Rock. He had been in America for years by then. When he arrived at what is now known as Cobbleway Park, he realized he'd gone too far. He got out of the car, and looked out onto the Sound. He heard the wind whispering to the trees, and beyond that he heard nothing, and, for the first time, he didn't miss Poland, or at least the Poland of his childhood. He saw how he could live and be happy in this place. How America could be a Poland of his own.

He drifted up and down the quiet streets until he happened upon a for-sale notice on a fence on Ocean Vista Road. He pulled to the side and peered over at the sixteen-acre plot of land that had been ravaged in a recent storm. The owner was selling it to pay off his gambling debt.

Zelig purchased that land with all that cash lying under his mattress and got to work on overseeing the onerous renovation of the main house and the rebuilding of the landscape. Lazer and his wife visited the estate to see its progress as it became a livable place. One day, Manya visited and looked around at the finished product—a beautiful home in the vast expanse of lush gardens, a greenhouse that Zelig was spending all his spare time in learning to grow plant life, the tacky European flourishes that immigrants of that era couldn't help themselves but to install, the thriving vineyard, the restored caretaker cottages, the sparkling new in-ground pool (unheard of!).

America! she thought. But what came out of her mouth was "Zelig, ir darft a froy."

Yes, Zelig realized. She was right. It was time. He needed a wife.

Meanwhile, just a few weeks later, over in Brooklyn, a young woman named Frieda Mutchnick was being forced by her mother to attend a singles dance at the Young Israel of Flatbush. Her mother was worried that Frieda was too outspoken and too tall to attract a man on her own and insisted she put herself up for auction at a veritable meat market so that a man could look at her through the prism of the aspects of her that made her a fine investment for marriage: a nonthreatening face, a large frame that would allow for prolific and easy childbirth.

Frieda didn't want to go. She wanted to go to college instead, and to meet a professional man while she took literature classes. But her mother screamed at her in Yiddish that she was going to be an old maid and a burden on them forever, like Tante Brocha. Tante Brocha, who was attending to some embroidery nearby, nodded sadly.

"Geyn! Gefin dayn mann!" her mother said.

Fine, thought Frieda. At least a dance was better than her mother's yields from the matchmaker. Attendance at the dance would allow her mother to think she was trying. So she put on her best Shabbos dress and some red lipstick, and left.

But she never made it to the dance. As the story goes, she was walking toward the synagogue at the same time Zelig Fletcher, who had been trying to park, had slammed his car, a Buick Roadmaster, into the bumper in front of him. The dance had started already, so the sidewalk was mostly empty of witnesses. There were only a few other people around, and the noise of the crash rang through the street louder than it would have on a busy street. Frieda stood on the sidewalk and watched as Zelig extracted the Buick from the car's rear bumper with such a jolt that now he crashed into the bumper of the car *behind* him. It wasn't a tight spot; the Roadmaster was a giant car, sure, but Zelig was a terrible driver.

He left the car and stood in the street, looking back and forth between both bumpers, trying to ascertain the damage. What an idiot this man is, Frieda thought. Finally he looked up at her and their eyes met. She saw from a shadow on his head that he was wearing a yarmulke. He was tall—did they make such tall Jews?—and blond, with blue eyes, features that were obvious explanations in those days for how a person had been able to escape Europe intact. What a novelty, she thought. To be tall and have blue eyes!

"This is what happens when you have cars," he said. He spoke in Yiddish. A thick accent, but those eyes.

"Not for me," she said, back in English, testing what he knew.

Her father had taught her how to drive when she got a job at the hospital in Coney Island and he didn't want her on the subways at night. "Do you understand me?" She wanted to marry an American husband. She had no interest in the haunted Eastern Europeans that surrounded them.

"I am cursed not being able to figure out how to fit in," he said, now in English as well. He was still looking at the car.

"What's your name?" she asked.

"Zelig Fletcher. What is yours?" He looked hard at her.

"Phyllis," Frieda said. "Here." She climbed into the car and parallel parked for him. Later, in rare moments of sentimentality, he would say he knew it then, right before he knew her name, that he'd gotten from this dance what he had come for.

He asked Phyllis if he could buy her an ice cream, and as they walked down Coney Island Avenue, he understood that fate had always been coming for him. Remember, he didn't not believe in God; he just hated Him. On the night of their wedding, and only that night, Zelig looked up on their drive home and gave a cursory nod to the sky.

Life had somehow turned out for Zelig Fletcher. On the estate, he spent his spare time in the greenhouse, where his plants were flourishing. He was a devoted husband and would soon be a devoted father, too. He stayed close to home, leaving the country only to go to Israel with his family on occasion and to Antwerp once a year for an annual meeting of chemists who discussed advances in polystyrene mold-making.

Phyllis began capital campaigns to help fund the new temple and its Sisterhood. Within one more year, Phyllis had given birth to a daughter, then, another year later, a son. In the tradition of the time, Zelig and Phyllis gave the baby his Hebrew name first and then took the first letter of that name for a passably American name, by which the child would be called. Zelig, who rarely spoke much in public, even in small groups, stood on the bimah at his son's bris, which was at the freshly built Temple Beth Israel, just a mile down from his estate, where he and Phyllis had been married, and where their children would attend Hebrew School and have their bar and bat mitzvahs, and where their grandchildren would, too. In his arms, he held the baby who would, twenty years later, be called home from college upon news that Zelig had collapsed right in front of Ike Besser, the young foreman who had succeeded his own father, Lazer, just a year before that.

But at synagogue that morning, Zelig held his baby and announced to the congregation that their son would be called Carl, but that his Hebrew name was Chaim, for the young man who had given him a chance at life when he was just about dead.

IF RABBI WEINTRAUB was correct, and all families are a Bible story unto themselves, then the history of Middle Rock and its people and the Fletchers of course doesn't end there.

Middle Rock flourished, a haven away from the horrors of its people's history. It became the first American suburb to achieve a full half-Jewish population, and within a few years, the place looked like a WASPy country club. When the Jews escaped from Europe to America en masse in the thirties and forties, they looked around at where they could most easily fit in and lay low, and they found cover in the WASPs that populated the country. In Middle Rock, they wore boat shoes and took sailing lessons. Every mother had canvas boat bags from L.L.Bean. They wore Bermuda shorts and Polo shirts with popped collars. They fixed their noses into pointy things and dyed their hair blond and founded pool clubs and boat clubs so that the transformation was complete and no one would be able to pick them out from the general population and send them into slavery or off to concentration camps again. Their very own Canaan.

In the second book of the Fletcher family testament, lo did the baby Carl grow to a man, too quickly, and when he was in college, his father died on the factory floor and he was asked to come home and run the family business. He took a wife unto himself, the woman Ruth, and thus went on to sire three children, but it was the last of them, a daughter, who arrived just past a crucial moment in the family history when all momentum of freedom and choice for her father and therefore her mother and brothers had been frozen. Jenny Fletcher was born unto hallowed, ossified land, to a hollowed, ossified family, to a mythology that had just been struck torpified coinciding with her arrival but having nothing to do with it.

But what she was also born unto was a seemingly limitless potential, a voracious mind, a capacity for achievement unparalleled in her family or her community. She was born beneath a bright sun, to privileged circumstance, but also: Her brain was amazing. The world was hers to lose.

And lose it, she did.

That is, unless you counted the 300,000 points she'd just scored arriving on time to work in Mogul, the videogame she was playing, alone in a home that wasn't technically hers, and that no one knew she had commandeered by something not quite but pretty close to breaking and entering.

She'd downloaded Mogul at the advice of her sweet, pudgy nephew, Ari, after spending an afternoon of her grandmother's shiva observing him and his more miscreant brother, Josh, play horrifically violent videogames on their iPads while, nearby, the twins' parents debated how best to prevent their precious sons from ingesting artificially colored foods.

Jenny had been sitting on her grandmother's wilted couch on day one or two—how the days were a circle during shiva—watching people trickle in and out. Ari was seated next to her, his mouth slightly open, his tongue slightly visible, as he pored with dead eyes over his screen. He was playing a game where sprites murder fairies with arrows. On her other side, Josh was in the same posture with a first-person shooter game, an Ally decapitating a Nazi with a blade, then shooting him with a gun, then urinating on his remains.

"This is horrible," Jenny observed over Josh's shoulder.

Josh looked up but she could see that his eyes didn't register her for a full second.

"They're Nazis," he said. "Nothing is worse than a Nazi."

"But maybe it's not good to simulate murder?"

He didn't understand, so instead looked back down and kept

going. "My great-grandfather was killed by Nazis," Josh said solemnly. Implied was that Jenny was the worst of them for not doing what she could to eradicate a digital Nazi population.

It was Ari, who was more sensitive, who pushed away from his murdered fairies, swiping to another screen.

"You should try this game," he said. "I like it sometimes, to calm down."

Jenny took the iPad from him and examined it. The game was called Mogul, and it was the opposite of a murder fantasy; it was a life fantasy. Or a fantasy that involved an indoctrination to a certain kind of life.

In the game, an avatar of the player gains points by successfully living a totally normal life: waking up, going to the bathroom, eating, dressing, going to work, being at work, leaving work, coming home, eating dinner, copulating with its spouse (though there are a million extra points if this copulation leads to conception of a child), going to sleep.

The player creates an ecosystem based on their choices: the gender of the Mogul, the kind of home the Mogul lives in, the kind of family (or not, but usually yes) the Mogul has in that home, what kind of car the Mogul drives, and, most important, the Mogul's industry. While the avatar is at work, it conducts the business of that industry—anything from a hedge fund to running a gas station—and then comes home for dinner.

"Who makes this game?" She pressed a small information icon on the bottom corner of the screen and the name of the manufacturer popped up: LIBERTARIFUN, a division of HAPPITALIST CORP.

She handed the iPad back to him.

"How do you win?" she asked.

"You don't win," he said. "Or, you win if you get to keep playing. You can die in the game, but you can't win. Winning is staying alive. Making it to the next day. That's where you get the majority of points."

He began to play in front of her. He led his avatar out the door of his house to his driveway and into his car. Ari's version of Mogul was set up thusly: He had a male avatar that wore suits and combed its hair with a sharp, neat side part. It was thin and tall and wore loafers with argyle socks, just like Nathan. It had a wife who was chubby and curly-haired, like Alyssa—loving your mother slightly more lavishly than is appropriate being a trait passed down from Nathan, Jenny supposed—and twin girls, not boys. The avatar drove a Mercedes to work, which was at a pizza place in the mall. It had waiters and waitresses reporting to it. It ordered food from suppliers. It hired and fired different line cooks. The challenge of the day was that its summer staff, mostly college students, were absconding back to school. It had to replace them with low-skilled labor from around town. It was an exhausting day for the avatar. The avatar barely made it home in time for a dinner of spaghetti and meatballs, which was its favorite, and to fuck its wife before she headed to bed early, since she had a yoga class in the morning. If the avatar was late, the dinner was cold and there would be no fucking.

"You keep going to work and you show up on time and do good work," Ari said. "Then you get more money so you can buy better stuff. A better house and car."

"Ah."

"Come eat something," Alyssa said to her kids. "Put the games down."

"Here," Ari said to Jenny. "Do you want to play while I'm eating?"

Jenny considered.

"It makes the time go faster," Ari said.

Sold. Jenny took the iPad and entered the game.

It was easiest this way to ignore what was going on around her. It was easiest to ignore her mother, ignore the woman who had just said that her grandmother had tried holding on just to see if maybe Jenny would get married and have children, ignore Beamer's looming presence when she was in no way ready to even look at him again, much less talk about what happened the last time they saw each other. She wished her grandmother hadn't died. She didn't mind Phyllis, but she did mind this.

According to Mogul, if the avatar arrived at work on time, it was showered with points. If the avatar overslept, it became anemic of points. If the avatar stopped at a McDonald's on its way home from work, it wound up too weak to drive home. If the avatar didn't answer an email from a subordinate within three hours, it was docked more than a hundred thousand points and also met with demotion from an alderman kind of overseer, which made no sense to Jenny, since wasn't the point that the avatar was the Mogul? ("Well, my dad is way high up at his firm and he has a boss," Ari reasoned.) The game was pure, uncut capitalist indoctrination, complete with the libertarian drippings of achievement that allow the player some accomplishment without any examination over what exactly we were doing here, meaning literally on this Earth, in the first place.

This didn't make Jenny any less entranced by it, though. By the time her high school friend Erica Mayer came to visit that afternoon—blessedly without her baby this time—Jenny had already downloaded the app onto her own phone and was knee-deep in the droll, boring play-acting of suburban living and dreary corporatization.

"What are you doing, Norman?" Erica said, standing over her.

"I'm living, Norman," Jenny replied, without looking up. "I'm finally living."

By the time her grandmother died, Jenny's life had fallen apart. She had ended her romantic life after she spent several years mixed up in a psychosexual relationship that nobody who knew her to be the calm, deliberate, in-control person she was would have believed she'd be involved in. She was not on speaking terms with the only member of her family she could tolerate. She was living in a self-imposed exile. She had no idea that her life could fall apart even further, and here she was. No one in the history of Middle Rock, of Long Island, of New York, of maybe America and therefore the world had had the potential and rigor for achievement that Jenny Fletcher had had. When finally she fell, it was from the top of the skyscraper. And like most such falls, it was a suicide.

But hold on. Like all the other Bible stories, it's best told from the beginning.

...

"THIS IS ALL just bullshit," Jenny said on the night she graduated from high school, when her grandmother and mother begged her to stay in town just so they could have some sort of celebration: A dinner. No? Fine, a barbecue. No? Fine, a fifteen-minute champagne toast to wish her well and make it seem like she hated them slightly less.

But Jenny was having none of it. "I'm not celebrating something that literally everyone I know can do or has done. It's tacky."

"Your brothers came into town for this," her mother said, as she watched Jenny pack her bags. This was as close to pleading with her as Ruth's anger would allow. Jenny was headed to Prague for the summer to get started on an internship at the National Gallery of Art. Her mother, who had made the mistake of letting Jenny make plans with the family travel agent on her own, hadn't realized that she had arranged to leave while her graduation gown was still warm and crumpled on her bedroom floor. "We are expecting company!"

"They saw the graduation," Jenny said. "It's enough. I'm not an animal. This isn't a zoo. I don't have to perform."

"You're being a little dramatic," Ruth said.

"I'm not an animal," she repeated. "This is not a zoo."

"Sarah Bernhardt over here!"

"They get it, Mom. Don't worry. They had the same graduation. They've congratulated me. It's over. It's OK for it to be over."

Ruth sat on Jenny's bed as Jenny zipped a canvas bag, then unzipped it when she realized she'd forgotten her gigantic volume of Gombrich.

"You'll be overweight with that book," Ruth said.

"I'm fine."

"And who exactly is taking you to the airport? Because I invited guests and I intend to greet them, even if I have to explain to them that the guest of honor couldn't be bothered to stay for her party."

"Beamer said he could. It's fine."

"I don't know how I gave birth to this person."

Jenny put her big hands on her mother's tiny shoulders that night in what was almost an affectionate gesture and looked at her. But Ruth had no love behind her eyes and her shoulders showed no give.

"You're not bringing your flat iron?" Ruth asked.

Jenny dropped her hands. "I've never used it. It is a wish you made, that flat iron. It didn't come true. I'm sorry. Most dreams don't."

"A refusenik I raised. How did I raise a refusenik? I should have told you to leave, then you'd stay."

"I'm my own person, Mom. You would take this all so much less personally if you could see that I'm not some disappointing extension of your life. I'm my own person. You should want that for me!"

But does the Bible go forth with a history of the family, or the one who branches off and tries to make a go of it? What does it say of deserters? Or refuseniks?

Well, Jenny, who never forgot a word she ever read, would tell you that Abram leaves Ur for Canaan and not only does he get to be the forefather of nearly half the population of the world, but he gets two extra letters in his name. Moses absconds from Pharaoh's palace and takes the Jewish slaves with him and what did he get but to be remembered as the great leader of Israel. Jenny would remind you that it's the ones who look back who turn into pillars of salt.

What Jenny got for her desertion, however, was not a nation as vast as the grains of sand. No, what she got was her mother's passive aggression, gripes, disappointment, every comment a loaded one, and this was how she was sent off into the world, and it was also what she received when she returned, which was perhaps why she did it so rarely.

The phone wasn't much better. Every Sunday, when she called to check in while she was in Prague, she got the same treatment, muted only slightly for her mother's awareness of how easily Jenny was capable of faking a bad connection and hanging up.

"Who leaves like they're being chased out of town?" Ruth was still saying on the phone, a month later. "You should see poor Brett."

"I broke up with him, Ma."

"Now I'm Ma. Like you were raised in the street. Bugsy Siegel over here."

"Mom."

"Does he know that? Does Brett know that? He seems to think you had plans together. He came over here to talk to me, to ask if I think he should go to Prague to surprise you."

"I hope you said no."

"I said that you didn't care about anyone but yourself, and if that was OK with him, he should surprise you."

"My mother, ladies and germs."

Jenny didn't want to hear more. She hadn't wanted to think about Brett, who was happy and satisfied with life as a general concept, who was not curious about the world and didn't hunger to understand all that had been kept from them in their cloistered suburb, who wanted to be an actuary, just like his father—an *actuary*—and who wanted to replicate the lives they'd been born into. At prom, which she'd only reluctantly agreed to attend at her friends' urging and Brett's bewildered begging, he told her he hoped they'd get married someday, and that sometimes he drove around Middle Rock, wondering where they might live with the children they had, and she spent the long night with this echoing in her ears and staring down the barrel of a life that ended her up exactly where she was standing. "I don't want that," she told him. "That sounds like a terrible life to me." The whole night she looked off into the middle distance, distracted and barely comprehending anything else he said to her. How did he not understand that that was a breakup?

She was only home for thirty-six hours between her internship and her departure for Brown. She was going to study art history and economics, having grown up a disciple of her friend Sarah's father, Dr. Richard Messinger, if not his common-law child for the amount of time she spent in the Messinger home. Richard Messinger was so erudite and interesting and so defined by his relative moneylessness—a condition for many totally middle-class people who lived in Middle Rock—that Jenny began to think of money as the condition that made you boring: wealth as a crippling starting position.

Dr. Messinger was so sure of the way that outsized wealth corrupts class systems and economies; Jenny would arrive home from his dinner table lectures and be able to see up close, in action, how it corrupted even the wealthy. When she looked at the world through Dr. Messinger's eyes, she saw only folly in the Fletchers' capitalist existence. In her own house, the money sat with them at the dinner table, then watched TV with them in the living room, and part of what made the Fletchers boring and dumb, in her opinion, was that they never talked about it. They never talked about what all this money *did* to them, how it made them look to others, or how it felt for them to have it, how they *behaved* because of it. The Fletchers might not have been the only wealthy people in town, but the majority of the people they dealt with were not as wealthy as they were, and wasn't it true that it seemed like people were always thinking about it when they looked at them, like the Fletchers were a Christmas ham with all the fixings in a Bugs Bunny cartoon? Her family didn't seem to see it, though, perhaps because they were fish and it was their water—but she was a fish and it was her water, too!—or at least they didn't say it, though they were always on their guard, too.

But just down the road, farther inland, the Messingers were talking. Dr. Messinger wouldn't talk about anything *but* money. He made an exuberant case for understanding the world through its economies. He lectured about the cruel pendula of finance and inheritance over every dinner table, his own children making comically elaborate snoring sounds, but not Jenny. Jenny sat googly-eyed for a father who talked about society and its ills—who talked about anything, really. Her own father was an automaton who went to work every day, then, at night, became a zombie, distracted always, until you said his name a few times. Dad. Dad. Dad! *Dad.*

At home, Jenny sat in the living room, openly reading the volume of Thorstein Veblen that Dr. Messinger had pulled off the shelf, unable to rip herself away, nodding vigorously at Veblen's old-timey thoughts about conspicuous consumption. Old-timey and yet so rel-

evant to her purposes! Yes! This! This was all the fuel Jenny needed
to reject the values her mother and grandmother had been trying to
pump into her since birth: that anything done in the interest of a
family's protection was warranted, that money is the only true safety
in the world, that the systems that had worked till now would be in
place forever so a girl had better be skinny and pretty and with the
same kind of processed hair and processed nose that all these people
had in order to get married and perpetuate a family that would conspicuously consume into the next generation, sitting on an estate
with an electrified fence that kept out not just kidnappers, but also
new ideas and revolution, and then we would call that success!

You could appear to relent to this point of view. You could appear
to roll over like a possum and just let them batter your apparently
dead body, the way her brother Beamer did, without ever saying a
word, a facial expression so neutral that a desperate mother could just
believe that he had acquiesced to what she was lecturing him on while
god knows what was going on in his brain.

Or you could submit fully, like her brother Nathan did: getting
married, staying in town, replicating your family's family with your
own family, pushing the boulder up the mountain of your mother's
approval, only to find that it was your mother herself standing there
at the top of the mountain, kicking it back down so that you had to
start over and over and over—that there was no submittal that was
complete enough, and if there were, she had the affliction of not
wanting membership into the clubs that would have her. (What if
Sisyphus was happy? Camus asked, though no one in her family read
Camus so the reference was lost on everyone.)

Or you could do what Jenny did, which was fight. You could fight
against the whole diaphanous premise that they based their greed and
clannishness upon: that whatever they had to do for money was justified because once, a long, long time ago, Jews trusting the world and
playing by the rules didn't go so well.

But this didn't stand up to Jenny's questioning. Why must we be
so suspicious of the world if we're also so well established in it? Why
must we be so fearful when we're also so safe? Why must we con-

stantly sing the liturgy of oppression—a liturgy where we constantly call upon God to punish our enemies—when we didn't seem all that oppressed and our enemies appeared to have dispersed, and it seemed like we were getting the last laugh anyway?

Of course, you couldn't say this out loud, because all of this was a recipe for having to hear about the Holocaust again. If you tried to poke one tiny hole in their way of life, if you tried to just push back on any of their strongly held identity of persecution in even the tiniest of ways, even from *inside* its stronghold, you got:

"They tried to kill us!" her grandmother would hiss. "This money you hate, it's all that stands between you and the gas chamber!"

"Ah," Jenny would say. This was the night she stood amid a sea of college acceptance letters and was innocently trying to figure out where to spend the next four years. "The Holocaust. How novel to bring up the Holocaust."

"You are a spoiled brat," her grandmother would say. "I did not know I'd live to see a grandchild rolling her eyes about the war."

"It just doesn't make sense, Grandma. What could the Holocaust have to do with me wanting to maybe go to Berkeley?"

"They hate Israel there!"

"And the Holocaust started in Berkeley?"

"Jennifer," her mother said.

"Hitler would have loved your help, Jennifer," Phyllis said, putting up her hands. "What can I say? You would have been an excellent apprentice for him."

"Oh, so I've gone from being a Nazi sympathizer to being a Nazi intern. Do you know how crazy you sound!"

"No, you just follow in a long tradition of Jews who side with their enemies in order to survive," Phyllis said.

"That makes no sense, Grandma."

"Don't you talk to your grandmother that way," her mother piped in.

"Jews have a long history of siding with their enemies," Phyllis repeated. "They think if they show how unacceptable they know they are that this will save them. Your grandfather, who hid on a ship with dysentery in order to give you a safe life, would tell you that doesn't work! Don't turn on your own people! You're not better than our enemies if you turn on us."

"Oh, so now I'm an *actual* Nazi," Jenny said. "Got it. Great."

Ouroboros!

She'd thought she could get them to see her point of view, or at least who she was. But for as smart as Jenny was, it became clear only after her brothers were gone off to college that there was no fighting any of it. Only when the house was finally that quiet and empty was she truly able to hear how her own voice matched her mother's in shrillness when she was angry. It scared her enough that it was then that she began to shut down. Her anger became glibness; her anguish became apathy, her anxiety a studied calm. Her fight was not to fight with her family, but to save her fight for later. For only when it was finally quiet could she finally, truly see her role in her family, which was to be the person running as far from it as she possibly could.

By the time she was applying to college, Jenny understood that her job in life the minute she was freed from that house was not only to undo what she'd learned in her own home about wealth and safety but also try a little bit to right the corrupted world that her family had contributed to with their wealth and the terrible damage they'd done to the world via their literal styrofoam factory.

But how? What did it mean to run in the opposite direction of her family? What was the opposite of a polluting, wealth-obsessed, productivity-obsessed family?

She had liked the sciences, so she had considered concentrating in, of all things, quantum physics, entranced and depressed by Einstein's entanglement theory. But she didn't want to live as a scientist, stuck in a lab, or a professor. She pivoted to poetry but even as an act of rebellion, she couldn't herself find any of the value in it. She tried her hand at European history, but it all felt so counterproductive, a way of not living in the world but retreating to her family's ongoing gripes. She had a dalliance with a double concentration in theater and acting.

In a panic, she resettled on a double concentration in econ and art history because she ran out of time deciding. She did not consciously enjoy the fact that the econ seemed like a rebellion, a lifestyle threat her family couldn't abide, and that the art history was a frivolous luxury her family would be too practical to endorse. But the unconscious is a layered thing, she learned in the psychology classes that almost caused her to switch her concentration.

She went home one Passover and was talking about all her classes, and somehow it came out that her parents and grandmother were actually gratified by her choices.

"Either way, you'll end up a professor," her mother said. "If I could tell my parents that I had a child who ended up a college professor!"

And Jenny returned to campus and found she could no longer take interest or joy in her classes.

She took a summer course in English and thought maybe she'd be a journalist. She took a class in Marxism and began to wonder if she shouldn't actually go whole hog and become a political scientist, maybe working for the government. She tried to picture what her life would look like then, but she couldn't. She could only see a blurred version of herself, indistinguishable from other blurred figures in a room, doing the same small thing, and hoping it would amount to something.

That was the problem. It *all* felt so small. Every single option felt like it would just lead to the life of an automaton. She didn't much believe in fate or destiny—it was too easy to go from that belief into fully hopping on the superstition trauma carousel with her family—but she did think that it would be folly to take the opportunity she'd been given, meaning the money, and do something small. It wasn't quite her goal to pretend she didn't come from where she came from; no, the question was, for her, what would she be if she hadn't? If she could answer that, she could perhaps begin to remediate some of the damage her family had done in the world. Plus, there would be the added bonus of direction for, you know, her life.

But as much as she had rejected her family's values and religious and superstitious inclinations, she had somehow internalized the idea—an idea that would be odious to her if she were truly conscious of it—that she was special and her privilege was extraordinary and to become just another working stiff would be to spit in the face of all of that. But didn't she want to spit in the face of it? Wasn't that the plan? Not out of teenage angst but out of the true and righteous impetus to change the world!

Ouroboros again!

The problem only got worse as her liberal arts opportunities became more vast. She switched her concentration to poli-sci, then doubled in linguistics to help her study the world's inequities through money and language, respectively, because who had time for art history, or any history, when there was a world to save? By the time she had left linguistics behind in pursuit of—get this—chemical engineering (the convoluted reasoning is not worth sharing in this space), a woman from the career development department reached out and asked her if she wanted to talk. Jenny said she didn't, but the woman insisted, and so she ended up in her office at the Center for Career Exploration in a brick standalone building on a late-spring afternoon of her junior year.

"When we see the kind of path you're on, we worry," the woman explained. She was in her fifties and spoke slowly, like she was talking to a mental patient. "We worry we haven't done the best job of helping you determine a general direction for your education here. We worry you've fallen through the cracks a little."

"Well, see, I thought college might be a place where you were supposed to explore those things?" Jenny said. "I didn't read in the catalog that you had to arrive here knowing exactly what you wanted to do."

The woman stared at her. It had been a hard few years, and lonely, too. Along the way, Jenny had developed certain personality traits that had either not existed or been dormant in her in high school, where she had actually been quite popular. She had become so afraid to commit to anything—to express an opinion, to sign up for anything long-term, to buy any clothing that made any kind of statement about herself, lest she find herself boxed in on something she wasn't wholly sure of yet—that she found herself incapable of showing up anywhere as human being enough to attract another. She didn't have many friends at Brown, or any, really; friends, too, require a declaration of some sort, and she just wasn't willing to do it. You have to join a club (but what club?). You have to go to a game (but are you a game-going person?). You have to have a passion and an interest, and as time went on, she found all such exploration—despite what she said in her own defense to that counselor—a waste of time as she began to feel time breathing down her neck.

She went on a couple of dates with a few guys she met in classes or at the V-Dub, but no one serious, since the exposure of only her negative spaces and not her positive, active ones created a self-consciousness that stymied her. On the rare occasions she had sex with someone, she wouldn't make a sound, then be so disgusted by her own participation—the way her body reacted to someone else's desire, or its own—that she would spend the postcoital period not admitting to even having been there during the act: "Was it good for you?" "Was *what* good for me?"

All this was the kind of thing that made Jenny seem aloof, and, with the mean streak she'd cultivated to forestall the kind of intimacy that would lead to declarations and commitments to being a specific, nontemporary person in the world, she wasn't the best company to keep. She had overheard her roommate, Diane, telling someone on the phone that Jenny thought she was better than everyone. Jenny wanted to grab the phone and tell whomever Diane was talking to that Diane only thought that because Jenny had once observed (aloud) that Diane's concentration, marketing, seemed to utilize all of human knowledge to use it against the humans it had knowledge of. She'd thought Diane might be grateful for the revelation, but, no, Diane had turned on her very completely after that.

"We don't need you to know *for sure*," the counselor was saying. "In fact, we *encourage* this kind of searching, you are correct. But right now you're not headed toward an on-time graduation." She looked down at a folder that was opened on her desk, which contained Jenny's transcript. "You won't have enough credits unless you return to art history."

"So you'd prefer I do something that I don't think is even ethically right at this stage, just so I can graduate on time? Makes sense!"

The woman squinted at Jenny. "No. Not at all. We just want to make sure you're aware—I'm sorry, did you say art history is unethical? As a concentration?"

"I don't mean unethical, exactly, but, actually, maybe I do. I feel like I have all this opportunity, this education, this *life,* and what am I going to do? Hole myself up in a museum? Teach?" She laughed. "I don't think so."

The woman ignored Jenny's implications with a blink and a micro head shake. "I guess I just don't see how a career in art history is a waste? Everyone has a calling. It takes all kinds to make a society. You could use your knowledge of art to change the world. Is that what you're talking about?"

And sure, yes, it was, but the world to Jenny was the ecosystem of symbiosis that she lived in with her family, something she'd never admit out loud but there it was. Now she was years out of that house and she was just as much a prisoner of it as ever.

Jenny tried to speak but instead shook her head, afraid she was going to cry.

"Do you need a second?" the woman asked.

She looked at Jenny with such sympathy that it angered Jenny. No. This was not a person she would share her tears with.

"Your undergraduate degree is just a first step, Jennifer," the counselor continued. "You can take a successful liberal arts undergraduate degree and go anywhere from there."

Jenny agreed, finally—she completed the coursework for her art history concentration—but the counselor had been wrong. You graduate from Brown with a degree in art history, with honors no less, and you have nowhere to go but graduate school for art history. And she just didn't have it in her. When it came down to it, she could not square the arts with a life of substance.

So she applied to Yale to get a graduate degree in economics. They let her in because of her diverse coursework and exceptional grades, and perhaps her ability to pay full freight, but she had to spend the summer taking several prerequisites. She learned she could take them at Yale, which was good, because her bile for Providence was too great to endure even one last season there. She packed and left and played her headphones loud enough to not hear the thought she'd had on moving day echo, which was that she was now zero locations for two in terms of adaptive, successful living.

She still didn't know if she was doing the right thing; she still didn't feel the urgent direction she had been hoping would take hold of her by now. Around her, people hustled for their basic survival, and she saw from the bleachers how their need to figure out how to make money and begin their lives focused them—how it made their direction clear to them, how it quashed mid-journey questions that might have emerged about whether or not they had chosen right. She realized once again that her money was weighing on her. Once again, she was plagued with the question of who exactly she'd be without all this money—what is ironically called an advantage, but was proving more and more a liability.

Her first two years of coursework at Yale were an act of the same kind of inertia that landed her there directionless in the first place. She watched her fellow students study frantically in groups for their oral exams, but she did hers alone. The advantage she had of having roughly twelve concentrations across college made her into quite a pantomath, which was a word she learned when she'd flirted with concentrating in classics.

In her third year at Yale, she began her work as a teachers' assistant, same as everyone else her year. She was in GPSCY (pronounced *gypsy*), grading papers for a behavioral finance class focusing on Bayes' Rule, a theorem that allows one to assess probability of an outcome based on prior knowledge of conditions. She resented Bayes' Rule, and all the easy and basic ideas that people had had the luxury to codify before everything was codified and there were no new ideas left. She looked up to refocus her eyes and saw, three tables away, two people clearly talking about her behind their hands.

Now, she hadn't made any friends at Yale, either, other than some passing acquaintances. She lived alone in an apartment on

High Street and Crown. She was never invited to parties or asked out. Her main interactions were with teachers and with undergrads she had to explain the grading system to. All day she daydreamed about getting in touch with her high school friends, to check in on Erica Mayer, who was already working as an audiologist for the Board of Education, or Sarah Messinger, who was working in fashion merchandising at Lord & Taylor, but she couldn't. Jenny was so afraid that in her condition she would get hypnotized into some placid Middle Rock existence that she had to resist. Her brother Beamer, who was now doing business as her best and only friend, was frequently unavailable, even more so lately now that he was in production on his new movie. She looked around and she was all alone. All alone in her apartment, all alone in Connecticut, all alone in the world.

And it was fine, she told herself. It was totally fine that she hadn't made a new, lasting friend in six years. But something in her, seeing people openly gossip about her, well, that was it.

"Excuse me," Jenny said. "Is there—do you want to tell me something?" She could feel her heart thumping in her neck.

The two grad students were a man and woman who expressed more annoyance than embarrassment that they were discovered. The man stood up.

"I'm going," he said to the woman. "I'll see you at the church."

Jenny watched and waited. The woman gave the man an exaggerated dirty look but decided to answer Jenny.

"It's just—you're pretty ambitious," the woman said. "We were talking about your ambition."

"I don't know what you're talking about?"

The woman started packing her notebooks into her bag.

"What's your name?" Jenny asked.

"It's Alice. We all know each other's names by now. You're Jennifer Fletcher."

"Jenny, yes."

"You should know my name. There are like forty of us in this whole program."

"Maybe if you talked to me instead of about me? What do you think of that?"

Alice laughed with cold eyes. "Wow."

"I really have no idea what you're talking about," Jenny said, then felt a prickling panic at the tip of her nose, like she might cry. She turned back to her papers urgently. "Forget I said anything."

She had been so popular in high school.

Alice stood up and came over and stood in front of Jenny until she had to look up again.

"Yes?" Jenny asked.

"Are you grading papers?"

"Yes. Why?"

"Hm."

"I don't understand," Jenny said.

"We're on a one-week action where we're not showing up for TA duties and it's one thing to not join the union, really. But to be sitting here in the open doing your work is just a slap in the face. But I heard you came from a lot of money, so I guess that makes sense."

"What are you—there's a *strike*?"

"An action. In the union. The very same one that fought for you to get your stipend. And vacation time? The one that is fighting for you to be put on tenure track instead of just exploited for labor?"

Jenny was stunned. The *union*? The grad school union, as yet unrecognized at Yale, was a random, chaotic borg that operated at Jenny's periphery. She vaguely remembered someone pressing a union card into her hands during her orientation a few years ago, and she certainly was familiar with the signage, and certainly she received the emails—if you could call filtering the emails from the union immediately into her trash unread "receiving" them. She'd seen the small, impassioned gatherings of the mostly male union leadership in the quad and at the pizza place on Wall Street. It all seemed, like every other part of the campus experience, like something that had nothing to do with her. That stipend, which was about nine thousand dollars per year plus some marginal benefits, was more trouble in terms of tax filing than it was literally worth to her.

"I really didn't know," Jenny said. "And if I'm not in the union, you know? I'm not really sure what my role in that is."

Alice rolled her eyes. "Your role? Is to *join* the union. You understand that?"

"What is the action for?"

"We're trying to get a higher tier of health insurance. We're being treated like apprentices, that's the whole problem."

"Well, we are, right?"

Alice sat down. "We're not. We're *labor*. They try to convince us that they're giving us essential workplace experience, but it's labor. They're *gaslighting* us. We should be compensated for our *labor*. Anyone who works should be compensated." Alice didn't seem angry anymore; her anger had been supplanted by a uniony fervor—scripted-seeming, but fervent nonetheless.

Jenny was quiet. She didn't know what to say. She kind of agreed with the university. She also thought back to her and her brothers' summers at their father's factory. That wasn't exploitation. That was growing up. Right?

Instead she said, "Alice." It felt so good to call someone by a name, even this girl who clearly hated her. "I really had no idea about this."

Alice stood up. "Well, maybe look into it? Maybe then you can figure out a way to not undermine your peers?" She walked out, and Jenny tried to summon umbrage, but by then, she was so exhausted and defensive, so sick of the quiet that surrounded her loneliness. And she couldn't help but notice that even just a direct conversation with someone who chose to sit down with her—for whatever reason—had flooded her system with the hormones of warmth and bonding that she hadn't felt since she last visited her brother in California.

She tried to stand up but immediately had to sit down. She wasn't just tired; she was weak and hot, like she had a fever.

No, it wasn't physical weakness. It wasn't a fever. It was something else.

It was shame.

Right, shame.

Oh god, shame.

It was like a dam broke, so vast and manifest was the shame. She stood up again and was overcome by the nauseated, skin-prickling embarrassment of not having seen what was in front of her. Of having sat through Dr. Messinger's lectures. Of having been an econ student. And here she was, a scab? A union scab without even knowing it?

She sat there at that table at GPSCY for it must have been an hour, laden with the weight of the shame. It wasn't a new shame, though. No, as she labored beneath it, she realized it was a shame that had been building up and collecting and tapping on her shoulder for so many years that right then, as she finally registered the tapping as something to turn toward and pay attention to, she realized she'd been using all of her mental energy to ignore it. Her exhaustion wasn't sudden; it was merely suddenly realized.

Somehow she was able to trudge her way across campus, though she was weak and so tired it was like she'd been given anesthesia. How could she have missed this? What was wrong with her that she was given the opportunity to finally be what she wanted to be in the world—to be someone who spoke truth to power or whatever—and she'd fallen so flat that she hadn't even heard the knock at the door? God, she was so full of shit she couldn't bear it.

She went to her apartment and collapsed. She stayed in bed for a week, answering to no one, missing two of her own classes and two more that she was supposed to teach at or proctor tests for.

But there she was, laid up in bed, covered not just with the idea of shame but the weight of a planet of it: the crust layer of this revelation, but then also the mantle layer of her listlessness and friendlessness. And then there was the planetary core of the shame, which was everything that had come before: her cruelty toward her family, toward Brett, the way she held her high school friends in contempt because the accident of their proximity didn't make them good enough for her, the way she dismissed the boys who liked her in col-

lege, the way she was shitty to her stupid marketing major roommate, the way she thought she was better than that career counselor.
The way she had watched people couple and laugh and kiss on this
campus now for years like she was in her living room watching a TV
show—a science fiction TV show.

The irony of it nearly crushed her. She had been locked in a debate
with herself her whole life about how to be good in the world, and
the only thing she left out of that very private conversation she was
having was the actual work of being a nice, normal human being. She
spent her waking hours of the days of this time excavating the layers
of her behavior, and all she could find was that shame, which was so
crippling that it hurt her to swallow. She did not know how to survive this. She didn't even know if she would.

"I haven't heard from you" went a message Beamer left on her
answering machine. "What's going on? Call me. I have news to tell
you—" But the machine beeped before he was done. The machine
was full. She had ignored the urgent, then pleading messages she'd
gotten from the professor who had been counting on her presence in
those classes. She'd been sitting next to the phone when he left them,
not picking up. The sounds of the way the urgency went to pleading
but then to anger were exactly what she needed to feel the shame
even more deeply. What is it about shame, that a teaspoon of it
weighs so much more than a teaspoon of happiness or any other innocuous emotion? What is it about shame that it always feels like the
truth? If she could only feel more of the shame, went her logic, she
could get at the actual truth, and a solution.

Eight days later, she awoke at four P.M. to an urgent knocking at
her apartment door. She staggered over to it and opened it up. She
hadn't eaten in a while and found herself woozy. For a second
she had a hard time recognizing the man who stood at her door. She
could only see his features one at a time, not as a whole, but she
stepped back and looked again and the features resolved into a face
that at first she thought was a hallucination; maybe in death your
brain grants your wishes. But it wasn't a dream. It was, to her great
relief, her brother Beamer.

•••

BEAMER SPENT THREE days with her in New Haven, away from the movie set that was currently filming the second *Santiago* movie. He was worried when he hadn't been able to get in touch with her, and he didn't want to call their mother and worry her needlessly, so he'd gotten on a plane.

For the first two days, he fed his sister and helped get her onto her feet. He forced her to shower. He took her outside. He listened to the whole sordid story, not just about the confrontation, but about everything that came before.

"Why didn't you tell me any of this?" he asked.

"I guess I kept thinking it was just a temporary adjustment."

"You didn't tell me because of your bravado. God forbid you not look like you know what you're doing."

Jenny didn't like that. Her relationship with Beamer worked best when they allowed each other the grace of their egos and their delusions. She fell back asleep.

Beamer cleaned her kitchen and sent her laundry out. He went through her answering machine, listening to all the messages as he deleted them.

"I can't believe I left that poor professor without a TA," she said.

"You had to," Beamer said. "You're in an action. It's like a strike. You just have to. Actually, it's the right thing."

"It's just." She was sitting up in bed, trying to stomach the soup Beamer had heated up for her.

"I know. I'm in a union, though. This is how it goes."

"You have to be in your union. This union—it's a bunch of rich kids who have no place to put their energy. They think they're Bolsheviks. They think this is real life. They don't know that their real life hasn't started yet."

"I don't know," Beamer said. "It feels like whatever is happening right now is your real life, you know?"

"I don't know. Sometimes I think, wow, I'm getting a degree for six years total? After four years of college. Is that real life?"

"Seems so. Seems like the time is passing no matter what you do."

"So wise," she said.

"Why, thank you."

The phone rang just then. Jenny put up her hand when Beamer went for it.

"Let the machine get it."

When it did:

"Jenny, hi. It's Alice. We met at GPSCY a little while ago. I just heard what you did. Honestly, we can't believe it. It was such a power move. And—what it did? We're having a meeting tomorrow night, and we'd love for you to come and talk to the crowd about what you did."

She went on to leave information about where and when the union met. When she hung up, Jenny and Beamer stared at each other.

"I have no idea what's going on," Jenny said.

"It looks like you got a fresh start," Beamer said.

"I can't speak to a crowd about this!"

"Why not? You're a revolutionary. You're a Bolshevik."

"I got sick and depressed."

"You should do this," he said.

"Why would I do that? I can't face these people."

"But you're their hero now."

Jenny put the half-eaten soup on her night table and lowered herself to a lying-down position. "I guess I don't understand why I didn't figure any of this out. It was around me. That's what makes me so upset. Forget why didn't I do this. Why didn't I *think* of this? Why didn't I *invent* this? When will I connect my good intentions with the actual world?"

"I don't know," he said. "You didn't invent it because you didn't have to. It was invented for you. Maybe you think this isn't real life going on because you don't think *you're* in your real life. You know?"

"You're an idiot," Jenny said. Then, "Did you say you had news? I just remembered you said something."

"Oh," Beamer smiled. "Yes."

"What is it?"

"I met someone. An actress."

"Is she Jewish?" Jenny asked.

"No, Mom. Sorry."

"Mommy's going to blame you for the Holocaust."

"I'm going to ask her to marry me," Beamer said.

"What's her name?"

"Noelle."

"Christ."

"No, Noelle. But close."

Beamer laughed but the news sent Jenny right back to sleep. The last thing she heard was Beamer saying, "Well, that's one way to react."

The next day, Beamer was gone and Jenny finally got out of bed and showered. She told herself she wasn't going to the meeting, but then she found herself getting ready for it.

Finally, the evening came and she went to the church the other grad students rented for these gatherings, just a few blocks away. She walked in and saw Alice and the guy who was there at GPSCY that day with her, the one who walked away, whose name was Andrew.

Alice was the shop steward for the department. When she entered the hall Alice first caught sight of her. She nudged Andrew, who was noticeably older than they were, and he turned to her. They were standing among at least a dozen other econ grad students that Jenny recognized and whose names she didn't know. The shame threatened to consume her again, and she almost turned and walked out.

That was when Andrew's face spread into a smile. Alice and the others began to clap, and you have to forgive Jenny—she was so depleted by then, she was so starved for affection and friendship. She allowed herself to smile back and then covered her face with her hands. She listened to the applause and it reminded her of standing there, on that stage, in high school, her whole life ahead of her, and all the people who believed that she was made of limitless potential.

"Well, look who woke up," Andrew said, and when she took her hands down from her face she saw them all bounding toward her.

...

JENNY DIDN'T JUST join the union; she became the union. The dregs of ambition in her combined with the hormonal wash of the approval of her peers she had for so long missed and she was now filled with purpose.

The union was social, it was scrappy, it was maximally involving, it was so busy that the questions Jenny had prior to this about how to live weren't so much answered as it was the case that it was no longer quiet enough inside her head to hear those questions.

Her life became a rolling roster of meetings. She was on a committee that was organizing a sit-in in the bookstore in order to protest the use of sweatshop labor for the college-branded activewear sold there. She sat on a council that was planning guerrilla tactics to get the college to negotiate with the union. She was on a subcommittee in charge of posters for the upcoming union drive across New Haven for the groundskeepers at the university.

What is the word for when you know everyone is taking something too seriously, that the way it's taking over your life isn't normal, that it's a little ridiculous, that it's clearly what a bunch of rich kids stuck in a decade of ivory tower schooling need in order to think of themselves as real, living people? What is the word for the displaced energy of young people chained to academia when every atom in your body is begging you to join the world? What is the word for when you think that, truly, but then start to have those beliefs replaced with earnestness? (One of them knew the word, probably one of the German-language doctoral students.)

She let the work consume her, and, in turn, the work helped her see her place in the world. It fostered the specific part of her that loved self-righteousness, which, hitherto, had only been this yawning, unused, yes, whiny energy, left mostly dormant since she'd left Middle Rock.

It was not hyperbolic to say the union saved her life. It was the antidote to the faded vanilla person she'd become. Everyone in this new world had a fire in them; they were enraged. They had strong, definitive points of view. They had *energy*. The more time went by, the more the urgency of the union's causes became glaring and her fellow members felt real to Jenny while the other people in the world felt like background noise—like the unawoken. Did it occur to her what sedition the joining of a union was for a family in the factory business? Was it a conscious choice she made?

Who cared? She finally had friends. By then, she was so desperate for friends that each one was a drop of water to rehydrate the desiccated husk of her sense of self. She loved them for that, but also for how purposeful they were. They weren't like her bland high school friends who were all falling in line and coupling and working and marrying and giving birth now. Her union friends had sharp opinions and spiky personalities and stood up to the status quo. They cared about everything; they didn't turn away from suffering. They sat in. They laid in. They *died* in. They marched. They plotted. They worked through the night. That was what they were doing in their constant meetings, taking over large swaths of the tiny, grubby Wall Street pizza store because the coffee place a few storefronts down seemed too corporate and entrepreneurial and not quite on-brand. Yes, they were so opinionated that they even had opinions like where they should be talking about their opinions!

Most passionate union workers have a story of thunderbolt radicalization. Jenny's radicalization was slower. Sure, she let Alice and everyone believe and tell the story of their confrontation leading to her radicalization. She let it get lost in the story of what happened when she found herself army-crawling back to her apartment and sleeping for the week: that the students in the class she was TAing, upon noting her absence and hearing that it was union-related, stood up and walked out of class. (Perhaps the professor would later ascribe this to a Bayes' Rule irony? If he had a sense of humor about things, which probably he didn't.) Those students walked out and it forced the university to have a conversation with the union leadership about how to get everyone back into class. The result was not the higher tier of health insurance that the group wanted but a new rule where it became illegal to fire a TA for scheduling a doctor's appointment during class time if no other appointments were available. A small victory, but a large one in spirit. Jenny, in her convalescence, had become a labor hero.

So, no, Jenny did not expound on the fact that it was her depression and not her Marxist instincts that led her to stay home from TAing that week. She did not admit that her radicalization's early origins, of course, were based in her desperation for human contact after years of social rejection from her peers.

But then there was a series of small events that kept her burgeoning radicalization on an upward trajectory: that Bayes' Rule professor eviscerated her for her abandonment, telling her she was "ruining a way of life"; the way her eyes were now open to how the administration kept ignoring the union members' demands, which were only based on what union members actually needed to survive; the way she was having a hard time squaring her reading and philosophizing with the urgent call for making the world better—the way her shame was now quelled, pushed back down so that it didn't seem to approach the crust of her earth again.

The last of these small, radicalizing events was when she and Alice were headed to the movies on the day Jenny's car was hit while it was parked. Jenny called the insurance company and Alice came to pick her up to take her to dinner and the movies to cheer her up. Alice insisted on paying. She said the car repair would be expensive enough, and so the whole evening was her treat. It was just a movie and a burrito, but later, when Jenny was trying to untangle what made her so grateful for it, she realized it was that she was finally in a place where her money didn't matter. And that might not seem like work toward radicalization, but for Jenny to no longer have to see herself through the prism of the prism the people who looked at her saw—her response was further devotion to the union. She was all in now.

The work was fruitful, and it was endless. New Haven was special in this regard. Yale was one of the few Ivy League universities that exists in a working-class town, which the administration believed made it harder to attract talent: Harvard had Cambridge, and Brown had Providence, and Yale had a town that all its custodial staff lived in and so created policies that would benefit the college but drive away the working class. When the union would shout that the administration was union-busting and that elitism was un-American, the university would counter calmly, explaining that Yale was older than America; it had its own values.

Now, Andrew wasn't a Yale student like Jenny had thought. He had been, several years before, and had dropped out of the grad school program, where he had been pursuing a music education doctorate, but stayed in New Haven and became boisterously involved in the grad school union.

He was handsome and had the kind of massive charisma that Jenny had only ever seen before in her brother Beamer; even then, Beamer had nothing on Andrew. Everywhere Andrew went, he was surrounded by grad students. He was always at the head of a table where they were sitting and plotting schemes and warlike tactics. He was on sidewalks, riling a crowd that was about to start knocking on doors to try to get Yale's maintenance and food workers to join the local. He was leading those workers down York Street in the hundreds to show the university that not acknowledging a union doesn't mean it doesn't exist.

He was a magnet. He had eyes that locked on you like you were a revelation. Jenny didn't know if it was her alone who felt that way. She knew that she overheard someone saying that the union was a little like a cult, and she knew that Andrew slept around with some of the students, which, this person was saying, made it a sex cult. She was at the meeting where an English doctoral candidate stood up and said that he walked in on Andrew with his girlfriend and her roommate, and could it possibly be ethical to be that much older than everyone and having threesomes with the people you're trying to organize?

Why did this make Andrew more attractive to Jenny?

Jenny and Andrew's relationship was never codified exactly; they were never on a romantic trajectory, until they were. They perhaps were people who got together because of the way proximity builds bonds. But one day they were sitting in at the student bookstore— sweatshop labor, again. They'd been sitting in there for hours and

Andrew decided to lie down with his head in her lap. Jenny found herself for the first time since she'd left high school with an identity strong enough to ask it what it wanted, and what it wanted was to take the little curl that dangled from his hairline and comb it behind his ear. So she did that; that was what she did. And he woke up and looked at her and smiled and she leaned down and the identity told her she could kiss him now.

Her relationship with Andrew was more like a disease than a romance. She woke up thinking of him, writhing in her bed for him—he rarely stayed over—a subcutaneous hunger pushing her through her day. She was consumed with his whereabouts, his thoughts, the feedback loop of his eyes to her loins to his eyes to her loins. She went to meetings because she knew he'd be there. She marched because he was leading. She had never, ever felt those feelings before.

Even still, in her hypnotized state, she recognized that he was largely mediocre. That he wasn't particularly smart or ambitious—that he had nothing to offer but the promise of an offer. And yet! Yet! Even as she knew this, she couldn't control her body and mind's reaction to him. She loved it. She had spent so many years by then feeling backed into a corner. Her only real relationship to speak of had been with Brett, whom she had just been passing the time with. She allowed Andrew to take over because, honestly, it felt so good to feel like a normal young woman again. Do not tell her mother that!

That summer, Andrew went to Mexico for a six-week retreat for union workers, and Jenny, to her family's shock, went home. If it was to parade her new, supercharged self in front of her mother, she was not aware of it. What she did know was that her apartment was being fumigated and wouldn't be ready to live in again until August. Besides, New Haven cleared out during the summer, and she didn't want to be alone again when the memories of her recent jag of years-long loneliness here were still so fresh. So she went home, and after just half a day, lying in her childhood bedroom, she called the factory and asked Ike if she could have a job for the summer.

"Are you kidding?" Ike answered her. "I'll warn everyone else to up their game."

Ike's son, Max, now worked there full-time. They were the same age, and Max, who had big, wet eyes and puffy lips, was in his third year of night school at Queens College, trying to finish a pre-law philosophy undergrad degree. He worked in inventory and production; she was in drafting, having taken those three undergrad classes in chemical engineering. She would lecture Ike and Max over lunch about how much better off they'd be if the factory was organized—even for Ike, who was in management, since it would take the layer of his job that was enforcement and worker manipulation away from him. At night, she and Max would smoke pot in the parking lot and then fool around a little. She and Andrew weren't exclusive or anything, and Andrew had been careful to clarify and confirm that when she drove him to the airport to say goodbye. They'd barely spoken since he'd left for Mexico.

Few of her friends from home had gone beyond their bachelor degrees except for the smattering of them who went to law school. They were all living in the city now—Sarah Messinger, Erica Mayer, the Palmolive twins, Joy and Dawn. They would come home on weekends to swim in their parents' pools, or go to the Hamptons with boyfriends or husbands and babies or even toddlers by now. She had dinner with them once but felt like she was watching people in a play that was a mockery of bourgeois boredom. She kept picturing what Andrew would say, how they would laugh if he was sitting there with her.

"Now, who is this Andrew?" Joy asked. "Is he cute?"

Their lives weren't real to Jenny. Erica was talking about getting married. Sarah was talking about a vacation her parents had taken her on. Joy and Dawn were renting a house on Cape Cod for a week. Ridiculous. Boring. Soft. Safe.

After that dinner, Jenny didn't accept their invitations. She was busy catching up on schoolwork, busy helping at home, busy at the factory, busy visiting her grandmother, so she said. She had to resist

the backward fall into her old life—even in her contempt of that dinner, she found a warm comfort to its familiarity—especially now
that she finally had direction. Plus, she had to spend her nights con-
tinually lecturing her family at the dinner table about how unconscionable it was that the family factory wasn't unionized.

"This is America," she said. "Say what you want, but workers'
rights are an American value."

"If your grandfather could hear you," Phyllis would answer her.

"He came over here because he wanted American values!"

"He came over here so the Nazis wouldn't kill him!" Phyllis
screamed back.

All the while, her father at the head of the table, looking down at
his food, hearing nothing.

"We have enough," Jenny said then. "We should now try to make
the world better."

"Karl Marx over here," her mother said, ending the conversation.
Then, "Do you know Brett is getting married?"

Jenny froze.

"She's an optometrist. Her name is Jenny, too." Ruth kept watching her, but Jenny was playing chicken with her face—she wasn't
giving her mother anything. "You should call and congratulate him."

The last time she'd seen Brett, he'd shown up at her off-campus
apartment at Brown, crying, asking if there was any chance for them
before he made the decision to try to move on. They'd been broken
up for three years by then, and Jenny couldn't hide her shock that he
thought they still had any kind of chance. She couldn't hide her disgust, either, and finally blew up and called her mother, demanding to
know if she'd given Brett her address.

"I can't remember," Ruth said. "Why? What happened?"

"You know what happened. You probably orchestrated this whole
thing."

Ruth made her voice exhausted. "Jenny, I don't orchestrate anything. I don't know what's going through your head half the time."

"Well, Brett just left here crying because obviously I'm not getting back together with him."

"That's a shame," her mother said. "It's a shame you can't see such a nice person in front of you. He would have taken such good care of you."

They hung up and Jenny tried to understand why what Ruth said was so devastating.

"No," Jenny said at the dinner table with her family, her face still locked expressionless. "Tell him congratulations if you see him."

That night, finally alone in her room, she allowed her thoughts to turn to Brett. It was her junior year in high school, she remembered, when she was writing a history paper on anasyrma, the concept in Greek art of exposing yourself. She had finished it just as Brett came over after his trumpet practice. She was fried from writing for the last three days—she'd get an A on it, like she did on everything—and asked him to proofread it for her, which he did, happily.

"This is sexy stuff," he said. He was sitting on her bed while she pinballed around the room. Nothing made her more wired than having finished something.

"This is sexy stuff," she repeated of him in a no-doy voice with a lisp, as she did whenever he said something that didn't live in the confines of the cool vernacular that she and her friends used.

"You can be very mean," he said, but his face was full of delight.

She danced around her bedroom that night. She was wearing a skirt, and every few steps, she would stop, turn to Brett and lift the rear of the skirt, say "Anasyrma!" like she was in a Las Vegas revue, then start bopping around again, then lifting her skirt again—"Anasyrma!"—over and over. First when she did it, she lifted her skirt an inch over her knees, then another inch farther, then another over her young, tan thighs, till the bottom of her underpants was showing. Brett sat on her bed, his dopey smile across his face, staring in unfettered, unabashed love.

Brett was a cornball. Brett was too sincere. Brett didn't know how to play it cool; he didn't even understand why he should. And when Jenny tried to explain it, the answer kept running out of her reach. Coolness for the sake of coolness, that wasn't her message, was it? She lifted up her skirt for real, and she stopped bopping across the room.

Sometimes she wasn't embarrassed at how much he was so thoroughly who he was; sometimes she could really get on board with him. That night, they had sex for the first time, right there on her childhood bed, with her parents downstairs, watching *Wheel of Fortune.*

Now, in her room again on this strange, regressive summer vacation, she stood and paced. What did she care about Brett? Everywhere was a nostalgia trap. She understood from the three psych classes she had taken how aging forced a warm fuzziness. She had to stop it. She had to remember the bad things, too, or she might end up a prisoner of this place once again. Oh, here's one: She couldn't pass the upstairs bathroom after all these years without remembering the day of Nathan's bar mitzvah, when Ruth had to run to the cleaners because she'd forgotten to pick up Carl's tallis, so she tried to wake Jenny up. But Jenny was napping on the couch and didn't want to go and pretended to still be asleep. Ruth called up in annoyance to Carl.

"Carl! I'm leaving Jenny," her mother had called up the stairs. "I'm taking the boys. I'll be back in twenty."

Beamer made some noises about having to go but Nathan was obedient, and soon they were gone. Jenny stayed on the couch on her back, looking up at the ceiling when the ceiling began to darken in the corner. She sat up straight, scared. It turned damp and wet and folded in on itself. She jumped up.

She heard a moan in the distance, like a dying animal. She looked back up at the ceiling, and there she found that the spot was growing. Jenny realized that the moan wasn't new. She didn't actually know how long the moan had been going on until she heard it, so quickly had it become an ambient noise that blended with all the other noises.

By the time the moan registered as its own separate, discrete noise, it was already changing into something that was more of a scream. But the scream had a voice to it. The scream was so familiar to Jenny that it felt like it happened inside her body. She was only five. She stood up, and, more afraid of the spot on the ceiling than she was of

the sound—the sound still could have been a heater or something—
she decided to run upstairs, deeper and deeper into the house, knowing her father was there.

Her father, when she was that little, was still a figure of protection
for her, more because of the marketing of fathers to American children than anything Carl himself ever did. She ran through the upstairs of the house, looking for him, looking for her father, until she
arrived at her parents' bedroom. She ripped open the door and ran
inside but it was empty. The screaming was louder now, but she
couldn't tell where it was coming from.

It was then that she turned to her parents' bathroom door, glowing with white light and steam coming out like at a magic show. She
walked slowly, one inch every two seconds, to the door, and finally
she reached the doorknob and put her hand on it. She turned the
knob softly, worried her father was in there and needed help. She
pushed open the door a few inches and saw Carl kneeling on the
floor, in front of the sink vanity, the cabinet to it open and the pipes
that were normally hidden exposed. He was staring at them and
screaming a disgusting noise that came from beneath his sternum,
beneath his stomach, from the depths of his bowels. He had been trying to shower, and had a white towel wrapped around his waist, but
the towel had fallen to the floor, and he was naked.

Jenny turned and ran, out the door, down the stairs. She was going
to head out the door—what was happening upstairs in her home to
her father was beyond her comprehension and would be for years—
but by the time she got to the living room, Beamer and Nathan were
waiting in their Mets yarmulkes and suits and she realized she could
no longer keep her eyes open and she lay down on the floor and went
right to sleep for real.

In her bedroom now, Jenny heard the phone ring. A minute later,
her mother called up to her.

"Jennifer! It's for you."

She picked up her phone, which she hadn't touched all summer.

It was Andrew.

"Hola," he said. "I am back!"

"Thank god," she said. "I can't take another minute of this shit."

AND THEN, THE next day, just as Jenny was preparing to return to New Haven, something happened that completed her radicalization for good. It had nothing to do with the factory or with the union at school. It came from out of nowhere, when her mother knocked on her bedroom door while she was packing and said she'd just heard that Amy Finkelstein's father had died.

Glenn Finkelstein had grown up in Middle Rock; in fact, he was a close friend of Carl Fletcher's all through primary school. As an adult, Glenn worked as a salesman for a local podiatrist who had dreams of selling the insoles he hand-made to a mass market. Glenn's job entailed bringing the insoles to one pharmacy after another and taking orders; he had a salary, but the bulk of his income came from commissions, and there were only so many pharmacies in the area and only so many feet. He watched, baffled, as hard work led the friends he grew up with toward ever-greater opportunity and wealth, but he was perpetually left behind, scratching for a means to survive.

And there was his daughter Amy, who was a cello prodigy. She had three sisters, and they were all very nice and smart, but Amy had picked up a cello in third grade and had just *known* how to play it. Her music teachers called their professors. Important people came to evaluate her. The Finkelsteins became convinced that if she could just obtain certain opportunities, she could be the family's financial savior. And forget money—God had given her a gift. Remember that! That Glenn Finkelstein believed that this was a gift from God, which would also mean he could justify anything in the name of supporting it. Because this particular gift from God didn't come with the money to support it, and the Finkelsteins were desperate to figure out how to make ends meet while they waited out what should have been a straightforward process, which is the discovery and reward of talent by the world.

But that podiatrist Mr. Finkelstein worked for retired suddenly, when Mr. Finkelstein was only forty-five. He quit sales and took a course in day trading. He played the stock market in the reckless, uninformed way a person who just arrived in Las Vegas plays roulette for the first time. Sara, Amy's mother, sold baby clothes out of the basement in a short-lived experiment they called The Boutique. Glenn taught bar mitzvah lessons on Sundays to local kids. You could say that anyone could predict what would happen next, but honestly, it's a story as shocking to retell as it was to hear the first time.

Glenn Finkelstein didn't start out planning or wanting to break the law; it all just got away from him. What happened was that he came into a small amount of money after the death of an uncle and decided to invest it, not in the stock market, but in something more tangible. When Amy was in ninth grade, he bought twelve burial plots in a New Jersey Jewish cemetery on a hunch—correct, as it turns out—that eventually, in several years, Jewish cemeteries were going to become overpopulated along with the rest of the world and the Jewish laws of burial, that a person be buried alone six feet underground, would cause logistical problems that would lead to a buying panic. So Mr. Finkelstein bought up Jewish death futures, let's call them, and pretty soon he sold off six of those at a huge profit to a young, healthy family from down the block. He kept six of them, thinking that he'd use the rest for his family—but the money, the money. Surely there would be more burial plots. And so he sold four to a family at B'nai Jeshrun, the Orthodox synagogue that Glenn Finkelstein favored, during Passover services.

But that night after Passover ended, Merrick Lewinsky came over to the house to give Mr. Finkelstein the cash for the plots and Mr. Finkelstein had a sudden idea and said he had to run a quick errand before he gave him the deeds. Mr. Finkelstein came back from the errand with the deeds, and got his money.

Apparently, on this errand, Mr. Finkelstein had made a hundred copies of one of the deeds, and from then on, he began to sell them—the same plot, plot A9462, over and over. He tried to be smart about it. He would only sell to young, healthy people. He tried not to sell to any more neighbors, lest they somehow be in a position to compare the deeds. The one time anyone asked why both his and his wife's new plots had the same number, Mr. Finkelstein said it was because the plots were a duo. The lie, it just came out of nowhere. He was a nice guy, the kind of father who knows a lot of trivia and can always find a quarter behind the ear of a child. It stands to reason that he made those copies in a moment of desperate inspiration. A person endures Passover services and sees the relaxed countenances of the fathers of other families and the ease with which other people go through life; a person wonders if God has abandoned him and becomes desperate. A person also wonders if maybe God was calling upon him to act in the name of his daughter's gift.

For a while, you'd see Mr. Finkelstein in town, taking his family to the Chinese restaurant on Sunday nights, everyone in new clothing. He bought a new Pontiac. Amy suddenly had a shiny, firsthand cello and private lessons; her sister had a word processor and another one a new boom box that could rotate six CDs at once. Mr. Finkelstein was exactly the kind of man who wouldn't be able to sleep over what he had done, but he was also feeling something entirely new, which was the feeling of yes being able to sleep now that he wasn't worried about paying for Amy's little sister's braces.

Plot A9462 was sold eighty-nine times before Neil Shondheim had a sudden massive stroke at the age of just fifty-four, and died. Amy was a senior in high school then. The problem wasn't that Neil Shondheim was the first person with plot A9462 to die; the problem was that he was the second one. The first one, unbeknownst to anyone in Middle Rock, was an old lady in Brooklyn whose son had been an assistant at the podiatry office where Mr. Finkelstein had worked—one of Glenn Finkelstein's first sales. The day after Neil Shondheim's funeral, Mr. Finkelstein was arrested.

The Finkelsteins used the remainder of their money to pay for a defense lawyer, but the money ran out and they had to finish the trial with a public defender. Glenn Finkelstein was sentenced to ten years in jail, with a chance of probation after seven. On the day he was sentenced, Amy's mother made her and her sisters part their hair clean on the sides and wear floral dresses from Laura Ashley—dresses she'd bought them the previous Rosh Hashanah with the money from the cemetery plots. She brought them to the Nassau County Supreme Court in Mineola for his trial, hoping that the judge and jury would look at his four daughters and feel a little sorry. Who didn't feel sorry for the Finkelstein sisters as they watched their father from behind as he stood and read an extenuating-circumstances letter while they cried in unified, stifled sobs?

After Mr. Finkelstein was arrested, Amy's mother had tried her hardest to leave Middle Rock before anyone learned what had happened. She didn't hire a moving truck. She had an uncle rent an apartment in Brooklyn and she and Amy took turns driving her car back and forth with as much inside it as possible. But she didn't move quickly enough. Everyone knew. The morning they packed the last car, it was almost dawn when Cecilia Mayer came outside to walk the dog and just stood there, watching them. The Finkelsteins had been close friends with the Mayers, but now Cecilia just watched as Amy's mother shoved lamps and suitcases into the Pontiac. She didn't say a word. She didn't wave or shrug. At one point, Sara stopped her packing and stood and just looked at her, and Cecilia looked back. Neither of them moved for a second. The sun was coming up. It was that gray, powerful weather. Sara finally broke the stare and went back to shoving, while Cecilia turned and walked slowly back into the house.

Jenny never thought about Amy Finkelstein after she left, really, except that she knew she'd become a music teacher for little kids at an elementary school in Brooklyn, near where they'd moved. Now her father was dead, and Ruth insisted that Jenny accompany her to the funeral. Jenny didn't argue.

Glenn Finkelstein had died in a prison transfer on his way to a parole hearing. He'd tripped and hit his head on his way to the van, and that was that. His shocked family stood at the graveside burial service. It turned out that Mr. Finkelstein had kept two of the original burial plot deeds, legitimate ones, one for him and one for Mrs. Finkelstein. He ended up buried in the same cemetery he had created a nightmare for with his defrauding; for years and years, the cemetery had had to explain to a bereaved person that their loved one's deed wasn't valid—to this day, an errant deed pops up now and again. But when it came time to bury Mr. Finkelstein, they stood aside and honored his deed, since it was one of the real ones.

Barely anyone showed up to the funeral—just the family and Glenn's brothers; two or three of their closest friends from Middle Rock; Rabbi Weintraub and his children; the podiatrist's widow; Ruth and Jenny, of course. Ruth was a passionate believer in honoring the rites of death; it was part of her post-kidnapping recommitment to religion and superstition.

"I don't get it," Jenny said as they drove home from the funeral. "Why did they have to leave Middle Rock?"

"They had no money," Ruth said. "Your grandmother gave her some money, but she used it for the lawyer. The mortgage was too high. Some people, they just don't have any luck. The Finkelsteins have no luck."

"They seemed fine when we were growing up," Jenny said. "I liked their house."

"They got out before the place changed," Ruth said. "It was before the Persians moved in. It was before you had to be overflowing with money just to go to public school here." She sighed. "But it was always going to change. You don't understand. You're a rich girl."

"Uh, so are you, Ma."

"Ma."

"Mom."

"I have money, but I'm not a rich girl. When you're born with money, you'll always be a rich girl, even if you lose all of it. If you were raised with no money, you'll never feel rich."

"You don't feel rich?"

Ruth closed her eyes for a brief second at a stoplight. "I don't." She opened them. "I think the bottom could fall out anytime."

"I would love to know that feeling," Jenny said.

Her mother turned to her sharply and, before either of them could see it coming, punched her daughter in the arm.

"Mom!"

"What is wrong with you! Did you not just see what I saw?"

"I'm just saying that it would be nice to understand the world a little better. I'm trying to understand the world."

"You're a spoiled brat," Ruth said. "You see people who are like this who are so unlucky and you envy them. That's what a rich girl would do. I look at them and see a fate that could have been mine."

"He was a criminal. That's not bad luck."

"The luck was that his grandmother never thought to take a thousand dollars and put it in an interest-bearing account, so that even if he thought of doing that now, the people like you with inherited wealth are so far ahead of him that his thousand dollars would be a pittance no matter how much interest it earned. That you got such a head start—that's all Glenn was trying to do, was give his daughter the same head start you had just by being born."

Jenny didn't say another word. Ruth and Jenny arrived back at the estate, picked up Phyllis and Carl, and brought them over to the Finkelsteins' apartment for the first night of shiva, along with huge, round platters of rugelach and stacks of turkey and pastrami sandwiches and pickles and tubs of spicy mustard from Beldstein's.

At the apartment, Glenn Finkelstein's wife and daughters and brothers gathered in low chairs and rended garments. Someone poured Mrs. Finkelstein a slivovitz and then another and soon she relaxed and someone started telling stories about Mr. Finkelstein. In his death, he was restored to what he'd been before, a gigantic, beloved character, no longer a tragic criminal, just at the point when the family had nearly forgotten that he'd ever been anything else.

One of the brothers told a story about the time when they were young, when he and Mrs. Finkelstein were getting married, and Glenn couldn't afford to help her buy a wedding dress, so they sneaked into the garment factory that was adjacent to the button factory where he worked at the time and stole some white fabric. But they realized that they didn't know what kind of white fabric she'd like—silk, tulle, organza, what. So they stole a bunch of it and they draped it over their heads so that it wouldn't touch the dirty ground, but as they were leaving the factory, they heard footsteps and froze.

They heard a security guard scream, "Madre de Dios!" and drop a cup of coffee and run. The security guard had thought they were ghosts!

These men, whom Amy and her sisters had never seen before, told all these stories about Mr. Finkelstein—what a ringleader he was, how charismatic, what good ideas he had, what creativity, how much he loved their mother, how much he loved Amy and her sisters. And they told more stories that indicated that maybe he actually had been a criminal that whole time: how he figured out how to get free cable for the break room, how he "helped" Ivan Yarlburg when his factory was underwater and insurance was the only way to get him out of it. Mrs. Finkelstein was laughing so hard from the stories by then. She had been so humiliated by her recent life, and now she was laughing with these small-time thugs, like she was remembering something about herself. Jenny watched Amy watch her mother smile.

"Were we gangsters?" one of the brothers asked through laughing tears. "No! But did we know how to start a fire?"

And they all collapsed in laughter anew.

———

JENNY WAS SORRY to report that she and Andrew stayed together through the revelation that he was sleeping with a couple of first-year grad students, one of them male. She was sorry to report that he was caught sleeping with a freshman whose father filed a civil suit against the union, which settled by firing Andrew. She was sorry to report that she stayed with him throughout all of this, less because she still felt the way she'd felt at the beginning, and more because she worried she'd never feel it again.

The thing that ultimately broke them up, to her great shame, was an incident from when she brought him home for Erica Mayer's wedding, which was in Middle Rock.

He arrived on the estate with his mouth open. He couldn't stop marveling at how rich Jenny was, but also how they'd been in a relationship for several years and he somehow hadn't known it. Jenny suggested this had to do with his refusal to engage in actual monogamy, which would necessitate him focusing on her.

"You said your father owned a factory," Andrew said.

"He does!" Jenny replied, but she heard how defensive she sounded.

"This is not factory money, Jenny."

"It is if you started it at a certain era in this country. That's the problem, right? That you can no longer even do that? Isn't that what we're fighting for?"

But he didn't want ideological arguments. He wanted to know if she had a trust fund.

For the wedding weekend, Andrew was staying at her grandmother's house while she stayed in her childhood bedroom—it was the house rule that only married couples could co-bed. She had gone over there to visit him and say good night and they'd ended up having silent, frantic sex, during which Andrew kept saying, "Take it, you rich bitch. Take it, you fucking JAP."

Their relationship was over soon after that.

Not that Jenny disagreed with his assessment, or his disgust. But she'd been exposed, and he'd spat where she was vulnerable, and then there were his statutory crimes, and then there was his interest in polyamory, decades before it became Brooklyn de rigueur, and so it had to end.

"I guess I'm just sort of shocked that you kept this from me?" Andrew said, as he packed his clothing. The wedding was later that day, and Jenny had encouraged him to leave Middle Rock before it started.

"I didn't keep anything from you. I don't see what my family's circumstances have to do with you. Or me, for that matter."

"Really?" he asked. "You don't understand that?"

Her face stayed placid and blank.

"It's that you can't really understand inequity if you can't even be honest about who you are. This"—he looked around the room they were in—"I don't understand why a person has this when most of this world can't figure out how to eat."

"That's my family, Kay," she said. "It's not me."

"Exactly!" he said. "Exactly! What happens to Michael Corleone is that it turns out he is just like them!"

"You're very righteous when you're not calling me epithets while you fuck me." She stood up and put on her shoes. "Now. I have to get ready for this wedding."

And that was it. Andrew, who stared at her for a second, unable to conceive that this wasn't a fight but the end of a relationship, had no idea who he was dealing with. By then, Jenny had walked away from her high school friends, from her family, from everyone. The only person she was attached to in the world was Beamer. There was no one she couldn't drop in a hot second.

ANDREW LEFT NEW Haven soon after he was fired and went to work at his father's hedge fund. Jenny was offered his job, and she took it.

But despite how ridiculous she knew he was, Andrew's reversal on her turned out to be a seismic event in her life. It wasn't fair, what he said. But suddenly, there was something about the near-million-dollar drops into her bank account each quarter that kept making her feel like she was a dilettante, a society lady playing a charity game.

That was when she realized that it was time to start giving away her money.

First she gave a large, anonymous donation to the union. Then she gave money to several national unions. Then to other unions within Yale and New Haven. She gave a gift to the city of New Haven, for a start-up fund to fight Yale encroachment.

She donated to union start-ups in other countries. She put these donations on automatic and was left close to a negative tax bracket, so that her entire (piddling) salary from the union was hers to live on. She tried to feel the panic of less, but it wouldn't come, so she gave away even more. And on the day all but a little money was left in her checking account, she sat and waited to finally feel what it was like to have no money.

But it wasn't so easy. Of course it wasn't so easy. How could she be so naïve? Giving away your money wasn't the same as not having any—this wasn't a game.

The years passed. She never joined Facebook, but her mother was happy to let her know about the goings-on of all of her high school friends, who had moved into adulthood without question, but also without much intention. And yet things were working out for them! Erica and her husband moved from the city back to Middle Rock. Sarah Messinger and Lily Schwartzman married the Schlesinger brothers. Brett had married the optometrist and had two kids. They continued to perpetuate the environment-destroying, climate-changing, downward-spiral-economy-sustaining, soul-crushing American ideal that the way they'd been raised was the best way to live. They all had these lives, and she didn't, but that was OK. She had meaning. Right? She was lucky to have work she believed in so passionately. Right?

And this all could have been enough for her. It was a smaller life than the one she had dreamed of, but she admired it for herself in a form following function kind of way.

Then things went south with Beamer and it began to feel like she was adrift in the wind, like she could be sucked into space, a late-in-life casadastraphobia setting in.

What happened was this: She went to visit Beamer and Noelle in Los Angeles in October, for Wolfie's birthday. She stayed with them, lounging anarchically at their pool, reading books about modern painters, and wondering aloud if she missed the boat and should have doubled down on art history.

"Maybe I'll go back to school for it," she told Beamer that night, as they smoked a joint together outside around the firepit, draped over lounge chairs. Noelle had put the kids to bed and gone to sleep herself. It was just as well, since Jenny was never sure where she stood with Noelle.

"Well, you never really left school, so," Beamer said.

Jenny sat up. "What does that mean?"

"It means, you would just have to register. You already live in a college town. What did you think I meant?"

Jenny relaxed. "I don't know. I guess, maybe I could still if any of my credits applied . . . I don't know."

"You should figure it out."

"Now what does *that* mean?"

"What do you mean? I'm not speaking in subtext. I think you're getting paranoid."

"Hm."

"Wow, that was a Mom 'hm' if I ever heard one."

"Hm."

"*Hm.*"

"What did you mean, though?" she asked.

"I meant you should figure it out. I meant no one here is getting younger."

Now she sat up again.

"I'm paranoid?" she asked. "You're telling me I'm getting old."

"Well, you are." He was laughing as he stood up. "I gotta go take a leak."

But he was gone for a while, or maybe it just felt like a while because Jenny was SO! AMPED! UP! from whatever was in that weed and so she wandered around their pool deck, poking her nose into various corners until she came upon Beamer's work bag. She approached and looked inside, hoping to find the antidote to how crazy she felt, or the provenance of the thing she was on now, which felt like it couldn't possibly just be weed.

She opened the bag, and instead of a pill bottle or two, she found something more like a litany. That was the word, *litany,* that went through her head as she rifled through what must have been twenty-five different baggies and tiny amber bottles. She thought she'd find evidence of the casual California user who never really grew up. This was something different. It was, what was the word, *troubled.* She had a turn of nausea that suggested that things were worse than she'd thought. But not because of the drugs, because of—

"What are you doing?"

Beamer had returned.

"I was looking for a downer."

"It's weed. You don't need a downer."

"I'm not sure it's weed."

"You could have just asked."

"You were in there for like an hour."

"I was in there for like three minutes."

"Beamer—"

He took his bag from her.

"I don't know what to say about this," Jenny said. "Are you sick? Are you OK?"

"Am I—no. About what? What would you say about anything?" He busied himself rearranging his bag and zipping it.

"Nothing." She stood up. "I have to go to bed."

"Jenny, what's your—"

"Nothing, I have to go to bed."

"It looks like a lot," he said. "It's nothing, Nathan." When she didn't laugh, he tried again. "You're being uptight, Nathan."

"Good night." Jenny walked inside.

She sat up for hours in their guest bedroom—Jenny! Who could sleep through anything!—not thinking about her brother's health, which she should have been, but thinking about the more imminent concern that her brother wasn't what she thought he was. He was troubled. He was *sick*. He was held together by string. How had she never seen it before?

She had always thought that Beamer was like her, a person who was born into their crazy family, and who chose the particular form of resistance that was standing at close distance and mocking the thing, which was how you remembered that you weren't the thing. She had thought that they were together in that. She had thought they were the same.

She should have been worried for him, but instead she just felt betrayed. Her last thought before she fell asleep that night was not about Beamer, though. It was about herself. About the fact that he was right about one thing. She was getting old.

In the morning, by the time Noelle and Beamer awoke, she was long gone, two days earlier than expected.

A few months later, her mother called her to tell her to come home to Middle Rock for Chanukah. Her grandmother was sick, and her mother had pointed out that she hadn't been home in three years.

"It's a very busy time here," Jenny said. "We're planning a drive."

"Oh, a *drive*," Ruth said. "I'll tell your dying grandmother that there's a *drive*."

"It's actually a hunger strike? It's an action of solidarity with the food service workers who were not given pensions."

"Look at you kids playing a war. You're getting too old for this, Jennifer."

Jenny agreed to come home just to get off the phone. It was true that her grandmother had a diagnosis of some kind of disease. It was true Jenny would feel bad if she didn't get to say goodbye. At least Beamer would be there. They hadn't spoken since she left, but she wasn't mad at him, just still a little startled by the whole thing—by the *litany*.

The first night she slept there, she was unaccustomed to being home and she woke up with panic in her throat at around two in the morning to a dark, silent house. She'd been dreaming she was at a bookstore, listening to her father read from a memoir he wrote, and only when she woke up did she remember that, yes, this was true, her father had once talked about writing a memoir.

It was slightly after her performance in *The Secret Garden,* when her father seemed like he was somehow on the cusp of becoming something new, and he was—it was crazy to remember now—trying to convince her mother that he should write a memoir.

"You don't want to open up a can of worms, Carl," Ruth said, not looking up from her cooking. "One thing will lead to another, and you know what will happen."

"Isn't my life—Ruthie, isn't my life worth this? Manufacturing, it's all leaving for China. I've held it down here. I've figured it out. I think people would be inspired."

"Let's talk to your mother," Ruth said, but she really just wanted to end the conversation.

That night, at dinner, Ruth had made noisy conversation with Beamer to forestall further memoir discussion and then continued on to ask Jenny what she was learning in school, which was as absurd a topic as any of them could think.

"About Missouri becoming a state," Jenny said. "With all the other states. The Missouri Compromise."

"Have you learned about the Long Island Compromise?" Beamer said. He had a way of smiling that was friendly but menacing if you knew that he was up to something.

Jenny coughed her soup.

"I don't remember the Long Island Compromise," Ruth said.

"You probably didn't learn it," Beamer said. "It's probably not something people learned when you were in school."

"I don't know what that means," Ruth said. Then, to Jenny, who was still clearing her throat, she said, "What's with you?"

"Wrong pipe," Jenny said.

"Hey," Carl said. "That would be a great title for my memoir."

"I'm sorry, what?" Beamer asked.

"Dad wants to write a memoir," Jenny said.

"I see," Beamer said.

"It's still very much up for debate," Ruth said. "He has a job at the factory. He has plenty to do around here."

"*Long Island Compromise*," Carl said. "I like it. It shows that I was strong in business, that I knew how to negotiate. That it's all up for compromise. Compromise is the key. Yes."

"I think that's a great title, Dad," Beamer said, barely keeping it together.

Ruth threw down her spoon.

"We're not talking about this right now," she said through her teeth.

But her father soon shut down again, and that was the end of the memoir idea.

Jenny couldn't bear another six hours of just staying in her childhood bed, so she got up and wandered downstairs, thinking she could possibly eat or find something to read to distract herself, and it was there that she found Beamer awake in the living room, watching a kids' Christmas movie.

"What are you doing?" she asked, and sat down on the floor.

"I drove around a little. Now I'm watching this."

"Does Noelle make you watch this shit? Is that why?"

He laughed. He was so clearly relieved that she was talking to him that it made her hate him a little for being so . . . scared.

"I just love what a big deal they make of this holiday," he said. "And every year, it's such a crisis for them. They all get depressed and suicidal, and it's really—Christmas asks nothing of you. Imagine these people on Yom Kippur."

She lay back on the carpet. "What's going on with you?"

"I'm trying to write this rom-com."

"You and Charlie?"

"No, no. I'm doing this on my own."

"Ah. Because he's on *Family Business* now?"

"Hey, what do you think of it? Of *Family Business*?"

"I don't watch it."

"You're the only one."

"I mean it's clearly about us."

"Ha, do you think?"

"Beamer, are you crazy? Of course it is." She laughed. "You know the one thing he gets wrong? All these kids, fighting over the family business. What Jew our age wants the family business?"

Beamer laughed until this thought occurred to him: "Wait, I thought you don't watch it."

"Hm."

"What are you up to?" Beamer asked.

"I'm organizing this hunger strike that started today, but apparently it's too much so the students are taking shifts not eating."

"Shifts?"

"Twelve hours each."

"So it's like an intermittent fasting strike more than a hunger strike." Beamer laughed. Then, at the screen, "Look at these goyim."

"The elves?"

"The reindeer."

"They're reindeer. They don't have a religion."

"No, they're Christian. Like everyone else." Then he added, "I don't think reindeer are even real."

Jenny started laughing. "Of course they're real."

"You think these things are real? Look at them."

"No, flying reindeer aren't real. But regular reindeer are."

"Have you ever seen one?"

"Yeah, on TV. Right now."

"We should ask Nathan. He'd know."

And something about this made them laugh so hard for either ten seconds or ten minutes that they couldn't speak anymore, and as their laughter petered out, Jenny suddenly became deeply sad.

"I hate Mommy," she said.

"Well, you two are on a journey."

"Oh, come on," Jenny said. "You see what she says to me."

"A thing you learn in couples therapy, Jennifer, should you ever have the privilege of sitting through it, is that all dynamics exist in a consensual kind of infinity loop."

"But she started it."

"But you agree to it."

"Amazing that you're so wise now, Beam."

"I'm serious. Like, look at what you do. You're a union organizer."

"Right . . ."

"That's really something in a family like ours. Like, it's not an accident. From a character development point of view."

"What is an accident? It's meaningful work. I have meaning."

"Right, right. No, of course." They were quiet for a while, but then Beamer said, "Just, you don't seem that happy. You know?"

"What?" Jenny straightened. The amount of alarm she felt didn't feel appropriate for the way Beamer was casually saying it. "What do you mean? I'm very happy."

"I just think, you know, you could do other things. It's not too late."

"Like write warmed-over sequels?"

"Well, that was shitty. I'm trying to say something nice to you, Jenny. I don't really understand what you're getting out of this."

"Are you kidding? I'm helping people."

"You're a low-level bureaucrat."

"I'm helping people."

"You're helping rich Ivy League kids who already figured it out. It was one thing when you were a student and looking for a social life. But now you have this life where you're surrounded by students all the time, not even people your own age."

"Right. I forgot. I'm old."

"I worry about you sometimes," he said. "You were always the most competent of us. You knew what you wanted and what you were doing. But now I don't really know if you're happy." Then, seeing her anger, he put his hands up. "I'm not the enemy here. I'm saying, you've done it. You've successfully committed sedition against your family. Now you can move on. You can do more. I don't know anyone who has a brain like yours."

"This is what I'm passionate about. Why do I have to do something impressive to you if this is what I'm passionate about?"

He pressed his lips together in sympathy. "You're not passionate about this."

"I'm sorry, but what? This is my career."

"This is your job. You're passionate about pissing Mom off and showing her your contempt. I'm in a union. Trust me. We struck in 2007. I know what passion looks like. It's not getting a few rich kids to skip a meal."

"Wow."

"I'm not trying to upset you, Jenny . . ."

"I'm not upset!"

"It's just, if you went out there looking for a way to not be defined by your family, I cannot think of what is more a reaction to your family than working to unionize people. It's, like, poetic levels of irony here."

"Well, it's not making movies about a guy who keeps getting kidnapped. You get the gold for family obsession. I barely medal."

"You're taking this too personally. I am trying to talk to you. I want to say this gently: Your life is passing you by. You are stuck in a college town and you are aging now with the rest of us."

"Wow."

"No, it's true. You keep having this battle in your head against Mommy and Grandma, and Grandma's nearly dead. Mommy will be, too. What are you going to do then?"

She stood up. "I have to go to bed."

"Jenny."

"I'm tired."

"It's OK for me to know this. I still love you even though you're like this. We're all like this. We're all broken from growing up in this museum, Jenny."

"I don't know what you're talking about, Beam."

"Jenny, don't be mad at me. I can't take you being mad at me right now."

"I have to go to bed. Go do more drugs."

It was almost dawn. She stared out the window at the tree that hovered just beyond it, the one she spent all of childhood looking at. It occurred to her all at once: Beamer was one of them. Beamer was not an observer like she was, huddled with her in a corner, wondering how they got there. That was an act. Beamer was a Fletcher.

She sat up. She stood up. She packed up. If there's one thing any of them should know, it was that Jenny was disciplined enough to chew off her own leg to free herself.

The sun was just showing through the trees when she ordered a car, standing out front in the familiar cold frost of her childhood home. The car came to pick her up and headed out of town. In the backseat, Jenny closed her eyes and swam down toward unconsciousness and didn't wake up until the car pulled right in front of where she had directed it, which was her family's brownstone.

One of her colleagues texted her that the hunger strike twelve-hour shifts were too long, and they were transitioning to six-hour shifts.

She took out an ancient key that was still somehow on her key ring and entered. She turned off her phone and dragged herself upstairs and fell facedown on the bed and went back to sleep.

———

THEN HER GRANDMOTHER actually did die, which was kind of unbelievable to her. They'd joke about how Phyllis was going to live forever, and maybe part of Jenny had kind of believed that that was true. Phyllis had kept not dying, after all.

That day, after the funeral, Jenny was wandering through her grandmother's house, dodging other people, looking all over for a place where she could take a nap. She'd found the whole funeral exercise exhausting, and she was trying to avoid further confrontation with her mother.

She staggered through the house. Her hair was curly and a little knotty, though her mother had offered to have her stylist blow Jenny's hair out for her that morning, since Jenny *clearly* hadn't had time to do any one of the straight-hair *or* curly-hair routines that her mother had tried to instill in her as the absolute bare minimum for how a person should show up in the world. Jenny's skin was freckly and a little dull, though her mother had offered her some of her makeup, since Jenny had *clearly* forgotten her cosmetics bag. Her eyebrows were thick and unruly, though her mother had offered her six variations of tweezers, since those tweezers had *obviously* been in the forgotten cosmetics bag.

In her search for a place to rest, Jenny remembered the large wicker chair and ottoman that lived in the solarium. She was headed there when a hand landed on her shoulder from behind. The *annoyance* that built in her before she turned to see who it was.

"Norman," Erica said. She was holding a snotty baby whose name Jenny didn't remember.

"Noooooooorman," Jenny responded, and in those extra syllables was her declaration of all the bullshit she'd endured right up until that moment. She felt a surge of self-loathing as she said it for how quickly she reverted to her younger version—the one who had not evolved away from this place—when called upon to do so.

"Where's that Bagel Man, Norman?" Erica asked. "I endured a screaming ride with this one because I knew you'd have some Bagel Man up in here."

Erica shifted her baby on her hip, saying that Scott was off watching "the big one." Jenny nodded because she didn't know how else to answer. Forget a name, Jenny could not remember Erica's older child's gender.

Erica said her hellos and condolences to Carl and Ruth on their way to the kitchen, and then to Nathan and Alyssa, but then smelled the baby's diaper and made a garbage face and asked where she could change her. Jenny took Erica and her baby upstairs to Marjorie's old room.

"This place," Erica said. She stared up at a photo of a ballerina, placed there by Phyllis in her daughter's room, almost as a wish Phyllis was making. "Oh my god, that *eulogy*." Erica started laughing.

"That eulogy," Jenny agreed.

"Your grandmother is going to haunt your aunt Marjorie till she dies."

"Literally. Figuratively."

"Hey. Remember when we did diet pills that night in here and were just screaming all night?"

"Ha, no," Jenny said. "This was the Night of a Thousand Shots here. With the college guys."

"But we started out in here." Erica leaned back on Marjorie's bed, a rolled-up dirty diaper near her head—god, what becomes of a person—and laughed. They'd been fifteen, and walking home from town, when two of the merchant marines from down the road who were jogging stopped them and started giving them the time. It was hot that day, and they'd ended up stealing a thing of peach schnapps from Phyllis's house and spending the evening with those guys behind the caretakers' cottages, getting to second base (they told each other; in fact, they'd each gotten to third with those guys). "Where was the diet pills?"

"My parents' place in the Village."

"Now." Erica had finished fastening something and the baby seemed pleased with her. "Bring me to that Bagel Man. Tell him I will give him this child if only he would give me his bagels."

Sarah Messinger-Schlesinger arrived with her parents and her sister-in-law, Lily. Jenny hated herself for her delight at seeing them.

"Charlie wished he could be here, but you know, Melissa can't travel now," Sarah's mother Linda was saying to Jenny. "She's on bed rest. I'm going to go. I'm going to stay for a month to help out. Just in time for the winter."

"All my mother talks about is this baby," Sarah said.

"What else is she going to talk about?" Jenny asked.

"What does that mean?"

"Nothing."

"Right," Sarah said, and left it there, but you could see on her face that she was remembering something.

Jenny hadn't meant to be mean, or she had no other way to deal with how seeing all her old friends, how being home—that she still called this home!—would trigger something feline in her, something that made her want to nestle into her old friends. She was not devastated by the loss of her grandmother, but she was jostled by its rendering of how time passes. It felt good to be with people who'd borne witness to the time passing, too, which is maybe the best way to describe a shiva.

Then arrived the Palmolive twins, who also had moved back after getting married within a year of each other, then a few of her mother's friends and something about the sense memory of the house, something about the familiarity of its scents and the voices and cadences, mixed with the precise acoustics of the place and its general familiarity, intensified these feelings in Jenny and created conditions for a stew of the exact kind of nostalgia she dreaded. Jenny had felt so proudly immune to nostalgia before—how disgusted she'd been when her father would drive through town and talk wistfully about how this used to be the bagel place and this used to be the other grocery store, which was better. But here in this house, at the advanced age of thirty-seven, Jenny's guard was becoming porous and her skin warmed to the temperature where it was in danger of becoming vulnerable to infection. She relaxed into the comforts of her youth, dazzled and bewildered that the people she could not wait to abandon were the only people she wanted to see, and maybe even more, that she had treated them so contemptuously (in her mind, in absentia, but still) and that they still wanted to see her—to be there for her in grief, to comfort her. What is life? Do you see why she was so exhausted?

"How's the good fight?" Richard Messinger, Sarah's father, asked her.

"It's good," Jenny said. "It's a fight."

"Don't ever stop," Richard said. "That hunger strike—we saw on the news. We're so proud of you, Jenny. What a correction for the values you were taught. You keep fighting, young lady!"

Until then, Jenny had never noticed that Richard Messinger's contempt for the rich was aimed at the Fletchers.

"Are you still painting?" she asked him.

"Full-time now," he said. "That's retirement. I'm painting portraits now."

"Of who?"

"My heroes. I'm working on a Thorstein Veblen one right now."

"You gave me his book. I still remember. Wow, that is wild."

"I did a Karl Liebknecht last year that was in a gallery show. In Brooklyn, but still."

"Brooklyn is where it's at now," Jenny said.

"Maybe. It sold at least. A few hundred dollars richer. Finally."

"Oh my gosh," Erica interrupted. "I forgot to tell you."

She stood up and handed her baby to her mother and pulled Jenny into a corner, like they were little girls.

"I kept meaning to call you about this," she said. "But I'm happy I couldn't. This is better."

"What?"

"I get to now tell you in person and see your face. Brett is getting a divorce." Erica opened her mouth the way she always did, miming a scream.

"He is? That's so sad."

Erica had wanted more from this interaction.

Jenny had seen Brett just a few times since that last horrible time, mostly in synagogue during high holidays when she returned home. The first time that happened, Brett had stared at her from the outside benches, forlorn. Over the years, she'd heard a little about him and his optometrist wife, Jenny, though apparently he would only call her Jennifer and not Jenny. Sometimes, at synagogue, she'd see Brett and the woman she and Erica referred to as Second Jenny and with whom he'd had two daughters. He was an actuary in his father's business, and Second Jenny had a shop on Spring Avenue Road, where she examined people and sold them glasses. Brett sometimes looked a little sad when she saw him, but maybe that was a projection. The truth is, he looked just like he was supposed to. He looked like Brett, but older. Nothing had changed. That was the problem. Nothing ever changed.

"Norman. *Norman.* Ask me details. *Second Jenny left him for another optometrist that she met at an optometry conference*" was what Erica was saying.

"That's terrible."

"And . . ."

"*And?*" Jenny acquiesced.

"*The optometrist she left him for was a woman!*" Erica's jaw went at it again.

But again: "Poor Brett."

"He says he's happy she's living her truth. I would die. She's moving to Cincinnati and taking the kids. It's the saddest. Cincinnati? What's he going to do? He's never lived anywhere else. Hey, how long are you in town? Should we all get together?"

"Just this week."

Later that night, Jenny and Ruth were putting food away in the kitchen while Arthur, to Jenny's annoyance, sat at the island drinking tea that Ruth had made him.

"You knew about Brett?" Jenny asked her.

"Of course I knew," Ruth said.

Beamer and Noelle walked in.

"Is there any tea?" Noelle asked. "Maybe peppermint?"

"You didn't think that would be information to share, with all the other information you tell me?" Jenny said to her mother. "Like maybe for once information I would want?"

"What information?" Ruth didn't look up from her Tupperware. "I'm not allowed to talk to you about anything."

"Oh look," Beamer said. "There's going to be a show."

"You tell me plenty," Jenny said.

Now she'd shown her mother some daylight in the dark tunnel of their relationship, and her mother saw it and was gunning for the exit.

"I don't even know what your values are, Jennifer. If you would even find it to be a big deal that someone you knew got divorced. With your bohemian life. At least Erica, of all people, settled down. She has kids and a husband and a life."

Nathan, Alyssa, and the twins walked in.

"Is there anything to eat?" Ari asked.

"Do you want Chinese? They sent over Chinese."

"Let's set the table and make it nice," Ruth said.

"Ruth," Arthur said, and the fact that this seemed to calm her enraged Jenny even more.

"My bohemian life!" Jenny said. "You could not know less about me if you tried."

"You have no values. You don't care about your family."

"My values are to not have a nose job. Or straighten my hair. That's all you have on me."

"Who has a nose job?" Josh asked.

"What's a nose job?" Ari asked.

"I am proud of my work, Mom," Jenny said. "I don't have to justify making different choices than you."

Alyssa leaned over and whispered into Ari's ear. Ari's mouth opened and he looked horrified.

"On purpose?" he asked his mother. "You do that on purpose?"

"You are in for quite a surprise, kid," Beamer said.

"Beamer!" Noelle said, laughing. Then, trying to make her face serious. "I thought we eat Chinese food on Christmas Day."

"Jews eat Chinese food all the time," Beamer said. "Literally all the time."

"That's funny," Noelle said. "We never eat Chinese food at home."

But Jenny didn't hear any of it. She walked out of her grandmother's house, down to her parents' house, middle-of-the-night exhausted at the hour of seven P.M.

There was a spell over her now, born of whatever grief she might have been feeling over Phyllis and the way a shiva's job is to fill the crevices of grief with love. The way her friends had shown up for her. The way they never accused her of thinking she was better than they were. The way they'd always accepted her, even as she ran from them.

She fell asleep as the shame resumed its encroachment.

SHE HAD BEEN planning to return to New Haven when she went to the brownstone all those months ago. Really she had been, but the shame returned, and this time it crushed her. She spent the next few days hiding out in the city, wondering what a miracle it was that she survived her fucked-up family unscathed. But the days went on and on, and she must have known from the way there was a sale on cranberry sauce at the grocery and that then the Christmas lights came down and the way her phone began ringing that New Year's had come and gone. She had been due back at work, but she was so tired, and she kept finding more reasons to sleep. She'd wake up and play a game with herself: Was this darkness early morning or late night? Was this late afternoon or just past dawn? The phone would ring and she would go back to sleep.

Eventually, the phone stopped ringing. In February, she received an email, terminating her employment from the union. She confirmed its receipt in order to get her severance, though what did she need it for? She could just sit here and wait for her quarterly replenishment, and then give most of it away and figure out her next step.

On some level, she had to assume someone was going to find her. But the days went by. Listen, she'd done a lot for the cause. She had convinced literally thousands of grad students that, yes, they were workers, that unions were for all workers, that they deserved fair pay and a career path. She had gone up against the pricey law firm that Yale hired to bust their efforts, which met with them and denigrated them at every turn, calling them glorified interns who should feel lucky. The union was now recognized by the university. She was done. She'd done her job. They'd be fine without her.

The days went by, formless and shapeless and made out of jelly. Sometimes they were fast and sometimes they were slow. There was nothing to organize her. The borders of the world became blurry.

She remembered a term she learned in a linguistics class for the way a word stops making sense if you stare at it for too long: semantic evacuation. That was what it felt like for Jenny. The world no longer had coherence. It was just a group of modules, diffuse components that dissolved into each other before you could even understand what you were looking at. The outdoors was a painted perspective of disparate objects. The houses were just bricks + doors + knobs + windows. The cars were just body + wheels + go. The people were cogs on an airport people mover. Look at the word *boat* sometime. You'll never unsee the way it just falls apart in front of you. Everything was its parts; nothing was its sum.

People who don't know the term *semantic evacuation* sometimes call this feeling *depression*.

Maybe she should be a climate scientist, or a marine biologist, or an environmental lobbyist. No! That would be a reaction to her parents, too, the super polluters of Middle Rock, with their styrofoam factory and their terrifying Rainbow River.

Her thinking was a frantic circle by this point. What would be worth her grade-A brain's efforts? What would give her *purpose*?

What would be something suitable for someone who had been given the world without having to work for it? What is a person supposed to *do* with her time? Her body? Her life? What is a life for, anyway?

She came up with nothing and retreated to books. She went to the library to reread some of the art history volumes she'd left in her apartment in New Haven. (What if she became a librarian? No! Stop!) She read an entire book that had been published about the modern painter Alex Katz by someone who had been in a class she had TAed. The book was not a recent publication.

Alex Katz had gone through a period of time where he kept trying to paint the water so that it looked like the water—not how water made you feel, but actual water. She thought about trying that, some experiment. Maybe painting the moon. You know the way the moon is so hard to actually capture? What if she could do it?

It took her a full week from then just to buy a sketchbook at the stationery store that was six blocks away.

She tried doing a few sketches, but she didn't just not have the talent, she didn't have the will. She was nearing forty and she was besieged by that same undiluted, straight-distilled shame that overtook her like a flu when Alice, who had since gone on to an actual career and family, had confronted her all those years ago and that she now realized had never really left her, a generalized sense of embarrassment over everything she'd ever done and everything she couldn't figure out she should do. Every day, she would wake up and think about her past, and every day she would squirm in the mortification of who she had been even before—thoughts she'd had and decisions she'd made. Every day she was new, and yesterday, whenever yesterday was, she'd been an idiot. And then so on the next day and the day after that.

This, too, people call depression.

But they also call it being a *dilettante.* They also call it being a *rich girl.* They also call it being *useless.*

Her only distraction came from her new videogame.

Her avatar on Mogul was a man who lived in a house and worked at a factory that produced unspecified widgets. Every day he would leave for work and oversee his staff and come home to have dinner with his family. He had jovial conversations with his children, a son and daughter, and then went to sleep, and then he did this over and over. The avatar gave his staff a bonus, and got docked 100,000 points. He allowed his staff to unionize and got docked 400,000 points. He set up strict schedules for them that included bathroom breaks, and he gained back 50,000 points. On Friday, he ordered them pizza, and was summarily fired by the overlord.

Jenny was in the middle of an HR meeting in Mogul. She had her avatar pleading for his job back, on his hands and knees, but the VP of HR kept saying no. Finally, the avatar started to do a slow, somewhat seductive striptease, pulling off first his tie, then his pants (over his shoes), then his shoes, then his socks. The screen went black briefly and Jenny was docked a *full million points,* putting her in a deficit for the first time. She looked at the screen and found that the avatar, who was naked, was lying there lifeless.

Jenny sighed and stood up and stretched. She pulled up a few apps on her phone, looking for a distraction. She opened her banking app to see if maybe the union, which was extremely disorganized, had continued paying her. It was right then that she noticed that her balance was unusually low.

Not empty. No, just low. But it was quarter's end and the same internal clock mechanism that made it so that she knew exactly when she was about to get her period without ever tracking or counting made her realize that she'd missed a distribution. She looked at the day of the week: nope, not a weekend. She looked at the day of the month: not a bank holiday.

Two days later, the money still wasn't there. She tried calling Beamer to ask if he'd gotten his distribution. He didn't answer, of course. Then she called her mother, who was with Nathan. Then she spent a good, long while sitting with the information she'd received.

She spent the evening conducting an inventory of her body to try to figure out if there was any pain, but she couldn't find any. In her scan, up and down and up and down, she searched for any negative reaction, maybe some panic—she searched for the feeling of drowning. But it wasn't there. What she found instead was something that felt a lot like calm, or no: It was bigger than calm. It was . . . contentment?

It took less than a day for Jenny to understand that she had been so dumb this whole time. She'd known the money corrupted her; she'd known the money had been the condition that created her torture. She was defined by this knowledge. Now, here was her chance. The money was finally truly gone.

Maybe this was a blessing.

She waited there, in the dark, to feel it: to feel what it might be like for a curse to lift.

———

WEEKS LATER, JENNY opened her eyes to the sound of ringing and the same old game. It was bright out around the borders of the blackout shades, so it was morning, probably, and the phone was ringing, so it was day, but obviously she'd left the sound on her phone on and hadn't woken up from any other noise, so perhaps this was the first sound of the day? It was early morning? She looked at her watch. Seven-forty-five A.M. Correct!

"What is it, Nathan?" she said into the phone. "It's early."

"I need to talk to you," Nathan said.

"What is it?"

"It's the factory. Mommy keeps saying we should sell it but we can't because Haulers owns the contract."

"Why aren't we giving it to Ike?"

"Ike was just supposed to run it in an earn-back. That doesn't help us. We need cash."

"It's not fair to Ike."

"Well, not to worry," Nathan said. "There's no way to sell it. I just had an inspector walk through. There's no way to transfer it. The leniencies won't transfer."

"Then no one should be there. No one should have been there the whole time. Those laws exist for a reason. It's kind of unconscionable that we—"

"They're grandfathered in. What do you want me to do?"

"Do you know the phrase 'grandfathered in' has its roots in slavery?"

"I cannot get into that right now. I have seven days to furlough the staff. Once you get an inspection like that, you have to send people home. I don't know why I got it inspected!"

"You sound upset."

"I just was trying for a fix where we could maybe quietly transfer the factory."

"So we could poison more people?" She thought for a minute. "So what's going to happen?"

"They're going to shut us down. Our contract will be null and void. I don't know how we're going to offload a Superfund site, though. The fines alone—"

"You're closing the factory?"

"Jenny, we're totally screwed. Why are you the only one who doesn't get that?"

She rolled over on her stomach and looked beyond the shades. It was winter, a cold and sparkling day that felt like a rebuke on her. How time was passing.

"I don't know, Nathan. Maybe this is the answer. Maybe this is our destiny. Didn't you always wonder what this would be like? Didn't you always wonder if maybe the money was the problem for us in the first place?"

Nathan didn't speak for a second. When he did, his voice was low and confused. "What exactly do you think our problems were in the first place, Jenny? Because my only problem is that I don't have any money left."

"Really? What did you do with all of it?"

"I'm saying in general. Forthcoming."

"You have a job, Nathan. You have a job and I know you and there's literally no way you've spent your money."

"This is existential for our family, Jenny. Do you understand that?"

"Do I understand what? Are you whispering?"

"I don't want Alyssa to hear me."

"She doesn't *know*? Jesus, Nathan."

"She doesn't need to know. Not yet. After the bar mitzvah. Maybe we'll figure it out by then."

"Nathan, I'm saying that we've had a good run. You know? All capitalism eventually fails, especially when it doesn't support its labor."

"This isn't really about labor!"

"It is. I knew people who were sleeping in their cars. We'll be fine."

"Well, I'm glad you saved your money, Jenny. Because it's not looking so good for everyone else."

She got off the phone with an uneasy feeling, but it wasn't about the money, or her bewilderment at her brother—though, if Nathan was that scared, did it mean he'd lost his money? Impossible. Maybe he was worried about their parents. Maybe this was more of an emergency than she thought, which was a thing she could only ascertain by speaking to her mother or Beamer, so she had to make peace with never ascertaining it! Or, no, maybe she'd just forgotten briefly that Nathan was his mother's emissary whom she'd fostered to codependently absorb all her anxieties. Yes, that last thing.

No, Jenny's uneasy feeling was about the factory. That was it. She got out of bed and dressed. She wanted to see the factory again, maybe for the last time.

IT WAS A good sign that she wanted to go out, right? She hadn't been outside in a couple of days by then, and she hadn't done anything beyond the errant errand for weeks.

She took the train to Elmhurst, then a bus. She'd never arrived at the factory before by simply walking up to it.

It was still morning, just ten-thirty, when she stood outside the door, ringing the bell. The factory had been locked for as long as she'd been around, but this was the first time, perhaps, that she hadn't been escorted in by someone who worked there full-time.

A man who didn't look familiar but recognized her greeted her when he saw her.

"Yes, it's me. Is Ike around here?" she asked. "Is he in?"

She followed the man through the floor while he tried to track down Ike. She waited, standing next to a giant drum of polystyrene pellets that were awaiting processing. She put her hands into the drum, out of habit, because she loved the way the pellets tickled her palms.

"He's in the office," the man said, hanging up the phone. "I can take you."

"I know where it is," she said.

She walked across the concrete floor, past the shiny brass steampunk aerators. The factory employees knew Jenny, each of them stopping her to say something like, "Hey, honey, how's your father doing?" She recognized roughly half of them. She climbed the black grate steps to her father's office, which looked down both on the drafting department end to the fore and the machine end of the factory to the aft. That was where she found Ike, sitting at her father's desk, hanging up on a phone call.

"Look what the cat dragged in," Ike said, standing up, smiling wide. "What are you doing here, honey?" He had pulled a rag out of his back pocket and was wiping something off his hands. "Does your father know you're here?"

"Nah, I just came over to see the place. I don't know. I was in town. Does he not come in anymore?"

"Not since your grandmother died."

Something about that disturbed Jenny in her bones.

"We're just finishing up our current projects," Ike continued. Then, leaning in, he said, "Trying to finish up. Of course, you don't want the workers to know yet . . ."

"You're doing OK?" Jenny asked.

"We're at the end here, Jenny," he said. He stopped for a second and laughed a little. "I keep thinking we'll get saved. Foolish."

"What will you do?" Jenny asked. "Are you just going to retire?"

He blinked in a way that Jenny couldn't interpret. "I'll be fine," he said. "I understand it. Maybe I should have been more worried about my future. But your grandmother—she told me not to worry. She told me that it would all be fine if I just kept a close eye on your father." He laughed a little. "I guess she kept me on like a babysitter. A kid grows up and a babysitting job ends, and what happens to the babysitter?" He smiled at her. "I was lucky to have this job for as long as I have. I'm old now. I'm going to retire."

"Maybe they'll figure out a way for this to work out," Jenny said. "Maybe they could fix some of the issues? Nathan thinks maybe Haulers might want to fix the place up so they could sell the contract as usable."

"I'm not worried about me," Ike said. "Look how old I am." He laughed. "I'm thinking of Max."

"I remember coming here just as a kid," Jenny said. "I loved it here. I remember—Ike, you used to do that thing with your thumb."

Ike laughed and wiggled the joint where his thumb got cut off so that you could see the interphalangeal joint moving around like a restless foot beneath a blanket.

"I thought Max could take over," Ike continued. "Once I saw that one of you kids wasn't interested, I thought Max would take over. And he learned everything he needed to know from me. Now what's he supposed to do?"

"Maybe you should have left while you could," Jenny said. "Maybe you should have organized here. A union could have helped maybe."

"Maybe," Ike said. "But your father didn't have to keep me on. He didn't have to hire Max. He could have sold this place twenty years ago."

"He wasn't ready to leave. It wasn't him being nice."

"Things happen. What happened with your father, I don't know what to say about it. And then the world changed. Private equity, boy oh boy. Who could have seen this coming? Your father was good to me. Your whole family was. I owe them."

"You lost your thumb in an accident," Jenny said incredulously.

"And he took me to the hospital and spent the afternoon there with me. And he paid for the surgery. Which he didn't have to."

"Right, right. And he didn't fire you. Such a hero. All things a union would have helped you with!"

"You're too hard on them. That's not the whole story. It's true. But it's not the story. You know, Mindy, she has this—she has a problem. It's not easy for her. She blames me, she blames everyone. She wanted to get ahead in life and she didn't get to, you know? She drinks too much. She gets upset. I don't know what to do for her. You should have seen her when she was young. Such a pretty girl. Always smiling. You never knew her like that but she was always smiling."

Jenny nodded.

"Right around after Max was born, she tried to take her own life."

"Oh, Ike. Wow. I'm so sorry."

"She tried to kill herself. She took a bunch of pills and then went out for a drive. She said she didn't know what she was doing, but I came home just as she was driving down the street—if you could call it driving. I caught her just in time."

"I didn't know that."

"I'm surprised your mother never told you. But your father— I told him because I had to stay home with her and make sure she didn't hurt herself. Or hurt Max! We didn't have anyone. Her parents were dead, my parents were dead. Your father sent me home for two weeks. He paid me for every day." He remembered the moment as if he was pitying it. "Then your grandmother called me to tell me she had made a reservation for Mindy at a facility upstate. I said, 'How am I going to go? I have this new baby at home.' I don't know if you know this, but your grandmother took in Max for two months. A newborn. He stayed at your grandmother's house. She hired a nurse, a babysitter. I came over every night. They were very kind to me. They were a family to me."

"You're like family to them, though," Jenny said. "Honestly. It sounds like they were just making sure you could still work."

He shook his head again, then looked at the ceiling as if he was talking to God. "I don't understand you. What happened to your father, Jenny. It changed him. It's not who he was. It's not who your family was. What do you do? It's like Mindy. She's not the same as when I met her. There was too much bad stuff. But what do I do with her? I throw her out? I move on? I save myself? I can't live like that. Who can live like that?" He stopped, bouncing himself out of the moment. "Max should come say hi! Hold on! I'll get him!"

Jenny walked over to the windows, where she saw the top of Max's head in the drafting department. He had lost a little of his hair, which she hadn't noticed at the shiva. She saw him receive the phone call from his father that she was there. She saw him acquiesce to joining them upstairs, but she also saw that after he hung up the phone, he just stood there for a minute.

But when he came in, his greeting was big.

"Jenny!"

"Max!" She walked into his embrace, which was quick and not as warm as it looked.

They caught up for a few minutes and talked about what a shame this all was, what an end this was to the era. Then finally, Ike said:

"Why don't you two go to lunch together?"

Jenny thought she saw something hesitant in Max's eyes.

"It's OK," Jenny said. "You guys are so busy here."

"We're behind on the microwave boxes, Dad," Max said.

"We can be behind," Ike said. "You kids go out."

Was she imagining the pause before Max said, "Sure, OK. It'll be nice to catch up. Let's go."

Ike hugged Jenny and she hugged him back. He smelled like Old Spice and dandruff shampoo. She clung to him longer than she should have. It had been so long since anyone had hugged her. Then he squeezed her face.

"Do you see this?" Ike asked Max, still squeezing her face. "This is my girl."

THE DINER THEY had gone to every day when she worked at the factory that summer she was home from Yale had shut down, but there was a low-rent burrito bar in its place.

"I'm fine with whatever," she said.

Amid the gaudy Mexican-food-themed decorations, Jenny could see the ghost of the diner. The booths were in the same place, and so were the kitchen and cashier. They ordered, and Jenny was finally able to look Max in the eye.

He was different. His eyes weren't wet like they used to be, and they were now colder than they were soulful.

"So what are you up to?" she asked.

He laughed, maybe a little bitterly. "What am I up to? I'm working at your family's factory until I'm laid off in a week."

"No, I mean, are you still thinking about law school?"

"I'm almost forty."

"That's nothing."

"For you, maybe."

"Is—is something wrong? Did I do something?"

He laughed again but didn't say anything.

"Max, you know I'm not my family, right? It's not my factory. I didn't make the rules. I organize unions, for god's sake."

He still didn't answer, and Jenny couldn't decide if she wanted to run, or if she wanted to lie down in the vinyl booth and just sleep.

"Do you want to go?" she asked. "It's fine. I didn't realize—I'm sorry for how this has all worked out. You know? I would have done it differently."

He nodded, but more to himself, staring down at the table.

"Maybe we should go," Jenny said. "I'll cancel the order." She looked around for someone to call to, but Max stopped her.

"I'm sorry," he said. "It's hard to see my father like this."

"Like what? He seemed fine."

"He's not fine," Max said. "He's scared, and he keeps going back to what he could have done differently. But there's only one thing. He could have not gotten into bed with your father. He could have had some legal agreement. If your father had gotten out when he said he was going to—"

"I mean, that was thirty years ago," she said.

"Exactly," he said.

"They took care of him. They gave him a bonus."

"They gave him money that he could put toward the factory."

"They treated him like family," she said.

"No," Max said. "They treat you like family. They tell my father he's family and they treat him like an employee, except sometimes they invite him over for dinner."

Jenny was now remembering that something desperate in her had seen the top of Max's head and felt a jolt of excitement. This wasn't what she had expected.

"This is starting to feel like an ambush," Jenny said.

"I just wasn't expecting to see you today," he said. "Sorry if I'm not prepared to be on my politest behavior."

The food arrived, and Jenny watched Max as he arranged his napkin and started to eat. She realized that since those nights spent on the hood of her car, she'd kept him in the corner of her consciousness as a friend, or maybe more—perhaps a place to run.

"What are you going to do now?" she asked.

"I'm going to get a job. You know? A job."

"I have a job," she said. "I work for a living."

He laughed. "I'm sorry, but no you don't."

"What are you talking about?" She looked at her plate full of sour cream and tortilla and realized she couldn't eat.

"You work, but your living is made elsewhere. Or, rather, someone else made it for you. We did. We're the ones who ran this place. My father ran this place."

"Yes," she said. "Your father is a worker. He worked in exchange for a salary, and job security."

"Right, job security. He wasn't fired when my mother was in the hospital."

"Max, I really didn't mean to upset you. I think I should go."

He looked up at her with an almost friendly smile. "You can go whenever you want." He put his hands over his face and shook his head. "I don't know why I'm so angry at you."

She was quiet.

When he put his hands down, his eyes were red and tired. "I don't know, Jenny. I don't want to be angry at you. But I feel like I look at you and it's all contained in you. All that we went through. All that trauma."

"Your father told me what happened with your mother."

"When? All those years ago?"

"Yeah."

He shrugged. "This is how it worked out for us. I accept it. Too much trauma. Trauma for all of us. Trauma for your father, I always have to remember that. That's how it started."

"Trauma. Right."

"What?" Max asked. "What do you mean?"

"Nothing. Go on."

"You don't think what he went through was traumatic?"

"I think it's a word that gets thrown around a lot. My father had a tough week. I don't know if it had to define his whole life. I don't know if it had to ruin his life. Or your life."

"Or yours."

"My life isn't ruined," Jenny said. "It happened before I was born. It doesn't matter to me."

"I've worked with him. He's there, he's not there. You can still see it on him. That's not trauma?"

"That's him. I didn't know him before. People are the way they are. I guess the way I think is that it wasn't my trauma, how could I be traumatized?"

"It's called inherited trauma. We talk about it roughly seventy-five times per AA meeting."

"I don't know," Jenny said. "My brother Nathan is a nervous wreck, and he was, what? Eight years old. He had no idea what was going on. What do you remember from being eight?"

"A lot, actually!"

"I don't remember a lot. I remember some stuff. But none of it informs who I am." She shrugged. "Everyone is traumatized. Literally everyone I've ever spoken to is. You know? You get traumatized going to pick up milk these days. I'm not saying he wasn't traumatized. I'm just saying that maybe he shouldn't be? He should pick himself up lo these forty years later and brush himself off. He got out. He should be relieved and grateful."

"I don't know if it's that easy," Max said. "You act like it's a choice. I think the *condition* of trauma as opposed to just something bad happening is the way it repeats on you. Honestly, I think of what happened to your father as a trauma of mine. My own. Really. I even think of his money as a trauma."

"Honestly, Max. I'm surprised you're so concerned with this stuff. So you're traumatized. By your definition, we all are. Move on. Were you a psych major? I would think you'd be more skeptical about all of this. I wouldn't think you're such a feelings guy."

"Why? Because I work at a factory?"

"No, I just—" She tried to regain herself. "Honestly? Now I think you're just messing with me, because none of what happened has anything to do with you. You were a baby. I wasn't even born. Honestly. I think if everyone is traumatized, then no one is traumatized." She looked at him hard. "You think I'm being heartless. I'm not. I'm saying it's something in between for him. There was a point where he could have been saved. He could have brushed it off. But he didn't. Or they didn't let him. Anytime he showed any emotion, they quashed him back down because they were so afraid of his feelings, that they'd explode all over the new rug or something."

They grew silent for a while, and Jenny, not knowing what to do with her hands, started to eat.

"Hey," Max said.

"Yes."

"Did my dad ever tell you about the project I did for school?"

"No," Jenny said, wiping her mouth.

"It was a pre-law class. It was this class about cases. We had to find a case that had been decided and figure out what had gone right and wrong."

"OK."

"I went to the Nassau County Courthouse and I dug up your father's case."

Jenny didn't know why a lump dropped through her stomach just then. She took a second and tried to make herself cool.

"Yeah, I just thought it would be interesting," Max continued.

"Well, what did you learn?"

"It was a long time ago. I don't know. I could look back at the notes. You know, neither of those guys was capable of masterminding dinner plans. They were slow-witted, you know? That's what the DA was worried about. My father always felt so guilty, hiring Drexel Abraham . . ."

Jenny noted Max's fluency with her father's kidnapper's name.

". . . but there's no way he could have done this alone."

"He had that brother."

"They were both slow. If I remember correctly, Drexel had stopped working at the factory and he never would have had access to it, much less to hold your father there and visit him day after day. There was something wrong with both those brothers. Lionel became convinced he participated in the kidnapping after a few hours in an interrogation room. He was nowhere near New York when it happened. His job swore to it. His family swore to it. He pleaded because he thought it would help his brother. He was misled by the police. Lied to."

"Honestly, I don't really know anything about it. This wasn't my—this has nothing to do with me. Like I said."

"And when the DA had suspicions, your grandmother told him to zip it."

"I don't believe that," Jenny said. Though why wouldn't she? She'd known Phyllis well enough.

"There is a collection of ten letters from prison in that file. Drexel wrote every month at first and was trying to meet with the DA again to talk about who planned the kidnapping. He said he'd been keeping secrets out of fear. But now he saw he was in prison and no one was coming for him, and the man who told him to sit tight while it all played out never got in touch with him."

"That's—" But Jenny had nothing to say.

"And then he died," Max said.

"I can't—"

"You can't believe it? You can't believe that money and power buy the ability to brush an innocent person under the rug so as not to upset your precious son?"

"Drexel was part of it."

"He was clearly just the bag man. He deserved five years max. They had an all-white jury. Those things matter."

"I don't want to talk about this anymore. I don't want you to malign my family anymore."

"I'm not maligning your family. I'm telling you what happened. In your family. And the implication of it, which still affects people. Those people. The Abrahams. I remember thinking, that cousin of yours, what's his name?"

"Oh, you don't have to pretend that you're trying to remember any of this, Max. It's clearly been top of mind for a while."

"I was just—it was a class. I looked into it. Arthur Lindenblatt, right? Did he come from money? Do you think maybe he couldn't, I don't know, that proximity to your money made him do this? Because being around it can make a person insane."

"Arthur is our cousin. He would never do that. And we don't—we don't still have money. Just so you know. A lot has changed for us."

Max paused for a second and appeared to be about to ask about what she just said, but then he thought better of it and continued. "Being around money like that, though. It tends to make people ask questions about fairness."

"We took care of your father," Jenny said.

"If you took care of my father, why is he broke? Why is he old? Why is his life over with nothing to show for it?"

Jenny stared at Max. For a second, she could ignore his aging. She could see him again over that summer when they used to make out on the hood of the car.

"That's enough," she said. "I think we're done here. I'm sorry you're traumatized by what happened to my father or by our money or whatever. I'm sorry you're obsessed. Honestly, I'm sorry to see what's happened to you." She stood up.

"Yeah, well, goodbye."

"Honestly, I think you're just obsessed with money, Max. There's more to life than money."

She heard the last thing he said as she walked out, though, because he shouted it at her back.

"Only rich people say that!"

JENNY ORDERED AN Uber and then sat in the back like a caged animal. The thing that had happened to her in that Mexican restaurant, it went so far past her ability to emotionally absorb or metabolize that she entered a kind of fugue state. It wasn't quite dissociation, but if she found that she was more comfortable sitting next to herself in that Uber than being herself, it was only because she was never given the tools to handle this kind of acrimony.

At this thought, she whispered to herself, "Dr. Phil over here."

She took out her phone and tried to find a place for her brain to rest, but she hadn't invested the time in any social media app to be native to it. She opened up the Mogul app and waited for it to load.

It was a hit and run, what Max pulled. That's what it was. It was a hit and run. Max had just run her over. No warning. Nothing.

The game was ready.

The avatar was filing for unemployment. After its horrific striptease, her avatar had been sent home to find the locks changed on the door to the family home. The avatar spent the night in its car.

Who else didn't she know hated her?

The unemployment office said it couldn't help the avatar. It had been fired for cause. But the officer at the agency gave the avatar some pamphlets for some local recovery meetings.

But also: How had she missed the one truth she could have inferred on her own, which was that all these people probably hated her and them. With good reason. The only people who didn't were people who were like them, and, well, she hated those people.

Ourobouros x 3!

It was getting cold, and sleeping in the car again might end the avatar, so that night, it tried to go find its friends, but it hadn't taken the time to cultivate them (minus 400,000 points) and instead ended up calling the coach of its son's soccer team and asking if it could crash there. The coach was reluctant but ultimately agreed.

Now that she'd gotten a glimpse, she couldn't go back.

"Here we are. Do I enter the gate?"

But Jenny looked up, and instead of seeing her family's brownstone, she realized she was in Middle Rock. She'd put in the wrong address.

"No!" Jenny said. "God, no. Um, I'll update the address. Give me a second. I'm so sorry. Do you mind—can you take me, um—I just realized I was supposed to go to the train station. I'm sorry, just."

Without waiting for an answer, she updated her destination.

But it overheard the soccer coach's wife fighting with the soccer coach about the avatar crashing. The avatar was of untoward character, the wife claimed, and could not sleep under their roof.

"Here good?"

She left the Uber and went to the platform for the westbound train. According to a digital sign, she had twenty-eight minutes to wait.

The avatar, upon hearing the fighting, sneaked out of the house and went back to its car and drove to the parking lot of its former workplace and got into the backseat and fell asleep.

Once perpetual shame leaves the body for a period of time, it's tempting to think that the shame was a glitch or an anomaly. The way it coursed back through Jenny, she understood that actually, for her, shame was the condition, and its brief absence had been the anomaly. She returned immediately to thinking that any previous version of her, even the one from a minute ago, was the ridiculous one.

But it's winter—the coldest winter in a while, and before long the avatar's biological processes begin to slow. The avatar feels a hazy euphoria— finally, a feeling!—but before it can truly enjoy it, it understands what it means. It means the avatar is dead. All points are forfeited, and the screen goes to black.

When this happened, Jenny yelped out, right there on the train platform. She began to cry for her avatar. People looked at her and she turned away but she didn't stop crying. The train pulled into the station and as she boarded it, she was so flustered that her phone fell from her hands but was saved by the platform edge of the train car. The door tried to close on it, but she was able to rescue it just in time.

"What is wrong, dear?" asked an old woman's voice, and for a second Jenny thought it was her grandmother.

"My phone screen is cracked," she said.

"Do you need to use my phone?"

"No, I'm fine. Thank you."

"Well then, cheer up," the woman said with a smile. "There are real problems out there."

"Shut up!" Jenny spat back at her and walked away and found a seat in another car.

In the dark of the tunnel to Manhattan she saw her face reflected back to her. This was who she was. She was friendless. She had no emotional connection to anyone. She had no prospects. She had rejected everything given to her so that by the time she realized how valuable it all was it was gone.

An hour later, she transferred at Penn Station to a subway to the Village. She was so tired by then that she could barely walk. She came out of the subway station to find that it was raining. She trudged home, hoping she could make it to the couch, much less her bed.

Finally she made it onto 9th Street. Everything had slowed down.

Everything was a videogame, and the avatar had no strength and the entrance to the refuge seemed comically far away. The avatar no longer had power, so it couldn't walk through the mass of slow-moving, vanilla-flavored college students coming out of the meditation studio on her block, and instead just dragged behind them listlessly, as slowly as they were moving. The avatar realized it had never fallen asleep standing up and walking but maybe there were still firsts in its future. The avatar lost all its points for not liking its friends' Facebook posts, for not remembering their children's names. The avatar realized that life had been going on even as it had been paralyzed by how to live it. It was looking like this particular Bible story would be ending tragically and unceremoniously.

But lo, the avatar finally made it unto its stoop. It held the wrought-iron rail and climbed the steps and fit its key into the door only to find the deadbolt unlocked. It pushed the door open, trying through the haze of fatigue to understand how it had left the door unlocked when it entered the living room and saw that on its couch, waiting for it, was its mother.

VEAL,
OR THE DYBBUK

FOLLOWING THE KIDNAPPING, in the years when Phyllis and Ruth were charged with Carl's mental and physical convalescence, Phyllis used the time to tell Ruth stories about the Fletchers, and about her own family, the Mutchnicks. Not even Carl knew all these stories. But, as quickly as you can say "ransom drop," Ruth had fast earned the place of confidante to Phyllis, so she had the privilege—Ruth would have used a different word—of learning some of the less savory things about the family she was now a part of.

The Mutchnicks were slumlords. Their main source of income came from renting out units of a dilapidated building Phyllis's parents owned in the Bronx, near what is now Co-op City. On the first of the month, Phyllis's tall brothers would be dispatched there on the subway in order to collect rent from the tenants.

The Mutchnicks were not rich, but their tenants—*they* were truly poor. They paid half their rent, or none of it, or offered the boys a meal in exchange for amnesty, or they wouldn't answer the door in the first place when those hardy knocks came on the first of the month.

Once, Phyllis told Ruth, her brothers were leaving the building when they saw that one of the doors of the vacant apartments was slightly open. Someone quickly shut the door from the inside as they approached. The brothers looked at each other. The bigger one walked over to the door, pushed it open, and inside they saw four families, all in one room—and when they looked closer they saw that two of the families were ones that Phyllis's father had evicted from a unit three floors up for nonpayment several months before. The next day, Phyllis went with her parents and her brothers back to the apartment building to physically pull them out of the place for violating the rule about multiple families in a single unit. Her brothers and father were there to do the pulling, and Phyllis and her mother were there to clean the apartment so that they could rent it out to the next family at now a higher rent. Phyllis described to Ruth what the families looked like, crouched in a corner, afraid, as her father and brothers came in like a SWAT team to remove them.

"Like mice," she'd told Ruth. "Frightened mice in a corner with no hole to escape into."

It was this last part of the story that came to mind when Ruth arrived to see that her daughter was squatting in the family brownstone—her daughter, whom she'd been told was a professional Socialist who lived in Connecticut.

There was a light on in the kitchen when Ruth entered the brownstone that afternoon, which was her first indicator that something was amiss. No one was home, but it was clear that someone was living there. There was milk in the refrigerator, a computer on the kitchen table, women's clothing in Beamer's old bedroom. Before she recognized it as the drab, direly unfeminine clothing of her only daughter, she thought of those families in the Mutchnick slums and how it was entirely possible that they'd so neglected this brownstone that a family now lived here without their knowing. Then she saw a pair of yellow sweatpants strewn over the side of the sofa in the living room—the same yellow sweatpants Jenny had worn each night after Phyllis's shiva, when everyone went home. They were as familiar to her as Jenny's face. (Ruth breathed through it. She was not going to say a thing about the sweatpants. She would not take this particular bait from her ingrate daughter.) It was then that she started wondering: How far back did the horrors of her relationship with her daughter go? When exactly did it start that she and Jenny ended up on this road, in which her own child would pretend to be living in another state just to avoid her?

Who knows what brought Ruth to the city in the first place? Not even she did. But let's chalk it up to that witchy quality her children often spoke about, the way she would sometimes know, just know, that Nathan and Alyssa were fighting, or that Beamer had gotten bad news, or that Jenny was not coming home from New Haven for Thanksgiving even though she'd gone so far as to confirm that she was.

All Ruth knew was that, upon waking, she wanted to visit the brownstone on 9th Street. Ruth had gone to sleep the night before thinking about it as her brain conducted its new nightly ruminations, which consisted of a full inventory on what the family had left in terms of property, items of value, wits even, and, as she floated down toward sleep each night, how she could leverage those things into her family's salvation.

She went to the city first, and with pleasure: to check on the brownstone's condition; to maybe derive some comfort from what could possibly be a source of sustenance for her family now; to leave Carl, who was an adult, alone and have a few goddamn minutes to herself. She had started thinking of the Manhattan brownstone as a secret savings account to raid to get them through their next and final winters now that the factory was a liability.

The trip to the city was good; the movement allowed her to stave off the unspeakable actual question, which was whether the solution to their problems was to sell the estate. Of course it was, yes. People without money don't get to live on an estate. But it would be an impossible negotiation with Carl. There was never the notion that the estate would not belong to Fletchers in his lifetime—that they'd pass it on to Nathan, probably, and then he to his kids. It wasn't something you could talk about with Carl. Carl watched TV. Carl nodded his head and looked off. Carl occasionally read a paper. But Carl did not engage. Whatever it is they did to him all that time ago, combined with how they all handled it, netted her a husband who might as well have been a sofa cushion. How the time had gone by. How long she'd been paying for her sins.

Further, it was impossible to untangle the estate as a place of healing and stability for him, and who knows what would be the effect of moving him right now, at his age, so soon after his mother's death. He was only seventy-one. His own father had died young, but look how old Phyllis was. It was clear Carl had caught her longevity. Meaning that there was so much more life to go. At this thought, Ruth could weep.

The truth was, she'd always seen them moving to the city once the kids were out of the house and Carl retired. They could finally live like civilized retirees, going to the theater and the museums, though maybe she'd only thought of it as a survival mechanism for the actual life she'd accidentally opted into when she was too young to know about consequences.

Forget the kidnapping. Ruth had hated Middle Rock from the minute she'd gotten there, a place that seemed so much like her dream of wealth that she hadn't realized the implications of actually living there.

There was no *life* there. There were only children and middle-aged people, all on a steady treadmill of routine and anxiety about routine, routine and anxiety about routine. There was no *chance,* no serendipity, no magical night, no arthouse movie theater, no youthful energy. There was no eating out after eight at night! How could there be serendipity if you were home by eight? What it does to the soul when you only see children and middle-aged people.

Plus, there was no anonymity. There was especially no anonymity when you married a man from a well-known family who had lived in that same town all his life; there was less than no anonymity when your husband was kidnapped and held for a terrifying week that paralyzed the town and riveted (she knew the ones who were *too* riveted) every single person who'd ever known him, which was everyone.

They'd bought the brownstone ostensibly for Beamer, but then to use as an investment property, or a pied-à-terre for themselves. That whole time, she knew she was buying it for herself. It was the kind of place that she would pass when she was seventeen, coming to the Village to nightclubs and going on dates with men because they would buy her dinner and cigarettes. She would watch the people who owned those places walk up their front steps and she would imagine herself into their lives—how easy it could all be if only she lived somewhere nice and centrally located, and not in four rooms with five kids and parents who didn't know how they'd afford to eat past their working years. Sometimes she could see a little behind an untucked curtain, or into an open door. She saw bright walls painted chic colors and lush curtains. It seemed so nice in there. She wanted to be inside there so badly.

Then, many years ago, just as Beamer was a freshman in college, Arthur, who was the only person who was still keeping track of her dreams, told her he saw a brownstone that was up for sale. She put an offer in before she saw the place, and then convinced Carl and Phyllis that it was a good investment, and look how much money they'd save on dorm living at the very least. The magic words for Phyllis were a reminder that all rent is throwing money away; the magic words for Carl regarding a purchase were that his mother approved.

Ruth had begun to dream of the brownstone again two Novembers ago, when Phyllis had started complaining about her joints hurting. Ruth assumed that it was because of the cold—all of Phyllis's friends had abandoned Middle Rock by then for Florida, some for Jerusalem, but not Phyllis. If she'd ever been longing for one of those places, Ruth didn't know about it, as predictable life had stopped for all of them on the day that Carl was taken away. Upon his return, Phyllis had moved the family onto the estate with her and announced that she would never go anywhere Carl was not again.

But along with the joint pain, a strange effect had taken over Phyllis's face. Her skin had started taking on a glow or sheen, and a puffing out of the cheeks like a 1930s movie star, pretty and youthful—there was no other way to describe it. People commented on it everywhere she went. All Phyllis had ever wanted was to look preternaturally young and beautiful, so she would smile her coy wouldn't-you-like-to-know smile, the same one from after her face-lift. But there would be a slight descent of her eyebrows with the smile, a shadow of confusion behind her eyes—something was not right. It could not be that this late in life, God had finally granted her beauty.

Ruth hadn't found Phyllis's new appearance remarkable, not even when Carl made some noise about it one night after the three of them had dinner at Phyllis's house. On the walk back to their place, he'd said, "My mother's face looks funny." But Ruth had just shrugged. Ruth, after all, had been watching Phyllis's face change for years. By then, Phyllis had had several elective surgeries that included an eye lift, a neck lift, a facelift that included a revamp of the initial eye lift and an additional neck lift—everything lifted so high that it appeared that gravity was just another force on Phyllis's payroll—and finally an emergency procedure in which her septum was reconstructed, as she had outlived all lifespan expectations but nobody had told her nose job that.

So Ruth had assumed, of course, that Phyllis had had another "procedure"—a series of those new fillers was Ruth's bet—and that they were having some kind of interaction with either Phyllis's Lipitor or her Losartan, and so Ruth took her to the doctor. It was there that they learned that what had been happening to Phyllis's face wasn't the result of a secret cosmetic surgery; it was that she had developed a syndrome called systemic scleroderma.

"Most people don't seek treatment for months," Dr. Halpern said. "They just think their creams and what have you started working better. It's only when there's pain that they come in. And then, well?" He indicated the patient in front of him.

"I waited for the pain to pass," Phyllis said. Her hair was now blond, as it had been in the ancient photos from her youth, but it was no longer silky. It was now teased upward to disguise how sparse it had become. She had taken to wearing large glasses that had an amber tint to them that faded on the way down—not sunglasses, but bifocals in disguise.

Dr. Halpern touched Phyllis's elbow and she recoiled. Ruth looked at her. She couldn't, in all these years, remember Phyllis ever complaining of pain.

"Yes," Dr. Halpern repeated gently. "When it doesn't pass, that's when people come in."

"I thought . . ." Phyllis had trailed off.

"You thought you were getting younger," Dr. Halpern said with a sad smile.

Phyllis opened her mouth and shook her head like she couldn't explain.

"How did she get it?" Ruth asked.

"Oh, it's genetic," said the doctor. "But that doesn't mean Carl or the kids will get it. Though you should be on the lookout for auto-immune in them in general. Jews. As you know."

The doctor told Phyllis and Ruth there was nothing much to do beyond the steroids he had given her, but that he had had good experiences with steroids for systemic scleroderma. Phyllis stood up to leave and the doctor told Ruth to linger to fill out a form. When Phyllis left, he told Ruth that there weren't a great many treatments for this for people Phyllis's age and they could expect this to be the thing that killed her.

"Something was going to, right?" he asked.

Ruth drove Phyllis home, up the long driveway, settled her into the house and then drove back down the long driveway back to her house. She looked at the estate as if it were her first time seeing it— the first time she realized that the young man who had flirted with her at a party was actually her salvation—and instead of finding it beautiful and ancient and high-class, she now found it to be entirely dreadful.

As Phyllis's condition grew worse, Ruth continued to dream about the brownstone, to dream about what could come next for her and Carl. Maybe with Phyllis gone, Carl could finally be the person she had always hoped he could be.

Did she really think this? Did she actually believe this could be true? She could no longer remember. Recent events had deleted all her hope and made her skeptical of any moment of optimism she'd ever had. There were not many to draw upon.

Then Phyllis was gone. She had not been inscribed for survival that year. That was what Ruth kept thinking while she organized the funeral. Phyllis had died—she by illness. She had not made the cut for another year. And Ruth, sitting in the brownstone now, waiting for her seditious daughter to show up, found that the only person who would understand her grief in this moment was dead.

Ruth's issues with Jenny predated Phyllis's death. Perhaps they even predated Jenny's birth. Perhaps they even went all the way back to those days in the Tudor on St. James Drive, when Ruth spent her days making coffee for FBI agents and answering the same questions over and over again while she waited for a miracle to show up. She was busy trying to manage her own children. Nathan wasn't the problem; she could usually hear him from wherever she was and he was always in her sight line anyway. It was Bernard she worried about. He was wilier and wild, writhing and running away whenever he could, terrified and thrilled at all the excitement in the house. She tried to hold on to him, but he'd wriggle away and then she'd get distracted, and in moments when she realized it was too quiet, she would freeze, unable to move, willing her peripheral nerve to spark at its most powerful setting until she spotted him. By then, she didn't even need to turn to him to see him. She had become like a cheetah in the jungle, all instinct and inhuman hearing, sensing her children rather than actually seeing them. When you're pregnant, all you can think about is the fact that you're pregnant. Ruth didn't think about the baby growing inside her even once that week. Was that where this all started?

But what if their issues went back even further? What if they went back all the way to Dale Scher? Dale, whom she'd met in an ac-counting class that they were taking together—it was an elective for him, a compromise he'd made with his father. She had wanted to be a buyer in a department store, but the city schools didn't have that major yet and so she majored in business management. Dale, on the other hand, wanted to be a gym teacher, and as they fell deeper in love, Ruth realized that one of the many things she had assumed would happen was that Dale would awaken from this silly idea and choose a profession that was serious, one where he could support a family. By the time Dale took her to an AEPi party three months into their relationship, he was still asleep, with no regard for practicality, unlike the other young man she met at that party, whose father's recent death had made him nothing but practical, and nothing but rich.

Carl wasn't a college student, or at least he wasn't anymore. He had been at UCLA, but his father's recent, sudden death had brought him home after his junior year, and he was spending his nights trying to maintain some kind of youth despite the fact that he was now a twenty-one-year-old boy in charge of a factory—in charge of a hundred workers, all grown men, his only counsel the guidance of Ike Besser, his father's employee who was only a year older than Carl himself.

Ruth remembered seeing Carl across the room, so young and clean-cut, so shiny and well-kept. Carl looked at her like he'd been struck.

"How do you do?" she asked.

Dale put his arm around her. "Isn't she a class act?" He made his voice fancy: "*How do you do?*"

"Charmed," Carl said.

But now Carl was staring at Ruth, and Dale—Dale knew something was up. He tightened his grip around his girl. There was the smell of beer on his breath. She felt herself wriggling from him.

"We have to go," Dale said suddenly, though they didn't.

Dale picked a fight with her on the ride home that night. She couldn't remember now exactly what it was about—probably the usual fight about him wanting to marry immediately and her wanting to wait till graduation—except that she saw clearly that he was asking for a reaffirmation of her love in all the ways that men do, meaning indirectly. She remembered thinking that she knew what he was asking for, and what did it mean that she was not willing to give it to him?

The next day, her mother told her a young man had called the house. His name was Carl. She canceled a movie date with Dale, citing a headache, and waited at home for him to call back. That weekend, Carl took her on a date to the Copacabana.

She wasn't a horrible person (she told herself). She loved Dale, yes, but love wasn't the only metric she thought a person should consider. She grew up with too many siblings and parents who loved each other just fine. What she wanted was security. What she wanted was to be able to make a decision without worrying it would be her ruin, and as she dipped her toes into adult waters, she'd been finding herself crushed by the possible terrible outcomes of living this close to the margins. She was barely able to rationalize sending herself to college.

She didn't finish school, in the end; she was already married to Carl by the time it was time to enroll in her junior year. By then, she already had access to more money than she could have earned over the next twenty-five years by simply working a job.

And she was *busy.* She was making the house. She was joining the temple. She was attending the meetings that her very imposing mother-in-law wanted her to attend at the Sisterhood and at the Hadassah and at the Historical Society, even though she didn't fundamentally believe in the concept of conservation. What's to conserve? She believed in progress. She had seen things get better. She was born in the echoes of the Great Depression; she came to exist just at the moment of Israeli statehood. She would live to see personal home computing and, she was sure, people living on the moon at this rate. Again: What's to conserve?

But there was no time for these arguments. Life came at her too quickly and one day she was pregnant. And then she was pregnant again. And then again. She would never work for a living, she knew that. But she had hoped she would travel and engage in the world. But then Carl was kidnapped, and she knew she wouldn't be able to make plans for a very long time. It took her too long to realize it would be never.

Those nights when the agents were in her house, she thought this:

that wherever Dale was, she knew for almost completely sure that he hadn't been kidnapped. She knew that had she married him, she would have had a normal life. She would have had children that she could prioritize—ones she could actually raise, instead of viewing them the way she viewed her actual children, which was as constant, potential threats to her husband's fragile psyche.

No, worse. She had thought she would have children who maybe resembled her a little more in their grit and energy. She had thought she would have children that she maybe thought more highly of. How she'd watch her three children flailing as they aimed to find meaning in a life where they didn't have to work for anything. She felt bad for them, because once you're born that way, even if you lose everything, the way they just had, you never feel the fire of survival in you. You never truly believe there's a reason to get out of bed in the morning, even if now there is. Ruth had felt the survival instinct in her strongly. That was why she'd married a rich man with no thought about what this might yield in terms of her children. The danger had gone away when she'd married Carl, but the fear never did.

Maybe her animus with Jenny went back that far. Maybe.

But maybe it was this: After the kidnapping, after she arrived home from visiting Carl at the hospital the second night he was there, she'd noticed some spotting in her underwear. She called Phyllis up and asked her to stay with the boys while she got into the car and returned to Long Island Jewish to see Dr. Mark. But on her way there, something in her reversed course without actually deciding to and instead headed to the other hospital, to North Shore, where she sat patiently in the emergency room like everyone else, staring straight ahead. When she was finally seen by a female gynecologist whom she'd never met, so much blood had collected into her sanitary napkin that she couldn't imagine that she could still be pregnant. But she didn't feel sad; no, she felt relieved. She was sorry that this baby was a martyr to this kidnapping, but better it than Carl or the boys. Better it than her.

But the baby was somehow fine. The doctor did a sonogram on

her and she saw with her own eyes that it had life in it yet. She heard with her own ears the watery whooshing of its heart and felt the crushing disappointment when the doctor smiled and told her that it's hard to shake a good apple from the tree.

Right on that table, the thought appeared, full-formed, in her brain: She didn't want this baby. She knew this baby was already tainted with everything that had gone wrong.

But she left without asking the unaskable. It was unheard of to get an abortion, a woman like her in her financial position. She went home, and starting that night, she did all the things the old wives would say would cause a miscarriage.

At the hospital, Carl kept saying that it was the baby that gave him a reason to hold on while he was in that basement. It was the only time he talked about anything that wasn't about his immediate terror and need. He wanted to hear if she could feel the baby move yet, if it felt like a girl—how he wanted a girl.

At home, she drank coffee, cups and cups of it. She drank wine. She bought cigarettes without filters. She went to one of the new aerobics classes in town. She went to *three* aerobics classes in a row. She took diuretics. She took laxatives. She took potassium. She stood on her head. She did the yoga poses in a book from the library that were advised against during pregnancy. In the shower, she punched her own stomach until she vomited. But nothing could stop this baby, and that October, Jenny was born.

What had been her choice? Following the kidnapping, she'd kept it together as much as she could with a mother-in-law who thought that pretending it never happened was what was best for her son.

"We have to make things normal for him," Phyllis whispered to her when she caught Ruth crying and smoking a cigarette on the back porch of her house while the kids were in school. "Put that out. You're having a baby, for god's sake!"

"I can't pretend, Phyllis." Ruth stubbed out her cigarette. "Everywhere I go, I think, what's going to happen next? Are they still out there? Is there someone else looking at us? Who is giving us the evil eye?"

"Does it make you feel better to say these things?" Phyllis asked. "Because I promise that the minute you stop talking about it, it will go away. It happened to his body. It didn't happen to him."

Phyllis walked away and Ruth lit up a new one. Sure, she thought. Nothing happened. It's all in the past.

Except that Bernard continued to wet the bed.

Except that Nathan always thought someone was behind him.

Except that, each night, at the point where Carl would fall into REM sleep, he would startle and scream, and this continued even after the baby came and Ruth was exhausted and her sympathies were waning.

She took Carl to his GP (without telling Phyllis), who told him about a new class of medication that was designed to help with a condition that had been proven to calm people having a psychotic break.

"I'm not psychotic, David," Carl said. This was so undignified, sitting in a gown with his wife on a chair, like she sat when the kids got examined.

Carl went home and took the medication. But these were early days for antidepressants. The side-effect profile of the pill his doctor prescribed was chilling: sweating; paranoia; vertigo; rabid, rapid blinking; dry mouth; tingling lips; a propensity for doing constant, repetitive advanced multiplication calculations in your head; constipation.

Carl experienced each one. In any other person, it was almost as if the side effects were the treatment, that they would distract you so much you wouldn't know you were in constant psychic pain. But in Carl, all they did was provide an unintentional exposure therapy for everything he'd been through. He was already sweaty and paranoid from being stuck in a closet; he was already dizzy and blinking like a maniac from being blindfolded for so long; sure, his mouth was dry and his lips were tingling; sure, Ruth woke up in the middle of the night and found him on the floor of the kitchen, her largest knife next to him on the floor, him sobbing, saying he could not stop calculating insurance premiums in his head.

Except that two years later, in 1982, "Make it simple!"—the same phrase the kidnapper had beseeched Ruth on the phone to do during his ransom call—would become the tagline of a canned soup company during a campaign to show how soup could be a good and fast marinade for chicken and steak, or add flavor to a stir-fry. The commercial was so annoying and so ubiquitous that a late-night sketch show did an elaborate gag where "Make it simple!" showed up in each sketch one night, and suddenly people in the street were wearing shirts that said *Make It Simple!* the way they wore shirts that said *Where's the Beef?* in 1984, or *Got Milk?* in 1993.

Except that Carl was at the reception portion of Marian and Ned Greenblatt's oldest daughter's bat mitzvah and the topic of money came up. This was less than a year following Carl's ordeal, when Ruth still had hope that it would one day be classifiable as a minor event in their otherwise long, happy lives. Cecilia and Frank Mayer and Bea and Walter Goldberg were at the same table for dinner following the candle-lighting ceremony when the conversation turned to money market accounts. Carl sawed away at a steak that was too well-done and listened to Bea bemoan that they had just lost twelve thousand dollars through a cousin who was an investor.

"I know what it is to lose money," Carl said suddenly. Frank and Cecilia Mayer looked at each other. It was the first thing he'd said that evening.

"I lost $221,934, as a matter of fact," he continued.

Well, this just stunned the table. Ruth closed her eyes. It wasn't the first time she'd heard this figure.

"You invested two hundred—I'm sorry, what was the figure?" Walter Goldberg asked, dabbing au poivre sauce from his mouth with a light pink napkin.

"It was $221,934. And I lost it. It was never returned to me. I got $9,479 back from one of them and $13,587 back from the other. Call it $5,000 for the used Datsun, which I never got back, because that's how it goes sometimes with evidence and what have you. But the total they got was $250,000, which leaves $221,934 unaccounted for. Now, I don't know where the rest of the money would be if these two split it evenly. If you ask me, I'd say that these two only saw some of it. Call it $30,000 between them, and they each spent a little. That means someone out there's got $220,000 of my money, still hidden somewhere."

It took just a few seconds for the table to realize he was talking about the ransom. Nobody moved.

"That's total," Carl concluded.

After a long pause, Cecilia said, "I didn't realize the money wasn't returned."

"Cecilia!" Frank warned her.

"It was not," Carl said. "The largest portion of it was not."

There was a desperate grasping at what to say. Ruth's eyes were still closed. She hated Cecilia Mayer. They had babies at the same time, both of them daughters, and Jenny and Erica were now in a Mommy & Me together. Each week, Ruth and Cecilia sat on the floor together, shaking rattles, and Cecilia asked Ruth angling questions about her life in a way that Ruth came to understand was the living, actionable evil eye at work.

When Ruth opened her eyes, she kept them downcast at her steak, which was inedible. The Greenblatts always went cheap.

"You never know where it'll turn up," Bea suggested cheerfully.

The table went quiet and Carl was the only person who continued to eat. It was the only time he ever would address the kidnapping or refer to it in so public or casual a manner again.

The next day, Ruth made Carl stop taking those pills.

Except that things kept not getting better. Carl was still distracted—catatonic, even. Ike picked him up for work every day, and drove him home. Carl wouldn't leave his office. Even after the trial, he was like a person stuffed inside a person, and Ruth was starting to forget who he had been in the first place, then *if* he had been in the first place.

After Jenny was born, Ruth made an appointment with her mother's internist in Brooklyn at the time, saying she needed to talk about her mother. But once she was alone with Dr. Schechter, she broke down and cried over her husband, who seemed broken forever.

Dr. Schechter gave her a tissue and put his hand on her knee (he was like that; it was a different time). "It could take a lifetime to heal from a thing like this," he said.

She shook her head; the words wouldn't come. She wanted to tell him that she didn't have a lifetime to wait, but of course she did. This had happened to all of them, not just Carl. The way Phyllis had spoken in whispers about the ordeal, it was as though it had only happened to him. But Ruth was almost widowed. Ruth was scared, too, and her fear didn't abate upon Carl's return; it only grew inside the same vacuum that her loneliness did. She gave birth to a new baby and wouldn't let her sleep outside her bedroom. No one ever wondered what had happened in Ruth's head during that time. At least Carl, in all of his suffering, had known he was alive. She hadn't known. Did anyone ever think of that?

Dr. Schechter wrote her a prescription for some kind of tranquilizer and gave her the name of a psychologist.

"But he already took pills," Ruth sobbed. "The pills made him crazy. He's still crazy from them!"

"This is not a guy with pills, dear," Dr. Schechter said. "You *talk* to him."

"Oh, Carl would never."

He removed his hand from her knee, and she found that her knee felt cold without it. "Just see."

A few days later, Ruth went to Manhattan to see Dr. Light herself to discuss the possibility of Carl coming in. His office was wood-paneled and featured a wall of books, one shelf of which was occupied entirely by a book he'd written called *Freeing You,* which had, according to his bookshelf, also been translated into German.

Dr. Light himself was bald and had a goatee, though the goatee was a darker color than seemed natural for his age and complexion. Ruth hadn't so far in her life ever considered that facial hair was a thing someone might dye.

"What brings you in?" Dr. Light asked.

Ruth rocked Jenny's stroller while she slept. She had told Carl that she was bringing the baby into the city to meet a distant cousin of hers. They hadn't had a baby naming because Carl couldn't yet handle a public event. (Was *that* how long back this all went? That Jenny hadn't been properly named in shul?)

"It's my husband," Ruth said. "He was kidnapped eleven months ago, and it's not that I expect from him that he should be fine." She stopped to consider what she should expect and didn't know, so she said, "He's just scared all the time."

"Why isn't he here with you?"

"I didn't want to upset him. I just want to help him. I was wondering if you had advice on what I should do." She told him about Carl's sleeping. She told him about the shaking at night. She told him about how scared he was to leave the house.

Dr. Light thought for a minute. They were facing each other, he in a giant club chair, she sitting upright on a couch that his other patients probably lay on. He looked Ruth up and down, his eyes staying on her exquisite ankles for more than a second. She had a baby with her, for Christ's sake.

"Very often, the brain receives a kind of injury during these moments," he told her. He smiled like they were sharing a joke. "I imagine you crying all the time isn't helping."

Ruth wasn't crying. At least she didn't think she was. She touched her face. All dry.

"Listen," he said. "Men and women are different." He chuckled lightly and pumped his hands up and down like a basketball referee calling double dribble. "Now, don't tell the feminists I said that!" He laughed again and shook his head. "But even the feminists would agree with me. What happened made you hysterical."

She waited.

"A woman isn't always hysterical," he said. "But she always has the *capacity* for hysteria. She's born with it. All you need is one big event and boom, the hysteria is dislodged. Think of it kind of bouncing around in your body, like a pinball. Do your kids play pinball?"

"This isn't really about me," Ruth said. "I was here to talk about my—"

"Yes, but it's all related, you see?" He leaned forward with his hands in his lap. "If you're calm, he's calm. You see?"

"But—"

"There you go again. Callllmmmm." He stretched the word out

like he was trying to lobby the concept of tranquility to her, to show her that inside the word itself were contours in which she could herself find some room for a full spa day.

There has never been, in the history of all human interaction, a way for a woman to explain effectively that she's calm when a man has suggested she isn't.

"Here's my advice," said Dr. Light. "I think you should come and see me twice a week. Maybe keep the baby at home." Boy, did he love her ankles. "It's most important that you remain relaxed because with incidents like what your husband went through, the real danger is in a torrent of excess emotion that could ignite a fire around him. Have you seen those Smokey the Bear commercials?"

"Yes," she said.

"Only you can prevent forest fires, Ruth." Off her speechlessness, he said, "The most important thing is to keep him calm."

"What . . . what can happen to him?"

"He'll never recover." Dr. Light shook his head. "It happens. What he went through is too big for him. There's no way for the brain to process it. He has to keep it inside, where he can suffocate it. If he starts feeling things, he'll never stop."

She sat back in the chair. It was close enough to an hour that if Jenny could just start crying or maybe move around, she'd say she had to feed her and leave.

"It's a new diagnosis. It's called post-traumatic stress disorder. They came up with it a few years ago. Vietnam veterans and flashbacks, you know?"

"What are you supposed to do for it?"

"There's nothing to do. It's just a diagnosis. So you hear me?" He stood up. "Keep calm around him. Make it easy for him to forget. Make it simple."

She shuddered.

"It'll be fine if you can help him *contain*."

She said goodbye and walked out of the office, cursing Jenny silently for not crying like a normal baby.

Was that how long it had all been going on?

Now Ruth's thinking migrated to wondering how long Jenny had been staying at the brownstone. A few days? A few weeks? A few years? Why bother wondering? What did Ruth know about Jenny anyway?

You could ask these questions all day, is the thing. You could even get answers, but none of them will tell you what you want to know, which is how did this all go so wrong?

"MOM," JENNY SAID, when she walked in and saw her mother sitting on the couch that afternoon. Jenny looked tired, or maybe she looked like a girl who was nearing forty and didn't own any makeup.

Jenny stood in the doorway to the living room.

"Jennifer," her mother said with some disgust. "What happened to you?"

"What do you mean?"

"*Jennifer.* What are you *doing* here?"

Finally, Jenny pulled herself together. She affected something close to casual and crossed the room to put her keys down on the kitchen table, biding time. She didn't once look back at her mother's face.

"I've been sitting here for three hours," Ruth said. "I've been sitting here trying to figure out how it could be that you could be living here for god knows how long and you didn't think your family should know."

Jenny continued to busy herself, now taking things out of her bag slowly and laying them on the kitchen counter for no real reason.

"So, you don't think I'm owed an explanation," Ruth said.

Finally, Jenny looked at her. "I guess I don't."

"Have you been crying?"

"No."

"You've been crying. What happened?"

"I just came from—I was talking to someone. I had an argument with someone."

"Why aren't you in Connecticut?" Then, something dawned on her: "Were you ever in Connecticut?"

Jenny sat down on the couch.

"Mom, I don't know what brings you here. If you want me to leave, it's your house, tell me, I'll be out tonight."

"Jenny, this makes no sense."

"Nothing makes sense, Mom."

"What's wrong with you?" Ruth asked. She could not seem to make her voice less angry. "Do I need to call a doctor?"

"No."

"What are you doing here?"

"I am trying to figure out, Mom, exactly how I ended up so fucked up. How I became rudderless. How I both failed to bond with my family of origin and to individuate from them."

"I don't have time for all this psychobabble," Ruth said.

"It's not psychobabble, Ma. It's feelings. It's other people's feelings. People have feelings."

"Sigmund Freud over here."

"You're not listening."

"You're *shouting.*"

Jenny laughed. "Mom. This is not shouting." But Jenny had no defenses left. All she had was her desperation. "I had this fantasy that if we didn't have money, I'd know how to live."

Ruth began to put her coat on. Her eyes became vicious.

"Where are you going?" Jenny asked.

"I cannot believe you came from me," she said. "All I wanted was to have children who didn't have to struggle. And now I see what you're like and I can't believe you're mine."

"Now I think you were maybe right," Jenny said. "I should have gotten a nose job. I should have gotten married. I should have kids, who could distract me from my worthlessness."

"My whole life I'm watching you kids with two loaves of bread under each arm. You have everything. It was all yours. You could have done anything you wanted in your life."

"How?" Jenny asked. "I wasn't even born when I was cut off at the knees."

"What are you talking about? You're a spoiled brat. You weren't even there for it."

"I was there for everything afterward," Jenny said. "You, and you and Arthur—whatever that relationship is."

"I beg your pardon, Jennifer."

"Nothing, forget it."

"No, you were implying something. Would you like to say it out loud?"

Just then, Jenny's phone rang. She glanced at it, barely able to see through the shattered glass, but then:

"I have to take this," Jenny said.

"Oh, you have to take it," said her mother.

"I'm—wait." Then, into the phone, she said, "Hello? Is everything OK?" She listened for a long moment while Ruth glared at her. "What? OK, tell me." And Jenny walked into the den and closed the door for privacy.

Ruth zipped up her coat and walked out. She had nothing left to say anyway.

RUTH REMEMBERED THAT when Jenny was in middle school, she did a report on veal calves being raised, how they were kept in crates, not able to roam around so that they could build as much fat on them as possible and be killed and sold at the heaviest possible weight. Jenny had presented these findings in the living room via a trifold poster, which later won the science fair at school for its use of an innovative styrofoam mechanism that showed the same baby calf from infancy grow, as you were taken through the presentation, into an incarcerated calf, into an animal on just the edge of cowhood that only gets to see the sky once in its life, which was from the crate that was its prison to the slaughterhouse. The last picture was of a fat, ugly, gluttonous family eating veal. Ruth recalled the moment when the calf leaves its crate—Jenny had rigged it so that a styrofoam calf would walk down from the crate, but it can't really walk. It doesn't have any muscle built, because it had spent its life so far in a cage, so it just collapses on the ground, and then the mechanism Jenny created drags the supine, scared calf to its death.

Ruth's children were the veal, she suddenly understood.

They were raised to be fattened, but never to reach a full and thriving adulthood. They'd arrived at the doorstep of life, unable to walk. Ruth used to hate them for this—hate them in a way you can only hate them because you love them—but now she saw how inevitable it was. Worse, now she saw that she was the author of their incompetence.

In the parked car, in front of the brownstone, Ruth stared out into numbness.

Arthur would have known what to do here. He would have known what to say, or how to handle it. Or at the very least he would have been a comfort to Ruth.

Or maybe not. Maybe the more time that went by, the more it seemed like Arthur never existed.

But he had. He had been there the whole time.

Even during the entire ordeal, Ruth knew that Phyllis would one day refuse to talk about it. Her children would not remember what had happened, they were too young, and in the absence of a fully present romantic partner, she was left with what she found to be a dear friend.

At first, Ruth and Arthur had plenty of business together because of the aftermath and then the trial. Then they had business because of Arthur's role as their lawyer and the way the wills had changed after Carl's ordeal. But then, as Arthur's duties around their legal situation lessened and all the issues regarding the kidnapping were as resolved as they would ever get, he just kept showing up. First to join them for dinner. Then to check in on them several times a week, at Phyllis's behest. Then, as the equivalent of an emotional support puppy for Ruth—someone to help her make decisions, someone to confide in, and then, finally, someone who did the Medal of Honor service of remembering exactly when and how her life had gone off the rails.

Then, one day, a few years after the ordeal, Arthur was over for dinner and Ruth asked where Yvonne was.

"Yvonne and I are divorcing," he said. He was eating soup and focusing intensely on it, not looking up.

Ruth was afraid to react. Both boys were in elementary school now, listening to dinner conversation more and more. Carl was there. Phyllis was there, too, watching, always watching.

"I'm so sorry," she said. She found that she was relieved he was telling her in front of everyone.

"It's OK," he said. "It happens."

And on it went for more than thirty years: Arthur showing up everywhere, Arthur able to communicate through wordless glances with Ruth. Jenny and Beamer sharing wide-eyed looks and then raucous laughter at a running private joke they had that she pretended she'd never overheard, first about Arthur being their real father, then about Arthur plotting to kill their biological father to become their stepfather.

And Ruth took great pains to never give Arthur room to say the thing that seemed stuck in his throat.

The last time Ruth had seen Arthur alone was just before Phyllis died. She was returning a dress to Bloomingdale's when she called Arthur to tell him she was coming to the city.

"Why don't we meet?" she asked.

They made plans to meet at Sette Mezzo. Ruth did some shopping on Fifth Avenue in the meantime.

Arthur was waiting for her at a table with his sad, loving eyes. He stood when she approached and held a hand out. She pushed her cheek against his in a close facsimile of a kiss and sat down.

Arthur immediately leaned forward.

"What is it, Ruthie? What's wrong?"

Ruth looked down at her menu.

"Nothing's wrong," she said. "I needed to get out a little. I'm tired of the phone, I needed some air."

When she looked up he was looking at her.

The waiter came to take their order, just in time, reading more than ten specials. Arthur's and Ruth's eyes found each other again as they waited it out; the longer it went on, the more hilarious they both found it, though if anyone else had been there they would have barely discerned a twinkle in either of them. Such was the nature of old friendship, or whatever it was that Ruth and Arthur shared.

"We'll both have the sole," Arthur said. "From the menu."

"Yes, sir," the waiter said.

"Burt Reynolds over here," Ruth said, as she watched him walk away. Then, turning back to Arthur, she said, "She's going to die soon."

"I know," Arthur said.

"She's just lying there in the middle of that living room. And I honestly do not know what's going to happen to him when she does."

"What do you think will happen?"

"I don't know. Maybe he'll throw himself on her coffin. Maybe he'll be a wreck."

"Or maybe he'll be free."

Ruth thought about that for a second. "You know, they say that when a man dies, his widow goes on to live many more years. But when a woman dies, her husband has a year left in him tops."

Arthur shook his head. "She's his mother."

"I've been trying to explain that to them both for years," Ruth replied, and the two of them laughed like the old friends they were.

Then it was the third day of shiva when Ruth got home after overseeing cleanup in Phyllis's house to find an envelope on her desk. She opened it up and it was a letter from Arthur:

Dearest Ruthie,

I waited for my dear aunt Phyllis to pass, and for the funeral and for you to feel settled before I left. I know this will come as a surprise, but I'm taking some time off from work. I know you will wonder why I didn't tell you. Do you know deep down?

I won't be in touch while I'm away. If you have questions regarding your legal needs, call Arnie at the firm. I'm leaving my phone, and I'm

not leaving my itinerary with anyone. I will be
safe, and I will be thinking of you.

                                 With love,
                                 Arthur

There must have been a hundred people in the house. She went upstairs, to her mother-in-law's bedroom, and she cried for an hour, slapping her own face from time to time at her schoolgirl silliness. What a child she was, to feel so alone in the world with so many people in the house looking for her.

Now, after leaving Jenny in the brownstone, Ruth pulled out of the parking spot on 9th Street and put the car into drive and headed over to Second Avenue and then drove over the 59th Street bridge instead of the tunnel. After all this time, she still couldn't bring herself to pay for a toll she didn't need to.

She realized as she drove over the bridge that the answer to all of this would not come from her children. They just weren't equipped. It was too late for them to learn how to be. The answer would come from Ruth. Who else?

———

IT ONLY TOOK two weeks before the scrappy, superstitious, desperate parts of Ruth—that girl from real, disgusting Brooklyn—rose to the surface and revealed the answer to her. It was shocking to her that it took her that long, but she was out of practice.

She didn't have Arthur to advise her, but she also didn't have Arthur to stop her. She didn't have Arthur at all, and so she was left to all of her own, semi-formed devices.

One morning, she waited until after breakfast and drove to Forest Hills to her sister-in-law Marjorie's apartment complex, one of those Soviet-bloc buildings on a corner of Queens Boulevard.

Ruth used her key to open the door to Marjorie and Alexis's apartment when nobody answered, but there was Marjorie sitting on the couch, staring at the door with wide, scared eyes.

"Why didn't you answer me?" Ruth asked when she saw her.

Marjorie didn't answer at first.

"Are you OK? Marjorie, what is going on?"

"I knew you were coming," she said. "I felt you in the building."

Ruth felt then how tired she was in her whole body.

"Marjorie, please. What is happening here?"

Marjorie couldn't take her eyes off Ruth as Ruth moved closer to her.

"Marjorie, what is wrong with you?"

"I'm just . . . ," Marjorie started. She sat under a crocheted blanket, hugging her knees, making herself into a tiny ball. "It's been a long time. I knew you were coming."

"How did you know?" Then, realizing she didn't want any more psychobabble, she straightened up and sat down on the overstuffed lounge chair across from Marjorie. "Listen, I'm here to talk to you about something. I'm sorry I didn't call. I know you're angry."

Marjorie recoiled further, holding the blanket up to her chin.

"You look just like her," Marjorie said. "You are doing a convincing job."

"I don't know what that means. What are you talking about? Where is Alexis? Is Alexis here?"

"She went to her class."

Ruth took a breath and made her smile her warmest.

"Now, Marjie, I care about you very much," Ruth said. "*We* care about you. I know how complicated it is. I know how scared you are about finances. I've been thinking of you. I'm worried now, because—are you listening, Marjorie? Marjorie!—I'm worried because Nathan says that we can't sell the factory, that no one will want it, and that there was an inspection and they found all kinds of things wrong."

"At the factory?" Marjorie appeared for the first time to be paying attention.

"Yes, the factory is a liability now. It's going to cost us a lot of money to fix it."

"What are we going to do?"

"Well," Ruth said. "I have an idea. Do you want to hear it? Marjorie? You can hear me, right? Because it seems like you're just looking at my face and my hair."

"You look just like her," Marjorie said, now more in wonder than in fear.

"I have an idea," Ruth said.

"What is it?"

"Do you know that the estate was not willed to your brother? Carl doesn't even know that. The estate wasn't put in your mother's will. You know what that means?"

"I don't."

"It means that the estate belongs to her next of kin. Which isn't just Carl. It's both of you. You're her daughter. Her older daughter. You have *rights*. I shouldn't even be telling you this. It's against my own interests. But I can't bear to see you left with nothing."

"You want me to have the estate?" Marjorie asked.

"I want you to have what you *deserve*. But the problem is I can't tell that to Carl. As you know, he's very emotional right now. Because of your mother. He doesn't want to leave. He won't leave. He doesn't want to. But if you were to talk to a lawyer, maybe? I could give you the name of a lawyer and you could talk to someone and make a claim. And then we'd have to sell the estate. We would just have to."

Suddenly, Marjorie was angry. "Then why didn't you give it to me? Why do you make me live like a pauper?"

"I didn't do that. What? I'm telling you, the estate, you should ask for your half. You must. It's owed to you."

Marjorie folded her arms, petulant. "My whole life you did that."

"I don't know what you're talking about."

"I thought I would be free of you by now."

"Free of me? Marjorie, we're your family. Why do you want to be free of us? I just thought, you should fight for your half of the estate. You should fight and tell Carl that you want to sell it. He can be a bully. I can't be part of it, of course. I can only help you if we keep this a secret. But you should demand it. That's what I would do. I would take what was owed to me."

"You always loved him more. I thought I would feel free from you by now. I was supposed to hear the shackles clanging on the ground. That's what Alexis said it would sound like when you died."

"Marjorie, I'm not dead."

"I can see that."

"I don't know what you're saying. Should I call Alexis?"

"She doesn't want to hear from you!"

"You have the right to take what is yours, Marjorie. And the estate is half yours. And if you want to sell it, well, I don't see how he can really stop you."

Marjorie leaned forward with her hand held out. Against her better instincts, Ruth sat still and let Marjorie touch her face.

"Is it true?" Marjorie asked.

"It's true. Now you don't tell anyone I told you. I'm looking out for you."

But Marjorie wasn't listening anymore. She was still just trying to touch Ruth's face. Finally, Ruth swatted her hand away.

"Marjorie, are you OK?" Ruth was asking with a squint.

"I'm fine," Marjorie whispered. "Just overwhelmed and exhausted. I'm so glad you're here. I've missed you so much. I miss you."

Ruth stood up. She'd had it.

"Pull it together, Marjorie. Listen to me. So all you have to do is go to Carl—are you hearing me?—you go to Carl or maybe even have Alexis do it and you tell him that you know your rights. That the estate is half yours, and . . . what?"

Marjorie stood up, too, now, and touched Ruth's nose.

"That you want to sell it, right?" Ruth prodded her.

"The factory is a liability," Marjorie said, suddenly serious.

"Yes. It will cost us too much money to fix. We need some money back. So, we agree? Would you—like me to talk to Alexis about this?"

Marjorie's face turned to warmth. "Of course," she said, her voice full of love. "Of course."

"I have to go now," Ruth said. "Remember, it's yours. Do you hear me? You make a big stink! I know you know how to do that!"

Marjorie nodded. She was smiling in a serene way that made Ruth want to scream.

"I have to go now," she said again.

"Will you visit me again?"

"Sure, of course. We're family."

Ruth turned away from that crazy smile and inched out the door, rotating half a turn before she left like she was going to ask something, but thought better of it and walked out the door. It was better just to leave.

LATER THAT NIGHT, on the estate, Ruth awoke with a start. She had been dreaming that the lighthouse that her mother-in-law had spent thirty years of her time in the Historical Society trying to restore was beaming at her, yelling at her every time that the light came around, and she saw that the yelling was constant but that she only knew about it when it was pointed to her.

It was still night, and into the dark room her phone was ringing. It was the landline, which hardly ever rang, now screaming for her, clear and ancient.

"Hello?" she said.

"Ruth?" It was Ike Besser. "Ruth, it's Ike. I'm so sorry to call you this late."

"Ike? Ike, is everything OK?"

"Ruth, I'm at the factory."

"What time is it?" she asked.

"Ruth, I'm at the factory. You need to come now."

Ruth sat up. She tried to make her eyes see in the room. The bedside next to her was empty. She had a feeling that someone was standing there watching her, but when she turned on the light she was alone.

"What is it, Ike? Are you with Carl?"

"Ruth. You need to come here. There's been a fire."

Part 2

THE PLASTIC HOUR

STYROFOAM

*N*OW, WHEN POLYSTYRENE burns, it melts and goes from a white, lightweight material into a pitch-black, tar-like liquid that, upon cooling, turns into a brittle solid. If, in the burning, the grinding of the polystyrene produces enough dust, then that dust, when dispersed, can result in an explosive mixture: large amounts of black smoke made up of carbon monoxide, total hydrocarbons, and smoke particulates. A molten, melting disaster.

Of course, the explosion element is secondary. The high heat itself would set off any number of explosions within the factory, a chain reaction from pressurizer to aerator. The drums of polystyrene burst in tiny combustions like dynamite Jiffy Pop. On the night that Consolidated Packing Solutions, Ltd., burned, the explosions did not decimate beyond the main building, but the ruckus could be seen from planes taking off at JFK.

The promise of styrofoam is its protection. It's built to be a dense, light layer that can absorb impact as it creates both shock absorption and distance between an object and the world. When it's set on fire, it softens, contracts, and ultimately melts. It releases a styrene gas and polycyclic aromatic hydrocarbons, a toxic brew that, if exposed to humans, could lead to permanent damage of the nervous system.

What a strange world chemistry is, how the very creations of protection can also cause so much damage.

By the time the fire department arrived, parts of the factory were on fire and a brown nest of smoke and dust was suspended over what was left of it, like a judgment—no, like a curse.

That night, the smoke alarms had gone off and the Consolidated Packing Solutions, Ltd., security system had summoned both the fire department and the Queens local police, sirens blaring, all lights narrowing on a shivering, nightgowned figure sitting on the loading dock of the factory.

It was Marjorie, of course.

Under the glare of those lights, she seemed even more birdlike and fragile, and even more disoriented than she'd been when Ruth had visited her just a few hours before. Dust coated her hair and her fingers were tarred black, and tears had streamed clean arteries through the dirt on her face.

Six fire trucks surrounded the factory, along with three police cars, and then six uniformed cops. The cops at first had drawn their weapons, screaming and threatening, trying to get Marjorie to raise her hands. But she was crying so hard that her arms were bobbing into a cactus shape, and the policemen looked at each other and holstered their weapons and approached her slowly, calmly, while a black sedan drove up and a tired detective in a rumpled suit tried to piece together exactly what had happened.

Ike arrived at the factory a few minutes later, having been alerted by the private security company that Consolidated Packing Solutions, Ltd., contracted. The area of Queens where the factory resided was deserted at night, and alarms would trip for reasons ranging from a mischief of rats scurrying across the entrance to a taxi that used the driveway to do a K-turn. Add to that the extra security measures that had been installed since Carl's return from his ordeal, and the place was a pinball machine of alarms that got tripped all night. There were so many false alarms over the years that, long ago, Carl had transferred the alerts to Ike's name, since Carl could not withstand the constant midnight ringing, and he wasn't about to go out to the factory in the middle of the night anyway.

At least not usually. But Carl was there. He had arrived in his Range Rover just as Ike showed up in his Ford Focus, though it was unclear who exactly had summoned Carl or where he had come from. Ike was talking to the detective, trying to explain that he was the foreman of the factory and that Marjorie was the sister of the factory's owner. The detective listened while one of the police officers handcuffed Marjorie, who couldn't stop crying long enough to answer any of their questions but who did have literal matches in her hand and couldn't stop coughing. Despite Ike's pleading, the police officers marched Marjorie over to their cruiser. She sat in the backseat, behind the window, looking out, a scared puppy.

One of the fire trucks was parked directly on top of Carl's parking spot, so he parked behind it. He jumped out of his car, leaving the door open, and then ran to the police car, yelling, "Stop! That's my sister!"

The police officer took a look at him. He was dressed in his nightclothes, a trench coat over them; his hair was crazy.

"That's my sister," Carl said again. "This is my factory. Leave her alone."

"It appears she burned it down," said the officer.

"It's my factory, though. I won't press charges."

"It's a public safety issue. Arson is a crime. It's not about pressing charges."

Marjorie was shouting something from inside the police cruiser.

"Please, just let me talk to her."

"We have to take her in."

Marjorie was wildly trying to explain something from behind the closed window. She was crying and her eyes were looking all over, left and right and up and down.

"I know, Marjie," Carl said to the window. "It's OK."

Ruth arrived then, her hair messy but otherwise dressed.

"Carl! Where have you been! I was sick!" Then, seeing Marjorie in the car, she pulled out her psychopath voice, the screaming front-loaded. "What is this?" She yelled at the closed window, "What did you do? What did you do?"

Marjorie, crying soundlessly, cowered away from her vicious sister-in-law. It was Carl who pulled Ruth away from lunging at the car, the most aggressive move he'd made in years.

"She's not herself, Ruth," he said. Then, to the officer, he said, "Can't you roll down the window? Let her tell us!"

The police officer looked at Marjorie and, seeing how pathetic she was, went to the driver's side to open the window, where Marjorie was in midsentence.

". . . came to me but she looked just like Ruth. I'd never seen anything like it. It was her, though. It was her!"

"What are you talking about, Marjorie?" Ruth said. "Crazy woman." She turned away from the car.

"She told me that I had to save the factory! That I could save it by destroying it!"

Marjorie looked up then, not at Ruth or Carl or the police officers, but beyond them, the siren's electric glow off her skin making her look otherworldly. "I was at home and Alexis was going to her class."

"Marjorie," Ruth said.

"Let her talk," Carl said, not taking his eyes off his sister.

"She came to me, but she looked like Ruth," Marjorie said. "But it was so clear. And Carl"—here she teared up—"Carl, it all made sense. She told me she loved me. She told me that she was going to take care of me. I just had to get rid of the factory. My half of the factory."

This time, it was Ike who stepped in.

"You don't want to say more, I think," he said.

"I want to hear what my mother said," Carl said.

"Your mother is dead," Ruth said. "Your sister has been in two cults, Carl. We have had to extricate her from two separate cults."

"We really need to take her in," the officer said, and rolled the window back up and got into the driver's seat and drove away.

Carl stood next to Ike and watched the taillights of the police cruiser, Ike's hand on his shoulder in support.

THE FULL STORY would not be pieced together until they'd been at the police station for three hours. What had happened was that Marjorie's cardiologist had recently increased her dose of Benicar when she would not stop ranting about all the slights—real and imagined, both of which raise a person's blood pressure—following her mother's death. This in addition to some Trazodone she'd been prescribed after her mother's funeral. Four hours after Ruth left, still unable to calm down, Marjorie imagined that the Trazodone had worn off and took two Klonopin, not remembering that she had also taken an Ativan. She hadn't remembered that the Klonopin was long-lasting, or maybe she never knew, or maybe by then her sense of time was so warped that she didn't even think in terms of hours but something more akin to wavelengths, or the reverberation of harp strings, or horse gallops. All of this combined inside her put-upon bloodstream, which, now swirled with these several classes of medicine, had set loose a wild delirium. The delirium led her to believe with certainty that Ruth, who had come over to manipulate her into forcing Carl to sell the estate, was actually a dybbuk of her late mother, telling her to destroy the factory.

"But how did she even burn it down?" Ruth asked. "I didn't think she could even pull that off."

"She knew how to get in," the detective said. "She had a security code. She knew if you hit the aerators first, you set off a chain reaction. She is saying that your dead mother guided the process."

"Jesus Christ," Ruth said. "Dead mother-*in-law*. Jesus Christ."

"It's a good thing she wasn't better at this," the detective said. "If she'd really known what she was doing, the whole neighborhood would be destroyed."

They were seated in the waiting area. The only other person at the station who didn't work there was a young Black man who had been caught with a joint after he was stopped and frisked.

"When can we go back into the factory?" Ike asked.

"There's no going back in," the detective said. "It's a tear-down now. There are holes in the walls."

Ike hit his hand against his forehead.

"Say, what happened to your thumb?" the detective asked.

Ike looked at his hand. "Lost it. Accident." He did the thing where he moved the joint around.

"At this job?" the detective asked.

"A long time ago," Ike said.

"Like I was saying," the detective said. "It's a good thing your sister didn't know how to set a fire."

Ruth had nothing to say, so she said, "Sister-in-law."

Several hours later, Ruth, Carl, and Ike were still in the police station, waiting for the detective to explain things to his superior. Ike had called Nathan, who was in the interrogation room with Marjorie.

Carl was silent. Ruth looked at him closely. His face was strange. He was doing something like marveling, quietly to himself, his lips moving, his gaze dreamy.

Ruth didn't ask, but Carl answered anyway.

"It was my mother," Carl said.

"Right. Your mother."

"No, Ruthie. You don't understand. I—I don't know what else to say. She came to me—"

"Dressed as me," Ruth said. "Or maybe she was the gardener when she came to you? Carl, do you want me to just start screaming here? Is that what you want?"

"I wasn't asleep," he said. "She asked me to go to the pool. I heard her voice exactly like I hear yours. She told me to go to the pool."

"And you went."

"I went. I was there, and I saw her. She was like when I was young. She was wearing a dress that I used to love."

"You sound insane," Ruth hissed. "You should keep it down or they're going to lock you up."

But Carl barely heard her. "She told me to come to the factory. She said that the money would be there."

"What money?"

"The money they took from us."

"The—"

"$221,934."

"The money from the—"

"Yes."

Ruth looked at him for a long second. She would not have guessed that he remembered his children's middle names, but here he was reciting the remainder of the ransom that was never found forty years ago as if it had been a ball of saliva waiting in his mouth this whole time. She had nothing to say. Instead, she stared straight ahead. How far back indeed.

Nathan and the detective arrived back in the waiting room.

"We're releasing her," the detective said. "Never saw an arsonist get off like this."

"We called the judge," Nathan said. "He spoke to her doctor. Do you remember Joe Villanche?"

"Joe, yes," Carl said. "I remember him well. He was the judge?"

"He was the judge. He says to just keep her off the streets for a while."

A female officer was leading Marjorie toward them. In her nightgown, she looked like a Victorian ghost. The officer released her from her handcuffs.

The detective looked at Ruth and Carl. "You're lucky."

The sound that came from Ruth just then.

"I'll drive Marjorie home," Ike said. "Nathan, you'll take your parents?"

"I have my car at the factory," Carl said.

"So do I," Ruth said.

"It's OK," Nathan said. "We'll figure it out tomorrow."

The young Black man was told he'd have to spend the night in lockup pending his indictment.

•••

BOTH RUTH AND Carl sat in the backseat of Nathan's car as he drove them home.

"Your mother is talking to you," Ruth said. "Waking up poor Ike. Like he doesn't work hard enough." Then, her psychopath voice rising, she said, "Can someone tell me when everyone in this family went insane?"

But they all knew the answer.

"You're saying Grandma came to you?" Nathan asked. "You saw her."

"I saw her. Clear as day. At the pool."

Now the sound that came from Nathan.

"You're going to give him a heart attack, Carl," Ruth said. "Is that what you want? Of all the times. We have your mother's unveiling and the bar mitzvah and we're not even done with the name cards, we're not done with the catering menu." Then, to Carl, she said, "Maybe you can call your mother and ask her to help with the name cards? Or ask if she thinks mesquite salmon and chipotle salmon are redundant?"

Nathan deposited his parents on the front porch of their house and then drove farther up the driveway to Phyllis's house, where Alyssa was waiting for him.

Carl lingered on the porch. Ruth turned around and found him daring to look serene.

"My mother came to me," he insisted. "I'm telling you. I know the difference between a dream and my mother." Then he added, "But it wasn't bad. She was sitting on our bed, like when I was little, waiting for me to wake up."

Ruth didn't look at him. "You said she was at the pool."

"No, first she was on our bed." Carl's eyes began to dart this way and that, and then finally, he looked at Ruth. "She told me the money was at the factory, that I could find it there right now. She said to rush on over, that it was there." He looked like a maniac when he spoke. "I didn't get a chance to go in and look, but she said it was there."

She closed her eyes. It was getting cold; it was too cold to be out here.

"It was more than a dream, Ruthie." He looked up at the sky.

"Shirley MacLaine over here." She closed her eyes, prayed silently for a beat, then opened them. "Carl, I don't know what to do. Maybe you can tell me. Maybe your mother can. We are out of money. We are going to have to sell our home. Do you understand that?"

She turned and put the key into the door. She opened it and walked in. Carl followed her.

"I didn't get a chance to go inside and see," he said again. "I didn't get to see what my mother was talking about. I didn't expect—well, who could expect something like that?"

Ruth turned again to Carl. This time she had no sharpness to her, just the ever-unfolding, deeper and deeper understanding of how irredeemably, irreconcilably beyond repair he was—how beyond repair he'd always been.

"I've had it, Carl," she said. "I can't listen anymore. Go to bed."

Carl went upstairs to sleep, but Ruth returned to the porch. It was morning now. On the Impossible Lawn, men had arrived and started setting up gargantuan white tents, the same as they did to prepare for all the other Fletcher family simchas. Another person would have found this overlap the beacon of comfort and stability. Not Ruth. She looked at this estate, just a headstone with more-than-average graveyard space, and wondered if Nathan's car had always been driving up the driveway, if the tents were always in a state of being erected. This estate—it was negative space. It was the space in between movement, the space in between growth, the space in between something nice, the space in between a home.

———

THE GHOSTS OF a family's troubled past will play out riotously in the soul and on the body of each member of that family in myriad ways. A staggering sudden impoverishment to the comfortable, a seismic event from which a person may never recover.

But have you ever tried to plan a bar mitzvah in the American suburbs?

Ari and Josh Fletcher's big day loomed.

On the estate, the tents were set up on the Impossible Lawn, erected over wooden dance floors and daises. Wine and water glasses were shined by uniformed waitstaff and held up to the midtent chandelier to check for smudges. At the synagogue, an event planner arranged orange Knicks-logoed yarmulkes and programs at the entrance; the Knicks were the only thing those two agreed on and so became the bar mitzvah's de facto theme, a logo with both Josh's and Ari's names woven into the basketball.

At Phyllis's house, Ari's and Josh's matching suits were hung on the mirrors of the bedrooms they slept in while they waited for their house almost a mile away to be rebuilt; their orange ties draped over the suits' shoulders.

In the guest wing of Phyllis's house, the Semanskys—Alyssa's parents and her four brothers and their families—settled in for the weekend. Alyssa busied around, looking for a washcloth for one of her sisters-in-law, and tampons for one of her nieces.

At Ruth's house, Ari and Josh hid upstairs, in their own father's old bedroom, playing on their devices. Ari played a version of Mogul in which he was an old man, retired, living alone in a house with a health aide who brings him food in his bedroom while he watches TV. Josh watched on YouTube a girl in a bra top with what had to be prosthetic nipples playing a first-person shooter game where a boy band opens fire on a water park. They each played in silence while they waited for the storm on the estate to pass.

At Phyllis's dining room table, Sidney Lipschitz, who had taken over his father's catering company fifteen years before, oversaw a series of uniformed waiters setting the table for a Friday night dinner for the family and making sure all the separate courses were up to specification. The matzah balls were checked for their firmness. The brisket was checked for its tenderness. A garnish of dill was applied to the small plates of gefilte fish that were being prepared.

And upstairs, in his bathroom, or, rather, in the bathroom at his grandmother Phyllis's, hunched over, trying his best to rid himself of the scourge inside him, was Nathan. It was supposed to be a happy day. Why didn't he feel happiness?

Following his meeting with Gal Plotkin, the former Mossad agent, the world had stopped. Life was over.

Nathan had sat in the car, cold in the late-winter air. The sun beamed through his windshield just to annoy him. There was no use in holding it off anymore. Nathan headed home, penniless for the first time in his life.

On his drive back to Middle Rock, he passed the corroded husk of a house that had been the place he had so far raised his own family. He could not bear to turn to look at it.

He turned the car onto the estate and drove up, passing his parents' house on the right. He could not look at that, either. He arrived at the top of the hill and got out of his car. He staggered inside the house and stood in the foyer, a soldier returning home, shell-shocked and paralyzed. In the distance, he heard Alyssa negotiating with a caterer.

Her voice got louder as she came with a placid curiosity to see who had let himself into the house. What a luxury, to not feel scared when you hear a door open. She arrived at the foyer and took one look at him.

"I have to call you back," she said into the phone. Then, to Nathan, "What happened? Are you OK? What happened?"

She began to descend on him, checking all over his body for injury.

"I have to tell you something."

She put her hand to his head. "You're burning up. We have to get you to bed."

But he took hold of her wrist and summoned his energy reserves to be as forceful as perhaps he'd ever been. "Alyssa, I have to tell you something. Please let me tell you what I have to tell you."

She stepped back, understanding that something was about to change.

"What is it?" she whispered.

•••

IT TOOK HER a long time to understand. When you are raised the way Alyssa was, money no longer makes sense after a person's basic needs are met. Still having at least some money to your name seems substantial, but Nathan made her see how it was not. He told her that they'd been trying to sell the factory but that nobody wanted a Superfund site with a concentration risk. He told her about his job. He told her about Mickey, and that all their money was gone.

She tried to take it all in. She stared out into the distance, adding and subtracting these pieces of information, the lies and the secrecy, the betrayals and the assassinations. She opened her mouth several times to ask a question, but the questions didn't feel substantial or complete. Finally, she shook her head, a decision made. She was not going to think about this anymore.

"The bar mitzvah is mostly paid for," she said. "I'm not canceling it, OK? I'm just not."

"No," he said. "Of course not."

"We will figure out the rest. What are we going to do?"

"I don't know. I might still have my job. I don't know."

She led him upstairs and into bed. She helped him off with his clothes and covered him.

"One day, we will have to talk about why you didn't think I should know any of this."

"I didn't want to scare you."

"That's not what marriage is, Nathan. It's not like what your parents do, where your mother protects him from having to be a person in the world. That's not partnership." She patted his head like she did the boys' when they were sick. "I think you should go to sleep. There's time to talk later."

He closed his eyes. He wasn't suffering. In fact, the chaos of atoms spinning around his worried head like flop sweat settled for a minute and he felt the singular peace of an emergency realized.

Finally. He'd been waiting for this. This was the best part.

He had reached the part of the emergency where he could finally exist as himself. He spent most of his life trying to warn the world that destruction was imminent, that the fail-safes were gone, that the walls were flimsy. And here, when he was faced with what was absolutely and incontrovertibly an emergency—one that no one could argue with—this is when the world finally started making sense to him.

The anxiety and fear were the only things that were real to him; they were the only things that never abandoned him. And when everyone else got to feel them, too, well, that was when he could finally relax. Now Alyssa knew. His mother, his sister, his brother—his father even. They all felt the emergency, too. Finally.

And—was this unspeakable? If it was, it didn't make it less true: If you wanted to know how Nathan felt about his father's kidnapping, well, he loved it.

Now, he wouldn't have exactly known how to say it. This terrible thing, this horrific moment in his family history, he remembered it so well. He remembered the people in the house, all the ways it was signaled to him that something was wrong. It was the first time—it was the best time. Finally, finally they were listening! Something was wrong! They were as vigilant and as scared as he was. And for that time, when he was allowed to sleep with his mother and people wrung their hands in anguish over him—when people pored over him with concern, that's when Nathan finally got to stop sounding the alarm about how the world was scary and how life was untenable. How scary it all is. What targets we are. The way a body can fail. The way systems can fail. That people can have hearts filled with violence and terrorism, and how those people could be lying in wait outside your home any day. The absolute chaos of the world.

Was he like this before the kidnapping? Certainly he was at least on his way there. But it actually didn't matter. Nathan now came as an emergency, equipped with a backstory that allowed him and others to make sense of him. Who would not consider that a gift?

Yes, that was the disgusting truth: that he loved his father's kidnapping. There it was.

Alyssa pulled the blanket over him and Nathan fell asleep.

———

MEANWHILE, DOWN THE driveway, Ruth picked up her phone and did her best to ask for the physical reinforcement and emotional support she needed from her family.

"Mom, hi," Jenny answered.

Ruth's voice came out as a growl. "Where the hell are you?"

———

ON THE DAY that her mother found her squatting in the family brownstone, Jenny had received a call, not from Beamer, and not even from Noelle, but from someone in the accounts payable department at a luxury rehabilitation center called—I kid you not—The Bluffs.

The Bluffs is a storied facility, with a legendary clientele and proprietary six-star accommodations that cater to the wealthy addict with nymphomaniacal predilections. It is the only rehab facility with a restaurant that has a Michelin star. It features private suites, in-room (chaperoned) massage, meditation classes, salt baths, infrared saunas, and sensory deprivation tanks.

Jenny received a call saying that her brother's bill was due and that his wife had directed the facility to call her, Jenny, instead.

"How long has he been there?" Jenny asked. "Is he OK?"

"Mr. Fletcher settled in fine eventually," the man in accounts payable said. "Yes . . . eventually. We had an incident at the beginning, but he's been a very good citizen since."

"Does he want to leave?"

"He would like to stay. He seems fairly bewildered that his wife is claiming that they have no money. Mrs. Fletcher asked that we call you and straighten this out."

"Oh, wow. OK. I'll call her and call you back—?"

"She asked that we ask you not to call her, either."

"Really? Wow. OK. I'm not sure what I should—how much is it? How much does he owe?"

"We charged his credit card for the first three weeks of his stay,

$85,000 on an American Express. But Amex wouldn't take further charges and his wife, well—she said you'd be able to help."

"One second. Where are you guys?" Jenny asked.

"Malibu."

"Can I call you back at this number? I have to check—"

"Yes, but please do. We have a large waitlist for a sudden influx of men who have been accused of various—"

"You mean all those Hollywood guys?" Jenny asked.

"They can all pay cash, and—"

"I'll call you right back."

————

ON THE NIGHT that Beamer had collapsed in front of Mandy Patinkin's house, the Patinkins had immediately called the paramedics and locked themselves inside. At some point, an ambulance arrived and took Beamer to the hospital.

Beamer writhed in a bed, in and out of consciousness for three days.

He wasn't quite comatose, but he certainly wasn't regular, either. He was cycling through hallucination, fantasy, wishful thinking, and night terrors, and the worst thing about it was that he didn't know which was which. He couldn't talk, or he wouldn't. He couldn't stop moving; or he was scared to. He would feel the cold touch of a hand and he would think he opened his eyes to find it was Noelle, and she would smile in angelic goodness and look down on him lit from behind like Jesus's mother (Was Jesus's mother also named Noelle? He couldn't remember now.) or whatever Christian figure he never committed to memory. But then he would blink and he could see through the smile that actually she was a swamp creature with a bloated face who hated him to her very bones. The hand of whoever this person or thing was would squeeze him hard as if it loved him, then squeeze him hard as if it were trying to warn him, and then it would puncture his hand—go right through the skin—and he'd open his eyes to see a cross-eyed male phlebotomist trying to find a vein. He would scream and the phlebotomist would run from the room, screaming himself.

Then the cycle would repeat. He'd feel a cold hand and realize it was Noelle, but this time he knew, just knew, that if he opened his eyes, he would see her angry and hurt, and so he squeezed them tight against the seething but then she was standing over him and suddenly he would hear an accented voice say, "I didn't do nothing to him. I was cleaning him and he just started crying."

He heard snippets of conversation about himself without truly being able to accept that they were about him.

"One of his kidneys has shut down completely and we're not sure . . ."

". . . a known allergy to leeches? Because we've never seen . . ."

"Has he been in contact with the Malawian River Nightmare Raccoon? He's displaying symptoms that are in line with . . ."

". . . fully one-third noxious gas . . ."

He grew very concerned for whomever it was that they were talking about. That poor fucker was doing badly.

Then he was a siwwy wittle boy who wanted a spanking.

He sat up in bed and screamed "*It's Wednesday*" with no proof of this (it was Saturday) and then said, more coherently than he had said anything in days, "I believe I'm running late for the Thai fifty-minute massage!" He didn't say it in any kind of incoherent mumble; he said it like he was making fun of an English fancy man who was trying to catch a train.

"No, he doesn't like massages." He heard a voice that sounded like Noelle again, but the voice was far away and he did not know who she was talking to and in the absence of a person or a voice that answered her, he filled the space out to be his cousin Arthur who, for some reason, was sitting on Carl's shoulders and wearing a propeller hat and licking an all-day sucker. But—and this was the craziest part of this already batshit scene—even with Arthur on Carl's shoulders, Noelle was still taller than them both.

At one point, the dominatrix he'd been seeing for years army-crawled in—he was sure of it—and slithered around the room on her stomach, reaching up when she passed the foot of the bed and pulling hair off his toes.

And then night would fall and everything was dark except for a line underneath his door that he knew, if he approached it, would open up into heaven. He knew it would open up into hell. He knew it would open up to his mother screaming at him in the kitchen when he was so small that he was only eye-level with her knees, "What did I do to deserve this?" and she was talking about him and one of his tantrums, which were really him just trying to explain things to her, something he attempted to do for years until he realized that the explaining was called a tantrum because she didn't want to hear from him at all.

He knew the door would open up into his fourth-grade music room, with his ginormously titted recorder teacher leaning over him to show him how to hold it just so, even though he knew and just wanted to lean his head against her chest.

He knew the door would open up to the room in the Radisson, where his hunger was deep and dark and it would take anyone it needed to down with it.

He knew the door would open up to Morah Rochelle telling him that after we die, we're made to watch our lives over and over, which is a good experience if you're good and a bad one if you're bad. He hadn't asked!

He knew the door would open up to his son and daughter in his bed at home, waiting for him to read to them, warm and safe and so fragile-seeming, like dolls, and he knew he had to busy himself so that they'd fall asleep before he arrived in bed because if he went near them, his poison would combine with their purity (he just knew) and just his touch would turn them brown and corroded in his hands.

He knew the door would open up to the first time he saw baby Jenny, home from the hospital, his mother lying down on the couch, gazing at Jenny with love, getting barely any cigarette ash on her, and saying to Beamer, "Do you want to see her?" And little Beamer walking toward her super slowly, not liking how small she was and how easy it would be to steal her.

"Come here, hold her."

He was more afraid of his mother yelling at him than he was of dropping the baby. He stood on his tiptoes and looked at her. She was asleep. He reached out to touch her. She was velvet. He leaned down to lick her cheek—he didn't know why, but he had to, and Ruth turned over and went to sleep while he stood, this four-year-old, watching baby Jenny and licking her face like he was a cat and she was his kitten.

He knew the door would open up to him in the backseat of his mother's car, sitting next to a paper bag that had hundreds of thousands of dollars in it. He knew his mother was in the front seat of the car, crying and talking to herself in a way he didn't understand, but fast and loud. He knew that the car was going too fast, that he was so scared, and then they were at the airport, and his mother told him to shut up, not with her mouth, but with her body and her face, which was scarier than words. They got back into the car and drove back home and his mother was now screaming in the car, just screaming and he froze to make it go away. He sat on the floor in the back and he peed his pants, and then he was afraid that she was screaming because he peed his pants. And then they arrived home, and both his grandmothers were there. His mother ran out of the car and they told her news that made her cry and made her fall to the ground. Beamer was still in the car, though. He was too young to open the metal levers on the doors. He didn't even know if they could open because he'd never been asked to try. He was covered in his own urine and this whole week was terrible, with the new people in the house all the time and his father was just gone but no one would answer his questions about it, and now he was stuck there—he was going to die in the car. Maybe his father had died in the car. Probably his father was dead.

He knew the door would open up to his father's home office. And

Beamer was small again, so small he had to stand on his tiptoes to open the door, but when he opened it up it wasn't night anymore. It was day, and his father was writing, and Beamer walked over to his desk. He stood on his toes to look.

The page was covered in his father's longhand, as familiar to Beamer as his own thoughts. He realized his father was finally writing his memoir. But all it said all over the page was LONG ISLAND COMPROMISE, over and over.

"Dad," Beamer said, but Carl didn't look up. He just began to sing:

"Race you to the top of the morning! Come, sit on my shoulders and ride! Run and hide, I'll come and find you, climb hills to remind you . . ."

And Beamer opened his mouth and the words came out, too. He didn't even realize he knew them. But he picked up and he and his father, now the same height and now the same age, sang together:

"I love you, my boy at my side!"

They stood, unselfconscious, face-to-face, finally able to express themselves, and finally Beamer knew it. His father loved him; his father had loved him all along.

His father walked out of the room, and Beamer knew there were terrible men waiting outside to take his father away. Beamer tried to scream to stop him, but all that came out was more singing:

"Race you to the top of the morning!"

And he ran after his father and down the stairs but didn't arrive in the living room, which was what should have been there. Instead, he was in a bed in a white room and the person whose face he could now see wasn't his father, or even his mother.

It was Noelle. He opened his eyes and he saw her.

"Is he singing?" Noelle asked.

There was someone else in the room, but he couldn't locate her. He wanted to speak and say to Noelle, "Yes! Yes! Me and my dad! Come join us! The whole world should sing with us!" but then everyone faded and he realized he was so, so tired. He was, wow he couldn't even form a sentence. It was bad. It was fading.

It was gone.

And then it was hours. It was days. It was weeks. It was months. It was years. (It was roughly seventy-two hours.) And he was being taken somewhere, up and out. Noelle, dutifully by his side.

But when he looked at her he saw that she wasn't just worried. She wasn't just tired. She was first holding something up to his face—his phone? Like she wanted him to see something, but instead she took it away and began to look through it. He fought to stay awake. He couldn't go back to the backseat of his father's Cadillac Brougham. He couldn't go back to the backseat of the Jaguar. He couldn't live not knowing what was beyond the door to this hospital room anymore. But he wrenched his eyes open and now Noelle was scrolling through his phone and his last thought before he followed that thought down his consciousness back into that backseat was that it was very bad for Noelle to be looking at his phone.

WHEN HE FINALLY woke up, he was no longer strapped to the bed. The room was quiet and peaceful and his body felt bright and drained. He turned his head and looked around. The room showed no signs of what he'd just endured in his hallucinations. But over to his right, in a chair next to his bed, was his wife.

"Noelle," he said.

But her face was devoid of everything.

"I know everything, Beamer," she said. "Or, actually, no. I just know enough. I'm sure there's more. I'm sure there are things I can't know—" Her eyes began to well. "I don't want to cry. I'm too angry. I'm angry at you. I'm angry at myself. I have to think that on some level I knew."

"Noelle."

"I have to think that I knew about this. I have to think this is why I was going to a psychic. She took one look at you and she knew. She knew! I am going to try to figure out for the rest of my life why I didn't know what was happening."

"Noelle."

"And yet, there is nothing I can tell you about your own behavior that you don't know. The only thing I can tell you is that I didn't arrive at the auditorium until after her solo. The only thing I can tell you is about Liesl, who stood on the stage, staring at two empty seats in the front row. She's seven. This isn't something you do. The teacher told me she just stood there, crying while she tried to play her flute. They had to stop her performance. They stopped the whole thing."

He began to cry big, fat, juicy tears. By then, he had been on an IV for three days and was hydrated and ready to mourn his life and the decisions he'd made. He reached for ways this could have been different, that he could have been normal, but none of them would hold up: If Noelle had agreed to have a third child. If he'd never found sex or drugs. If Noelle had been a kind of person who would have understood anything other than the straightest way of living. If his family hadn't been what they were; if his father had never had anything bad happen to him.

At the bottom of it all, the common denominator was him. Noelle watched him as he cried—nothing in her face at all—and when he finally could speak, he said, "Do you understand that I spend my whole life doing things that will make me able to function as a normal person for you? Do you understand that?"

She looked at him for a long moment and stood up and walked out the door. Beamer tried to sit up to follow her, but dark descended on him again, and he was back asleep.

———

THE GUESTS OF The Bluffs were not so much men who had hit bottom as they were men who had been caught and—for reasons either of negotiation or contract, or to keep their wives from leaving them—were going through the motions of redemptive abstinence. Certainly the CEO of the big tech company who was caught with hookers was. Certainly the rock star who had stopped his car in the middle of a highway (in the left lane), climbed to the top of his car, stripped, and begun urinating on cars passing by so that a digital tabloid had a photo of him that was partially in yellow splash was. Certainly the congressman who got his dick stuck in a glory hole when his desire for and access to such a mechanism coincided with Viagra's very real side effect in which an erection lasts for longer than four hours. Those guys all moped around, constantly jockeying to be the king of the place, or the most aggrieved of the place, or the saddest and deepest of the place. They got into fights in group therapy, trying to talk over people, saying things like, "You know what you need?" to which the facilitator would respond with, "No, Bob, we are all equals here. No one here is in management."

But Beamer didn't care about dynamics in this stupid group, these men all in contest for the most important and most self-made. He had bigger problems. Like, mainly, how much he loved being there, and how deeply fucked up he knew it was to love being there.

When he woke up in the strange room, a day after he last saw Noelle, he didn't know where he was and he panicked, so he made a run for it, and three men with tasers tackled him to the ground from behind, and he couldn't move any part of his body but his terrified eyeballs. He knew from beneath the weight of these men on him that he couldn't get out no matter how much he screamed and cried and negotiated. He was in a vault, he was a prisoner, he was unaware of the state of the world, controlled by a rigid set of someone else's set of expectations. He was kidnapped. He was *kidnapped*. He was finally kidnapped.

He had never been happier in his life.

After two days, he'd been led into a gray and tan living room—themed room where he sat with a gentle, friendly man in a shawl collar named Ed who got him to work. It was with Ed that he figured out that his entire life had been lived in the shadow of a kidnapping he wasn't even online for; it was Ed who explained to him that trauma can be inherited the same as hair color and that of course in a family of unresolved trauma, in which emotional displays were verboten, of course someone like Beamer was disciplined and denied love. Of course his sister found it threatening to hear that she was in a symbiotic relationship with the family she kept running from. Of course he stopped having tantrums when his mother punished him for them by taking him on a ransom drop. Of course a woman he married because he was too afraid of himself was also not someone who could listen to him and understand him. Of course of course of course.

Ed had his own protocol he had to work through, since time at The Bluffs was of great use if you got to understand why you were the way you were, but The Bluffs promise was that you would be dissociated from your habits to the degree that you could guarantee reentry to the world with a plausible vow to your family and employer that you were a new man. So: Beamer had to list all his erotic triggers, what Ed called a project of free association. Here was Beamer's list:

1. Any kind of deviance
2. Social pressure
3. Work pressure
4. Running late
5. Running early
6. Being on time for something
7. Sour cream & onion Lays/Ruffles, the way the chemical smell that creates the sour cream & onion combination smells somewhat vaginal in nature
8. Boobs
9. Butts
10. Stomachs
11. Some feet
12. Porn
13. Women
14. Some men
15. The words "The Bluffs"
16. Shawl collars

17. Discussing sex addiction
18. The stigma of sex addiction
19. A couple of large, sinewy mammals, though to be clear, these only aroused him. He'd never do anything about it.

This was all so humiliating . . .

20. Humiliation

Beamer committed to the program, submitting to the rigors of it, and served it like a master. He avoided all the captains of industry, mulling around in their linen pants, unsure of what to do with their hands when they had no phone or machine.

He wore the linen pants, too. He had six pairs of them, with a drawstring and a white V-neck, and he was responsible for doing everyone's laundry on Mondays. They mixed their clothing so that no one knew what underwear belonged to whom but that was part of the program, to have your identity and peccadilloes and skeeves ripped from you. He loved to show up to therapy on time. He loved to show up to meals on time. He loved to show up to smoothie hour on time. (He also loved to show up to smoothie hour ten minutes late and get a tongue-lashing from Nurse Sarah, that little minx.) This was all he had ever wanted, to be held within the confines of an arbitrary rigidity, sure he could find happiness within the strictures.

And he did, he did. He tanned and had lost fifteen pounds. He was back to being Beamer, but the Beamer before this recent meltdown. The one with clear eyes and vigor to him. The one who could think straight. The one who could finally see himself from the outside for the first time in years. Or maybe for the first time in forever.

Some of the men would hit on nurses, or orderlies, or security guards. Some would masturbate by humping the ladder railing in the facility's Lapping Waves pool . . .

21. Extra the words "Lapping Waves"

. . . or by rolling down their bathing suits so that the part of the pool that recirculates water in a rush after it's filtered would blow directly into their assholes until they came. (At this, of course, the pool had to be cleared and the water removed and then refilled and so if a person was responsible for that, he would have to apologize to each other guest of The Bluffs, which, frankly, some of them quite enjoyed.)

They were to keep themselves unstimulated. They were not allowed to wear spandex. They were not allowed to wear tank tops. They were to pull their trunks up high. They couldn't be in the pool alone together, lest one got it into his head to give another one the old Long Island Compromise.

There was music piped into the place, but it was like music at a cheap, all-inclusive resort, covers of popular songs, all sung in a drone by one singer who would not meet the song's emotional pitch, instead just singing it as words without feeling. No TV. No phones. No books. No photos. Nothing that would bring about emotion or revelation except in the highly controlled environments of therapy— two hours of group a day, four hours individual.

He went swimming. He used a kettle bell. He meditated. He did yoga. He did Pilates. A woman waved her hands over him and called it energy work. A technician stuck a hose up his ass every afternoon and injected water into it to scrub out his colon till it was whistling clean, till you would eat a sandwich off of his colon. He sat in endless circles, talking and listening, crying and touching his heart—cohorts at The Bluffs were not allowed to touch. He prayed to a God he'd never thought about twice since Hebrew School but was glad was still there. He ingested smoothies with no fewer than thirteen superfoods and absolutely no refined sugar.

They ate poached scallops. They ate wild salmon. The chickens they ate were grass-fed; their steaks had come from cows that went to the finest schools. Everything had morels or truffles in them— everything, even the oatmeal. They were only allowed desserts on Tuesday nights—a low-key, sugarless, flavorless pudding that was only discernible to be dessert by the fact that there were raw cacao nibs sprinkled over the top. But the dessert wasn't guaranteed. If one of the people on campus behaved poorly—made sexually lewd comments, came on to a nurse, masturbated publicly—dessert would be taken away. This was The Bluffs' way of reteaching a collectivism that its rich clientele had forgotten.

In therapy, he was making a breakthrough. He sat with Ed every day, first in a group, and then alone. He talked about his appetite and everything he'd done in service to that appetite, an endless loop of noticing it, then nurturing it, and then protecting himself from it over and over. He was realizing now that the drugs and sex were not to service lust but in service to danger—how he had been reenacting his father's near-death experience for his entire life, trying to make sense of it, trying to have some Freudian wisdom about who he was and where he came from, and the eternal question of the Fletcher family, which was this: What would they have been like if this had never happened to them?

The question hurt so much to ask. It hurt the way the sunshine or a cool drink of water hurts when you hate yourself. He'd had no one to consider the question with. His parents wouldn't talk about any of it. His mother scolded him if he made any reference to a thing that could later be a trigger to discuss The Thing. His father was frozen in a block of ice that he couldn't blow-dry fast enough to reach him inside. His brother, Nathan, who was supposed to be his older brother—who was supposed to lead him—was so fragile that a wind could blow him away. And his sister, Jenny, she just wanted out. She had done the ultimate sin of creating a life with him as a child (they had loved each other so much) only to grow up and become the most mercenary motherfucker he'd ever imagined. And so who could he talk to? Noelle? Beautiful Noelle who didn't know even a fraction of how fucked up he was?

Maybe he would have gotten some answers, too, if one day a man from accounts payable hadn't come to his room to say that he had to pack up and get out. His sister was coming to pick him up and the room had to be turned over by three P.M.

So much for his fresh start.

•••

JENNY PICKED BEAMER up and took him on a plane to Newark. There, she rented a car and drove him out to Yellowton, where there was a new state-endowed rehab facility that was actually attached to the town's new Giant's. It's the first of its kind, this rehab that's part of a superstore like that. (Unbeknownst to Jenny or Beamer, Dominic Romano was able to get the Giant's in Yellowton open if it could also be somehow categorized as a healthcare facility, so it offered highly discounted rehab services for all kinds of addicts and now the Giant's had the tax status of a folding table set up by an errant Girl Scout to sell cookies. Land use!)

"There's nothing else?" Beamer asked.

"I used my last money on two more weeks at The Bluffs," she said. "I loved it there."

Beamer spent eighteen days in Yellowton, trying to recapture the spirit of healing he'd had at The Bluffs—The Bluffs Giant's Detox N' Rehab was not—before he broke and called Jenny from a pay phone to pick him up.

Now he came out with a small overnight bag with the linen pants that The Bluffs had let him keep. He was holding a bargain brand kiwi lime seltzer—they'd had rose quartz water with purifying healing qualities at The Bluffs—and looking less tired than she'd seen him in years.

How savagely handsome her brother was, thought Jenny.

And there is my sister, thought Beamer.

As he got into the car, her phone went off again with her mother's tenth text message of the morning:

Are you with Ben Hur? I haven't heard from him or no well question mark question mark stop stop stop

Beamer stared out the window as they passed through the Hamptons in silence.

"Did you hear anything from Noelle?" he asked.

"I didn't. She wouldn't talk to me. Is—what's going on?"

"It's not looking great," he said. "Not great."

After a minute, Jenny said, "I'm sorry I said what I said."

Beamer said, "Me, too."

They drove in silence, and in the quiet space between them, the bond they always had forged even tighter—a chemical alliance, borne of biology and shared experience. Jenny's whole life, she thought that they had chosen each other, that it was a terrific kind of coincidence that they were both born into the insanity of this family. But they hadn't chosen each other; they didn't even have to choose each other. They had been chosen for each other, and now they lived in the kind of exquisite stuckness you can't even opt out of.

"Where are we going?" Beamer asked that day, from the backseat of the car.

"We are going to the twins' bar mitzvah," she answered.

"Oh Christ," he said. They drove a little and he looked over at her. "Hey, do you know that one of my Hebrew School teachers once told me that the afterlife is just you watching your life and feeling either good or bad about your choices? And that heaven and hell is the same thing. It's you watching your life and you either feel ashamed or delighted by your choices. Were you told that, too?"

"I was not."

"There are things you tell a child when they're so young and then they can't ever forget them. You know? It's so delicate to be a child. Everyone who says fucked-up things to you knows that."

"Are you OK?" Jenny asked him.

Beamer closed his eyes. "Yeah," he said. "I'm just sad. I'm just really, really sad."

———

JENNY AND BEAMER went barely noticed when they arrived at their parents' house the night before their nephews' bar mitzvah. They absconded to their childhood bedrooms without saying much to their father, only to bump into their mother at the foot of the stairs.

"Hi, Mom," Jenny tried.

Ruth stopped long enough to make sure that Jenny and Beamer registered her annoyance, her lips pursed into a sphincter with the umbrage of a person who knew that secrets were being kept from her but would not stoop to asking questions.

"It's Nathan's weekend," was all she said. Then, looking them up and down and seeing Jenny in jeans and Beamer in the post-rehab wear of a sedated mental patient, "You aren't going to ruin this for him."

———

THE TWINS' BAR mitzvah ceremony was a rousing, unmitigated success: well attended, beautifully decorated, sumptuously catered—the sanctuary was positively doused with flowers, all of them orange, to highlight the Knicks theme. Lily Schlesinger later asked Alyssa who she used as a party planner, what with her daughter's Sweet Sixteen coming up. A rousing success indeed. All those private lessons had paid off. Both Ari and Josh had performed their sections of the haftorah expertly. They had each taken half of the parsha as well. Their mother's brothers had each taken a portion of the morning prayer, then Musaf, and a group of Semansky cousins, aged two to twelve, all sang Adon Olam and Aleynu at the end to envious applause. It went beautifully; it was flawless; it was the complete triumph of a family that had endured a difficult year but had gotten through it gracefully.

At least, that was the story that Alyssa would tell afterward to every acquaintance who wasn't invited and every distant cousin who couldn't attend. It wasn't untrue, but it excluded some details.

What had happened instead was that when the Fletchers and the Semanskys arrived at the still-empty synagogue, Ruth allowed herself a rare sentimental moment, saying to Carl, "It feels like the morning of Nathan's bar mitzvah. It feels like we took a time machine."

Alyssa was fussing over her sons, pinning their yarmulkes to their heads. Hershey Semansky was idly looking through a prayer book and Elaine was scouting out seats for them and their other children and grandchildren. Jenny and Beamer—Jenny in an old dress and Beamer in one of his brother's suits—stood nearby.

"But you weren't there," Beamer said to his mother. "Remember?"

"What are you talking about?" Ruth said.

"You weren't there," he repeated. "You didn't go to Nathan's bar mitzvah. You disappeared that morning."

Nathan froze. Alyssa looked up from bobby-pinning Ari's yarmulke.

"What do you mean?" Alyssa asked.

"It's true," Jenny said. "Our parents didn't go."

"That couldn't be," Alyssa said. "I don't understand."

"Heh," Beamer said. "Neither did we."

Alyssa turned to Nathan. "It couldn't be that your parents didn't go to your bar mitzvah. I've seen pictures. Haven't I?"

Jenny spoke for him. "It's true. I'm telling you. They weren't there. The pictures were taken the day before."

Ruth's eyes narrowed. "Jennifer, this is a crazy thing to say."

"You weren't there," Jenny repeated. "You stayed home."

"This is the craziest thing I've ever heard," Ruth said. "I did not realize that you would use my old age to malign me—no, to *libel* me."

"It's slander if it's spoken," Jenny said. "Libel if it's written."

"It's slander if it's false," Beamer said. "It's not false. You weren't there."

"I think we should all calm down," Hershey said. "We're all very excited."

"That's so crazy," Ruth said. "I don't know why you do this, why you kids do this."

"You weren't there," Beamer said again. "You didn't go to Nathan's bar mitzvah. Grandma and Arthur took us. We didn't see you the whole day. You didn't come."

"This is the most ridiculous thing I've ever heard," Ruth said. "I'm walking away."

"It's true," Jenny said. "You didn't come. And we slept over at Grandma's."

"And Grandma told us about dybbuks," Beamer said. Nathan, who had been looking down, looked up at him and Beamer met his brother's eyes. "How a dybbuk must have possessed you and that's why you couldn't be normal. I remember it like it was yesterday."

"How could this be?" Alyssa asked Nathan. "How could it be you never told me this?"

Nathan's mouth was open but he just shook his head. He couldn't think of what to say. The truth was, he hadn't really remembered it till now. It was always there, but it was like it was hiding.

The party planner approached Alyssa with a tiptoeing face. "Can we grab you to just come outside for a question?" she whispered.

"Of course, of course." She looked at the Fletchers and then took Nathan's hand. "Nathan, come with me."

Ruth and Carl took seats in the front pew, where Alyssa's parents directed them, as if it were their synagogue. Beamer and Jenny sat down next to them, as directed, as well, but Ruth wouldn't look at them. She just stared stonily ahead.

And then the room filled and the service began, and the kids—they did great. They really did. They received their aliyot; they each did half of the haftorah; they each gave a speech about the Torah portion they'd just read, and at the end of that speech, they each thanked their families, and especially their parents.

"You are always there for me, Mom," Ari said. "You always worry about me and make sure I have everything I need."

"I can always count on you, Dad," Josh said.

Beamer took Jenny's hand, and it didn't burn either of them.

Nathan and Alyssa, in the front pew, stood up and walked the three steps to the bimah.

"Now Nathan and Alyssa will bless their children," Rabbi Weintraub said.

Nathan put his hands on Ari's head but found he couldn't speak. No, it was worse. He found he couldn't breathe. He had started crying—no, he had started *sobbing*.

"We all know what an emotional moment this is," Rabbi Weintraub explained to the congregation, as everyone laughed lightly at Nathan's display. "We know what it means to stand before your community and pronounce that your children are ready to enter the world in a meaningful, participatory way."

Well, that didn't help. Nathan was now not just openly howling. His body was overtaken and he was bent over, gasping for air.

"Nathan," Alyssa whispered.

Alyssa's parents started walking up toward the bimah. Elaine Semansky arrived up there first and put her arm around Nathan. She led him gently to the chair at the back wall that was reserved for the president of the congregation. She jutted her head toward Alyssa, indicating that she should sit with her husband, and so Alyssa came and sat down next to him.

Nathan tried to stand up. "I can—" He hiccupped.

But Hershey came over now and put his hands on Nathan's shoulders.

"Don't worry, son," Hershey said. "Don't worry. You have a family. This is what your family is for."

And so Hershey Semansky, the failed clarinet player, instead approached his grandchildren. He put his hands on their heads and blessed them, one at a time, asking God to make them brave like their forefathers, to give them good and courageous lives, lives that would mean something. He asked God to grant them ease and peace.

"You are entering into a tradition of manhood, or personhood, in this troubled world," Hershey said. "You are taking a full responsibility for the Torah and its laws, and you are responsible not just for perpetuating Judaism but for making sure that there are still Jews in the world. On this day, we ask of you that you build a Jewish home, that you feather it like a nest, that you keep it in one place and that you don't move it around, so that the children you bring into the world will always know how to find you. Darling boys, you are beloved. You will live a long life and sometimes you will wonder what your worth is in the world, and at the lowest moments of this, you will remember how proud we were of you on this day, and how precious you are to all of us."

The Semanskys moved in a coordinated ballet of knowing how to do this, a beautiful harmony in what was—was that?—it was joy. What it looked like from the pews was this: Hershey Semansky holds the boys by the head and recites those blessings by heart. Elaine Semansky hangs nearby, her hands clasped, watching. Alyssa leaves Nathan and makes a speech that talks about the origins of the bar mitzvah in general, and then the origins of the boys themselves—how hard it was to conceive them, how she prayed for them, how she never forgets her gratitude to God for them, not ever. She talks about their individuality and their attributes, and now, suddenly, they aren't just a couple of screen-obsessed, nose-picking boys, but they are people— real people, with a mother who believes in them, who has put every part of herself into their launch into the world, which will be ongoing until she's gone, surrounded by them and her grandchildren on her deathbed. She turns to the congregation and invites everyone present to see her sons through her eyes, to see how they contain the potential of the world, the continuity of a people, and suddenly, those two boys are the shining, golden future of the room, and the congregation sits in awe, not just of the Fletcher twins but of God and His miracles.

In the first pew, Beamer and Jenny couldn't move. They had watched all this, as the understanding of what had really gone wrong in their lives revealed itself to them, which was that the tide pool you're born into is only manageable if someone gives you swimming lessons. Or, put more simply, in order to be a normal person, you had to at least see normal people.

But the alternative was true, as well. What bonded them was what they alone had seen. But what evaded them was what they hadn't. That was what Jenny thought right then, and when she truly understood it, it found her breathless: that if you don't know to do the things that the Semanskys were doing it's because that was an inheritance, too. If you never saw it, you couldn't have it—no, if you never saw it, you couldn't even know that you were supposed to want it.

Instead, what they had was this: the three of them—Nathan, Beamer, and Jenny—who were bound by only one tether, which was what happened to them, which marked them forever as people who would only ever make sense to one another. Beamer understood all that the minute she did, and she gripped his hand back, because they had arrived at the end of all this time to find that they at least had each other and their big brother.

On the bimah, Nathan stood up and walked to his family—not the Fletchers, who were seated and gnarled, but the Semanskys. Nathan was still crying so hard he couldn't stand fully upright, but now he managed to hug his sons and his wife and take his place right next to his in-laws, who put their arms around him and told him how proud they were of him and how much they loved him.

There was no answer to the question of who the Fletchers would be if Carl hadn't been kidnapped. It not having happened wasn't one of their options. The only thing worse than realizing that it was a question with no answer would be to mull it over inside your head forever and ever and not realize that your life was passing by at the same exact rate it was for people who weren't obsessing over questions like that. What would they be like if this hadn't happened? What did it matter? It had happened, and you couldn't reason your way out of that one, basic fact.

"Do you see that?" Jenny asked Beamer, unable to take her eyes off their amazing big brother and his beautiful family. "Do you see that we never stood a chance?"

THAT NIGHT, IN a tent on the Fletcher estate, Beamer and Jenny danced in a circle around Nathan and Alyssa. They helped lift Nathan's sons aloft in their chairs. Jenny took one of Alyssa's brother's daughters' hands and crossed them with her own and spun in a circle till they were both dizzy, the same way Marjorie had done with her at Beamer's bar mitzvah. Beamer stood behind the most obnoxious of the bar mitzvah motivators and did impressions of him, so that his sister and brother and even his sister-in-law whooped with laughter. Nathan showed off a hitherto unknown-to-even-him flexibility doing the limbo. Josh did a wooden slow dance with a chubby little girl and Ari jumped in a circle with his friends, what thirteen-year-old boys call dancing.

Ike and Mindy slow-danced while Mindy began to stumble. Richard and Linda Messinger showed off their swing dancing lessons. Erica Mayer and Sarah Messinger-Schlesinger laughed with Jenny in a corner. Alexis made the DJ play a Hebrew song as she dragged Marjorie onto the dance floor so that they could show off the Israeli folk-dancing classes they'd been taking.

Ruth, at her seat at her table, whispered to Carl that the eighth-grade girls were dressed like hussies. Then she watched as into the tent walked Brett Schloff, who had been invited by Alyssa because they were on a school committee together. She watched as he made his way over to Jenny at the bar, who had just ordered a Joshuatini, which was a piña colada. Brett put on a light-up necklace and a lei and one of the plastic fedoras that the bar mitzvah motivators had handed out, and the two began to talk. Ruth was so entranced by this that she didn't notice that Carl had left the table.

He had wandered outside. He had been at the table with Ruth when he saw his mother at the doorway to the tent. She'd beckoned him over, and he'd followed her, of course he'd followed her, until he was standing outside under the starry sky and couldn't see her anymore.

"Mommy?" he called out. "Mommy?" He thought he saw a glimpse of her, running into the vineyard, but just as he was about to give chase, he saw her again on the other side of the tent. He watched as she appeared here and there, and he stood still, content to just know she was nearby.

He had now lived without her for nearly a year and it didn't seem to feel any better these days than it did in the early ones. He tried to think of what she would tell him. She would say: *This is happening to your body, it is not happening to you.* Was death the same? Was this grief the same? Because it felt so physical to him. There was no way to ask her, which felt like suffocation. The only thing that had changed this year was that he went from being someone who was sad that his mother hadn't lived long enough to see him get well to being someone who knew he never was going to.

When Ruth's mother had died all those years ago, she had cried all day, saying, "This is the end of my youth." Carl didn't feel that way about Phyllis's death. His father's death was the end of his youth, a youth that hadn't been long enough for him to process. He went from being a child to a man with nothing in between, and then he froze in amber that day he was kidnapped, a prisoner of his own body. His life had happened when he wasn't looking. He was an old man now. He was an old man and he was still under that hood.

He was kidnapped, and he was returned, but he had long since realized (and then he realized it again and again) that he had actually never returned. On that horrible day, he stopped being able to re-member basic things about himself, like what he'd liked to do in his spare time. And that became the story of his life. His memories, his feelings, his reminiscences—they existed only in those five days. Everything before that was precursor. Everything after that was af-termath. Under that hood, he couldn't picture his own wedding any-more. He couldn't picture the births of his sons. Something about the placement of the hood on his head had created a disorientation, a mortal rocking of his vestibular system, which is the system that tells you which end is up.

What was asked of him when he got home? To hold it together? And he did. Didn't he? There were some leaks, but he hadn't ever truly broken down. His whole life, and his only accomplishment was not breaking down. This happened to his body, it didn't happen to him.

But in his mind, he was still always under that hood. Or part of him was. Part of him was replaying the reel always, and the other parts were not understanding how other scenes were playing for everyone else. What other movie was there to watch?

That morning of the kidnapping, after they drove off the estate, he strained momentarily to keep track of where he might be but no longer could; the weight of the man on top of him only compounded his disorientation. By the time they set out on the highway, Carl no longer knew where he was and so, eventually, he stopped trying to understand the car's movements. Instead, his mind shifted to wondering how this would end, and by the time the car reached its destination either minutes or hours later, his imagination no longer contained a mechanism that could help him see how it would be possible to survive this.

By then, Carl had been driven out to his factory—his own factory, it would turn out! How he never got over this!—where he was handcuffed by his right wrist and his left ankle, in his three-piece suit, to an exposed pipe on the floor of a closet in what he believed was a basement, since he was sure he had felt some kind of descent down one or two sets of stairs. Two men remained in the room with him for that first day. One of them, the one who sounded more educated and had a growly voice, called him "Jew scum" and said he was going to bring over a gang of men to rape his wife and murder his children—in subsequent days, those men would be Puerto Rican, and then Black, and then they were Arabs. Every morning that Carl was in that basement, this man came in and relieved the other man, who had stood over Carl in the night, sometimes waking him with a scream, sometimes urinating onto his head while Carl writhed to turn away. The second man barely spoke, but he grunted a baritone grunt when he kicked Carl in the stomach and the head.

Or maybe there were three men? Carl didn't know. In the black of his eyelids behind his blindfold, he couldn't see changes in light and he couldn't see his captors. He had no idea what time it was or how long he'd been there and he couldn't answer their taunts; he couldn't even answer the questions that were screamed at him about where he kept his money and what time his kids came home from school. For the duration of his time in that basement, his blindfold never left his face and a bandana held his tongue down so that the area in the back of his tongue jerked as he tried to swallow. In his time down there, he was never able to take a good swallow.

Carl spent five days tied to that pipe, unwashed, in his own piss and shit. The first captor, whom Carl began to think of as his main captor, yelled at him sporadically: He called him kike, hymie, pig, sheeny, over and over. They forced water down his esophagus with such force that his swallowing complex couldn't stem the tide of it. Via the same method, they fed him a vile, grainy liquid that smelled like the vanilla diet shake that Ruth sometimes had for breakfast. Every day the main man came in with the same taunts and threats: "I raped your wife. I left her on the floor, bleeding and crying. I'm going to cut her throat tonight. I have a band of men"— again, of various ethnic minorities—"fucking her right now. Your sons are watching. YOUR SONS ARE WATCHING HER GET FUCKED!!!"

Each morning, when the first man arrived back at the factory, he would say in his crazy grumble that he'd left the night before and had raped Ruth himself and made the kids watch, then murdered the kids in front of her. It didn't matter that the man had said this same thing the previous day. It didn't matter that it made no sense. Carl wailed into his muzzle every time.

Later, when he was home, Carl couldn't open his mouth too wide anymore lest it hinge open right exactly at the angle where his mouth had been gagged and, honestly, he could not predict how he'd behave if that happened, so he began to talk like a gangster from the 1930s. He didn't go to the dentist for years; he couldn't be in that supine a position with his mouth open again. It would be months before he could smell his own shit again without going into paroxysms of terror.

For years, Carl would wake in the middle of the night with an urgent request of his throat to initiate a swallow, just so he knew it could. In the brutal dark, he waited two seconds for the swallow to come, and it always came, but in those two seconds you could not have convinced him that it would, and so by the time his peristalsis proved to be in good working order he was cold to the touch and the smell of his own doom had once again filled his nostrils.

Following his homecoming came the depression, a grayscale view of the world without joy that whispered menacingly in his ear that this was how it truly was, that his other view of life was a lie. Then came an anxiety that shook him so hard that he didn't feel that he could sit still long enough to identify it as anxiety.

One morning, he awoke amid a too-vivid dream in which someone he couldn't see was hurling numbers at him that he had to add or multiply from the previous numbers. He stopped taking the pills that day—abruptly, angrily (fits of rage, unexplained or otherwise, were another side effect), and he had to deal with a kind of chaos in his brain he'd never encountered: flashes of blinding electrical charge, like he was a lamp that had been delivered a surge of energy bigger than he could accommodate; they happened every two minutes or so and they left him breathless. But three and a half weeks later they were gone, and he learned never to share his mental state with Ruth again. No, Ruth was there for comfort and support; she was not there to fix a broken person. He could not be a broken person. His family needed him to be a leader. A man. He had to put this all away where no one could see it. That was what his mother meant, he thought, as the last of the electrical charges surged through his ragged brain: that he could just try to move on like it didn't happen; that you could treat it—and what was it but five terrifying days?—the way you treated lost time in surgery. You could shrug and put it away. It happened to his body. It didn't happen to him.

He was let loose back into the world. He was trusted to go to work. It was asked of him to be normal. To be a father. To be a husband. But he couldn't get better. He just couldn't. He began to see all of time as happening simultaneously, or close to it. He began to see that he could be at work, or at Nathan's baseball game, but he could also be locked in that basement. He sat at a Passover seder and saw that this thing that had happened to the Jews, their slavery in Egypt, seemed so ancient, but it wasn't. It was like yesterday. All the periods of time you thought were so long ago were so much closer than you thought they were, just a breath away. Moses was parting the Red Sea and Zelig was stowing away on that ship and Ruth was giving birth to Nathan and Carl was being chained to a pipe all at the same exact time. How can you get over anything if it all is just constantly happening?

He remembered Ruth telling him about post-traumatic stress disorder, back when she still thought things could be different. He laughed at that: *post*-trauma! Anyone who named it that didn't really understand it. There is no post. There's only trauma. Over and over. Time moves on, but you stay there forever. No wonder there was no treatment. How do you treat what is now called your life?

What weighed on him the most was what the kids were saying today. He hadn't ever thought about it again, Nathan's bar mitzvah. But they were right. Just this afternoon, as he sat on the bed, watching Ruth get dressed for tonight, he said, "Ruthie, what did we do?"

And Ruth said, "What are you talking about?"

And he said, "We didn't go to Nathan's bar mitzvah. We hurt him."

"What are you talking about? Of course we did. They're lying. They play tricks on us, Carl."

"No, think about it, Ruthie," he said. "Do you remember? Anything about Nathan's bar mitzvah?"

"Of course I do. We made him Mets kippahs. He looked so handsome in his suit."

"But do you remember any part of it?"

Now Ruth was screaming at him. "Don't you start, too! Don't you start right now, Carl! I can't take it!"

And he placated her, and patted her, and said he was sorry, but she went into the bathroom to put her makeup on and he remembered being in the bathroom. He remembered he was taking a shower for the bar mitzvah, and Ruth screamed that she had to run to town for something, and he screamed back it was OK. And then he was in the shower and the thing that happened to him was the same thing that happened to him sometimes in those days: He went somewhere in his mind that he couldn't account for. He zoned out, went black, disappeared. And usually that happened and it was a soft, startling experience, a haze to enter and exit, but it was ultimately usually fine. Just on this day what happened was that he went dark, but when he came back there was so much steam in the shower that he couldn't see anything. He couldn't see enough to get out of the shower. It was like he had that blindfold on. He could smell his own shit again. He could feel the deep terror in his stomach of his life being over. So he screamed and screamed, but he didn't realize he was screaming. He was just trying to survive. But then he fell, and he was on the floor, and his little girl came in—the little girl he tried to keep all of this from. She saw him naked and screaming and he remembered that he had this fantasy from the time he was in the hospital in the days following the kidnapping that he was going to be better by the time she was born and awake and alive. And he saw her in her dress and she ran, and he knew it was too late. That it had always been too late. He knew he had ruined her, too, just like the boys.

Ruth came in. She called his mother, who raced over. He couldn't stop screaming. He couldn't stop shaking. The blindfold had gotten hold of him again, and he might as well have been back in the closet. He couldn't find his way out.

"I'll stay with him," Phyllis said.

"No, I'll stay with him," Ruth said. "You tell them we have the flu, or that we're sick. You tell them we were in a car accident. I don't care. But if one of us goes and not the other—just say we were sick."

Phyllis turned to him and grabbed the lapels of his bathrobe and said it again, but this time so, so angry, "You remember. This didn't happen to you. It happened to your body."

Oh, he was so sorry about all of this. He was so sorry his mother never got to see him well. He had no idea where to find her anymore, except that at night, he felt that she was in his blood, a globule or a clot, worming her way through him and trying to tell him that she was with him. He dreamed of her all the time—once he told Ruth and she looked at him like he was crazy (he shouldn't have told her). It's not fair to have to live without a mother. He had already lived so long without a father.

"Carl!" screamed someone now. It was Richard Messinger.

He and Linda had come outside the tent to leave and had seen Carl lying on the ground. Richard crouched by his side, and Linda ran back in to get help.

Ike was the next to run out. He just sat down on the ground, holding Carl, his head in his lap. Beamer and Jenny followed, then Ruth and Nathan and Alyssa and the kids.

"Dad!" Beamer kept saying. "Dad! Dad!" He and Nathan knelt and Jenny crowded around him. Someone was on the phone with 911.

"Oh my god," Ruth said. "Oh my god. Is he OK? Carl!"

But Carl was not in pain. He was confused at first, but not in pain. He tried to figure out what was happening, why everyone was so upset, but then he realized that he was no longer standing where he had been and he was no longer attached to his body.

Carl was OK. He was fine. He was finally what his mother wished for him, fully separated from his body.

He looked around. He stood up. Carl heard sirens in the distance. But what was the emergency? He found he had freedom of movement, that he was no longer heavy but light. He could will his way to the right and to the left. He could do a flip in the air. It was all so wonderful.

With his new freedom, he ascended upward—where else?—where he saw in the air the flow of his mother's face and he yelled out in joy that he could see his mother. How could he not have known that his mother wouldn't go anywhere without him? She followed him up and up and there he found his father, who was not like his father at all. Zelig, frozen in time as the strong, middle-aged man, had a different kind of face than Carl remembered. It was relaxed; it was kind.

They were in some kind of chamber now. A dining room in a

palace? Zelig sat at a long table, backlit in a golden glow. Carl looked to the left and right, and as he did, the scene filled out and he realized he was in his parents' dining room, at their table. His mother was seated at it. The nice Pesach china was out. The entire table was set but it was only Zelig, Phyllis—smiling placidly, as if that was who she'd been—and Carl. He saw that the empty, setting-less spots at the table numbered his family: one for Marjorie, one for Ruth, oh god one for each of his children, oh god oh god one for each of his grand-children.

"Is this it?" Carl asked. "Is this what happens? It's not so bad! It's not so scary!"

When Zelig spoke, it was with all the layers of a voice that Carl, who had not seen or heard him in more than fifty years, had forgotten—the distinct lilt of his Yiddish/Polish accent, the way his *d*'s were pronounced by a tongue rubbed up further against his teeth than normal, owing to a childhood injury.

"It's time for your judgment now, mein zeis," Zelig said. "I had mine. Your mother had hers. And now it's for you."

"What is it?" Carl asked. "What is it like?"

"What is it like?" Zelig repeated. He looked at Phyllis and they shared a secret smile.

"It's not what you think it is," Phyllis said. "It's not judgment like on Earth. It's *understanding*. It's the ability to look at your life and find yourself justified."

"Justified," Carl repeated. "I don't understand."

"That's what it's like," Zelig said. "It's like forgiveness."

"Forgiveness?" Carl asked.

Forgiveness? What would that be like? It had never occurred to him to consider it. Forgiveness for the way he wasn't strong enough to fight off the men who took him; forgiveness for the way he didn't even have the decency to die while he was chained up in that base-ment. Forgiveness for not ever being able to orient himself again. Forgiveness for the ways he absolutely saw around him that he had stopped life for his family. He wanted to tell them to go on without him, that he'd catch up, but he couldn't see his way to do it.

He'd seen how Ruthie suffered—his beautiful Ruthie—how he stole her life from her and maybe even drove her into his cousin's arms. He saw, too, that he, Carl, was not man enough to even ask if this was true. How could there be forgiveness for that? Who could forgive him that?

Zelig seemed to understand from Carl what he was worried about. And at this, he and Phyllis smiled again. Phyllis nodded to Zelig, permission of sorts, and Zelig accepted this permission and began to tell Carl the story of his life:

Some of the story was familiar. The childhood in Poland. The rise of the forces that began to limit their movement. The dread. The aborted education. The father that was shot in front of him; the brothers sent away to die elsewhere. The guilt that he'd survived alone.

"The boy who helped me," Zelig said.

"Chaim," Carl said. "You named me for him."

"He wasn't dead when I woke up on the morning that I left," Zelig said. His face had changed and he and Phyllis were now looking at Carl carefully.

"What do you mean?"

"He was still alive when I left," Zelig said.

"He gave you his ticket to the boat. He gave you his formula."

"No," Zelig said. "I took it. I went to take it from his hand and he woke up and fought me and I punched him, and I don't know what happened after that. I ran. I ran and ran, and I never checked. I went to the boat. I came to America. I never found out what happened to him."

Carl shook his head. "No," he said.

"I had to save my life," Zelig said. "That's what a war does to you. It turns you into a question mark, and there's only yes or no. And by then I had no other answers. I had to keep trying. You don't know when to stop trying when you're constantly being asked like that."

"So what happened?"

"I lived with it. I came here. It was a new world, and I tried to be a new person. But I dreamed of him every night. I wore him like a chain around my ankles. When I died, his face was the last thing I saw."

"Oh no," Carl said. "Oh no."

"I'm forgiven now," Zelig said. "Don't you see? I was judged and then I was finally forgiven."

Carl looked at his father. His father looked back at him. His father was younger than Carl was now and yet, to Carl, he still looked like the platonic ideal of a grown man and Carl himself still felt like a little boy.

"I didn't go to Nathan's bar mitzvah, Daddy," Carl said. He found that he was crying. He was crying so hard he couldn't speak, which was part of why he said it again. "I didn't go to my boy's bar mitzvah."

"You are forgiven," Zelig said.

"I couldn't figure out a way through, Daddy," he said.

Again: "Forgiven."

"I couldn't keep a thought in my head. I was so scared all the time."

"Forgiven."

"I was terrible," he said, and he stood up because sitting couldn't contain him. "I saw it in their faces. It was a living hell. It was—"

And Carl, overcome, sat back down and folded his hands and put his head on the table. He cried then for all the terrible things he had had to endure. He cried for all that poor Ruth had had to live through. He cried for the glimpse he'd seen of Ike, in his front yard, throwing a ball with Nathan when it was Carl who should be teaching his boy how to throw a ball! He cried for the ways that his bright boy, Beamer, was broken, and then he cried for the ways that he knew he, Carl, didn't do anything to address it—how he couldn't even bear when Ruth would mention it. He cried for Jenny, who couldn't seem to find a home in the world. He cried for Marjorie, who had never been able to get enough love into her to patch the wound of being his sister.

And then Carl looked again at his parents, here now at this dining room table, just like at Phyllis's house, only he wasn't small anymore.

He was big now, and now he cried in relief to see his parents again, that it was not just a rumor that he could be with them again, and because he understood now that one day he would have peace, that the ultimate judgment on him would be forgiveness, and so, then, finally, he cried in sadness, for the fact that he now understood that he was dead, and so he cried in mourning for himself and for his own life. He had tried so hard as a person could. He had tried as hard as everyone else.

He looked at his parents and he was both a little boy again and a wizened man of the oldest age he'd ever reach, and he knew now that the only thing he ever had to apologize for was that he hadn't recognized that the kidnapping was there to show him how every single other moment of his life, he was not being kidnapped. That there was danger and there was safety—neither of them are passive creatures—but he'd only ever acknowledged the danger. He hadn't realized that the safety was aggressive, too. He hadn't realized that for every single moment of his life that he was not in that basement, chained to a pipe like an animal, he was free like a king.

"Oh wow, oh wow," he said, because he knew that what awaited him was more of this understanding. "Oh wow oh wow oh wow."

It was from this realization that he understood that there was a new person in the room. It was Mandy Patinkin, and he was dressed in billowing robes of white. Carl rose to look at him.

"I know you," Carl said.

And Mandy Patinkin looked at him—he didn't even need to say anything more than with his eyes. But Carl heard it as clearly as if Mandy had said it.

"You are forgiven."

"Oh wow oh wow oh wow," Carl said.

"It's time to say goodbye," said Mandy Patinkin.

"Mandy," Carl said. "Mandy. They said it happened to my body and not to me, but now I have to go and tell them—it's the same thing. Me and my body are the same thing."

Mandy Patinkin nodded sadly. "They know that now," he said,

and he opened the door to the chamber so that Carl could take one last look down at Earth.

Never again did a prophet rise up from Israel like Carl. The last thing Carl saw on this Earth before he closed his eyes were the anguished faces of the people who had loved him the most in the world—the people who fretted over him and lived symbiotically with him and existed with him inside the unique syzygy that is a family. The whole universe lines itself up to make a family, and the family takes it from there.

Back on the estate, Alyssa held on to Nathan as he tried to understand what was happening. Marjorie put her arms around Ruth and sobbed, and Ruth, who now saw the whole of Carl's life—who now got to see how it ended, and understood for the first time what a tragedy it was—put her arms around Marjorie, too. In that instant, Marjorie became something different than an opposing force; she became a fellow mourner, a person for Ruth to sit beside in a short chair for seven days in the next week, and then, in some sense, for life.

Beamer and Jenny knelt and held their father's hands as they watched him take his last breath, which he did, in the arms of his trusted old friend Ike Besser, who had stood loyally by their father's side, who had filled in the gaps where he could, who had offered their father something they never could following his ordeal, which was dignity, and in whose backyard shed were 220,000 mildewing, rotting, marked, unusable dollars, which had been there since 1980 and which would not be found until Ike's death four years later.

LASS, WOULDST THOU 'LOW ME REST HERE? I'VE RIDDEN QUITE FAR

T HE NEXT MORNING, on the estate, the Fletchers awoke, one by one, to the cold disbelief of their loss.

It was supposed to be the day they unveiled Phyllis's headstone. Now it was also the day they'd be burying Carl Fletcher.

Up in Phyllis's house, Nathan hadn't slept at all and woke Alyssa up with a cup of coffee.

"I have to bury my father today," he said.

In the house farther down the driveway, Jenny awoke, clammy, and staggered downstairs, waiting for anyone else to join her in the kitchen. Beamer arrived there soon. And Ruth woke up thinking about that old saying about a man not being able to live a full year after his wife's death. Perhaps it was Phyllis who was the love of his life, and not Ruth. She turned to see the space where Carl would normally be.

Jenny and Beamer went upstairs to dress for the funeral. Ruth was in her kitchen, in her old black velvet robe, preparing coffee when she heard a voice that might as well have come from inside her, for all she believed it was real.

"Ruthie."

Still she turned around, and there he was.

"Arthur."

He was dressed in a suit, as usual, with a trench coat over it, as usual. He had a suitcase next to him. He was tanner, and a little older looking, but his face organized into something so loving and so needed by Ruth that she actually gasped.

"Ruthie, I'm sorry."

"Arthur," she said, and almost started to cry when her anger big-footed her grief. "Arthur! Where have you been?"

"I left you a note. Did you not get it?"

"I got a note saying you were going away," she said.

"Yes."

"Where were you? You have no idea—I didn't know if you were ever coming back."

"I wanted to attend the unveiling, to pay my final respects."

Ruth had no words. She sat down, in her robe.

"May I?" And Arthur sat down, too.

"Arthur . . ."

"No," he said, in as forceful a way as she'd ever heard him. "No, I have to say something."

She was too tired and stunned to talk anyway.

"I had to leave, Ruthie. I had to go and figure out what exactly I was doing spending my life waiting for you. I don't know when I fell in love with you." Ruth opened her mouth but Arthur preempted whatever she was going to say. "I know we both know it and don't talk about it. We're so old now. And Carl hasn't—Carl is still Carl. And it was a crazy thing to imagine in the first place."

"I've never given you any reason to hope, Arthur."

"No, but you knew that I did."

"I'm a married woman! I'm a mother!"

"Let me finish," he said. "I left because I needed to be able to re-view this situation from where I could no longer smell it."

"Shakespeare over here."

"No, listen." His voice was dreamy and his eyes were a melted pool of feeling. "I went away. I went to Paris, to visit Yvonne. Her husband just died. But I watched all the lovers in the street, and no matter how familiar she was to me, she still wasn't you. I went to Israel, where I prayed at the Wall for God to alleviate this love from me. I went to Greece, to see how things that were older than me could survive. I went to India—I went to an ashram, and I learned how to sit with my thoughts, but then I realized that my thoughts were never the problem. You were."

"I never gave you any reason—"

"I know. But this isn't a court, Ruth. This is my life. And I'm an old man now. And now I'm home, because I am tired of trying not to love you, and I guess I'm stuck this way. But I had to find out. I'm glad I tried."

Ruth sat and looked at him. What is this question, she wondered. What is the love he's talking about?

"Carl died yesterday," she said.

"Ruth. What?"

"He died. At the kids' bar mitzvah." And for the first time she cried. "He's dead."

"Ruth. I'm so sorry. I came home for Phyllis's unveiling. It's supposed to be today. I didn't want to miss the—I still get emails from the shul."

"Well, it is, but it's also a funeral. Did you see that email? Arthur, you don't know what happened. We're destitute now. The factory is gone. Marjorie—you'll never believe this—Marjorie burned down the factory. But before that, a private equity firm took it away. And it all just stopped. We don't have a penny left! We're going to sell the estate. I hope there's something left after we pay these fines. Ike thinks they'll be in the millions."

"That's impossible."

"That's what I thought, too. But yes, this is it. This is the reality now." She turned angry. "And I could have used your help! You can't change the rules on a person after all this time! You have to give a person some warning!"

It was the closest thing she could have said to the truth, which was that she might have loved him back if she were capable and allowed—if she hadn't been kidnapped, too.

"No, Ruthie. I'm saying it's impossible."

"It's all gone. I promise."

"How long did you know Phyllis for? You know how they didn't trust banks. You know how they would never let the government near their money."

Ruth stood still.

"Those trips Zelig used to take when the kids were little. To Belgium."

"Right, Antwerp. To chemistry conventions."

Arthur shook his head. "Those—Ruth, those weren't chemistry conventions. You think they had chemistry conventions? For polystyrene factory owners? In *Belgium*?"

She was quiet.

"Come with me," he said.

"Where?"

"Just come with me."

He took her hand—she let him—and walked her outside the house and down the driveway, in her robe, right to the old greenhouse, into the corner beneath the old terra-cotta flowerpots that hadn't been used in a quarter of a century. He got down on his knees, in his suit, right there in the dirt, and he began to dig.

Ruth stared at him and held her breath.

IT WAS DIAMONDS, of course.

Zelig had watched his family lose all their money and property to the Nazis and knew that there would be a time when this great, new country caught up with the rest of the world and came for the Jews, as well. In other words, he wasn't so keen on banks. He took half the earnings of his first ten years owning the factory, back when people would sometimes pay in cash for a discount, and bought diamonds with the money. That was what he was doing in Belgium every year, because, as anyone could reasonably imagine, Antwerp is not home to an annual meeting of chemists to discuss innovations in polystyrene molds. He returned home with the diamonds and put them in Maxwell House coffee cans and buried them in the greenhouse, where, yes, he did also enjoy the life-affirming art of gardening, but mostly he liked to dig up his diamonds and look at them and remind himself that what had happened to him could never happen again, that his family was protected by the only means that mattered, money—that he was safe.

He told Phyllis about them after Carl was born. Phyllis eventually told Arthur, soon after Zelig died, fearing that something would happen to her and nobody would know about them. They discussed transferring the diamonds to cash, but the tax laws were terrible through the nineties and Arthur couldn't figure out a way to turn the diamonds into money without losing half of their value.

Should they need cash, of course, there was Phyllis's collection of Israel bonds, buried in yet another can beneath the flowerpots that used to hold the ferns. Over the years, Phyllis had buried close to $200,000 in Israel bonds, which she meticulously kept track of and renewed at maturity.

Ruth was no longer stunned by what she had heard three hours later, when the limos arrived to take the family to Carl's funeral. Of course Phyllis had put in place a mechanism that would stop them from self-destruction. Of course it was based on the very principles that Zelig had ruled over his house with, which were paranoia and a belief that all measures to protect yourself were righteous and none of your business.

Ruth's children got into the limousine with her and Arthur and Marjorie. Alyssa and the kids and her parents took a second limo.

Ruth thought about her husband, waiting in a coffin at the synagogue. She was going to have to face that box. How her devil's bargain had cost her so much. She thought back to who she was when she first drove onto this estate. She hadn't been able to believe her luck. She was so happy she wouldn't have to struggle. Her struggle to survive was so gigantic that she refused to pass it on to her unborn children.

And yet, sitting in this limousine, there was something in Ruth that couldn't bear that her children, now fully born, hadn't suffered at all.

How she couldn't forgive them for this.

The car was silent inside as it found its way to the expressway, each of them in their own worlds.

"I'm thinking about your grandfather," Ruth said to her children. This was a strange enough thing to say that the kids looked at her. "You know that story about the boy he left behind to save himself to get to this country so that he could have children and hope that they made something of themselves, too."

"Yes," Nathan finally said.

"Your father was named after him. Did you know that?"

They nodded that they did.

"You know," Ruth said. "Your grandfather killed that boy."

Beamer looked at her, struck. "What do you mean?"

"Your grandmother liked to tell the story about this young man sacrificing his life, or dying, or the natural order of things," she said. "But it wasn't true. That boy your father was named after—your grandfather stole his formula and the information for his ticket to America, and then took his food and water. The boy was too weak to fight back."

"Mom," Jenny said. "What are you saying?"

"It's true," Marjorie said. "My mother told me that. She never told Carl because she thought it would upset him too much."

"He did. He killed him. He killed to get what he wanted," Ruth said, turning to her horrified children. "That's what people have to do sometimes."

But they just stared back at her. They had no idea what she was talking about.

———

THAT NIGHT, AFTER all the well-wishers left the house, Ruth told the children about the diamonds that had been buried beneath the greenhouse. She told them she was going to sell half of them and keep half of them. A quarter of the cash would be for her future and for Marjorie's future, and a quarter to invest in several irrevocable trusts that would be controlled by Arthur. The other half would be distributed among her children, who now had more money than they ever had before.

See? A terrible ending. There would be no growth, no revelation, no coming of age, no plastic hour brought to fruition. There would be no reckoning with all that happened or resolution. Their problems were solved, and there was no need for any of that now.

But what are you going to do? That's how rich people are.

Part 3

THE FLETCHER DISAPPEARANCE

THE TERRIBLE
ENDING

THE DAY AFTER the shiva for Carl Fletcher ended, Ruth and Marjorie put the Fletchers' Middle Rock estate on the market. It sold within a week to a Persian neurosurgeon who had grown up in Middle Rock and done his residency in Los Angeles. He'd married a girl from Beverly Hills, where they had tried to settle. But the neurosurgeon found the culture in Los Angeles lacking, and the people boring, and the schools substandard. He had been indoctrinated to Middle Rock, same as all of us, and he'd found nothing else that was good enough—not even Beverly Hills—and so he decided to return.

Now that the factory was an unstable structure, it could be razed and paved over without the bureaucratic red tape that would have plagued it had it only been merely condemned. Because of the fire, the insurance (Haulers's liability insurance, not their fire insurance, since fire insurance doesn't cover arson) was forced to cover Haulers's end of the damage. Once the factory was torn down and there was no trace of it, a mall developer bought the lot at a premium, which allowed the family to easily pay off the federal and local EPA fines they'd accrued without having to dip into their own accounts, and even settle a burgeoning lawsuit with the neighbors, who did not enjoy the rainbow residue left over on their children's shoes when they played in the local park.

Nathan and Alyssa, meanwhile, decided there was no reason to stay in Middle Rock with the estate (his mother) gone. They crossed two rivers and moved to Livingston, right near Alyssa's parents' house, where Nathan bought a bankrupted development and gated it off and built houses on it for him and all of Alyssa's family. He never joined the New Jersey bar, though. Instead, he learned how to manage his money, and spent all day choosing the most conservative possible yields so that his money could grow slowly and steadily for his children.

Beamer and Noelle reconciled less than a year later, in time for his investment in a wellness business she was starting up with her dermatologist. Beamer began writing a new feminist version of the *Santiago* series, where Santiago is actually Chilean and a woman who helps trafficking victims, but everyone who read it thought it was too much of a bummer and it was never sold or made.

Marjorie and Alexis packed up the apartment in Forest Hills and moved upstate to something that was called a "residential wholeness community for the mature" but was actually a benign cult led by a charismatic former insurance salesman. It was there that, absent all the attempts at being saved by her family who thought they knew better, Marjorie actually began to thrive for the first time in her life. She spent six hours a day in therapy, and the rest of the time gardening and doing yoga and eating vegetarian meals and sometimes having to have group sex with the former insurance salesman. What could she say? Some people are born to be in a cult.

And Ruth distributed all of Phyllis and Zelig's possessions among her children—the china, the furniture, the albums, the silver candlesticks, the seder plates—throwing out the ones that they didn't want. She spent the week before leaving Middle Rock buying herself memberships, which she was now old enough to receive a discount on, to the Met and the Guggenheim and Film Forum, and subscriptions to the ballet at Lincoln Center. When she arrived at the brownstone, she set her bag down and left immediately to take a walk through Soho, where she found a set of simple bamboo candlesticks, which were much more her taste than any of the crap that had been in the house in Middle Rock. She put them on the dining room table in her new home, which she'd bought from a Danish furniture dealer upstate. As she sat at the table looking at her new candlesticks, how relieved she felt to remember what her taste was.

And elsewhere, Max Besser is rejected from another job at his interview, for the fact that he only has factory experience, and for the veneer of palpable bitterness that he can't quite drop. And Charlie Messinger stands on a soundstage and watches the screen from his producers' village, headphones on his ears, as Mandy Patinkin plays out an arc in which he, the patriarchal uncle, gets kidnapped in backstory, which explains why the family is so fucked up in the first place. Mickey Mayer does burpees in his prison cell—waiting out a six-year sentence because Ruth forbade Nathan from asking the judge for clemency on his behalf—and uses the time to conjure a wire fraud scheme that he hopes technology will catch up to while he is on the inside. And under the cover of night Lewis Squib pours oil at the front steps of what will forever be called the new Giant's, coming back in the morning when a security guard is there to witness him fall and break his leg while his nephew, who is pretending to record himself doing dirt bike tricks in the parking lot, gets the whole thing on video. And Beamer's dominatrix stands with her foot on a man's neck, daring him to peek up her skirt while she does and then kicking him in the groin because being a massage therapist, it turns out, doesn't pay the bills. And Phyllis, Noelle's psychic, looks hard at Noelle and makes her own eyes tense as she expresses her concern that she could see quite clearly that Noelle's new business partner has secrets, and that Noelle should come back again tomorrow to cleanse her aura, this time for five thousand dollars, which would allow the psychic to truly see all the ways Noelle is getting manipulated and lied to. And Amy Finkelstein takes her students through one last rendition of "Hot Cross Buns," as she applies an anti-inflammatory cream to her joints, having used up her health on instruction and after-school tutoring for spoiled children who did not love music or even seek to understand it, but wanted an exotic instrument to pad their college applications. At night she pulls out her cello, but she can't play it that well anymore, owing to the arthritis, and though she long ago accepted that she would never play for the Philharmonic, it seems to her that she's in a constant state of accepting this, that it never really lands. That something in her wonders if this will get sorted out somehow, even as time goes on and there's no indication that anyone is coming to save her.

And even as we know that there is no such thing as a mechanism that can guarantee your safety, and even as we know that there's no such thing as a dybbuk, not really, except for the way the prior generation haunts you forever—the rest of us arrive at the next class reunion and what we talk about is the way things have changed: how most of the people we know are in finance now, leveraging the Talmudic reasoning that is also our inheritance to short markets and figure out how money could make money for itself. How the middle class is disappearing, how the Jewish intellectual class is dwindling. How the generation who worked and fought for our ability to live how we wanted to would be shocked to see not a painter, or a poet, or a concert violinist, or even a philosophy professor among us.

That's when, inevitably, our conversation turns to the brief moment when the Fletchers nearly had to face the same reality we all do. That time there was a dybbuk in their works, when they almost were forced to understand what it meant to not know how the future might go. We comfort ourselves by suggesting that it was not to their great benefit for their problems to be solved so easily—that they may have been bred to not have to fight for their security, but how could that be a fulfilling life? Yes, we comfort ourselves that perhaps the phantom limbs of their potential tingle enough to tell them that they missed their opportunity to rise from their comfortable circumstances and become the real people that only true adversity and fear can make you into. Genes can lie dormant, but they don't dilute—even the recessive ones stand backstage in full dress, waiting for their turn to go on.

Perhaps, sometimes, when it is quiet, the Fletcher children still feel the dregs of the genetic imperative of their mother, of their grandfather Zelig, of Phyllis's menacing brothers collecting the rent of their tenants in the Bronx, of any member of their family who was wily enough to make it out of Europe alive—of any person suddenly called upon to fight for their survival.

Though probably not. The body and mind being efficient machines, they bury what they don't need anymore. Dregs aren't enough to make for a real, complete person. And there is little to no chance that any of these thoughts crossed the minds of any of the Fletchers ever.

Maybe that was the real Long Island Compromise, that you can be successful on your own steam or you can be a basket case, and whichever you are is determined by the circumstances into which you were born. Your poverty will create a great drive in your children. Or your wealth will doom them into the veal that Jenny described at her science fair, people who are raised to never be able to support a life so that when they're finally allowed to wander outside their cages for the first time on their way to their slaughter, they can't even stand up on their own legs. But the people who rise to success on their own never stop feeling the fear at the door, and the people lucky enough to be born into comfort and safety never become fully realized people in the first place. And who is to say which is better? No matter which way it is for you, it is a system that fucks you in the ass over and over, in perpetuity, and who is to say which is better?

Or maybe that's just what we had to tell ourselves to move on, knowing that the Fletchers of the world were out there and that they'd always be saved and the rest of us were battling basic solvency and survival in a tournament setting that would never end, a tournament whose field of play sat on an abyss, a vast cauldron whose tiny precipice the rest of us live on, our legs dangling over the edge, the vertigo alone threatening to take us down. We tell ourselves it is better to be able, better to have the ability to survive and to be competent—to be any other animal but a veal calf—but, man, as I grow older, it's getting harder and harder to believe it.

———

JENNY WAS THE last of the Fletchers to leave Middle Rock. Her mother had called her that last morning before the new owners arrived and asked her to double-check that there hadn't been anything left in Marjorie's old room on the estate. Jenny checked, walking through the house one last time, but nothing was left.

She walked out of the house and boarded the passenger seat of Brett Schloff's idling car, which contained a final several boxes in the back that were going to make their way on a drive to the house they'd bought in Cincinnati, where they were moving to be closer to Brett's children, and where, in just two years, they'd bring home their baby daughter, and then one year later, their son.

The day she left, their SUV drove off the estate, driving through the gate and, for the first time in her life, not closing it or locking it. Brett tried to make a right to head out of town, but Jenny instead directed him left. She wanted to drive through one more time, this place that, now that she was leaving it, had somehow suddenly become beloved to her. So they drove through town, past the Bagel Man, past the Poultry Pantry, which closed the next year, the owner saying that it was a miracle they won over the Persians—no way could business withstand the Orthodox and Asian apathy to his product now that those two groups were Middle Rock's majority. They passed the butcher, which was now kosher and run by the Beldsteins' grandson; past the Manufacturers Hanover Bank that Ruth had procured her marked bills for the ransom from, which, in the intervening years, had become a Chemical Bank that was now a Chase. They passed the gutted Duplo's Ski and Skate Shop, which was being renovated into the town's fifth CVS.

Brett drove on, and Jenny watched the scenery go by: the high school, the Mayers' house, Brett's childhood home, the library, Cobbleway Park. She told Brett to hook a left onto St. James Drive and to slow down until they arrived at the old Tudor where her father's life had effectively been cut short when a person who loved him but could not abide him had lifted him violently from his peaceful life and taken with him the story of the Fletcher family. Brett slowed to a stop and Jenny got out of the car and stared at the house and she cried for a full, gorgeous minute. She returned to the car and said, "Let's get out of here," and Brett drove her out of town and into the rest of her life.

The next day, a bulldozer came onto the estate and began work on the demolition of the grounds. A wrecking ball went into Zelig and Phyllis's house first, then Carl and Ruth's, so that the white painted brick sat shattered amid shards of black shutters on the ground. The caretaker cottages and garages were razed in one bulldozed swoop. The greenhouse was dismantled, pane by pane. The old strawberry bushes were mowed to the ground. The concrete that formed the pool was removed from the ground and the hole that was left was filled in with dirt and covered with sod.

In place of all of that, the new family put in a gigantic Georgian-style house with three smaller houses in the same style scattered along the driveway. The Impossible Lawn was dug up and a long reflecting pool was put in its place. On the expanse of lawn between the house and Sound, a platform was erected that included a brand-new pool that hovered over the water, along with a tiki-themed cabana featuring a built-in barbecue and outdoor shower. The estate was theirs now; it bore no trace of the people who came before them, or anyone who came before them.

The Fletchers were a great Jewish American family. That was what Rabbi Weintraub had said at Phyllis's funeral, and then again, a year later, at Carl's. He meant that they'd survived and proliferated, that they'd come to this country, observed the landscape, and deftly assimilated into it. They did such a good job of this that, ultimately, they disappeared undetected into a completely different diaspora, fully absorbed by the America outside Middle Rock and in no need of a place like that anymore. That worked until it didn't.

That day, Jenny and Brett drove off Ocean Vista Road, made a right on Shore Turnpike, and followed it all the way down to the parkway. She looked out the window as they passed the other side of the Sound, where she could see the lighthouse that her grandmother worked to restore, and, beyond that, the estate where she'd grown up. Brett sensed sorrow in his periphery—the feeling of an ending—and he put his hand on hers and they drove and drove and drove until they had left Long Island far behind.

The Fletchers were gone for good now, and we never had to hear their terrible name again.

AUTHOR'S NOTE

THE KIDNAPPING IN this book bears resemblance to the kidnapping of Jack Teich on Long Island in 1974 for good reason—that aspect of this novel was inspired by it.

I've known about the kidnapping for most of my life, as I've known the Teiches personally for that long, as well. My father grew up in the same town as Jack, and, for a period, worked as a computer consultant for their steel and partition company in Brooklyn. I would see the Teiches periodically when I was growing up myself, and when I was laid off from one of my first jobs, Marc Teich, Jack's eldest son, took me to Stew Leonard's and bought me a refrigerator full of groceries and gave me a job doing data entry at the company for the summer. Marc and I have remained in warm touch over the years, though I only have a passing acquaintance with his siblings.

Jack never spoke openly or publicly about his kidnapping—not to me, nor, apparently, to his family. He was returned safely to his home after his family paid his kidnappers an exorbitant ransom. He chose to move on with his life and insulate those he loved from the details of the horrors he was subjected to beyond what was revealed in the news articles about the crime and at his kidnapper's trial. He has since thrived and lived a successful, fruitful life with his family, full of gratitude.

A few years ago, I met with Jack to discuss a novel I wanted to write that would use a similar kidnapping as a central plot point. He gave me his blessing for this book and, in turn, asked me for some publishing advice. He told me he was thinking of writing a memoir. He wanted to finally speak about what happened to him all those years ago. Now that he was older, he didn't want to pass on without his family understanding what he'd been through, during his kidnapping, the years-long investigation that ensued, and the public and private aftermath of all of it. Roughly eighteen months later, he sent me a copy of *Operation Jacknap: A True Story of Kidnapping, Extortion, Ransom, and Rescue*—"Operation Jacknap" for the name the FBI gave the case. If you want to learn more about Jack Teich's kidnapping, I encourage you to read his excellent book.

Needless to say, the Fletchers are wholly figures of my imagination. The Teiches bear no resemblance to the Fletcher family—not in biographical detail, not in occupation, not in physical description, not in personality, and certainly not in spirit. I am grateful to them for their kindness and their continued friendship.

In addition, I gratefully acknowledge the poet Timothy Liu, whose beautiful poem "The Lovers" was posted on the New York City subway as part of the MTA's Poetry in Motion program during the time I was writing this book. That poem, which I read every day on my commute, inspired the conversation that Beamer and Noelle have after their tarot card reading.

Thank you to Marsha Norman for her gracious permission to use lyrics from *The Secret Garden* in this book; to Mandy Patinkin, whose mesmerizing performance in that show stayed with me all these years; and to my aunt, Lois Akner Fields, who took me to that musical (and many others) when I was in high school. I was lucky to be there.

—Taffy Brodesser-Akner
NEW YORK CITY
2024

ABOUT THE AUTHOR

TAFFY BRODESSER-AKNER is a staff writer for *The New York Times Magazine* and the *New York Times* bestselling author of *Fleishman Is in Trouble,* which has been translated into more than a dozen languages. She is also the creator and executive producer of the Emmy-nominated limited series of the same name for FX. *Long Island Compromise* is her second novel.

ABOUT THE TYPE

This book was set in Bembo, a typeface based on an old-style Roman face that was used for Cardinal Pietro Bembo's tract *De Aetna* in 1495. Bembo was cut by Francesco Griffo (1450–1518) in the early sixteenth century for Italian Renaissance printer and publisher Aldus Manutius (1449–1515). The Lanston Monotype Company of Philadelphia brought the well-proportioned letterforms of Bembo to the United States in the 1930s.